THE LAST STAND OF
MARY GOOD CROW

The Crystal Calamity, Book 1

Rachel Aaron

Copyright and Publishing Info

Aaron Bach, LLC
"Writing to Entertain and Inform."
Copyright © 2022 Rachel Aaron

ISBN Paperback: 978-1-952367-05-2

Cover Illustration by Luisa J. Preißler
Cover Design by Rachel Aaron
Editing provided by Red Adept Editing

Chapter 1

June 1876.
Somewhere beneath the Montana Territory.

Mary Good Crow knew from the start they weren't going to pay her.

She couldn't say how she knew. The miners had looked as good as any when she'd agreed to be their guide: no liquor in their breath or notches on their guns. They hadn't even grumbled overmuch when she'd told them it'd be half up front. Those were all usually signs of a quality customer, but they hadn't been underground an hour before Mary started getting the crawlies, and the crawlies never lied.

The staring was what bothered her most. Being half Lakota in a place where people acted like that equaled being half rabid dog, Mary was fair used to getting the hairy eyeball. It was why she hid her face under a hat the size of Dakota and covered her body in an oilcloth poncho so huge she looked like a rag pile with feet. She claimed it was to keep off the drips, but really, Mary had never minded cave water. It was other people she wanted to make distance from, 'specially the men.

They weren't all bad sorts, of course. Most were friendly enough so long as she was careful to let them see her as only a talking hat riding on a pile of cloth. It was when the geniuses put two and two together and realized someone named Mary was likely to be smuggling lady bits under all those layers that things got ugly if they were gonna. Even then, though, she had her ways.

Guiding, for example. The crystal mines below Medicine Rocks, Montana were a wellspring of wealth, but only for those who could avoid the pitfalls. To actually get to crystal, miners often had to crawl through squeezes no bigger than a child's arm or find their way through darkness no light could penetrate. The mines held poison spiders and rock leeches and clouds of fetid air that could kill a man before he even knew he'd breathed wrong.

Most first timers would be dead in two days without someone to hold their hand, which was where Mary came in. She was one of the few living souls who knew how to get past the cave dangers to the crystal on the other side. It weren't much of a leg to stand on, but when your know-how was the only thing between a man and his death, even the worst ones tended to remember their manners.

That was how it typically went, anyway. But this latest batch of miners was slipping below Mary's rock-bottom expectations. The moment she'd caught the bearded one ogling her backside despite there being nothing he could possibly see through her poncho, coat, second coat, waist satchel, rope coil, and denim overalls that were thicker than bullhide, she'd known this would come to no good end.

She should've ditched them right then in hindsight, but a cave guide was only as good as the clients who survived to speak well of her, and she'd needed the money bad. Other than the staring, they hadn't actually tried anything, so Mary'd done as the nuns who'd raised her would've wanted and given them the benefit of the doubt. She just hoped her gut was wrong about the whole "not-paying" thing. Only one way to find out.

"Welp, here we are," she announced cheerfully, holding up her big kerosene lantern to show the miners the water weeping down the green-streaked cave wall that dead-ended the narrow tunnel she'd been leading them down for the last quarter hour. "One hundred feet of virgin rock not half a mile from where the Rinker Brothers struck it rich just two weeks ago. It's got fresh water, sweet air, and a straight path back to the Main Gallery so you can find your own way home when you're done. No other guide could've done you better, so I believe that settles our agreement. If you'd be so kind as to hand over the rest of my fee, I'll be out of your hair and let you boys get on with the business of gettin' rich."

She finished her usual speech by sticking out her hand palm up, fingers wiggling. But instead of dropping coins like he ought, the big miner scowled at the walls.

"I don't see no crystal."

"It's in there," Mary promised, scraping off some of the green slime to show him the glitters underneath. "This whole side's packed with formations. Listen." She tapped her lantern's metal edge against the biggest bit of shining flecks, making the whole wall ring as the crystal echoed the sound back in its beautiful, pure voice.

"See?" she said with a beaming smile. "A fortune, just like I said. All you gotta do is dig it out."

That might've been stretching the truth a little. There *was* plenty of crystal in the rock, just maybe not of the size and worth she was implying. They'd actually passed a richer vein on the way over, but that one had sung so beautifully, Mary couldn't bear to point it out. 'Specially not to these men with their crawly-causing stares. But she'd had to throw 'em something iffen she wanted her five dollars, so Mary had compromised. There were plenty enough small crystals here to keep them busy and make her not a liar, which was all Mary cared about. Now she just needed them to pay, but rather than digging into their pockets as they should've, the four miners fanned out across the narrow tunnel, blocking her into the dead end with their bodies.

"Looks like you *do* know what you're doing," the big one said, stroking his bristly beard in a way that set Mary's crawlies kickin'. "That's good for you, 'cause me and the boys been thinking. We mined plenty of gold back in Deadwood, but this is our first time digging crystal. You clearly know your way around the stuff, though, and these caves ain't safe for a lady alone, so why don't you stay with us? I'm sure we could come to a new arrangement."

"The old one suits me fine, thanks," Mary said, pulling her lamp back in so that the little flame was between her and them. "I don't mine crystal. I just find it, which is what you hired me to do. I appreciate your concern, but I assure you I'll be perfectly fine on my own as soon as you pay me what you're owin'."

"You can't be serious," the bearded miner tsked, crowding in closer. "Little thing like you and half Injun besides. We're at war with the redskins, you know."

"I'm aware," Mary said, taking another step back.

"Then why don't you stay?" he pressed, closing the distance she'd just made. "Boys and me could keep you safe, and you could keep us company."

"You could be our cave squaw," one of the other miners said excitedly, pushing in next to the bearded man. "Bet you're hiding something good under all them coats. Give us a gander!"

He lashed out to grab her, but Mary danced away across the slick rocks, sure-footed as a newt. "I don't think that's a good idea for any of us," she said, still trying to salvage the situation as she raised her lantern one last time. "Now I'm asking you fellas nicely to pay me what you promised. Gentlemen don't go back on their word, and y'all are gentlemen, ain't ya?"

"How gentle we are depends on you," the bearded one said, reaching for the pistol on his hip. "You keep quiet and don't bite, and we'll take real good care of—"

He cut off with a squawk as Mary lifted the glass of her lantern and blew out the little flame inside. The moment the light vanished, darkness fell like a hammer. Not night dark, *cave* dark, the sort of blackness that took the eyes of anything that lived in it too long.

All the miners shouted in panic when the blackness fell. The leader recovered first, swearing and lunging at the spot where Mary had been, but she was already gone. The moment the darkness covered her, she'd shot up the seep, scaling the wet stone and wiggling her body into a narrow crack she'd taken note of weeks before in preparation for this exact situation.

"You red-skinned *whore!*" the big miner bellowed, groping blindly at what he'd thought was a dead-end corner. "I'll skin you like a buffalo!"

Mary was sure he had every intention of making good on *that* promise, but she wasn't worried they'd catch her. She'd never be foolish enough to let anyone drive her into an actual dead end, and situations like this were why she carried the big lantern. It burned a fortune in fuel, but the bright, steady flame meant that none of her clients bothered with lanterns of their own. That way, when things went south as they so often did, all Mary had to do was put out the light and *poof!* Guaranteed escape. While the miners cursed and fumbled for their tinderboxes, blind as newborn rabbits, she was free to move as she pleased, because unlike them, Mary had never needed light to see in this place. All she needed was the music.

The music was always there. Anyone could hear crystal when it was struck, but Mary was the only person she knew of who could hear it all the time. Even in places that had been mined out ages ago, pebbles and flecks were always left in the stone. They kept their voices small when light was near, but the moment darkness fell, they roared up like a river, filling the tunnels with music that never faltered.

Mary'd thought she was going mad the first time she heard it. To be fair, when she'd first come down here two winters ago, she might've been a little. But even in those dark days, the caves had bid her welcome, singing her to peaceful sleep for the first time in years.

From that night forward, the tunnels had been her dearest friend. With the cave music in her ears, Mary no longer needed eyes or light to find her way underground. All she had to do was listen, and the crystal told her where to go, painting its paths like a picture in the darkness of her mind. Even with the miners screaming bloody murder behind her, it was easy to follow the music flowing through the crack she'd crammed herself into, following it over the crystal-studded wall to another gap in the rocks a dozen feet behind where the men thought they'd had her cornered.

By this point, the miners had gotten their own lamps lit. Peeking out of her hiding place, Mary saw them huddled in the tiny pool of their lights with their shoulders hunched all the way up to their hats, staring helplessly at a darkness that must've looked endless from their perspective.

It would've been easy to end their story here. This section of the mines was forever having collapses, and thanks to the cave music, Mary knew the ceiling above her head was already weakened. One good whack with her hammer and they'd be buried back there forever. It was no more than they deserved given what they'd been planning, but Mary didn't reach for her tools. Not because she was saintly—Lord knew that wasn't it—but because bad things done in the caves always came back to bite you.

Their miserable lives weren't worth that kind of trouble. There were too many ghosts down here as it was. Four more who blamed her specifically would just make life that much harder, so Mary let them be, turning around on cat-quiet feet to start the trek back toward the Main Gallery Trail.

Toward but not to it. This part of the mines was the current favorite: far enough out that you still had a good chance at finding crystal but not so far out you risked finding something else. The popularity meant the main tunnels were a highway, and since Mary found people much more worrisome than anything else that lived down here, she always took care to go around. It meant a bit more walking, but the same poor mining practices that caused all the cave-ins meant the side tunnels in these parts were so chopped up, you could always find a way to sneak between them. 'Specially if the caves themselves were helping you along.

It was fun, too. After four days of guiding folks who seemed to forget which foot was which the moment they lost sight of the sun, moving at her own pace again felt like flying. Keeping to the side tunnels meant she had to pass close to active claims and the trigger-happy miners who worked them. But with no lantern and deer-skin boots that turned her footfalls to whispers, Mary was able to slip by most without them even realizing she was there.

The only ones who did raise their heads were the wild-eyed sorts who'd been down here way too long. Too much time with crystal did funny things to men's brains. Mary'd never had a problem herself, but she only guided and listened. She didn't touch crystal unless it was still in stone, and she *never* mined it. The men she guided never understood why Mary didn't just lead herself to fortune after fortune, but miners didn't see themselves as Mary saw. They didn't see the mad greed that crystal sparked in their eyes or the back-shot corpses left behind by claim jumpers she was constantly burying in her ongoing mission to make the dark tunnels a little less haunted.

Mary didn't know if it was the crystal's revenge for being chiseled or the fact that pretty colored stones were worth five times more than gold ounce for ounce, but she'd never seen a miner's story with a happy ending. Even the lucky ones who struck it big seemed to end up dead in the same ditch as the poor bastards who envied them.

Mary's life weren't no fairytale, but she was still alive after two years in the caves, which was more than she could say for the men she guided. She also had her living, the sturdiest of stone roofs over her head, and beautiful music anytime she wanted to listen. Now if her clients would just stop cheating her, there'd be nothing to complain about, at least not down here. Town was a whole 'nother matter, but that mess was still miles away. With only two sausages and a bit of biscuit left in her pockets, she'd have to surface soon. For now, though, Mary was busy enjoying the best part of her work: getting to be alone with the music, swimming like a fish through the glittering black.

It was so nice walking free again after days of being on guard that Mary didn't realize how quick she was moving until she ran face first into the Dark.

The Dark was most people's first true taste of the caves on account of how close it liked to stay to the entrance, and it was Mary's least favorite by far. Unlike the Slip or the Holes, which were easy to avoid if you knew what you were doing, there was no going around. There was also no predicting when you'd hit it, since it looked just like any other darkness from the outside and was given to roam. The moment you were in it, though, you knew, because any flame you were carrying would instantly put itself out.

No lights worked in the Dark. You could set yourself on fire, and the only way you'd know you were burning was from the pain. Nothing else—not the heat nor the smoke nor even the smell of burning flesh— would make it through, 'cause the Dark wasn't just a lack of light. It was a heaviness that hushed every sense, leaving you groping through tunnels that started winding like tangled yarn as soon as the light vanished.

Mary wasn't sure if the Dark caused the tunnels to twist or if the maze roamed along with the blackness, but it was the only bit of the caves she truly feared. Even the music was muted here, forcing her to slow down and put her hand on the wall to keep from getting lost. Those who didn't have the cave song to guide them had to hold on to a string some intrepid soul had strung up along the main path back when the Dark was first discovered. Stringing worked well enough when the line was intact, but since miners were no-account hoodlums who seemed to feed off screwing each other over, the string was cut more often than not. Sometimes, really evil people would deliberately run it down the wrong path, usually right off a cliff.

If Mary could've seen the ghosts down here, she was sure they'd've been packed cheek-to-jowl. Their constant moaning and muttering was so loud that even normal people could hear it despite the Dark's hushing, but Mary's main complaint was that they talked over the song, forcing her to stop again and again to make sure she was still following the hum that led to the surface. She was shuffling along in this slow fashion when her straining ears caught the distant sound of someone yelling for help.

The noise was so faint she thought it was another ghost at first. They liked to do that sometimes, luring you off the trail with distant pleas until you stepped off a cliff and joined them forever. These cries didn't sound like the dead to Mary, though. They were too hoarse, rasping and giving out midscream the way only a real live throat could do. It was hard to tell which direction the noise was coming from through the Dark's shushing, but that was definitely a living soul crying out there, and from the sorry state of his voice, he'd been doing so for a long, long time.

This realization put Mary squarely in the horns of a dilemma. On the one hand, approaching a man when she was alone was a proven bad idea. There was also still the chance this was a trap. Ghosts weren't the only dangers in this place. Ambushers, bandits, and everyone else who got their crystal with a gun instead of a pick also loved the Dark, and they could yell like living men just fine.

She was in no hurry to make herself prey for that lot, but on the other hand, there was an unspoken rule down here that whenever someone asked for help, you gave it. Mary was all too aware how easily it could be her screaming alone down here one day. She wouldn't want someone else deciding she was too much trouble to save if the situation were reversed, so she unclenched her hand and pulled off her glove, fumbling over the wall with her bare fingers until she found the sharp edge of a tiny bit of crystal.

Keeping one finger on the spot so as not to lose it, Mary dug her pocket knife out from under the folds of her poncho. Moving carefully to avoid cutting herself in the blindness, she flipped the blade open and tapped the metal tip against the grain of crystal, sending out a wave of fresh ringing to paint the cave around her. Even this clear sound was hard to hear through the Dark, but it gave her a feel for how many tunnels crisscrossed the main trail she'd been following and which ways they went. Straight down was the answer for most, but one fork sounded like it ran the same direction as the cries, so that was the one Mary tried first, tapping her knife against the wall as she walked to keep the crystal ringing.

It was slow, slow going. Most hazards in the caves were just that: hazards, dangers, pitfalls to be avoided. They could be quite deadly, but in the way of a storm or a wildfire; things that just were. Here again, though, the Dark was different. It had a malevolence about it, a weight it pressed down whenever you were doing something it didn't approve of, like not getting lost. It was pushing hard on Mary now, dampening the crystal's singing to something softer than a breath despite all her tapping.

She could've rung it louder, but Mary didn't want to give herself away in case this was a trap. Hard as the Dark pressed on those it didn't like, it was just as quick to help those it did. Even she could tap herself straight into a knife if she wasn't careful, so Mary took it slow, sliding her boots along the ground to make sure she didn't step off a cliff. But while she was now certain she was going the right direction, the cries for help weren't getting any louder.

That gave her a fright for sure. A few frantic moments of listening later, though, Mary realized she was overcomplicating matters. The screams weren't staying the same because the Dark was tricking her. They were getting quieter because the man doing the yelling was getting weaker.

In the end, she found him only by his breath. Her probing boots had just discovered the edge of a drop when she heard panting from below. There was no looking over to see what was doing it—this was still the Dark, after all—but it sounded like a hurt man. Physically hurt, not pangs-of-eternal-damnation hurt, which was a relief. Mary still wasn't entirely convinced she hadn't fallen for a ghostly trick. There'd be no saying for sure until she laid hands on him, though, so she screwed up her courage and got down on her stomach, crawling her hand over the cliff edge and down the muddy wall until her fingers landed on a head of soft, thick hair damp from the mist of the caves.

They both gasped in surprise when she touched him. Mary was snatching her hand back when the man's flew up to grab her wrist. "Who's there?" he croaked, his hoarse voice barely more than a wheeze after all that yelling. "Who are you?"

Mary freed herself with a scowl. The man was asking in French, which struck her as unusual. The only French talkers she'd met in this part of Montana were Canadian trappers looking to be somewhere else. Greed spoke all languages, though. Maybe this Frenchman had traded his beaver traps for a mining pick?

She puzzled over that for a second before deciding it didn't matter. Whatever tongue he spoke, it was obvious he needed her help. The pit he'd fallen into couldn't be too deep, since she'd touched him so easily, but he must not be able to climb out or he would've done so already. Mary's bet was a broken leg. Not much she could do about that, but she could help with his dry wheezing, grabbing the water skin off her pack to toss it down.

The Frenchman had no questions about that. The moment the water-filled pouch landed on him, he started sucking it down like this was his first drink in a year. For all his need, however, he didn't drain the whole thing, stopping himself just shy of the last few sips before passing the water back up.

"*Merci beaucoup.*"

"You can have it all," Mary told him in the same language, pushing the nearly empty skin back. "I can get more."

The rapid gulping that had already restarted stopped with a surprised choke. "You speak French?"

French was Mary's first language. The nuns at the tiny mission where she'd been raised had allowed nothing else. She hadn't actually learned English until a few years ago, when she'd been forced to leave the Lakota and strike out on her own. But these were things Mary didn't like to talk about and none of his business besides.

"Where are you hurt?" she asked instead.

"It'd be easier to say where I'm not," he replied, sounding more like a man of good spirits now that he wasn't dying of thirst. "But my left leg's the worst. I think I snapped something when I fell into this thrice-damned pit."

Mary gave herself a pat on the back for guessing right. Too bad her prize was hauling a man who couldn't walk. An especially annoying turn considering it shouldn't've been necessary.

11

"How did you even get all the way over here?" she scolded him. "Why didn't you follow the string like everybody else?"

"Because I thought..." The man trailed off with a shamed sigh. "I thought I heard voices of people I'd lost, and I let hope make me stupid."

At least he knew it. "I'm going to tie a rope to haul you up," Mary said, pushing back to her feet. "You stay put."

"Staying put I can do," he assured her. "Thank you, my friend. I owe you my life. I promise you'll be handsomely rewarded when we get back to town."

Mary perked up at that. She hadn't been thinking so far ahead, but now that he mentioned it, a reward would be most welcome. She was already dreaming of the food she could buy—actual fresh, *hot* food!—as she untied the coil of rope from her pack and looped it around the nearest jut of rock, tossing the rest down the hole.

She only had to pull him a few feet, but it was a harder haul than it should've been, since the man couldn't use his legs to help. If he hadn't been so light from near starvation, Mary never would've gotten him out. Even after he made it up, though, he still couldn't stand on his own. Not only was his broken left leg unable to bear any weight, his right was strained and weak from all his efforts to escape before her arrival.

A pair of crutches would've solved the problem. Mary didn't have anything like that, though, so she made do with her shoulder, sliding herself under his blind-groping arms to haul him up. It was going great until her body came up flush against his, and the Frenchman jumped away as if burned.

"*Merde!*"

"What's wrong?" Mary asked in a panic. "Did I hurt you?"

"No, it's not—I'm not—you're a *woman!*"

Mary'd thought that would have been obvious from her voice. But the Dark did strange things to your senses, and the man had clearly been down here far too long. "Is that gonna be a problem?"

"Of course not! It's just..." His hoarse voice began to quiver. "Are you an angel?"

Mary'd been called a lot of things in her twenty years, but that was a new one. "Did the fall break your head as well as your leg?" she asked, laughing at him.

"My head is fine," the man insisted. "And I think it's a fair question. You appeared from nowhere when I thought I was dead, not even making a sound. You pulled me out of that horrible pit, spoke to me in my mother tongue with your beautiful voice." He sighed. "You are either an angel of mercy or a cruel phantom of the crystal madness. I know which I prefer."

Mary chuckled again. Poor man. He must be crystal addled indeed if *she* was an angel. Still, "If you want to think I'm heaven-sent, I ain't gonna stop you," she said, sliding her arm back under his shoulder. "It's a fair sight better than what I get called most times."

"You are most certainly *my* angel," he said, leaning more heavily on her now that he'd been allowed. "What is your name, *mademoiselle?*"

Mary pursed her lips. It was the natural question, but giving her name to a man she'd met in the Dark felt like too big a risk. "What's yours?" she asked instead.

"Lieutenant Jean-Jacques Lucas of the tenth U.S. Cavalry," he answered proudly.

Now it was Mary's turn to jump away, shoving the poor man back so hard she nearly sent him down the hole again. Of all the people she could've pulled out of that pit, she had to go and rescue a *cavalry officer*. A hero in the war America was fighting right now against people who looked just like her!

What was a soldier like him even doing in the caves? They were supposed to be up top with their horses and forts, not down here with the riffraff. This was Mary's safe place, darn it! She got harassed enough by his sort above ground. It weren't right she had to put up with it below as well, and there'd certainly be no getting any reward now. She'd be lucky if this

Lieutenant Lucas didn't shoot her the moment the Dark wasn't hiding her half-Lakota face.

At least she'd been smart enough not to tell him her name. As soon as they got to the edge of the Dark where it was safer, Mary would dump him and run. The Dark liked to hover near the cave entrance, which meant they were probably only a few miles from town. The tunnel out was always super busy, too, so he'd probably sit only a few minutes before someone else came along to scoop him up.

Plan made, Mary wedged her shoulder more tightly under the lieutenant's and started hobbling them back toward the main trail quick as she could. The rapid pace forced the soldier to lean nearly all of his weight on her, a fact he seemed ashamed about, but Mary was too worried over her own skin to mind his pride. At least he was a polite burden. Despite being forced to cling to her like a baby squirrel, the lieutenant's hands never strayed anywhere they shouldn't, and he tried hard not to slow her down by hopping forward best he could on his still-working foot.

Mary was sure he wouldn't be putting himself through so much trouble if he knew he was leaning on a "filthy Injun," but it was nice to be treated with care for once. A bit too nice, maybe, for when they made it to the spot where the unnatural Dark gave way to normal underground blackness, she found it surprisingly hard to let him go. He might've only been doing it 'cause he had to, but that didn't change that the lieutenant's arm around her shoulder was the first kindly touch Mary'd had from another person in years.

Feeling like a proper sad sack, she forced herself to let go, dropping poor Lucas a little too hard in the process. His gasp of pain when he landed stabbed her conscience, but she'd dawdled too long already. The Dark seemed to get bigger every time she went through, but it must've really stretched itself this time. They were almost back at the start of the caves now, which put them in range of the cavalry patrols that guarded the entrance.

If one of those squads caught Mary with a downed officer, they'd shoot her dead before Lucas could speak in her defense, assuming he even remembered who she was. He already seemed more confused now that she'd set him down, his breathing speeding up in distress as she untangled herself from his grip.

"Where are you going?" he asked fearfully.

"Away" had been Mary's intent, but it didn't seem right to abandon him in this state. "I'm going to get you help," she said instead, pressing him into a hollow just off the path so that no one would step on him by accident. "Wait here."

He clearly didn't want to wait anywhere. He actually tried crawling after her. But while they were no longer in the Dark, there was still no light, which meant he was still blind as a cave fish. For Mary, though, the music was back clear and bright, giving her a good view of the exhausted lieutenant's shape as he flopped back on his face with a *thump*.

"For the love of—"

Mary hurried back over, picking the addled man up and returning him to the hollow with an angry huff. "Stay put this time," she ordered. "If you try to follow me, you'll just get lost again. Sit here and wait while I get you a rescue."

He tried to argue, but his words were too jumbled to make sense anymore. Being left alone in the dark again, even normal dark like this, seemed to be more than he could take. Mary might've been in a hurry, but she wasn't made of stone, so she sat with him a while, holding his hand until he passed back into something like sleep. When she was sure he wasn't going to hurt himself chasing after her again, she slipped her fingers out of his and sneaked away, following the cave music up the slope toward the mine entrance.

The path became more dirt than stone as she got nearer the surface. The Dark really had dumped them far up this time, so much so that Mary didn't realize how close she was to the checkpoint until she nearly walked right into it.

15

She skidded to a stop just in time, darting down one of the many dead-end tunnels prospectors had blasted into the soft sandstone of the Front Caves during the early days of the crystal boom. Plenty of miners saw her—the entrance was where everyone bottlenecked before spreading out to their individual claims—but hiding from the tax table was a perfectly normal activity, so no one paid Mary any mind. She was wondering how to tell the troop of blue-coated soldiers searching miners' bags for hidden crystal about Lucas without getting arrested when she spotted a rare friendly face.

"Oliver!"

Coming up the tunnel from the town side was an old man scarcely taller than herself and carrying even more gear. All that weight had made him stoop so low his long beard dragged on the ground. He straightened when he heard her call his name, though, and his wrinkled face broke into a big toothless smile.

"Mary, Mary, Never-Contrary!" he called in delight, his tied-on cook pots rattling a merry chorus as he scurried over to join her in her hiding tunnel. "Looking to skirt the law? I can fake an attack of the chest pains if you need a distraction."

"That's mighty kind," Mary said, truly touched by the offer. "But no. I'm actually in need of the opposite. There's a cavalry officer up near the front edge of the Dark who's in a bad way. Someone needs to tell the others about him 'fore he dies, but me being me... you know..."

Oliver raised his calloused hands. "Say no more, dearie. I spy the picture you're painting. But why're *you* stoopin' to help a cavalry boy? Did he blow his bugle at you when you passed? Threaten to cut off your pigtails with his saber?"

He reached out to give one of Mary's thick braids a good-natured tug, but she shook her head. "He called for help."

Oliver's joking face grew dour. He'd been working these caves even longer than Mary, and while his mind wasn't what it once was, he knew what that meant same as she.

"Guess I'd best go 'n fetch him, then," he said, gripping the straps lashing his clanking backpack to his wiry body. "How far's the Dark today?"

"Barely any distance," Mary promised. "And he said there's a reward out for his rescue. Bet'cha it weren't just air neither. The cavalry's too short on officers to lose one to the caves. They'll probably fork out big for him."

"Don't know 'bout that," Oliver said, scratching his beard. "Cavalry's stretched thin in every direction these days, 'specially when it comes to coin. But an officer oughta be good for a drink at least." He smiled again. "Thanks for the tip, Mary-lamb! I owe ya one."

She gave him a salute and sent him on his way, watching his huge pack bob like a turtle shell as he boldly approached the tax table and started yelling about a downed officer just like she'd asked. The soldiers looked at him sideways at first—as well they should, given he'd just scuttled in past them not a minute previous. But Oliver never was one for quitting once he had a good holler going. No matter how many times they told him to get lost, he kept at it until the soldiers caved and called for a brace of men to follow him into the mines and see what the fuss was.

Oliver flashed her a winner's grin as he marched past with his escort. Mary pressed her hands together in thanks and started taking off her own pack, untying all the worn-in knots that kept her supplies together in preparation for the tax table.

It was a lot of undoing for someone who carried no crystal, but Mary'd learned that having everything already open and ready greatly cut down on the amount of trouble she got from the soldiers. Doing this wouldn't get rid of all of it, but she had no other way out of the mines she was willing to take. Wearying as it was to deal with soldiers, they at least had to pretend to be law-abiding. The smugglers' tunnels had no such compunctions and a much quicker trigger.

Fortunately, the cavalry tasked with collecting taxes today were too busy making fun of Oliver to pay her much mind. They still dumped her bag out on the ground and kicked her things through the dirt, but it was a halfhearted, lazy sort of harassment. There were none of the usual demands that she crawl on the ground or show them an Injun dance.

Not that Mary knew any of the Lakota's dances. After the nuns told her she was too old to stay, Mary had gone to the tribes, thinking there at last she'd be where she belonged. But she'd scarcely lived four full seasons with the Lakota 'fore they'd told her to leave. She'd never known why. They welcomed other half-breeds with open arms. No matter how good Mary'd tried to be, though—learning their language, following their traditions, doing whatever work she was asked—it hadn't been enough.

It was still a sore subject, but there weren't no time for moping. Another glut of miners was already making trouble at the table behind her, so Mary picked her things out of the dust and put them back in her pack, settling her hat down low over her eyes again as she climbed the last few feet to the exit to go remind herself what the sky looked like.

Big and clear was the answer. Coming out of the tunnels was always a bit like waking up from a dream. Mary hadn't even realized it was morning until she saw the bright sun rising over the curve of the huge Montana sky. She gave herself a moment to breathe in the fresh warm air before hurrying through the wooden gate that marked the end of the crystal mines and the start of the boomtown that fed off them.

She swore the settlement at Medicine Rocks got bigger every time she came back, but this morning had to be the craziest yet. Coming out of the mines should've put her at the end of Main Street, but Mary couldn't even see the road through the crowds of miners, cart drivers, gunhands, and cowboys cramming themselves into every nook and cranny. They were even standing on the porch of the Wet Whistle whorehouse, a place no one stepped unless they had money or a death wish.

Keen to see what could make so many folks take leave of their senses, Mary darted away from the mine gate and squeezed over to the copse of pines that sheltered the town's public water pump. It was a sad, dusty little grove, but she knew from experience that the biggest sapling could hold her weight. She shimmied up it quick as lightning, peeling off her gloves to dig her cave-hardened fingers into the scaly bark as she pulled herself above the field of hats to see what the commotion was.

Her guess was yet more soldiers coming to cram themselves into the already stuffed wooden fortress at the top of the hill. But while a lot of armed, uniformed men were coming down the road, they weren't dressed in cavalry blue. Their coats were brown, and they were riding in tight formation around the biggest, nicest, fanciest carriage Mary had ever seen. Dang thing looked like a snuffbox on wheels, a veritable painted palace bouncing down the rutted dirt of Medicine Rocks' Main Street straight at her.

Chapter 2

June 20, 1876.
Medicine Rocks, Montana Territory.
An ungodly hour of the morning.

Not fifty feet up the crowded road from the caves' entrance, in the basement of the enormous split-log whorehouse known as the Wet Whistle, a building strategically positioned to be the first thing miners saw when they emerged back into daylight with crystal burning a hole in their horny pockets, a gunhand called Tyrel Reiner sat on a three-legged stool, contemplating a corpse.

It was a fresh one. Nobody Rel knew personally, which was a relief. Not that knowing the poor bastard would've changed anything. The job was what it was, but Rel always found the work went easier when the bloodless face didn't come with a name already attached.

Eager to get this over with, Rel pushed off the stool and tromped across the board floor to the old pickle barrel currently serving as their liquor case. Inside were a dozen pristine bottles of rotgut packed in straw. The whiskey came from a farmer in Colorado who didn't paste labels or ask questions. The booze gleamed like honey in the orange light of the kerosene lantern hanging off the floorboards of the bar above, but the taste was closer to turpentine. Good thing, then, that taste wasn't the point. Neither was the buzz this morning. The only reason Rel needed the whiskey was because strong spirits were the only thing potent enough to make what came next possible.

Shaking like an old ether addict, Rel stepped over the corpse to unlock the iron railway safe bricked into the basement cell's stone wall. Inside were the usuals: gold, guns, a two-gallon jug of laudanum shipped up from El Paso at great expense. But these were merely distractions from the real treasure in the back: a glass-stoppered apothecary jar filled with carefully folded paper sachets.

Stomach clenching in anticipation, Rel grabbed the bottle, shook one out, and placed the folded paper on the stool next to the whiskey bottle. Next came the tin cup, which was hung on a hook by the safe for just such occasions. Working carefully so as not to spill a drop, Rel poured the whiskey. When the cup was as full as it could go without spilling, Rel unfolded the paper sachet and tipped the contents in, trying not to look as the shimmering powder hit the booze and sank straight to the bottom like the rock it was.

You shouldn't do this, warned the crystal-embellished pistol strapped to Rel's hip. *You just took one yesterday.*

"Shut your trap, old man," Rel grumbled, picking up the tin cup. "No one asked your opinion."

Facts are not opinions, the gun replied pertly. *Even crushed to powder, crystal is crystal. What you're drinking is basically pulverized glass suspended in a solution of grain alcohol. I shouldn't have to explain why that's a bad idea, especially when the last dose you drank is still working a bloody path through your intestines.*

Hard to argue with that, since it did indeed feel like a thousand tiny knives were going to work on Rel's insides. Normally there'd be a day at least between doses, but this trick only worked when the body was fresh, and the bastard on the floor hadn't been polite enough to wait.

Suit yourself, the gun grumbled as Rel lifted the cup. *Just remember: neither of us will get what we want if you die from internal bleeding in a brothel basement.*

Rel replied with a rude gesture and tipped the tin cup back hard, draining the contents in one gulp.

As always, the whiskey hit first, burning its way down like sour cinders. This was a good distraction from the crystal, which hurt a lot more. Even with the alcohol to wash it through, every pulverized grain felt like swallowing a broken bottle. The pain of its passing brought tears to Rel's eyes, but that was just a preamble to the real sucker punch of shooting crystal: the *sound.*

It went off like a cannon, blasting the breath straight out of Rel's chest. It wasn't a real noise—at least, not one that a person who wasn't flying on crystal could hear—but it boxed Rel's ears all the same, making them bleed rivulets as the gunhand dropped to the bloodstained floor.

I told you this was a bad idea.

"Shut. Up." Rel panted, heaving for breath as the violent eruption of noise shook through every inch of flesh. Like always, it felt like it would never end. Like always, though, it did, leaving Rel soundless and shaking, staring at the dead man, who no longer looked so dead.

Nothing on the surface had changed. The corpse was still a corpse without breath or pulse or twitch of life. But deep within the waxy flesh, something was quickening. It shimmered in the body like a heat mirage, rising in pulses that kept time with the waves of nausea pulsing through Rel's abused guts. Finally, after what had to be fifty cycles of this bullshit, the shimmering condensed into the see-through image of a man. A very confused man who immediately started to panic.

"Where am I?" he demanded, looking around the prisonlike basement cell with wild, glowing eyes. "What happened?"

"You died," Rel informed him, removing the bottle of whiskey to plop back down on the stool.

"I did not!" the ghost cried, indignant. "I think I'd know if I was dead. I'm just drunk is all."

"You *were* drunk," Rel corrected. "Drunk enough to try forcing yourself onto a lady you didn't pay for, which is how you earned that badge on your chest."

The ghost looked down at the red-black stain coating his shirtfront, and his already bloodless face went paler. "Merciful heavens."

"I don't think that's where you're going," Rel said. "Gentlemen like you typically travel the other direction. But you had the poor judgment to die in the Wet Whistle Saloon, which means you ain't going nowhere until you pay your bill."

"Are you shittin' me?" the ghost demanded, fear changing to fury. "I'm goddamn *dead,* and you want me to pay my bar tab?"

"You'll be paying a lot more than that," Rel promised. "Miss Shandy, the lady you paid the ultimate price for trying to force your attentions on last night, is one of our top-shelf items. The only reason she deigned to look at your ugly face is because you were flashing crystal like lightning. Since you're a miner, we assumed that means you struck a good claim. A claim you won't be needing any longer."

"Like hell I won't!" the ghost snarled, flashing his teeth, which were already sharpening with the malice of the dead. "I don't care how demised I am. I ain't giving up my crystal to no one! 'Specially not to some humphouse gunhand for a whore I didn't even get!"

"That ain't no way to talk," Rel tsked, pulling the crystal gun from its holster. "But it's never too late to learn manners. Is it, Daddy?"

The gun heaved a disgusted sigh but obeyed, rising from Rel's fingers as if lifted by an unseen hand until its bone-inlaid barrel was pointed straight at the ghost's face.

The dead man jumped away. "What in tarnation is *that?*"

"A gun," Rel said, unnecessarily. "But as I'm sure you've noticed, this ain't no ordinary firearm. This gun can shoot anything, even you. You think you're safe because you're already going to hell? Hell ain't shit compared to what I'll do if you don't spit out the precise location of where you got that crystal."

"Y-You can't do that!" the ghost cried with a furious sputter. "This is robbery!"

"It's a choice," Rel corrected, staring the ghost in the eyes as the pistol hovered closer to the dead man's face. "Way I see it, you can take your chances with St. Peter, or you can take 'em with me. Peter's a saint, so he might still show mercy. I, on the other hand, will absolutely shoot your soul to confetti and let your broken pieces drift across these Great Plains for all eternity, so I suggest you start talking."

"All right, all right," the ghost said, putting up his see-through hands. "I'll tell you, *Christ*. Just make that devil gun put itself down!"

Rel flicked a finger, and the pistol returned itself to its holster, grumbling all the while. Nothing loud enough for the ghost to hear, though, so Rel was free to pretend it wasn't happening.

"Tell me where you found the crystal."

The ghost was already opening his mouth to point out how impossible that was when Rel walked back over to the safe to pull out a carefully folded map. Not one of the normal useless paper maps that went out of date five minutes after they were drawn since the caves changed themselves like showgirls whenever no one was looking. This was a square of fine leather embroidered with shimmering crystal thread. Each stitch was no bigger than a pinhead, but they twitched in the leather like hairs in living skin, creating a map that breathed and shifted as easily as the caves themselves. It bled, too, if you pricked it. A fact Rel sincerely wished to unlearn.

"What the hell is that?" the ghost demanded, horrified.

"Something bigger than you," Rel replied, touching the map as little as possible as it unfurled. "Now show me where the crystal is."

The ghost did as he was bid. It took him several minutes to figure out how the moving embroidery lined up with the dark paths underground, but eventually, his glowing finger pointed at a fork near the map's end. Not the end of the caves. Those went on forever for all anyone knew, but this map only showed the currently explored territory. How it knew all the tunnels and kept up with their turnings, Rel had no idea, but it was a lucky break the dead bastard's claim was inside its reach. If they'd had to go off the map, things would have been a lot more work.

"I can't believe that thing is real," the ghost grumbled. "What's a treasure like that doing in a cheap whorehouse?"

"We ain't cheap, and that ain't your concern," Rel said, making a mark at the indicated spot with a bit of charcoal before folding the twitching leather up again. Damn creepy thing growled like a bear at being put away again, so Rel shoved it into the safe as quick as quick could, slamming the door on it before it decided to do worse.

"There," Rel huffed, turning back to the dead man now that they both weren't in danger of becoming ghosts. "You gotta claim deed for that strike?"

"Nah," the ghost said. "I jumped it. Original owner's down a hole somewhere in the Dark. Didn't think to get the deed off him before I kicked him in. Bad planning in hindsight, but the tax table's easy to con if you hide your crap good enough. I also thought I'd only be doing a few weeks 'fore I got rich enough to ditch this shit pit. Just my luck I'd get shot."

Luck had nothing to do with him being a sack of stupid, but Rel saw nothing more to be gained from kicking a man who was about to be six feet down.

"That'll do, then."

The ghost's face lit up. "You're letting me go?"

More like Rel lacked the stomach to keep him. The effects of the crystal shot were already fading, leaving only nausea in their wake. No need for the ghost to know that, though.

"Ain't got no right to hold you now that your debt's been settled," Rel said instead. "Move along to wherever you're going, and if you get another chance at life, try to do better next time."

That's rich coming from you, the pistol said, but the ghost seemed comforted. He was already closing his eyes, his transparent face glowing with the reflection of whatever it was the dead saw once Rel released them. Heaven's light or Perdition's flames, there was no telling. Rel was just glad it was over, rising from the stool with an exhausted sigh as the ghost faded from this world.

His bloody corpse was still on the floor, but that was someone else's problem. All Rel had left to do was hand the marked map over and fall into bed, preferably until the next sunrise. Alas, no such luck, because when Rel turned to unlock the heavy door that kept the drunks and other undesirables out of the Wet Whistle's real business, a great tall beanpole of a man was already leaning against it.

"*Christ!*" Rel shouted, jumping back a good two feet. The man chuckled at the sight, which only made Rel madder. "What the hell's wrong with you? You know I'm to be left alone when I'm working!"

"Tyrel, Tyrel," the other man tsked, pushing up his hat to reveal the charming smile Rel had never been stupid enough to trust. "Is that any way to talk to your superior?"

He said that like it was a joke, but there was never anything funny when Apache Jake was around.

That weren't his real name, of course. No one in this mad murder-parlor of a flesh house went by their Christian names, Rel included. But Apache's *nom du crime* was especially ridiculous, 'cause he weren't Apache at all. He was Black. Not even one of those Cherokee half-breeds but a perfectly normal Negro, which was why he'd named himself thus. According to Jake, no one was afraid of a runaway slave, but he'd yet to meet the man—Black, white, or Indian—who wasn't scared shitless of the Apache.

That weren't just posturing either. Even when it happened in broad daylight, no one ever heard or saw Apache shoot. The men he faced just sprouted bullet holes and leaked out while he kept smiling and smiling. He was like the map locked in the safe: another of the Wet Whistle's terrifying oddities. Most folks likely counted Rel among that group as well, though, so what was there to say?

Plenty.

"I meant no offense, sir," Rel said, talking over the pistol so it wouldn't get any ideas. "Though I'd appreciate if you didn't scare the life out of me. We got enough bodies buried out back as it is."

"Always room for one more," Apache said, peering over Rel's shoulder at the dead miner on the floor. "And speaking of, did you get that lump of meat to talk?"

"The meat wasn't the one talking, but I got it. Location's marked, map's back in the safe, and the soul's moved on."

"Nice work," Jake said, patting Rel's short-cropped mahogany hair like a puppy's. "Especially with the soul. Always nice to know we won't be getting any more haunted than I'm sure we already are."

He had no idea.

"I'll send one of my boys to take care of the mess," Apache continued. "And I'll get a crew down to our new crystal mine. Dirty work, mining, but it takes a lot of crystal to keep up with the way you guzzle it down."

Rel shrugged. "You were the one who ordered me to make him talk."

"And what good work you did," Jake said, wrapping a long arm 'round Rel's shoulders. "*Such* good work, in fact, that I've got another job for you."

"I can't," Rel said, ducking out of his hold. "I just took a shot. If you don't give me a few days off to heal, all I'll be good for is upchucking blood."

"This ain't crystal-taking work," Apache promised, circling his arm back around Rel like a clamp. "Have you seen what's going on outside?"

Rel snorted. "How could I? I've been in a windowless cell threatening the dead since you woke me up 'fore dawn."

"Then this should be enlightening," the gunman replied, guiding Rel up the narrow ladder-stair to the large saloon on the building's ground floor. A room that, oddly, was no brighter than the cellar below.

Rel blinked in surprise. This far into summer, the sun should've been well up the sky by now, yet the saloon looked dark as midnight. It *had* to be morning, though, because the drunks were all asleep, passed out on their stools or under the card tables. Yet there was no sun coming in through the pine shutters they used in place of panes, since not even the Wet Whistle could afford glass on windows that had idiots getting tossed through 'em every night.

27

Rel was worried this unnatural darkness was due to some house-ripping, sky-darkening storm that occasionally pounded the plains without warning, but the truth turned out to be much simpler and much stranger. When Apache walked them over to the saloon's swinging door, Rel saw that the windows were dark because a crowd of people was standing in front of them—and everywhere else.

All of Main Street was packed butt to gut. Miners, townsfolk, wagon drivers, laborers, *everyone* was out gawking at something Rel couldn't see on account of the mob. Even the whores upstairs were awake and leaning out their windows in their nightdresses, shading their tired eyes to catch a glimpse of whatever had so captured the town's undivided interest.

"What's going on?"

"The only thing that unites this town," Jake replied with a grin. "Money. Seems old Sam Price's next of kin has finally shown up to collect their inheritance."

The gun in Rel's holster jumped at that. *Sam?* the weapon asked desperately. *Sam's family is here?*

"What next of kin?" Rel said at the same time, grateful as ever that no one else could hear the old piece of junk. "Sam Price didn't have any children, and he'd burn his money before he left a cent to the rest of his relations."

"That's precisely what I brought you up here to ask about," Jake said, squeezing harder. "You're a friend of the Price family, ain't you?"

"Something like that," Rel muttered. "But that was a long time ago."

"More time just means a dearer reunion." Jake assured, dragging Rel behind him as he stepped outside, scattering the crowd packing the saloon's porch like pigeons as he did. "Whoever's come out here, they're at least as rich as old Sam was. Just look at that carriage!"

It was quite the piece of work. Rel couldn't fathom how they'd gotten something that huge down the rutted wagon tracks that crisscrossed the plains, though from the look of its wheels, it hadn't been without consequence. The top was still piled with fancy luggage trunks, though, meaning whoever was inside intended to stay a spell. Still.

"What's this got to do with me?"

"You're our in," Apache said, smiling down oh so pleasantly. "You're the only person in this town rarefied enough to claim a personal connection to the Prices. Whoever's in that carriage, they likely know you. I want you to lean on that connection. Be a friendly face in this harsh new world. Get 'em comfortable and trusting so they believe you when you tell 'em it's in their very best interest to sell us everything Sam left them for cheap."

Not much left these days could make Rel balk, but that came close. "Why the hell would I do that?"

"Because you work for us," Apache replied jovially. "Ain't no one else 'round here got enough crystal to keep you fed."

"That ain't why I'm here, and you know it," Rel snarled, fighting to get out of Apache's snakelike embrace. "I hate that damn crystal, and I ain't doing this. I was hired for shooting and ghost talking, not betrayal."

"Who are you betraying?" Jake crooned, locking Rel tighter. "This is a mission of mercy. Think about it: this town's been talking for months about how Old Sam found something on his last crazy rich man excursion to the caves. Everyone with a brain knows it's nothing but miner talk. Buried treasure, that sorta nonsense. But folks here are honed in keen on the idea, and—"

"And they think Price's heir will know how to find it."

"Now you're catching on," Apache said cheerfully. "This town's chock-full of no-account killers who'll happily shoot the toes off a rich easterner for a chance at the sort of crystal Sam Price used to bring in. That's why you're gonna do this for us, 'cause unlike the rest of these animals, we're civilized folk. We're willing to pay good money—"

"I thought you said you wanted it cheap?"

"Any amount's better than getting tortured until you spill a secret that ain't even real," Jake argued. "Which is precisely what's gonna happen

29

to the body in that carriage if they don't take our deal first. Look at it that way, and you're practically saving their life."

Rel let out a defeated sigh. "What exactly do you want?"

"A buyout," Apache said. "Shouldn't be a tough sell. Price Mining's fallen hard since its glory days. I don't see the point myself, but the boss wants everything Sam Price touched in her pocket."

Rel's head snapped up. "The boss ordered this?"

"This job's her baby," Apache said, smiling wider. "She and Old Sam had their philosophical disagreements, but I can't think of anyone more suited to honor his legacy. She's certainly a damn sight better than some know-nothing silver spoon who thinks rolling in here with a carriage the size of Texas is gonna impress anybody, and it ain't as if we're asking you to work for free. Get this deal for us, and I promise you'll be well rewarded."

"How well?" Rel asked suspiciously. "'Cause I've heard that promise before. The whole reason I signed onto this flea circus was because your boss promised she could get me the name of the man who killed my kin, but it's been four months now, and I ain't got shit."

"Ah yes," Apache said. "Your noble quest for justice."

"Don't you dare mock them," Rel snarled, ripping out of Apache's hold at last. "My family was gunned down in cold blood. Your boss promised to find me the no-balls bastard who did it if I did as she said. Now I've kept my end. I've guarded your whores, shot handsy miners, and shaken down every ghost you've ever brought me, but the only thing you've coughed up in return is a lot of hot air and excuses. I'm about at my limit already, so why the hell should I go out on this limb for you and screw over the people who put a roof over my family's heads when my father couldn't be bothered just so your boss can finally get one over on a man who's been dead for six months?"

"That is a most unfair accusation," Apache said, removing his hat and pressing it over his heart. "You asked us to find the villain who killed your daddy—"

"I don't give a shit about that bastard."

"All right," the gunman said, backing up. "You asked us to find the man who killed your mother and baby brother without giving us anything to work with. No description, no name, not even what kind of gun he used to do the shooting. All you could tell us was that it happened on Christmas Day at a cabin in the Dakota Badlands. That ain't a lot to work with."

"I know," Rel growled. "I came to you because I couldn't do it, but *you* said *you* could."

"And we will keep that promise," Apache said. "But you gotta do your part. The boss has a lot on her plate at the moment, things far more pressing than avenging folks who aren't getting any deader. I know you're on fire for this, but we at the top gotta think about the bigger picture, of which you are but a small portion. *However*." Jake leaned in close. "That pecking order can change. You get us Sam's legacy no muss, no fuss, your stock with the Wet Whistle's gonna go up, up, up. And those who go up move to the head of the line. You see what I'm saying?"

He's playing you again, the pistol warned. *Those are just rewrites of the lines he fed you when you signed up for this racket. Don't be the idiot who falls for the same trick twice.*

Rel hadn't fallen for them the first time. Now same as then, though, there didn't seem to be any other choice. Rel had already tried and failed everything else, but the Wet Whistle had reach no other could boast. There wasn't a bit of criminality involving crystal they didn't hear about, and crystal was what had brought that gunman to the Reiners' tiny cabin in the middle of nowhere.

And my research, the gun added. *He only took a few ounces of the crystal I was experimenting on, but he stole an entire bookcase worth of my notes. That's the real loss here. Crystal comes and goes, but the papers he stole from me were priceless. Knowledge collected by generations of Reiners over centuries—*

To hell with his notes. Rel had seen the old man's body, how he'd locked himself in his workshop with his precious research while a stranger had shot his wife and teenage son to rags. That sort of butchery took time, but the old bastard hadn't even poked his head out to cry stop. He'd just

31

cowered in there with his crystal and his papers, and what had it accomplished? As soon as the murderer got done slaughtering innocent victims, he'd kicked down the workshop door and shot Rel's father anyway. In Rel's opinion, killing the coward Bernard Reiner was the only thing that damn criminal had done right.

That's a lot of opinions for someone who wasn't even there, the gun said coldly. *You want to talk about cowards who abandoned their kin? Look in a mirror.*

"Shut up," Rel snarled, turning back to Apache, who'd been watching the internal struggle with great amusement. "All I gotta do is convince Price's heir to sell, right?"

"That's it," Jake promised. "Just a little bit of sweet-talking. You don't even have to lie."

It would take a boatload of lies to convince someone who'd come all the way out here from Boston expecting a mogul's inheritance that they should sell everything to a whorehouse for a loss instead, but Rel didn't care anymore. The Price family might've taken the Reiners in, but they'd never let them forget it was charity. They'd always been a load of stuck-up, selfish prigs who saw everyone who wasn't a millionaire as mentally and morally deficient. They deserved to be swindled and sent home with a pittance, and if doing so saved them from being tortured by the locals over the location of a treasure that didn't even exist, then that was the Reiners' debt paid.

"All right," Rel said. "I'll do it."

"I knew you would," Apache said with a wink. "This is top priority, so take all the time you need. Just mind you don't take *too* long. I myself am the soul of patience, but the boss is eager to have this matter finished, and you know how she can get. I'd hate to be picking up pieces of you off the street."

"If you're gonna rush this, we might as well not bother," Rel said, starting down the stairs. "You want Sam Price's legacy on a platter? Get out of my hair and let me work."

"Have it your way," Jake said, putting up his hands. "But don't say I didn't warn you."

"Yeah, yeah," Rel muttered, walking across the street toward the huge empty shadow of the Price Mining building, the crowd parting like the Red Sea all around for fear of bumping elbows with the Wet Whistle's monsters.

Chapter 3

June 20, 1876.
Medicine Rocks, Montana Territory.
Same ungodly hour of the morning.

The mining town of Medicine Rocks was both larger and smaller than Josie had expected. Positioned just over the Montana side of the Dakota border, the town sat on the plains like a swirl of flotsam in the great grass sea of the open prairie. The buildings, many of which had been constructed right up against the namesake boulders to save on lumber, showed little sign of sophistication or civic planning, but at least they were legitimate structures. That put them miles above the squatter tents and modified wagons that made up most of Medicine Rocks' housing.

At least it seemed well protected. Atop the area's tallest hill—which wasn't saying much out here in the plains—was the biggest cavalry fort Josie had seen yet on the frontier. Like everything else here, the fortress was built in and around the giant boulders that lay scattered all over, but the sections of wall that weren't stone were made of quality pine timbers sharpened to points. Troops of blue-coated riders patrolled the town's perimeter, and the hills to the west were covered in hundreds of picketed horses grazing under the soldiers' watchful eyes.

But while it was heartening to see the US government taking its commitment to protect the world's only known source of the miraculous new substance known as "crystal" seriously, the rest of Medicine Rocks seemed to be doing nothing of the sort. Josie had already noted the copious squatter tents thrown up to house the thousands of miners who'd rushed over here from Deadwood and other gold-mining towns chasing the even more valuable crystal, but that didn't explain why the town's permanent structures also looked so ramshackle.

Obviously, lumber was hard to come by out here in the grasslands, but Medicine Rocks had been a boomtown for two years now. Josie had expected to find the place overrun with shops, hotels, and banks looking to catch the spillover of wealth as miners removed it from the ground, but there was scarcely even a proper road. Just a rutted dirt gulch lined with even muddier pine buildings that some extremely optimistic soul had labeled Main Street.

It was disheartening to see just how much dirt and horse excrement she would have to lift her skirts over, but Josie reminded herself that even this was an opportunity. Growing up in Boston, she had little experience with wilderness or frontier life, but unmet demand was something she understood very well. All those missing amenities were needs just begging to be met. It wasn't as if the citizens of Medicine Rocks couldn't afford nice things, after all. Crystal was worth more per ounce than any other substance on the planet right now, and the poor men who mined it were stuck out here with nothing to spend their wealth on.

But while Josie's head was already dancing with all the low-hanging fruit she could kick into her coffers, she wasn't free yet. The greatest hurdle of her journey was yet to be cleared, and given the size of the crowd gathering to watch her carriage roll into town, doing so was going to be a spectacle. One she was as prepared for as any soul could be, but that didn't stop her hands from shaking as she gathered up her papers, which the bumpy ride had scattered all over the carriage bench.

As one of the first and only legitimate businesses founded in Medicine Rocks, the Price Mining Company commanded a choice spot one block up the hill from the crystal mine entrance. With its milled board walls, bright-red paint, and shining metal roof, her uncle's headquarters was hands down the nicest structure in town, although not the largest. That honor went to the building across the street: a three-story, tarred-log monstrosity labeled the Wet Whistle Saloon.

Whorehouse, more like, Josie thought, noting the brightly colored stockings fluttering like flags from the upper windows. Not that such places didn't exist back home, but even after months of travel, it was still odd seeing a vice house just sitting out in the open for all the world to see.

The same went for the guns everyone here wore prominently on their person, even the few ladies Josie spotted in the crowd.

She'd thought her uncle had been waxing poetic when he'd called Medicine Rocks an ulcer of violence, vice, and dirt, but it seemed he'd meant the description quite literally. Not for the first time, Josie wondered if she wasn't in over her head, but there was no turning back. Her overloaded carriage was already slowing to a crawl, pushing through the now astonishingly dense crowd like an icebreaker ship before rolling to its final destination in front of the impressive but oddly boarded-up Price Mining building.

Checking her papers one last time, Josie tucked the packet into the hard leather document satchel provided by her lawyer and sprang to her feet. The coachman hadn't even finished climbing down from his perch when Josie threw open the door and hopped down on her own. A decision she immediately regretted when the narrow heels of her quilted carriage boots caught the uneven planks of the boardwalk and twisted, sending her legs in different directions.

What a thing it would be to start her grand entrance to Medicine Rocks by falling on her face! Fortunately, the Fates were merciful, and humiliation was avoided. She had a bit of a wobble but was able to right herself again by grabbing the still-open carriage door. This handy purchase also gave her balance to fluff out the wire hoops that shaped the skirt of her walking dress, which had gone rather flat after so much sitting.

She'd much rather have worn one of the sleeker modern dresses that did away with hoops entirely, but Josie's wardrobe hadn't been entirely hers to choose for this venture, so she'd worked with what she had. She'd just gotten herself together again when she heard the heavy *clump* of boots on the boardwalk behind her, followed by the unmistakable throat-clearing of a man who wanted attention.

Here we go.

Plastering the brilliant smile she'd been practicing all the way from St. Louis across her face, Josie turned to face the man who'd stepped out of

36

the crowd. Unlike the rest of the shabby gawkers, he was well dressed and clean-shaven with thick chestnut hair that had been ruthlessly pomaded into a neat swoop beneath the brim of his spotless cream hat. No way was a man looking that polished a miner, but all was explained when Josie noticed the silver star pinned to the fresh-brushed wool of his lapel.

"Sheriff," she said, putting out her gloved hand with all the drama of a steamboat actress. "How absolutely delightful to meet you. I'm Josephine Price. Thank you for coming out to welcome me to Medicine Rocks."

"The pleasure's all mine," the sheriff said, not looking pleased in the slightest as he took her hand for the shortest second he could get away with. "I'm Mitch Brightman, sheriff of the municipality of Medicine Rocks. I presume you're here about Old Sam."

"Sam Price was my uncle," Josie replied, a little too promptly. "I've come to take charge of his affairs."

Sheriff Brightman glanced pointedly at the empty carriage. "By yourself?"

"As you see," Josie said, pulling herself straight, which, thanks to her unusual height, put her just slightly taller than the sheriff. "I am his sole inheritor, so there seemed no point in bringing anyone else. I have a copy of his will from his lawyer in St. Louis if you'd like to see it."

The sheriff put out his hand, and Josie dutifully passed him the folded sheaf of paper she'd been carrying on her person every day for the past four months. She just hoped he could read it. His office notwithstanding, men out here were not known for their literacy, and the legal language was quite dense. If he had any difficulty with the document, however, Sheriff Brightman hid it well, scanning the long sheet of notarized parchment from top to bottom before handing it back.

"Ain't that just like Sam Price," he said with a smile that didn't reach his eyes. "Everything in order even past the grave."

"He was quite meticulous," Josie agreed, tucking the will back into her legal satchel. "Now if you'll please excuse me, I have much to—"

"But I'm afraid his word ain't the final say in the matter," Brightman said over her. "I'm sure Old Sam was just trying to ensure that his niece was provided for, but inheritance is a serious matter, particularly given the value of the properties in question. This ain't some small family business. Before Sam's death stopped operations, Price Mining was the largest employer in town. Given the law as written, I'm afraid I can't allow a young lady like yourself to just waltz in and assume control."

"But that *is* the law, sir," Josie said, actually feeling more confident now that he'd challenged her on facts. "It just so happens that I have a copy of *Laws of the Montana Territory* with me."

She reached back into the carriage, retrieving the brick-like book she'd been lugging for fifteen hundred miles from its basket on the floor. "As you can see," she said, flipping the tome open to a well-worn and carefully marked page, "it states right here under the Women as Sole Traders Act of 1871 that a lady may purchase, hold, or inherit property within the Territory of Montana under her own name for the purposes of business provided that she first declares her intention to an elected official, which I have done." Josie plucked another paper from her bag and thrust it at the sheriff. "Here is my statement of intent as presented to the territory governor. You may observe his signature there at the bottom."

Brightman did so with great reluctance, taking the paper and shoving it in front of his rapidly reddening face. But while Josie had never met the man who tolerated being proven wrong by a woman gracefully, particularly in front a crowd, she made no move to alleviate his discomfort. This was Medicine Rocks' first introduction to Josephine Price. If she showed weakness now, she'd be paying for it all the rest of her days here.

"I've also obtained written approval of my intent to resume operation of my late uncle's mines from the Land Bureau, the U.S. Geological Survey, and the Supreme Court of Montana," she added with cheerful relentlessness when he took too long to acknowledge her legitimacy. "Would you like to see those documents as well?"

"No, no," the sheriff said, taking off the hat he should have removed before speaking to her to wipe his brow. "There's no denying you're Sam Price's kin, rolling in here with every *i* dotted and *t* crossed. I'm still of the opinion this is no place for a lady, but I ain't one to countermand what seems to be every government office in the territory, so welcome to Medicine Rocks, Miss Price. Can I get one of my deputies to help you with your things?"

"That won't be necessary," Josie said triumphantly, gesturing at the dozen armed men who'd ridden in with her and who were already frantically untying her trunks from the top of the carriage. "As you see, I have plenty of assistance, but thank you for the offer. It was most polite."

Only politeness, she was sure. The sheriff was acting as his office demanded, but his sour expression left no question about his real opinion, which the rest of the town also seemed to share. Uncle had warned her in his letters that Medicine Rocks could be a backwards, unfriendly sort of place, but Josie hadn't expected such open hostility. Grumbling, certainly, for who liked it when an outsider walked into the town's most successful business with seemingly no effort? But she'd thought any upset would be quickly tempered by promise of jobs and income that restarting the mining company would bring.

Obviously, she was in error. No one here seemed happy to see her in the slightest. Even the dirty-faced men wearing old Price Mining Company jackets were scowling murder at her, making Josie wonder what in the world had transpired in the six months since Uncle Samuel's death.

There was nothing to do but see for herself. Satisfied all legal matters were settled for the present, Josie bid the sheriff and the rest of the glaring audience adieu and hurried up the stairs to the massive, empty building that was her new home.

It was every bit as astonishing as the letters had described. Mining offices weren't supposed to be fancy, but Sam Price had always had a flair for the dramatic, and his parlor did not disappoint. There were horsehair couches every bit as fine as the ones in Mrs. Price's best sitting room back in Boston, a Persian rug with a pile thick enough to lose your comb in, and two Georgian marble end tables set with magnificent brass parlor lamps.

The ceiling went up two stories to make room for the built-in bookshelves that held Samuel's prized library, or at least the handsomest portion of it. Even this room wasn't big enough to hold all the volumes he'd brought with him from California, but what there was made for a welcomely civilized scene. A bright one, too, thanks to the copious windows fitted with actual glass shipped in at enormous expense. Most of it was still intact, but the spectacular main window—a giant pane of lead-joined colored glass that spelled out *Price Mining Company* in artistic, swooping letters—had been smashed clean out, leaving a six-foot boarded-up hole in the middle of the parlor's street-facing wall.

Seeing it made Josie feel as if someone had knocked a hole in her as well. Despite never having set foot in it before this moment, Josie knew every nail and fixture of this building. She and Uncle Samuel had worked together on its design, planning out all the features of the flagship headquarters for what was supposed to be her uncle's greatest achievement. He'd been even more excited about crystal than he had about railroads, coming out here months before anyone else in the country had even heard the name Medicine Rocks.

Josie had already been in close correspondence with him for years at that point, so while this had always been his dream, she couldn't help feeling a part of it. All of it now, she supposed. But standing in the diminished shadow of the place she'd heard so much about brought the pain of her uncle's death back as sharp as the day she'd first heard the news. It was a loss Josie didn't think she'd ever stop mourning, despite never having actually met the man.

The first time Josie had heard the name "Samuel Price" was the winter she'd turned eight years old. Born the heir to the Price family's shipping fortune, Samuel had balked at the idea of living idle on someone else's money and surrendered his coming inheritance to his younger brother, choosing instead to go west and make his own fortune. The rest of the Prices had proclaimed him mad and stopped talking about him altogether until Sam had suddenly come home one Christmas as a self-made millionaire.

As it turned out, he'd taken the money he'd made selling gold-panning equipment to miners in California and invested in the railway, making a killing when stocks shot up. He'd then taken that money and built his own local rail line connecting several far-flung mines, turning what had been a three-week journey getting gold out of the Sierra Nevada mountains into a one-day train ride. The new railway doubled his fortune again, giving him more capital for more investments until he'd made himself even richer than the Prices whose fortune he'd turned down.

Naturally, the rest of the family took this as a personal affront. Apparently, getting rich on one's own was even more unacceptable than being mad. Josie hadn't even been permitted to meet the "terrible man" who was "determined to ruin us." Despite all this, Mrs. Price, being the proper Boston society lady that she was, declared that *someone* still needed to write to Samuel to keep up the appearance of family unity, and since Josephine was the youngest and most talkative Price, the onerous duty had fallen to her.

And so it had begun. No one had known then what the correspondence would become, but Josie had been of a lonely age, and Samuel was a fascinating and dramatic man who thought nothing of sharing his business with a nosy, excitable girl. In hindsight, it was inevitable that she'd attach herself to him like a barnacle. The only surprising part was that he'd let her.

Of all the Price relations she'd been forced to correspond with, Samuel was the only one who talked to Josie as if she were capable of thinking for herself. He'd encouraged her unusual interests by sharing his own, inviting her into his magical world of books, business, and adventure on the wild frontier. His letters gave Josie ten times more than anyone else ever had, and she'd given her best in return, writing him volumes upon volumes so that he'd always know that someone back home cared.

The mining company was the first venture where she'd worked with him as an equal. He'd been running his ideas by her since he'd first realized she also had a head for business at ten, but it wasn't until he'd moved to Medicine Rocks that he'd really needed her help. Naturally, Josie had pulled out all the stops, using everything he'd taught her about contracts and trade to take care of all the details it would be impossible for him to manage from so far away. She'd sourced the picks for his miners and ordered hundreds of deadlight kerosene lamps that wouldn't catch fire in the caves. She'd gotten him the lumber for this building, bringing the price down to nearly nothing by promising the logging company crystal payments on future contracts.

Anything she could do to help she did, because Uncle Samuel deserved it and because it was fun. No one knew you were a woman in a letter. Doing business on her uncle's behalf had been like stepping into another life, one Josie had liked *very* much.

She'd gotten so good at it by the end that Samuel had started calling her his partner in his letters. He'd even written the family telling them he was leaving her his fortune when he died, since, as he loved to taunt his brother, Josephine was the only Price who could be trusted to manage anything properly. No one had believed him, of course, until the lawyer had shown up at the Prices' mansion in Boston to inform Josephine that she was now the sole owner of Price Mining and the richest person in Montana.

The other Prices had thrown a fit when they realized he hadn't been joking. They'd immediately contested the will, bringing in their own army of lawyers, but Sam, being Sam, had left them no opening. Once they realized they couldn't pry away control of the money legally, they'd started plotting to marry Josephine off to someone more tractable and gain control of her new fortune that way. After the third idiot suitor tried to force her into a compromising position, Josephine had decided she'd be better off on her own, booking a ticket to New York on the pretense of visiting her sister, only to switch trains at the very next station for an express to St. Louis.

And now Josie was here in Medicine Rocks, in the company they'd built together. In a place where she no longer had to bite her tongue all day. A place where she was finally free to live as she liked. She'd been dreaming of this for so long, and yet the only thing Josie wanted to do right now was meet the man who'd made it possible. The stranger who'd been as dear to her as a father and whom she was finally realizing she would never, *ever* get to see in this life.

It was enough to make a body cry. Josie hated crying, but there was no stopping it. She was digging out her handkerchief to at least save her powder when a voice sounded from above.

"Miss Price?"

Josie looked up with a start to see a man standing on the open landing of the second floor where the staff bedrooms were tucked away. He was dark-skinned with thick black hair going gray at the temples and an impressively large mustache that probably caused most people to mistake him for a Mexican vaquero. But while that was undoubtedly the aim, Josie wasn't fooled for an instant, and her face broke into an enormous smile.

"*Mihir!*" she cried, running forward to embrace him as he reached the bottom of the stairs. "It is you, isn't it? What a pleasure to finally meet you!"

"And I you," Mihir replied, squeezing her back like the daughter he'd always made her feel she was. "Welcome, Josephine!"

Just like Uncle Samuel, Mihir had been an irreplaceable part of Josie's life. He was Sam's oldest and dearest friend as well as the competent manager who'd kept all her uncle's wild ideas rooted in reality. Unlike the natives who fought the cavalry, Mihir was an actual Indian from the subcontinent, one of the many poor souls who'd been lured from his homeland with false promises to work for the railroads in slavery conditions. Samuel had discovered him hiding under his cabin in

California twenty-five years ago. Impressed by the young man's daring escape, Sam had invited Mihir to stay with him, and once they'd discovered their shared love of reading, the two had become inseparable.

Mihir was the reason Sam boasted such an impressive library. Even out on the frontier, where books were scarce, he was a genius at finding titles, corresponding with authors all over the world to secure works that might never find their way west of the Mississippi otherwise. Samuel's letters had always included a list of books Mihir thought Josie would enjoy, and she always had. Just like Uncle, Mihir had thought and cared about her in a way no one else had ever bothered to, and in her current weepy state, Josie couldn't have stopped hugging him if she'd tried.

"Forgive me for accosting you," she said when she'd finally gotten hold of herself. "But I feel like I'm meeting long-lost family. Sam talked about you constantly."

"Not half as much as he talked about you, I'm sure," Mihir replied with a warm smile. "Though I wish it were under happier circumstances, I'm delighted to finally speak with you face-to-face. Forgive me for not coming out to greet you earlier. I wasn't expecting you until next week."

"I wasn't expecting to be here so soon either," Josie said. "But we got lucky with the weather, and my escort was in quite the hurry."

As if they'd been waiting for their cue, the soldiers who'd ridden her out here burst into the lobby, hauling Josie's traveling chests behind them as if participating in a timed event.

"Are those your men?" Mihir asked excitedly.

"No," Josephine admitted, feeling suddenly as if she'd failed him. "I was able to ride the Northern Pacific railway all the way to Helena to meet the governor and settle my legal affairs, but there's no train that goes by Medicine Rocks yet. I was planning to hire local workers and drive the last distance on my own, but I couldn't find anyone willing to make the trip to Medicine Rocks for love nor money. It was absolutely ridiculous. You'd think there'd be a river of men ready to travel to a boomtown on someone else's dime. But between the Sioux and the bandits, the roads have become so dangerous that no one was willing to risk escorting a carriage. If the governor hadn't loaned me a company of state militia, I'd still be in Helena. Frankly, I think he only did it to get me out of his hair. I caused him quite a bit of extra work, I'm afraid."

"It was the least he could do," Mihir said. "Before it shut down, Price Mining was responsible for a third of all the crystal coming out of Medicine Rocks. The whole territory needs this company up and running again, and we could really use some more security." He cast a longing look at the men. "Is there any chance you could convince them to stay now that they're here?"

"I could try," Josie offered. "But they've been talking of nothing but going home since we started. That's how we got here so quickly. The sergeant had us moving sunup to sundown every day, and I'm sure they'll be heading back at the same pace as soon as they're finished disgorging my things."

The men truly did seem to be flinging her luggage everywhere. The instant her last trunk hit the board floor, Sergeant Mallory, leader of the militia unit that had escorted her here so efficiently, rushed over to Josie with a piece of paper.

"Right, Miss Price, we've seen you safe to Medicine Rocks as requested. If you'd just sign here, confirming that we've done our part, me and my men will be on our way."

He was hopping from foot to foot as he said this, glancing over his shoulder at the exit as if he were afraid of catching the plague. It wasn't a promising sign, but Josie took a chance anyway.

"Could I not convince you to stay another week?" she asked, taking the paper over to what had been the front office secretary's desk in search for a pen. "I'll gladly pay you for your trouble."

"I'm afraid that's impossible," the sergeant said without even a second's hesitation. "Medicine Rocks is no place for honest men, and speaking frankly, miss, I don't think you should stay here either. I know this is your inheritance, but between the redskins taking scalps and the bandits taking everything else, this town's a death sentence waiting to happen. I'm not presuming to tell you your business, but we'd be more than happy to take you back with us to Helena if you want."

"I appreciate your honesty," Josie said, locating a writing utensil at last and leaning over to scribble Josephine Price's name on the space he'd indicated. "But I'm not going anywhere. This is my company now. I will not be frightened away."

"Suit yourself, miss," the sergeant said, clearly ready to wash his hands of the whole affair. "Your things are all unloaded, and we've put your carriage in the shed 'round back. I believe that settles our business, so we'll be on our way."

"Won't you and your men stay for breakfast at least?" Mihir asked desperately.

The officer shook his head. "Thank you kindly, sir, but I'd rather have miles behind me than any meal in front. Good luck to you both. You'll need it."

With that, the sergeant and his men all but ran out of the room. Mihir watched them go with a terrified expression on his face, and Josie returned the pen to its nook in the desk's dusty drawer with a sigh.

"All right," she said when they were alone again. "How bad is it?"

"Let's just say I'm very glad you're a week early," Mihir replied, sinking onto one of the parlor's horsehair sofas like a collapsing souffle. "I've managed to avoid selling the furniture so far, but if you'd actually arrived on the day expected, you'd likely have walked into a very different office."

"How did things get to this state?" Josie asked, lowering herself onto the settee across from him. "You just said this was the biggest crystal operation in Medicine Rocks not six months ago. I know uncle's death was a blow, but at the risk of sounding like an unfeeling capitalist, mines don't stop producing just because their owner dies. Especially not with someone as competent as yourself at the helm. What went so wrong that you were put in this dire position?"

46

"It'd be quicker to say what *didn't* go wrong," Mihir replied, running a hand over his despairing face. "As you said, we were doing very well. We had over a hundred claims and twenty mining teams bringing in crystal by the bucket. Then, last autumn, Samuel went down in search of another strike."

Josie sighed. "Let me guess: he went alone."

"You know how he was," Mihir said with affectionate exasperation. "He was fascinated by the caves but had no patience for waiting on others. He ran off to the tunnels every chance he got, so I didn't think much of this particular trip until three weeks passed and he hadn't come back."

Josie's gloved hands curled into fists on her dark-green skirt. "I thought he died of pneumonia."

"I'm not to that point yet," Mihir said, shaking his head. "Sam *was* down longer than usual, but he came back whole and hale. The problem at that stage wasn't his lungs. It was his mind."

Josie didn't like the sound of that. "What was wrong with his mind?"

Mihir shifted uncomfortably. "You know how obsessed he was with crystal. We were planning to retire from the railway business and move to San Francisco when his old college friend Bernard Reiner sent him a packet containing four crystal pebbles. The moment Sam saw them, we were off to Montana. Since that day, there's been nothing that could keep him out of the caves. Did he ever tell you how he could 'hear' the crystal, even though no one else could?"

"God, yes," Josie said, smiling at the memory. "He wrote pages about the 'music of the caves,' though he failed to mention he was the only one who heard it."

"Well, there's music, and there's music," Mihir said. "All crystal sings a note when struck, which is why all our miners carried tuning forks as part of their standard equipment. But Sam didn't just hear the crystal when he tapped it. He claimed he could hear the rocks singing all the time, even through solid stone. There must have been something to it, because he could walk through the caves and point out veins that other prospectors had walked right by. That ability was how Price Mining did so well. My only contribution was hiring workers fast enough to keep up with all his discoveries."

"That is no small feat," Josie assured him. "But what happened to Uncle? Did the crystal start speaking to him in tongues?"

The remark was supposed to be a bit of levity, but Mihir's face turned ashen. "I'm not sure what he heard, but whatever it was, it changed him. Before that trip, Sam had always been excited about what we were bringing out of the caves. He used to say that mining crystal wasn't just about making money. We were bringing to light a new power that would build a better future for all mankind. He believed we were at the forefront of a technological revolution on the scale of the discovery of electricity. That was the Sam who went into the mines, but when he came out again, the very first thing he did was fire all our miners."

"Fire the miners?" Josie repeated, shocked. "*Why?*"

"To stop them from mining," Mihir said with a shrug. "He said he'd made a terrible mistake and that everything had to stop right then. I begged him to explain, but all he could tell me was that he'd been wrong about everything. The guilt was consuming him, so while I didn't understand, I did as he asked and shut everything down. Laid off our miners, our office staff, everyone."

No wonder those miners in the crowd had looked so angry. Josie had assumed the company's decline was due to Sam's death, but if he'd fired everyone before he'd even gotten sick, that meant no mining had been going on at Price Mining for seven months at least.

"Did you not try to talk him out of it?"

Mihir ran a sheepish hand through his graying hair. "Honestly? No. Crystal was Sam's obsession, not mine. I was hoping his reversal meant we'd finally be going home to California. I'd even started packing up the library when Sam suddenly announced he was going back in."

"I thought he wasn't mining anymore?"

"He wasn't mining," Mihir said. "He was just... *going*." He slumped over on the sofa. "Please know, Miss Price, that I did my best to talk him out of it that time. It was midwinter, and he already had the cough. With no more miners to worry about, I saw absolutely no reason for him to risk himself, but Sam said he had to. He claimed the crystal was calling to him."

"Oh," Josie said quietly, fiddling nervously with her dress. "I've... I've read about the effects prolonged exposure to crystal can have on the mind. Do you think...?"

"That he had crystal madness?" Mihir sighed. "I've asked myself the same question a thousand times. But I've seen plenty of miners lose themselves to crystal, and Sam wasn't acting anything like they did. He was as clear and calm as ever, no shakes or growths or paranoid visions. Aside from completely changing his mind on everything related to crystal mining, he seemed perfectly normal. Even his insistence on going into the caves was as usual. He'd never been able to stay out of them for more than a month at a time since we got here."

Josie released a long breath. "I take it that was his final trip?"

Mihir nodded sadly. "He was down there for over a month. Doing what, I have no idea, but when he finally came out again, the pneumonia was thick in his lungs. I tried my best to save him. Hired the best doctors, kept him warm, even let him drink the last of the whiskey I'd brought from Kentucky, but nothing helped. He died a week later. After that, the real trouble started."

Josie's head snapped up. "There's more?"

"I told you it'd be easier to say what hadn't gone wrong," Mihir reminded her. "Before he went on any trip into the mines, Sam would always leave me a detailed plan for what to do in case he didn't come out again. Your uncle being your uncle, it was always arranged down to the last detail, including what to do with the crystal stockpiles we still had left over from our aborted mining operation. Per his instructions, I went to the Mining Office to ask about selling all our remaining crystal to the government in exchange for a bond in your name, since you were his heir.

When I spoke to the officer in charge, however, he told me I could not make any such arrangements because I was not a citizen of the United States."

"But that's preposterous!" Josie cried. "This is the Montana *Territory*. We're not even in the States!"

"That's what I told them," Mihir said. "But even after I showed them Samuel's will specifically naming me as executor of his estate, they refused to acknowledge his wishes."

"Perhaps that was for the best, though," Josie said, trying to look on the bright side. "Surely all that crystal would sell for more in the private market than to the government?"

"It would indeed, *if* we still had it," he said. "That's the next act of the tragedy. That very night after the Mining Office denied my transaction, our office was robbed."

"Good Lord," Josie said, reaching out to take his hand. "Were you hurt?"

"No," Mihir said. "That's the oddest thing. We'd already let all the other staff go, so I was the only one left in the building, but I don't even remember going to bed that night. I just woke up the next morning to find the vault door ripped off its hinges and all our crystal gone."

Josie closed her eyes with a silent curse. "Well," she said at last. "At least that explains what happened to the window."

Mihir nodded, but he was staring down at his hands. "I know what you must be thinking. After hearing myself tell it, I can't help but think the same. But I assure you I would never—"

"Don't even say it," Josie interrupted, reaching across the table. "Uncle trusted you more than any person on the planet. There's not an argument in the world that could make me believe you had a hand in this atrocity. If nothing else, the fact that you're still here telling me about it is proof of your innocence, were it even in question, which it is not."

"It's a relief to hear you say so." He squeezed her offered hand. "I hope you still feel that way once you've heard the rest, for it's most

50

damning. Sam and I have had problems with thieves since we moved here. Buddha knows this town is full of them, but the men who robbed us this time were different. They knew exactly what they were after, because once they'd emptied the crystal vault, they walked right past this parlor without touching a thing to ransack our offices, including Samuel's private study and bedroom."

"That is suspicious," Josie agreed. "What were they looking for?"

"Deeds," Mihir said angrily. "I had multiple copies of our paperwork distributed throughout the building so that no single disaster could wipe us out, but they found everything. They even dug up the emergency strongbox I'd buried under the kitchen. They knew exactly where and what to look for, and when they were done, every claim deed and land note we had was gone."

The blood drained from Josephine's face. "But—but those were just documents!" she sputtered. "Possessing a piece of paper doesn't give you legal claim to what's written on it. Surely the Mining Office has their own records that prove our ownership?"

"They *did*," Mihir said. "Except there was also a fire at the Mining Office that same night, which means—"

"Which means whoever stole our deeds now has the only paperwork," Josephine finished, flopping back onto the sofa. "How very *convenient.*"

"I'm not worried they'll try to steal the land," Mihir said. "We had hundreds of miners working those claims. Everyone knows they're ours, so anyone who tried to present papers saying otherwise would just be outing themselves as the criminal. The problem lies in the crystal. Thanks to the Mining Office's efforts to halt the rampant spread of claim jumping, no one is allowed to remove crystal from the caves unless they can show proof that they own a mine it could have come from, and without our deeds—"

"We can't do that," Josie finished, scowl deepening. "That's it, then. They're trying to run us out of business!"

"We were already out of the mining business," Mihir reminded her. "I suspect they were after our claim locations. There's a stake number written on every deed. With that information, anyone could mine our crystal and then declare that it came from one of their claims when they got to the checkpoint. It'd be an especially good scam to pull right now, since we're shut down. The thieves could have mined our claims dry in the months since Sam died, and we wouldn't even know."

"Whatever they're doing, it's criminal," Josie said angrily. "Is the sheriff investigating?"

Mihir's expression turned sour. "He claims he is, but I've seen no evidence. He didn't even come here to look at the damage, nor has he investigated any of the other robberies that have happened since."

Josie's jaw dropped. "You mean there've been *more?*"

"Scores, unfortunately. The first group of robbers only cared for crystal and paperwork, but once they showed everyone how weak Price Mining had become, we started having break-ins every few days. The storehouse is in shambles. We've lost tools, guns, lanterns, even the cookware from our kitchen. They would have stripped this room to the walls as well if I hadn't taken to sleeping on the sofa every night with my shotgun."

"Oh, Mihir," she said. "I'm so sorry."

"Not as sorry as I," he said bitterly. "I abhor violence, but Sam and I worked decades building this collection. Tools and furniture can be replaced, but I'd shoot a man myself before I let him touch our books."

The image of kind, bookish Mihir turning murderous was a tragedy Josie hadn't been prepared for. "I'm so sorry you had to go through that," she said again. "But I promise the hard times are over. If the sheriff won't help us, we'll help ourselves. Look here."

She hopped off the sofa and hurried over to the trunks her escort had left in a pile at the foot of the stairs. Standing on her tiptoes, Josie grabbed the smallest—but still quite heavy—chest off the top. One she'd lowered it safely to the floor without crushing any toes, she opened the lid to show Mihir the treasure glittering inside.

"They're silver dollars, fresh from the mint," she told him proudly. "I got the banker to fill this whole trunk with them before I left St. Louis. They were supposed to be for travel expenses, but as you see, I've still plenty left. We can use this to hire new miners and get back to work. You still know all the locations for our claims, right?"

"Inasmuch as one can be certain of any location in the caves," Mihir said. "But I already told you, there's no point. Even if we mined it all, we can't legally remove crystal from the mines without those deeds."

Josie shook her head. "I'm not about to give up all of Uncle's hard work over some bad-faith legality. If everyone knows those locations are our property, then let's mine them! If someone challenges our right to do so, we'll challenge them right back to show us proof that these are not our claims. If they can't produce the evidence, we keep mining. If they try to use our own deeds, we've found our thief. It's a win for us either way."

"That's a bold plan," Mihir said, stroking his mustache. "Very like something Sam would've come up with, actually. But there's still a problem."

"What is it now?"

"We can't hire miners with silver," he explained patiently. "It was always going to be difficult for us to replace our workforce after your uncle unceremoniously fired everyone, but this is Medicine Rocks. No one in this town gets out of bed for anything that isn't crystal. Even if you filled that chest with gold, I'm not sure you could convince anyone to swing a pick for Price Mining right now, given how unpopular we are."

"Then what am I supposed to do?" Josie cried, slamming the coin chest shut. "We can't be a mining company if we're not mining! And I already promised I'd start sending profits back to St. Louis before the end of summer!"

Mihir looked confused. "Who's in St. Louis that you need to send money to?"

53

"No one," Josie said quickly, furious with herself. Furious with everything, really, because it had all gone so *wrong*. An hour ago, she'd been on her way to being a millionaire. Now it looked like they wouldn't even be able to keep the building.

The timing of the crimes left no question that this series of events had been orchestrated for precisely that purpose: to steal her uncle's fortune and leave her powerless to reclaim it. But Josie wasn't ready to surrender yet. If life with the Prices had taught her anything, it was that enough money could convince people to do anything. Samuel's rash decision might have hurt their standing in town, but Josie was sure she could get things running again with the right amount of capital.

There was plenty of money left from Samuel's railway bonds, but retrieving it from the bank in St. Louis would take months, by which point the entire building might be stolen right out from under them. If she was going to salvage the situation, Josie needed something quicker, but what? She was wracking her brain for ideas when Mihir cleared his throat.

"I don't know if it will be any help," he said, rising from the couch, "but Samuel was trying to write you a letter when he passed."

Josie's heart clenched, forgetting all about money and deeds in the joy of possibly getting one last conversation with her uncle. "May I read it?"

"Of course," Mihir said, reaching into his coat. "Though I'm afraid it doesn't make much sense. He was delirious with fever at the end, but he told me several times that this was for you, so..."

He handed her a folded square so creased and worn from being carried around in his pocket that the paper had gone as soft as fabric. Josie took the flimsy thing with trembling fingers, unfolding it as delicately as she could to uncover her uncle's last, precious words.

My little Dido, it read, *never forget that She Wolves don't read.*

"What in blazes?" she muttered, turning the note over, but that was all there was. Ten shaky, scrawled words, none of which meant a thing to her.

"Do you have any clue why he's talking about wolves?" she asked Mihir.

"Not the foggiest," he said, shaking his head. "I was hoping you would understand. Sam seemed lucid enough while he was writing, but I was busy with the doctor and didn't think to ask what he meant until it was too late."

"It's not your fault," Josie said quickly, reading the message over and over as she began to pace the room.

If he truly hadn't been delirious, then the note was almost certainly a riddle. Uncle had loved riddles. He used to send them to her constantly when she was younger. He'd slowed down once Josie got old enough to intelligently discuss business, a topic he'd loved even more, but seeing that he'd addressed her as Dido reminded her of a game they used to play.

It started with him writing a letter as usual, but instead of speaking to Josie, he'd write the whole thing as if he were corresponding with some literary or historical figure. Her job was to figure out which story he was referencing, read it, and then write him back with her thoughts on why he'd chosen that particular person. Looking back, Josie was certain it was a ploy to fool her into reading more widely than just her tutor-approved schoolbooks, but she couldn't remember him ever using Dido before.

"I can see why he chose it," Mihir said when she'd explained all this. "Dido was a princess who fled her controlling family to become Queen of Carthage. Seems quite appropriate to your current situation."

"I don't recall there being any wolves in Dido's story, though," Josie said, resuming her pacing. "And why does it matter if they read or not? For that matter, why did he say 'don't'? Wolves *can't* read, so it's not a matter of—"

She stopped suddenly, smacking her forehead with one hand. "Good Lord, I'm an idiot."

"You're not an idiot," Mihir said at once.

"Thank you. It's very nice to hear someone say that." Nicer than he could know, actually. "But I am absolutely overthinking this. Do you have a copy of Virgil's *Aeneid*?"

"Original Latin or Gavin Douglas's Scots translation?" he asked, turning to the bookshelves.

Josie had no idea, but it turned out not to matter, since the two books were shelved right next to each other. The Latin edition was a lovely leather-bound tome with gold-leaf embossing that turned up nothing. The Scots translation was far less ornamented, but the moment Mihir handed it over, Josie knew this was the one. Not only did this book show more signs of wear with its fraying cloth-bound cover and fading print, it sat more heavily in her hands than it should. Sure enough, the moment she cracked it open, an object fell out of the thin pages into her waiting palm.

It was like nothing Josie had ever seen: a crescent-shaped shaving as long as her hand and thin as a pane of glass. The white color and curved shape made it look like a large scrap of onion, but its surface was as hard as granite when she tried to bend it and slightly warm to the touch, like a rock that had been left out in the sun. Strangest of all, though, was how the thing glowed. Even with the morning sun streaming through the windows, the slender stone lit up her gloves with a white light all its own, making it look as if she were holding the crescent moon itself in her hands.

"What the devil is this?"

"It's crystal," Mihir breathed, his dark eyes wide with wonder.

Josie nearly dropped the thing in astonishment. *This* was crystal? Everything she'd read had led her to believe it looked like colored quartz, not this marvelousness.

"Is it valuable?"

"Incredibly so," Mihir said, reaching out to touch the dazzling stone. "But I never knew they could glow."

Josie's heart began to pound. "This isn't normal?"

Mihir shook his head. "I'd heard stories about glowing crystal from when the mines were first discovered, but I've never seen any myself. Samuel thought there might still be some in the Deep Caves, but he was always coming up with excuses to run down there, so I didn't think anything of it. I never imagined he'd actually found one."

"If he hid it even from you, it *must* be important," Josie said, mind whirling. "In one of his many letters where he was trying to describe the sound of caves to me, Uncle talked about clusters of crystal being part of a larger whole, like colonies of coral in the ocean. He claimed that while each crystal had a note of its own, they could also sing together in a harmony and that they would keep singing to each other even after they'd been broken apart." She held up the crystal crescent, turning it over to show him the sharp-sheared edge. "You've worked with mountains of crystal. Would you say this looks like a piece of something bigger?"

"It's very possible," he said. "I've certainly never seen a crystal grow into that shape on its own."

"Could it still be connected?" she asked in a rush. "We know Uncle found something that changed his mind about crystal mining. What if he found one of those singing clusters still glowing way down in the Deep Caves? What if this is a piece of it?"

"I suppose it could be," Mihir said skeptically. "But I'm still not entirely convinced his stories about music weren't overblown. You know how dramatic he could get."

"I remember," Josie said fondly. "But there must be some truth in it, or he couldn't have found all those claims." She looked at the lovely stone in her hands. "He hid this for a reason, Mihir. If it was just a valuable rock, he would have left it with you along with all the other crystal in the vault. The fact that he went through so much effort to make sure that I and *only* I could find it means there's more to this crystal than meets the eye." She sighed. "If only I could hear the crystal like he could. I bet that would tell me something."

"You are his blood," Mihir said hopefully. "*Can* you hear it?"

57

Josie already knew she couldn't, but she put the stone to her ear anyway. As expected, though… "Nothing," she said, shaking her head. "I can see it glowing and feel its warmth, but I don't hear so much as a whisper."

Mihir looked crestfallen, but Josie wasn't near ready to give up. This was a riddle just like the note, she was sure of it, and while it sometimes took longer than she liked, Josie had never not solved one of her uncle's puzzles. Her mind was already spinning with what to try next when the bell on the front door jingled.

Josie jumped at the sound, shoving the shining crystal into her pocket like a child caught with her hand in the candy bowl. She wasn't normally so skittish, but Mihir's stories about thieves and criminals were fresh in her mind, and the figure in the doorway wasn't helping.

It was a man dressed all in black. More than that was hard to say, since his hat was tilted down over his face, and his body was smothered under a duster that was far too big, probably because he was so short. If he'd been a lady, he'd have been perfect. As a gentleman, though, he must have felt lacking, for when his too-large coat swung open, Josie spied no fewer than three pistols holstered on his belt: two plain ones and a godawful gaudy piece of work decked all over in bone ivory and colored glass.

No, she realized. Not glass. The gun was covered in *crystal*. Not the lovely alabaster-thin sort like the glowing crescent in her pocket. These were the classic crystal cabochons as illustrated in the papers. Giant gems as big as Josie's knuckle held onto the gun with silver claw-shaped fasteners.

Josie didn't know if the rounded stones were meant to do anything or if they were merely decorative, but they made for an intimidating display. Mihir certainly seemed alarmed, for he jumped back to the bookcase, grabbing the pistol Josie hadn't realized was strapped underneath the shelf until he turned it on the intruder.

"Stop right there," he ordered, pointing his shaking gun at the stranger's chest.

The black-dressed figure did nothing of the sort, clearly unimpressed by the threats of someone so much less used to violence. But despite his dramatic entrance, he didn't seem interested in a shoot-out. He mostly looked confused, shoving his hat up to give them a good view of his face at last. A face that, Josie realized with a shock, she recognized.

"Reliance Reiner?"

"Josie O'Connor?" the stranger said at the same time, the name squeaking out in a shocked, high-pitched voice that didn't match his terrifying gunslinger image at all.

"O'Connor?" Mihir repeated, shaking his head. "You are mistaken, sir. This is Miss Josephine Price."

He glanced back at Josie, waiting for her to agree, but all she could do was gape, leaving Mihir looking back and forth in bewilderment at the two figures gone still as statues in the dusty morning light.

Chapter 4

Rel stood stupid in the doorway, crystal-sliced guts clenching in horror. Aw, hell. What was *she* doing here?

At least someone remembers the name I gave you.

Rel smacked the crystal gun into silence and stalked forward, glaring daggers at the little girl who'd grown into an absurdly tall lady. Josie at least had the decency to look ashamed, dropping her eyes to the floor as Rel approached. The old man with her, though, Samuel's pet foreigner—

Mihir.

Whatever. The mustached man had no such sense. He shoved himself into Rel's path and threw out his arms, as if that would do anything.

"Who are you?" he demanded. "What do you want with Miss Price?"

"Miss Price?" Rel repeated, pointing a finger at Josie, who was looking paler by the second. "You think *that* is Josephine Price?"

"It's all right, Mihir," Josie cut in before Rel could say more. "This is… this is an old friend."

At least Mihir was bright enough to give her the scowl that whopper deserved. "He doesn't look very reputable."

"I'm more reputable than she is! Have you ever seen the real Miss Price before? Like in person?"

"What kind of question is that?" Mihir huffed, blowing out his impressive mustache.

"I take that as a 'no,'" Rel said, smirking. "So you don't have any actual proof that this woman is who she says she—"

"Perhaps we could discuss this somewhere more *private*?" Josie said urgently, shoving her giantess body between Rel and Mihir.

"I'd like nothing better," Rel assured her, glancing back at Mihir. "Scram."

"You can't tell someone to 'scram' from their own home," Josie scolded, causing Rel's eyes to roll.

"I see you haven't changed a bit."

"I wish I could say the same for you," Josie muttered, turning primly to Mihir like she really was the rich heiress she was pretending to be. "Is there a room we might borrow?"

Mihir leaned in close and began whispering frantically, clearly attempting to impress the dangers of sequestering oneself with a gun-toting stranger upon Josie's pig-stubborn sensibilities. As typical, though, the lanky girl didn't listen to a damn thing, whispering back just as fiercely until the poor man gave up and unlocked a door at the back of the ridiculous parlor.

The door opened into what had clearly once been a very nice office. There were well-made desks and chairs for a half dozen clerks. But something terrible must have come through in the meanwhile, 'cause every stick of furniture in the place had been smashed to pieces.

Some were more pummeled than others. The chairs were still mostly intact, for example, but the desks had all had their drawers ripped out and broken, and the heavy wooden cabinet used for filing papers had been hacked to smithereens with an ax. Even the papered walls had been knocked full of hammer holes, a sure sign of someone's search for hidden safes.

"We were victims of a burglary," Josie explained despite Rel not asking. "Someone ransacked our offices and stole all our crystal the night after Uncle Samuel was cremated."

Rel arched an eyebrow. "*Uncle* Samuel, huh?"

Josie's powdered face scrunched into a scowl, but Mihir was still standing right there. Scowling deeper, she grabbed Rel's hand and closed the door—which still had a big crack down its middle from being kicked open—in the man's mustached face. She stomped to the far side of the ruined office next, pulling Rel with astonishing strength until they were as far from listening ears as they could get and still be in the building.

"Reliance Reiner, what in blazes are you doing here?" she demanded when they were finally alone. "How did you come to be in Medicine Rocks, of all places? And why are you wearing that ridiculous outfit?"

"I could ask you all the same questions," Rel replied, removing her hat and taking a seat on the still mostly intact oak counting table. "Josie O'Connor, it's been an age. Where'd you stash the real Miss Price? Is she hiding in that fancy carriage while you do all the hard work, as usual?"

Josie's flinch told Rel she'd struck true, but the answer that came next wasn't anything close to the excuses she'd expected.

"Miss Josephine is still in St. Louis," Josie whispered, finally sounding like the lady's maid she actually was instead of the lady she'd been impersonating. "When we learned of her uncle's death, the Price family's reaction was… undesirable. Miss Josephine needed to secure her inheritance quickly before her father's lawyers found a way around the careful language of Samuel's will, but she was too afraid to go into such wild country herself, so it was decided that I would come to Medicine Rocks and claim Price Mining in her stead."

"She sent you out here *alone*?" Rel cried, suspicion turning to fury as she realized what had been done. "That selfish spoiled sow! Her uncle dies and leaves her a fortune, and she can't even be bothered to come pick it up herself?"

"Actually, it was my idea," Josie said, twisting her gloved hands nervously.

"Did you have a death wish?"

"Quite the opposite," Josie assured her. "I volunteered to come out here because I wanted to, and because I knew Miss Josephine couldn't possibly do the job herself. You see, I was really the one writing all those letters to Samuel."

Rel snorted. "I should've guessed. Josephine always used to make you do her schoolwork. Why not her correspondence as well?"

"I never meant to deceive anyone," Josie said, hands twisting faster. "It was only supposed to be one letter to appease her mother, but I enjoyed Sam's reply so much that I just kept going. Miss Josephine didn't even know I was still writing him until we got the notice that her uncle had left her everything, thinking she was me."

"Guess you shot yourself in the foot, then," Rel said, leaning back against the hole-pecked wall. "But that's what you get for letting Prissy Missy Price walk all over you."

"I was doing my job," Josie said angrily. "My family has served the Prices for three generations! My mother even named me Josephine in Miss Price's honor. I owe them everything: my education, my housing, the clothes on my back, the—"

"Oh, I'm *very* aware of what you think you owe the Prices," Rel said testily. "I spent five years in that house listening to Mrs. Price and her daughters remind you of it every chance they got. Last I checked, though, servants weren't slaves, so what the hell are you doing risking your neck for their sake out in this shithole?"

"Language," Josie scolded. Then she smiled. "And I already told you. Coming to Medicine Rocks was my idea precisely because it got me away from them. I was the one who convinced Miss Josephine that running away would free her from her family's attempts to control her new fortune. Once we got to St. Louis, I left her in the care of Sam Price's lawyer to live as an independent lady of wealth while I went on to Medicine Rocks to claim the company *I* helped build. With fifteen hundred miles between us, we could both be 'Miss Josephine' and live as we wanted. It was the perfect plan!"

Rel arched an eyebrow. "Was?"

"I've run into a few complications," Josie admitted. "I was counting on Price Mining's crystal to supplement the actual Miss Josephine's income in St. Louis. Samuel used up most of his fortune building this place. There was still a good chunk left in the bank when I got on the train, but you *know* how the Prices spend. She'll blow that in a year. She already gave me

63

all her old clothes just so she'd have an excuse to buy herself a new wardrobe."

"That sounds like Josephine," Rel agreed. "And this didn't strike you as a problem?"

"It wouldn't have been! She'd just inherited the largest producer of the world's most valuable substance. Everything would have been fine if all I had to do was take over an already functional mining operation, but as you can see..."

"Price Mining's been stripped down to the nails," Rel finished with a nod. "Typical of anything left unsupervised in Medicine Rocks."

"It's not just the building," Josie said in dismay. "Our claim deeds were stolen as well, along with all our leftover crystal and most of our mining equipment. I'm practically starting over from scratch."

"Seems like a lost cause to me," said Rel, sensing her opening. "But you know, Josie, there's no need to sit here flogging a dead horse. I know some businesspeople in town who'd be willing to take this mess off your hands."

"For a pittance, maybe," Josie said with a snort. "No one's going to give me fair value for an already burgled building with no employees and no assets."

"Even a pittance would be more than you've got," Rel pointed out. "You're kidding yourself if you think you can restart Price Mining from nothing. I wasn't even in town yet when Sam Price fired all his employees, and I *still* hear miners grousing about it. There's no love for the Price name here and no profit neither. I know you've got grand visions, but you'd be much better off if you sold this place to someone who can actually handle it. A lump sum payment would give you all the cash you need to get back to St. Louis in time to stop the real Miss Josephine from squandering her entire fortune."

"I don't care if she squanders her entire fortune!" Josie cried. "Weren't you listening? I came out here for *me*! The only reason I'm sending money to Miss Josephine is because she'll take me down with her if I don't. I might be the one Uncle *thought* he was leaving his company to, but legally, that's her name on his will. She could destroy everything I've worked for in a heartbeat! And if you think she won't do exactly that the moment the money spigot runs dry, you've forgotten what it was like to live with the Prices."

As if Rel could ever forget what it was like to be at the mercy of such spiteful snobs. She hadn't been as easy a target as Josie, who, as the daughter of Mrs. Price's fanatically loyal housekeeper, was generally considered family property. But the Prices had never missed a chance to remind Reliance that she and her family were also inferior, charity cases taken in only because Bernard Reiner and the Price brothers had all been chums at Harvard. She admired Josie for getting her own out of them—she really did—but Rel had her own business to take care of.

"I understand what's at stake for you out here," she said, trying her best to sound reasonable. "But you should know better than anyone that hoping doesn't make things so. You can't just will this place back into profitability, and you might well end up losing more than your money if you keep trying. Medicine Rocks is not a nice place. There's a lot of dangerous people here, and you just taunted all of them by riding into town on that fancy carriage. You're nothing but a money bag waiting to be pilfered to that lot, so if you don't want to end up in the same sorry state as this building, you should take my offer, take the buyout, and take yourself away from this place. Hell, they'll be paying you in cash. You could take that money for yourself and run to California. You never have to see a snooty Price face again if you don't want. So what if Josephine bankrupts herself then? You'll be free! Free and *alive*, which is more than I can promise if you stay here."

Rel thought she'd made a pretty solid case, but Josie was staring at her like she'd just suggested lighting her hair on fire.

"I will not be threatened into giving up my life's work!" she cried, pulling herself to her full, ludicrous height. "Uncle Samuel and I put years into building this place together! It's all I have left of the only person who's

65

ever really believed in and loved me for who I was! I will *not* sell it for any sum, and I am *not* leaving!"

Rel jerked away from the tirade with her hands up. She didn't remember Josie being so feisty, but damn. So much for an easy sell.

Ask her about what Sam Price found in the caves, the gun suggested. *Maybe she has a legitimate, nonhysterical reason for refusing to sell that she's not telling us.*

Rel's usual reaction to anything her father said was to do the exact opposite, but the bastard had given her a good idea just now. Not that Rel believed in Old Sam's secret treasure—if Apache Jake said it was rumors, then it was rumors, 'cause he'd already be all over it if it weren't—but the town's belief that it was true made a good scare tactic. It was easy for Josie to stand there and scream down from her high horse when nothing truly bad had happened yet, but she might not be so damn cocksure once Rel gave her something real to be afraid of.

And you call me *a bastard.*

Rel swatted the pistol to shut it up. When she raised her head to give her new strategy a try, though, Josie was already looking like she was about to cry.

"What?" Rel said in alarm, scooting back on the table. "What'd I do?"

"Nothing," she said, clasping her hands in front of her ruffled skirt. "I'm the one to blame. You were just trying to help me, and I came at you like a tiger. You didn't deserve all that, it's just… I've worked *so* hard for *so* long trying to make this happen. Now it feels like everything's blowing up in my face, and I…" She trailed off with a huff. "I'm sorry. It was wrong of me to yell at you, and I apologize."

"Not your fault," Rel said, trying to remember the last time someone had said the words "I'm sorry" in her presence. "I can see how it's a sore subject."

"More like an all-consuming one," Josie said, pulling out an already damp handkerchief to wipe her eyes. "It's clearly eaten all my manners. Here I am talking endlessly about myself, and I haven't even asked how you've been. The last time I saw you, I was pinning your hair for Mrs. Price's cotillion. How in the world did the Beauty of Boston end up way out here? And where's your mother and little Chase? Though I suppose he must not be so little anymore. Are they living in Medicine Rocks as well?"

Rel'd known this had to be coming, but the innocent questions still felt like punches to the gut.

"Momma and Chase aren't here," she said after a long pause. "They… they died. Last Christmas."

"Oh, Rel," Josie said, wrapping her in an embrace Reliance hadn't expected or asked for but found herself unable to reject. "I'm so sorry."

"Weren't your fault," Rel said gruffly, sinking into the hug like a steer into a tar pit.

"That doesn't mean I can't be sorry," Josie said, pulling back. "How did it happen?"

"Doesn't matter," Rel lied. "I got my own life now as a hired gun working for the Wet Whistle Saloon."

"The brothel?" Josie scrunched up her face. "Is that why you're dressed like a man? So that you're not…"

"Mistaken for a whore?" Rel shook her head. "Not that I take issue with the profession. Forget the mines, those girls make the best money in town. But I didn't come here to get rich. I got my own reasons for living in Medicine Rocks, and dressing this way makes my life easier. Reliance Reiner wasn't getting anywhere, but Tyrel gets respect."

"So I see," Josie said, looking her up and down. "You certainly do look the part of the menacing gunman, but do you have to talk in that ridiculous fashion? You used to be a refined young lady who could speak German and Latin as well as you could English. Now it sounds as if you've never heard a proper sentence."

She makes an excellent point.

"I'll talk how I please," Rel snapped at them both. "And it pleases me to not stand out like a poodle in a pack of hounds. You'd better start thinking about that shit as well if you're serious about staying. Medicine

67

Rocks ain't a place to fool around. There's people here who'll kill you soon as look at you, 'specially when crystal's involved."

"I'm safe on that score, at least," Josie said, far too blithely for Rel's liking. "I don't have any crystal at present."

"That's not what the people in town think."

"Then they're blind," Josie laughed tragically, waving her arm at the destroyed room. "Does this look like anyone's idea of a functional mining company?"

"It ain't the company they're interested in," Rel said, leaning closer now that Josie had finally given her the chance to put her strategy into play. "Weren't you curious why so many people came out to watch you drive in? It wasn't because they were keen to see the rebirth of the company that fired half the town. They're curious to see what Old Sam left you. Now I don't know what he wrote in his will, but word here is that Price found something in the mines 'fore he died, something *big*. That's likely why you've had so many break-ins. People are turning this place inside out looking for whatever it was he must've left to show you the way."

Rel paused to let her stew on that a moment before playing her next card.

"I'm only telling you this 'cause I'm worried," she said, doing her best to sound like the concerned friend Apache had sent her here to be. "Whether Sam left you something or not ain't my business, but so long as folks here *think* he did, you're in hot water. They ain't gonna stop coming, Josie, so I suggest you reconsider selling this place. You've made it clear what Price Mining means to you, but all that love and hard work don't mean nothing if you're dead, and I'm sure Sam would never want you to suffer for his—"

"What if it's true?"

Rel blinked. "What if what's true?"

Josie lowered her voice to a whisper. "What if Uncle—I mean Sam Price—really *did* find something in the caves?"

Rel opened her mouth and shut it again, too startled to come up with a clever answer. Josie must've taken her silence as assent, 'cause she started hurrying around the trashed office, lowering all the blinds that were still attached. When the whole room was shuttered, she rushed back over and took a seat on the counting table beside Rel. She was about to ask what the hell this was about when Josie reached into the pocket of her dress and pulled out something Reliance had never seen before. Something small and sharp and shining white as the moon.

My god, her father whispered.

"Holy shit," Rel agreed, red-rimmed eyes widening as Josie placed the crescent-shaped sliver of crystal—*glowing* crystal!—into her hand. "Where did you get this?"

"From Uncle," Josie whispered, her powdered face shining as bright at the stone. "It was the last piece of my inheritance. I didn't know what it was for at first, but after hearing what you said about rumors, I understand. Sam *did* find something down there! Something he knew others would be after just like you said, so he hid this where only I could find it."

"Okay, but what *is* it?" Rel asked, turning the crescent shard over carefully to avoid cutting her fingers on the sharp edge. "I mean, I can see it's crystal, but what is it supposed to do?"

"I don't know!" Josie said excitedly. "But I think it's a key or guide of some sort. I'm sure I'd understand everything if I could hear crystal like Uncle did, but unfortunately, I don't have that ability. That doesn't mean I'm giving up, though! Uncle can't be the only person in the world who could hear crystal. You've lived here a while, Reliance. Have you ever heard of anyone else with that ability?"

A couple of leads actually popped into Rel's head before she realized what she was doing. "Oh no," she said, popping off the table like a cork. "You are *not* getting me involved in this."

"Why not?" Josie asked. "You're the one who told me."

"Only because I thought it wasn't true!" Rel yelled. "I didn't realize the stupid rumors were right!"

Really? her father asked. *It never crossed your mind that maybe the man famous for finding crystal could have... found crystal?*

"Shut up," Rel hissed at him, whirling around so Josie wouldn't see. "Apache thought it was bullshit, and he—"

He's a professional liar, her father pointed out. *What makes more sense? That you were rushed over here to buy out a broken-down mining company no one wanted or that they were using you to scare Price's heir into handing over her greatest treasure before she had a chance to realize what she had?*

"But he didn't say—"

Of course he'd tell you the rumors were false. If you'd known what they'd really sent you in here for, you'd team up with that serving girl and take Price's treasure for yourself, which is exactly what you should do.

"I'm not going down into those caves," Rel snapped.

"Really? Because I think you'd be perfect," Josie said.

Rel spun around to see her friend standing right behind her, smiling beatifically, as if she hadn't just witnessed Rel talking to herself like a—

Like a madman?

"Sorry," Rel said, smacking the pistol with her hand. "Picked up a bad habit of talking to myself. Too long on my own, I guess. Now, what did you say?"

"I said I think you'd be the perfect person to come with me into the mines," Josie told her excitedly. "I know you wanted me to sell so I wouldn't get hurt, but you know Medicine Rocks, and I know you. If we stick together, I'm certain we can find whatever Uncle left behind! It could still be nothing, but if it *is* a giant crystal strike, that's exactly what I need to save my mine and get everything back on track!"

"Absolutely not," Rel said. "Knowing the town ain't the same as knowing the mines. Plus I already have a job." And the boss would kill her a thousand ways from Sunday if Rel went behind her back to help Price Mining.

"Come on," Josie coaxed. "You can't *really* want to keep working at a muddy old whorehouse. This could be a great opportunity for both of us! I remember when you took up sporting pistols because Miss Josephine was terrified of the idea of you with a gun. You're still a good shot, right?"

"Damn good," Rel said proudly. "But—"

"Then what's there to worry about?" Josie rolled on. "You're already hiring out your services, so why not work for someone who actually cares about you? I brought a whole chest of silver with me from St. Louis. It's not enough to lift up an entire company, but I'm sure I can pay you twice whatever the Wet Whistle's offering and even more in crystal once we find what we're after."

"Whoa, whoa, whoa," Rel said, putting up her hands before Josie moved on to planning the rest of her life. "Why are you so dead set on this?"

Josie blinked at her. "What sort of question is that? I'm going to need help if I'm going down into the caves, and you're obviously the only person in town that I can trust besides Mihir."

"You can't trust me," Rel barked. "You haven't seen me in almost ten years. You've got no idea where I've been or what I've done."

"Does that matter?"

"It matters 'cause it matters!" Rel yelled at her. "You can't trust someone you don't know!"

"But I *do* know you, Rel," Josie said with an infuriating smile. "Do you remember when Josephine's middle brother hit me over the head with his polo mallet?"

Rel didn't see how that had anything to do with it, but it was a good memory. "Of course I do. Knocking his teeth in for it was the highlight of my year."

"Mine too," Josie said, smile growing bigger. "No one else in that house ever said or did anything where the Prices were involved, not even my own mother. But you never hesitated to stand up for me."

71

"Don't read too much into that," Rel warned. "That boy was an ass. Anyone would've enjoyed having an excuse to lay him flat."

"But you were the only one who actually *did*," Josie insisted. "You were also the one who helped me downstairs and held my hand while Mama stitched me up. Even when my cut got blood all over your dress, you didn't leave my side. If that's not a foundation for trust, what is?"

"That was a long time ago," Rel said, looking down at her calloused hands. "I can't go with you, Josie."

"Why not?"

Yes, why not? the pistol demanded. *This trusting idiot is offering you the keys to the kingdom. There could be a mountain of crystal down here! Do you have any idea what we could do with that much power?*

"The Wet Whistle has something I need," Rel reminded them both.

"You don't have to quit if you don't want to," Josie offered. "Just take a leave of absence for a few weeks. Surely the Wet Whistle can spare you for that long. They seem to have plenty of employees, and I'll compensate you well for your time."

Yes, yes, listen to the clever servant, her father urged. *She was always better at her lessons than you were, and now I see why. She has vision!*

Rel gritted her teeth.

Look, it's very simple, he continued. *You were sent here to play a patsy, but we have nothing but a lying whoremonger's promise that the Wet Whistle can even produce the information they've promised. If you go back in there with news that "Josephine Price" not only won't sell but has the key to Sam Price's final discovery and is going down to find it, you won't have to worry about her future. They'll kill her for you, take the crystal, and give you nothing but the next false promise to keep you on the hook. But if you can stop being a gullible fool for ten seconds, you would see that we've been presented with a priceless opportunity! If you go with the false Miss Price into the caves, and there is no crystal, she'll become disillusioned enough to actually listen to your sales pitch, giving you something to take back to your masters. But if my supposition is correct, and there is a fortune down there, then you'll be one of the only people who knows where it is. That's information you can lever over the Wet Whistle's whore queen to* make *her tell you what you want.*

Rel's heart was pounding by the time he finished. She'd learned years ago that her father never said anything except to benefit himself, but she couldn't find the trap this time. It really did sound like a legitimately good plan. One that made vastly more sense than Apache's now that she thought about it. Even Jake had claimed not to understand why the boss cared so much about buying out the ruined Price Mining, because it didn't make any sense. But if she was after this place because it was where Sam had hidden the key to his last fortune for Josie, *that* lined up.

Now you're starting to get it.

Rel shook her head to knock his voice away. If she was actually gonna consider this, then she had to be more careful about it than anything else in her life. She'd seen what the Wet Whistle did to traitors, but if she could pull this off, Rel would finally be able to squeeze those bastards into doing what *she* wanted for once! She'd force them to cough up the name of that murdering bastard, and then Rel would drag that son of a bitch all the way back to the Badlands. She'd kill him on the same bloody doorstep where he'd murdered her family, bleeding him like a stuck pig until Momma and Chase finally knew justice.

Why am I never included in these revenge fantasies? I died too.

"No one cares about your sorry carcass," Rel whispered, rising from the table with a deep breath as she turned to face the still hopeful Josie. "All right, I'm in."

"Really?" she said excitedly. "What changed your mind?"

"Inevitability," Rel lied. "I realized you were going to go down there no matter what I said, so I figured I might as well tag along. I'm not saying I'll make it any safer. The caves are hell, and don't you ever forget it. But if my oldest friend is dead set on doing something stupid, I'm not going to let her do it alone."

"Oh, thank you!" Josie cried, leaping up and throwing her arms around her friend with far more emotion than Rel had been prepared for. "Thank you *so much*! I can't tell you how much this means to me!"

73

Her old friend wouldn't be saying that if she knew what was really going on in Rel's head. There was no prying Josie off, though, so Reliance gave up and let herself be hugged.

"Sorry," Josie said awkwardly when she finally let go. "I don't mean to keep accosting you, but it's been a very emotional day."

"It ain't gonna get any easier," Rel warned, glaring at her friend for serious now that she'd decided to go all in. "If we're gonna pull this off, we need to move fast. Before the rest of the town figures out what we're up to."

"I can be ready to go by tomorrow morning," Josie promised, shoving the glowing crystal back into her pocket. "I wish I could be quicker, but I suspect we'll be down there for at least two weeks, and most of our dry goods and equipment have been stolen. I'll need time to buy new supplies."

"That's fine, 'cause I still gotta find us someone who can listen to that crystal," Rel said. "I have a person in mind, but I don't know if she's in town or not."

"If she is, we should bring her here immediately," Josie suggested. "Keep in mind, this is still all supposition. If that crystal doesn't actually do what I think it does, we're not going anywhere."

"That's a risk we'll have to take," Rel said, shaking her head. "People are loyal to whoever pays the most. Getting her in today would let us know sooner, but if this crystal listener learns what kind of trip she's on before we're ready to go, she could sell us out and get us robbed before we've even left town."

Josie paled. "Is it really so cutthroat here?"

"That's nothing," Rel promised. "But for what it's worth, I think you've got the right of it. Sam wouldn't have left you that crystal if it didn't do anything. We'll just have to throw everything together tomorrow morning and hope it works out."

"I'll go ahead and purchase supplies for three, then," Josie said, grabbing a piece of paper and a nubbin of pencil off one of the smashed desks to start making a list. "You, me, and the guide. Let's say a three-week trip, out and back. Food, water containers, mining equipment, kerosene for lamps..." Her voice faded to a mutter as she finished writing everything down. "I think that's all the basics covered. Anything special I should add?"

"Just a zipper for your lips," Rel said, walking toward the door. "Get the stuff together, but don't tell *anyone* what it's for. Say you're prebuying for the new hires you've got coming in from Helena or something. Just don't give people reason to think you're going into the mines yourself."

"Right," Josie said, sliding the list into her pocket. "I'll go over this with Mihir and—"

"Didn't I just say not to tell anyone?"

"I have to talk to him," Josie argued. "I've barely been in town an hour, and I've never set foot underground. I don't even know where the General Store *is*."

"That's easy. It's down the—"

"I was being hyperbolic," she said dryly, crossing her arms over her chest. "The most important part of success in business is knowing yourself, and I *know* that I have zero idea what I'm doing. This is my inheritance, Mihir is my expert, and I trust him with my life. I'm bringing him in."

"Fine," Rel groused, slapping her hat back on her head. "I'll find the guide and meet you back here at sunrise tomorrow. *Sunrise*, Josie. No keeping lady's hours."

"I'll be on time," Josie assured her, then she smiled. "Thank you again, Reliance. I couldn't do this without you."

That was the damn truth, but the sincerity of the remark was still enough to trigger Rel's shriveled sense of shame. She couldn't even bring herself to look Josie in the eye as she scuttled out of the room. Passing Mihir, who'd been standing as close to the door as possible without actually looking like he was eavesdropping. The Indian gave her another nasty look as she went by, but Rel was already bolting for the door, rehearsing mentally how exactly she was going to spin this new turn to Apache without raising his suspicions.

He'll be easy, her father promised. *Just tell him Miss Price is too dreamy eyed about the riches of the mines to see reason, so you're taking her underground to let reality scare her into selling. It's close enough to the truth, which is always what you want in a good lie.*

"You've got an awful lot of opinions about lying for someone who claims he's never done it," Rel muttered, pulling her hat down low to hide her face from the vultures who were still milling around Josie's door.

I am a man of many skills.

Rel rolled her eyes to the sky and picked up the pace, jogging down the dirt road toward the wooden mine gate where the cave guides were lined up looking for work.

Chapter 5

Mary woke to a growling in her stomach.

After watching the fancy carriage roll in, she'd climbed higher, trying to see what was inside. The crowds had been too thick for her to catch a gander, though, so she'd taken advantage of the distraction and gone to buy an onion roll from a chuck wagon that was usually swarmed under. The skinflint cook had given her the smallest bun in the bin and still charged her full price, but he didn't normally sell to her sort at all, so Mary couldn't complain.

Given how much the little bread cost, Mary had hoped it would keep her 'til evening, but she'd barely gotten back to the caves and down an empty nook where she could sleep safely when her stomach started gnawing again. She ignored the feeling as long as she could, but hunger was a powerful force that was hard to deny, and too soon, she was forced back into the town in search of more food.

It was about the worst time she could've picked. Night was dark, and men were drunk, making them easy to slip by. Mornings were bright but slow, with most folks too busy yawning to pay her any attention. By midday, though, everyone was up and riled, and the heat made folks mean. There was a reason men dueled at noon.

If her hunger hadn't been so biting, Mary never would've dared it, but there weren't nothing she could do. Much as she loved the caves, belly filling wasn't one of their strengths. Everyone came up top to resupply, even her. But while the rush of new miners this summer had brought plenty of new food wagons looking for their own slice of the crystal pie, sundries were hard to come by out here in the middle of the plains. To make up the difference, the cooks had resorted to dirty tactics like adding sawdust to their flour or wrapping old meat in sage and mesquite to hide the smell of rot.

It wouldn't have been so bad if they hadn't priced the junk so dear. Mary wasn't one to turn up her nose at a meal just because it was edging toward the wrong side of well-aged. But with so many hungry mouths and money to be made, stalls were demanding top dollar for what most folk wouldn't feed to pigs, and these days, they only traded in crystal.

Mary didn't have none of that. Fortunately, the proper shops along the road still took coin. *Un*fortunately, those establishments were run by people who'd actually lived in Medicine Rocks longer than it took to strike it rich or die trying, which meant they knew Mary's measure. They didn't always kick her out, but the redskin tax was steep, and she didn't exactly have palm-greasin' money. Unless she wanted to walk out into the grass and try her hand at catching a rabbit, though, there weren't nothing for it but to try. So Mary sucked it in and hiked her carcass up the road, pulling her big hat low over her troublesome face to reduce her chances of getting shot.

Where to try, though? If Mary was judging on quality, the Medicine Rocks General Store was the best hands down. The owners had ins with all the ranchers and wagon drivers, which meant they got first pick of everything, *and* they didn't gouge too hard on price. Every other guide swore by the place, but the man who worked the front counter was a God-fearing Baptist who'd served proudly in the Confederate army, which made it a no-go for her.

There was the Wet Whistle, which was officially a whorehouse but would sell anything to anybody if they had money. Mary had bought from them a few times when she'd been desperate, but she hated going near the place and not just 'cause they charged an arm and a leg for what should've cost fingers. There was something about the tar-smeared building that set her jeebies crawling like a spider under her hat. Pity, too, because the women who worked there were always eager to buy the baby-stopping moss she found in the caves sometimes, and the fella who ran the place—the tall, scary-lookin' dark-skinned one who always dressed in black no matter how hot it got—was the only man in town who tipped his hat to Mary when she passed.

It weren't much, but when you never got nothing normally, little things like that felt big. If she hadn't been so certain terrible acts were happening inside, that little bit of politeness would've made the Wet Whistle one of Mary's regular stops. She had neither the cash nor the gumption to show her face there today, though, so she kept walking way up the hill toward Sampson's, the other big saloon in town and her option of last resort.

It had only just become an option at all. Thanks to its spot two buildings down from Fort Grant, Sampson's was where the cavalry drank. Mary had avoided the place like a rattlesnake since it opened. Then one day, completely by accident, she'd discovered that the barkeep, Carlo, was so homesick for his ranch back in Laredo that he'd do just about anything you asked if you did so in Spanish, including sell her leftovers under the table. Mary hadn't known a word of the language at the time, but she'd always been a quick learner, and the longer she let him teach her, the lower Carlo cut the price.

Between his patience and her greed for cheap food, Mary could now hold a half-decent conversation *en Español*. She was already practicing her opener in her head—"*¡Buenas tardes, Carlo! Te ves muy guapo hoy*"—when she peeked over the saloon's swinging doors to see Sampson himself standing behind the bar.

Mary ducked her head right back under. It was just her luck Carlo wasn't working. Maybe she'd come too soon? It *was* just past noon, pretty early for a place that did business 'till sunup. Her stomach was hurting too bad for her to wait, though, so Mary took a chance, pulling her hat even farther over her face as she pushed her way in through the swinging doors.

Bless her lucky stars, the saloon was dead. Some kind of commotion was going on up at the fort, so the normal crowds of cavalrymen were missing, leaving just a few laborers smoking over a card game by the potbelly stove. But while Mary managed to make it across the empty room without drawing untoward attention, Sampson himself was like to be another story.

She'd never once seen the old man smile. He was scowling fit to blister at the moment, standing over the washbasin cleaning mugs like he was imagining wringing someone's neck. Eager not to give him a target, Mary stopped just shy of the bar and waited to be noticed, staying quiet as a mouse until, after nearly ten minutes, grumpy old Sampson finally looked in her direction.

"Sorry, son," he said, far kindlier than she expected. "Didn't notice you there. What's your need?"

Mary hadn't intended deception, but being mistaken for a boy made her life easier, so she rolled with it.

"Is Carlo around?" she asked in her deepest voice.

Sampson's scowl deepened. "Not anymore. Carlo met his maker two days ago. Got between two drunks trying to kill each other, and the crazy bastards threw him straight through the ceiling."

There was no way Mary'd heard that right. "*Through* the ceiling?"

He nodded up at the no-foolin' canvas-covered hole in the bar's roof, and Mary's blood ran cold. "*How?*"

"It's those damn caves," Sampson said angrily. "Used to be a mining run would only take a few days to get a man what he needed. Now, though, all the good crystal's been pushed so far back, folks are staying under for weeks at a time. All that dark and crystal's no good for a man. Even the usually levelheaded ones have been coming out tilted, and I don't just mean their tempers. I've seen men do crazy things when the crystal's fresh in their lungs, things no living man ought. Poor Carlo found that out the hard way, and now I gotta hire someone who can write Spanish to pen a letter to his widow that her husband got cracked by a rock-crazed idiot. It's a sorry state this world is in. If this gin mill weren't earning me ten times what I got for slinging the same slop back in Kansas City, I'd pack out myself."

He looked to Mary for agreement, but she was still too shocked to speak. She'd also noticed miners were staying under longer and getting worse for it, but throwing a man through a ceiling was a new one. Most folks had to put the crystal literally inside their bodies to get that sort of power. Gunslingers and other fighty types mixed crystal with whiskey for exactly that reason, but miners were normally too cheap to waste their precious finds on short-term boosts, 'specially considering what shooting crystal did to your insides.

Now that Sampson mentioned it, though, Mary could see how breathing in crystal dust for weeks might get the same result and the same problems. She was just broken up that Carlo was the one to pay the price. He hadn't deserved such a fate, and where was she going to get food now?

That was an awful, selfish way to think about a good man's death, but Mary was too hungry to be virtuous. She'd light a candle for Carlo later, but if she didn't want to pass out right here on the bar, she needed to be bold. When she looked to ask Sampson if he could spare her something, though—sprouted potatoes, beef trimmings, leftover brewer's mash, she wasn't picky—Mary found him already staring at her with the shocked expression that never meant anything good.

Aw, corn nuts.

"Wait a minute," Sampson said loud enough to get the attention of everybody in the saloon. "You ain't no boy! You're that half-Injun witch! The one what lures men into the caves with promises of guiding them to crystal and then leaves 'em to die!"

"No, no!" Mary said, waving her arms frantically. "That ain't me! I mean, I do guide, but I ain't never killed nobody!" At least, not directly. "Please, sir, I don't mean no trouble. I'm just trying to buy some—"

She stopped with a yelp as Sampson whipped a shotgun out from under the bar and stuck both barrels in her face. "Get out of my place!" he shouted, cocking the hammer. "I don't serve your kind, devil's squaw! Now get scarce 'fore I call the cavalry!"

"I'm going, I'm going!" Mary cried, dropping down on all fours to give him a smaller target as she scrambled for the exit.

"And don't come back, you red-skinned traitor!"

Mary wasn't sure if he was accusing her of betraying America or the Lakota, but now didn't seem like a good time for discussion. She was already hightailing it away, diving through the gap below the swinging doors and running full tilt into the crowded, dusty street, which is how she didn't see the other man coming 'til he grabbed her.

"Gotcha!"

Mary shrieked in fear, whirling around to beat on the hand that had grabbed her up by the neck of her poncho. She'd just managed a good whack to his elbow when she finally calmed down enough to see who she was punching. It was one of the Wet Whistle's black-clad gunmen. Not the tall, smiling boss who tipped his hat. This was the short, pale-faced, hard-eyed kid who always had the ring of sour crystal. He was humming particularly strongly today, his long duster coat gaping open to show the three six-shooters on his belt, one of which was covered in a fortune's worth of crystal.

Why a person with two hands would need three guns, Mary couldn't fathom, but she knew that she was dead. Other than the cavalry itself, the Wet Whistle was the most powerful force in town. They did whatever they pleased, and the sheriff didn't lift a finger to stop them.

Mary didn't mind that most times since, again, the Wet Whistle was one of the few places—maybe the only place now—that would sell to a half-breed, but that didn't mean they were safe. If Mary ran afoul of the wrong person, she'd be just as dead as all the other stiffs that got carried out of that giant coffin of a building. The kid who'd grabbed her was one of their rising stars, too, which meant she was done for. Good as gone. But just as Mary started panicking in earnest, the gunman eased up.

"Whoa there," he said, loosening his grip but not yet letting her go. "I don't mean no harm. I just can't have you running off. I've been looking all morning for the guide they call 'Good Crow.' You her?"

Mary didn't know if this boded good or ill, but lying to a man packing three kinds of murder felt like a stupid idea, so she nodded. "Yes'sir."

"Good," the gunman said, smiling, which made a strange sight. Men who killed for a living usually looked worse when they smiled, but this boy had such a pretty face with his fair skin, blue eyes, and silky bark-brown hair that any menace he might've had was ruined. Mary wondered how many of his victims had been suckered by that innocent look. A goodly number, she was sure. Good thing she wasn't so stupid.

"Why're you looking for me?" she asked in a cautious voice, pressing her deer-hide boots into the dirt in preparation for a quick getaway should opportunity present.

The gunman arched an eyebrow. "Why do you think? I need a guide."

"There's plenty of those at the cave entrance," Mary offered, edging a half step away. "We all do the same thing. Why come looking for me in particular?"

"'Cause you're the only one who came recommended," the young man said, pulling her back with the exasperated look of a mama bear wrangling a wandering cub. "I'm not going to try anything nasty. I'm just looking for someone who can hear crystal. *Actually* hear it, none of this circus-trick crap. I asked nice and then not so nice, and on the second go-round, all the other guides agreed that the only person who fit the bill was you."

Mary kicked her useless feet in the dirt. Curse those prattle-mouth cowards! All guides claimed to have ways of finding crystal, but the fact that Mary actually had ears for the stuff was something only a few of her oldest fellow guides like Oliver knew. Knew and swore to keep their traps shut about, because if word got out how good Mary's crystal finding actually was, someone was going to slap a collar on her and turn her into their very own crystal-finding dog. Someone like a Wet Whistle gunhand, actually, which meant it was time to run.

"Stop that," the boy scolded, yanking Mary's poncho again before she'd even tensed to bolt. Saints in Heaven, how fast was this kid? She was planning to sacrifice her oilskin cover like a lizard's tail and escape that way when the pretty boy said the magic words.

"I'll pay you thirty dollars."

That got Mary's attention. "You for real?" she asked, ceasing her struggle.

"I am if you are," the gunman replied, leaning in even closer. "Prove to me that you can really hear crystal, and I'll pay you thirty right there plus that much again when the job is done."

Mary's throat dried up at the thought of so much money. Sixty dollars was what she usually earned in six trips, assuming no one cheated her. Making so much off a single run was unheard of. Too good to be true, really, but before she could think of a way to test the situation, her stomach gave its loudest rumble yet.

The gunman laughed at the noise. "Sounds like you could use the work," he said, letting go of her poncho at last. "Come on. I'll buy you supper while you think about it."

Mary was ashamed that the offer of food tempted her harder than the dollars, but she was just so hungry. The gunman's case was further helped by the fact that, unlike her, he was actually welcome in places. He hopped right up the steps of the General Store as she watched, purchasing two pork sandwiches with pickle and a slab of yellow cheese from the counter and bringing them back to her.

"Here," he said, thrusting the food into Mary's hand. "Feeding strays makes them loyal, right?"

"That sorta rude talk's no way to win someone over," she said around the half sandwich she'd already crammed into her mouth.

"Does that mean you're not interested?"

"I didn't say that." Mary took a moment to chew, partially to think but mostly so she wouldn't choke. "Ain't no guide can turn down that kinda money, which I'm sure is why you offered it."

"That was the idea," the boy said with a chuckle, pointing down the hill toward the huge fancy building with the boarded-up window across the street from the Wet Whistle. "If you ain't lying about hearing crystal, meet me at Price Mining first light tomorrow. I got a test for you in mind. You pass it, I'll pay up, and we'll head down to the caves right then and there. If not, no hard feelings, and you're free to go. Either way, the sandwich is my treat. Sound fair?"

It sounded better than fair. The boy was being extraordinarily generous for someone who could've made her work at gunpoint, and she'd never heard of a Wet Whistle killer cooperating with a legitimate business like Price Mining, particularly since Price Mining weren't even in business anymore. But crystal made all sorts of strange bedfellows, and with sixty dollars on the line, it was certainly worth playing along.

"I don't see the harm in trying," Mary said, cramming the cheese and the rest of the sandwich into her pack before he could change his mind. "I'll be there, Mr...."

"Tyrel," the gunhand said, sticking out a pale, thin hand. "Tyrel Reiner."

"Nice to meet you, Mr. Reiner," Mary said politely, removing her dirty glove to shake his hand properly. "Am I expected to bring my own food? 'Cause if so, I'll need an advance on payment."

"We'll provide all your supplies," Tyrel replied, darting his sharp blue eyes around. "I don't want to say more on the street, but if your ears are really what they say, we'll be moving quick. In case the big fee didn't tip you off, we're in kind of a hurry."

"I can do hurry," Mary promised.

"Then I'll see you at dawn tomorrow. Don't be late."

Before Mary could say she was never late, the gunman walked off with his hands in his pockets. Mary watched him suspiciously all the way down the hill, where he turned in to the Wet Whistle. That told her nothing she hadn't already guessed, but it was still so odd to see one of their lot working for someone else. The Wet Whistle didn't usually tolerate moonlighting, but he was still alive, so he must've known what he was about. So long as his money was good, Mary supposed it didn't matter

85

who he took orders from. She was just glad she'd gotten a job *and* a sandwich with so little effort on her part.

That was a terrifying amount of good luck for one afternoon, so Mary hied her way back down to the mines to light two candles—one for Carlo's bad fortune and one in thanksgiving for her good—to the Blessed Lady of her namesake who was so clearly watching over her.

Chapter 6

Lieutenant Jean-Jacques Lucas woke up in the dusty-white glare of the medical tent. This was a magnificent surprise, since, after his rescuing angel had vanished as suddenly as she'd appeared, he'd never expected to see the light again. He still wasn't quite sure he was seeing it now. Lucas had imagined the sun so many times down there in that pit that the idea that he might actually be free didn't feel real, especially since his broken leg no longer pained him.

If the tent hadn't smelled so awful, he'd have been convinced he was dead. Lucas was certain heaven wouldn't smell of old blood and dust, though, and the cot, hard as it was, was still too comfortable to be from the other place. This could only mean that his angel had been telling the truth. She *had* gotten help. He really was saved!

He was lying in the wondrous joy of that when the tent flap Lucas hadn't realized was resting against his bare toes got whisked away. The culprit was a uniformed man with a long rifle strapped to his back, a precisely trimmed mustache curled at the tips, blond hair parted perfectly down the middle of his head, and half-moon spectacles covering a pinched, worried face that Lucas hadn't seen in ages.

"Well, I'll be," the newcomer said, his air of constant fretting dispelled momentarily by an enormous smile. "It appears the notorious Jean-Jacques has cheated death once again. And here I thought only cats had nine lives."

Lucas laughed in delight, then winced as the motion jostled his… well, everything. Now that he was no longer floating in the happy shock of being alive, he realized that, while his leg felt much better, the rest of his body was still covered in scrapes and bruises of every sort. He felt like he'd gone nine rounds with the champion of *Rue Champlain* and lost every one. But even the pain couldn't keep him from reaching out to his brother-in-arms and oldest friend in the cavalry.

"Townsend, you old stick-in-the-mud! What are you doing way out here?"

"Wishing I weren't," Townsend replied with his familiar old sourness, removing his long gun to take a seat on the edge of the empty medical cot across from Lucas's so as to keep his immaculate blue officer's coat away from the dark stains that pooled in the center. "I was happily minding my own business running the accounting office at Fort Worth when I got a letter from the major general himself that I was to drop everything and lead a newly recruited infantry company up to reinforce your position at Medicine Rocks. Not that eight hundred more idiots who can barely avoid shooting their own feet will be much good to anyone, but I got a promotion out of the deal, so I can't complain."

"If you ever stopped complaining, I'd worry you were dead," Lucas said, noting the new bars on his friend's sleeve. "Though I suppose I'd have to salute you first, *Captain* Towns—*ow*."

He'd been raising his hand for the salute, but the motion jostled the sheet covering his legs, sending a lightning bolt of pain from his toes to his spine.

"*Merde!*"

"The doctor said you're not to move that," Townsend informed him belatedly as Lucas fell cursing back onto the cot. "The surgeons have been at you since one of the mine patrols carried you in this morning. Apparently you sat on that broken leg so long it had already started to heal crooked. The field doctor tried telling General Cook it needed to be re-broken and reset if it was to have a chance of ever being straight again, but the general insisted he didn't have time for you to be lying around useless and paid to get you a crystal sawbones instead."

Lucas was in too much pain to make sense of most of that, but the last part struck him as important. "Crystal sawbones?"

"A local 'expert' named Dr. Pendleton," Townsend explained with a frown. "Though I don't know if I can rightly use the term 'doctor,' since I've never heard of that title being awarded to a *woman* before. But legitimacy of her degree notwithstanding, she did good work. Straightened you right out. See?"

He lifted the sheet off Lucas's lower half to reveal seven crystal nails shining like jewels in the exposed flesh of his shin right above the Indian cobra tattoo circling his ankle. Now that he was looking at them, Lucas realized he could *feel* the crystal pegs holding his bones in place. He braced next for the horrors he'd come to associate with crystal inside the skin, but aside from a slight humming in his bones, he didn't feel anything. His broken leg didn't even hurt unless something touched the pins directly.

"That would be the crystal working," Townsend explained. "Dr. Pendleton claims you'll be walking on your own in a week. I'll believe that when I see it, but no one can say she wasn't thorough."

He pointed at yet another crystal spike that had been nailed into Lucas's left arm between the crude dagger on his elbow and the elegant naked mermaid swimming up his bicep. Still more had been driven into his chest between the flames of the Sacred Heart on his left pectoral and the three-mast ship sailing across his right.

"How many cursed pins did she put in me?"

"Twelve, I believe," Townsend said, looking obnoxiously amused. "She had a hard time avoiding all your... artwork. Apparently all your 'conflicting patterning' could disrupt the 'healing harmonics' or some rot like that. It was quite the entertaining spectacle. I had no idea you were so decorated."

"Relics of my wayward youth," Lucas said, reaching for the shirt someone had mercifully left beside his pillow.

"Ah, yes. You were a sailor before enlisting, weren't you?"

"Something like that," Lucas said, covering himself quickly before Townsend decided to probe any deeper into the origins of his "decorations." "But I'm grateful the general valued my service enough to spend so much on my return. Hopefully I'll be able to repay him with a speedy recovery."

89

"You're already doing scads better than you were this morning," Townsend assured him. "You were quite off your rocker when they brought you in, raving about crystal gardens and ghosts and an *ange des cavernes,* which I believe means 'cave angel' if my French hasn't gone too downhill." He smiled indulgently. "Considering how you started, the fact that we're conversing like this is nothing short of miraculous. But Dr. Pendleton *did* promise her crystal pins would fix your head as well as your bones, so perhaps she isn't as much of a quack as I thought."

Lucas frowned at the glittering spike he'd just noticed in the back of his left hand. "How did crystal make me less mad when it was the crystal that made me so in the first place?"

"I'm sure I haven't the foggiest," Townsend said. "I'm still new to this insanity you all live in. I'm just happy you're well."

"And they say the English have no hearts," Lucas said with a warm smile. "That was *très doux,* my friend."

"Don't puff your head," Townsend scolded. "I'm just looking forward to you taking some of the work off the rest of us. We barely have enough officers to keep this place functional, and General Cook has been up my backside every half hour about when you'll be well enough to give your report."

"That sounds like the general," Lucas said, bracing himself to sit up only to pause. "She was real, you know."

"Beg pardon?"

"The angel," Lucas said. "She was not a figment. She found me in that cursed Dark, spoke to me in French, and pulled me out of death with her soft wings. How else could I have made it back to the main tunnel on a broken leg? She was *there,* Townsend! She saved me."

"That's just your overly dramatic Frenchman brain feeding you fantasies," Townsend said. "I paid the man who rescued you myself. He was a toothless old coot with a bug-infested beard as long as my arm. Definitely no one's idea of an angel."

"But—"

Townsend shushed him. "If you think there's any ladies, let alone angels, in those caves, then we need to call Dr. Pendleton for more pins. There's nothing down there but filthy, greedy miners looking to strike it rich while our soldiers die guarding their backsides. And speaking of backside guarding, you have another visitor."

Lucas looked to see another soldier standing at the tent flap, cap clutched in his nervous hands. His dark skin and the insignia on his blue jacket marked him as a member of the 10th Colored Cavalry, the ones the Sioux called Buffalo Soldiers. His face looked so different in the bright daylight, though, that it took Lucas several seconds to realize that this was the man who'd been his greatest help through the hell of the caves. One he'd thought he'd lost forever weeks ago.

"*Chaucer!*"

"'Ello, Lieutenant," Chaucer replied in that familiar Cockney accent of his, thick as old peas. "You're looking mighty lively for a man what's supposed to be dead."

"I could say the same for you, my friend!" Lucas replied gleefully. "I can't say how happy I am to see you, but how are you alive? The last time I saw you, you were shoving me out of the way of a rockslide. We all thought you'd been crushed!"

"I very nearly was," Chaucer said. "Lucky for me, I'm wiggly."

He gave his lanky body a shake to prove his point, and Lucas laughed. "You always did have the Devil's luck. But what of the men behind you? Did any of them make it out as well?"

Chaucer's happy face grew grim. "No, sir. I was quick enough to catch a pocket, but the other lads with me caught the rocks. I nearly starved in there meself 'fore some deep miners heard me yelling and dug me out. It's thanks to them that I made it back, but unless there's still someone else lagging behind you, we're the only ones."

That truth sat so heavily on Lucas he sank into the cot. Just two. Of the twenty-four men who'd gone with him into those caves—two dozen brave, battle-hardened souls—only he and Chaucer had survived to see the sun again. It didn't feel fair. It *wasn't* fair. They'd been good soldiers all. They hadn't deserved such a dark bitter fate, not after how hard they'd fought.

"What happened down there, Lieutenant?" Chaucer whispered, crouching at the foot of Lucas's cot. "My group got cut off, but the rest of you kept going, right? Did you make it all the way? Did you finish the mission?"

He sounded desperate for someone who'd already survived, but Lucas knew what he was really asking. He wanted to know if it had been worth it, that his fellow soldiers hadn't died in vain. Townsend was also paying close attention, his smart mouth clamped shut for once. As much as Lucas wanted to tell them what he'd seen, though, the story wasn't yet his to share. His soldiers had given their lives so that he could bring what they'd discovered back to the commanders. He couldn't just blurt everything out in a canvas medical tent where God knew who could be listening.

"I'm sorry," he said, and he was. Truly, truly sorry about everything, but… "That information is classified."

"Can you at least tell me if we made a difference?" Chaucer begged. "That was my company down there! I might not be an American born, but they bled for me like true brothers. I don't have to know the strategic details. I just need to hear you say they didn't die for nothing!"

"It was never for nothing," Lucas promised. "You and the others are the only reason I made it as far as I did. Without their sacrifice, we'd be blind to what is coming. They saved the mission, which might well have saved us all."

Chaucer lowered his head at that, and Townsend took the opportunity to clear his throat.

"On that note, I think it's time you made your report. The general gave me strict orders to bring you to him the moment you were lucid even if I had to drag you in on your cot."

"We should get moving, then," Lucas agreed, bracing to haul himself up only to discover that he couldn't. His leg might not hurt him anymore, but it was as useless as ever, hanging off his body like a dead branch.

Luckily, Lucas had more than just one angel's mercy this time. Chaucer and Townsend were both there to help him out of bed and back into his clothes, which some prince from the quartermaster's had had the good grace to launder. When he dressed again as befitted an officer of the cavalry, Lucas turned one last time to Chaucer.

"I promise the family of every man in our company will receive the full death benefit," he swore to the soldier. "And I'll make sure that you get paid the endangerment bonus the general promised when we started."

"Thank you, sir," Chaucer said nervously. "But, um, can you do that? They just announced we're all going on half wages 'cause the payroll wagons keep getting hit by bandits. I don't see them jumping to send coin to widows thousands of miles away when fighting men ain't getting paid."

From the snort he gave, Townsend clearly agreed, but Lucas held firm. "I'll make it happen. Fair payment is the least we can offer the families of men who gave their country everything. If there's a penny left in the coffers, I swear they shall have it."

Townsend rolled his eyes at the grandiose offer, but the vow made Chaucer smile again, which was all Lucas cared about. "Thank you, Lieutenant!" he said as he bounded out of the tent. "Thank you very much!"

"I wish you wouldn't say such reckless things," Townsend muttered when the soldier was gone, sliding his rifle back onto his shoulder as he leaned down to lift Lucas up. "You know damn well you can't control what payroll decides. Even if he is just a Negro, it's cruel to get his hopes up like that."

"They were soldiers who died in heroic service," Lucas argued, clutching his friend for balance as he tested his unbroken leg, which could fortunately still hold him. "That money is theirs by law. Surely it's not reckless to say the US government will honor its promises?"

"Of course not," Townsend said, though he didn't look nearly so sure. "But you shouldn't have made it sound as if they'd be getting the money soon. The whole point of hiring Black soldiers is that they cost less than white ones, and you know damn well these frontier wars are bleeding us dry. We're supposed to be cutting expenses and delaying payments whenever possible. Not promising cash on the barrel to a bunch of sharecroppers who likely don't even know where Montana *is*."

"So what if they don't?" Lucas said fiercely. "That doesn't change the fact that their men are gone. The death benefit for a Black soldier might be a pittance, but I'm still going to make sure they get it. It's the least I can do for those who died to save us all."

"All right, all right," Townsend said sourly as they hobbled toward the tent flap. "No need to make a speech about it."

"I'll make whatever I must until you stop being so unfeeling," Lucas snapped. "An army is more than numbers."

"If you saw the numbers I did, you'd be numb too," Townsend said. "But fine. If it's *so* important to you, I'll have a word with the quartermaster and see what we can manage. If I do that, will you *please* start moving toward the general so we can finally hear what's so bloody important?"

Lucas motioned grandly for Townsend to lead the way, hopping on one foot as his friend supported him out of the medical tent and into the dirt yard beyond.

The center of the fortress was even more crowded and chaotic than Lucas remembered. The officer shortage had left everything slapdash, but between the 7th and 10th Regiments plus however many infantry Townsend had brought up, more soldiers were now crammed into Fort Grant than the outpost had ever been meant to hold. They were well past the capacity of their wooden barracks, which meant all the Black soldiers were sleeping outside in tents. That was going to be a real problem if they

94

didn't solve the crowding issue come winter, but no one was in mortal danger so long as the summer held fair.

Struggling to walk across the yard now, Lucas's biggest issue with the tents was how they impeded traffic, filling the paths with stumbling stakes and tripping ropes no officer had yet found the time or attention to fix. There wasn't even a proper grid laid out, forcing Lucas and Townsend to take the long way around the sandstone boulders that poked out of the hilltop like the fins of a sea monster.

The fort's central keep was nestled between two such formations: a two-story pile of uncut logs thick enough to stop bullets wedged in between two giant stones so that its roof could serve as an entry point to the cannon nests the general had ordered built on top of the boulders. From this protected vantage, gunners could move between any of the base's twelve-pound Napoleons, using the height of their position to extend the cannon's otherwise short range up to nearly a mile.

"Ho, there," Townsend huffed when he and Lucas reached the foot of the tower, turning to show his new rank to the men guarding the front entrance. "A little assistance, please?"

The soldiers rushed to take Lucas at once, nearly dropping him as they attempted to salute the new captain and open the heavy door all at once. Fortunately, yet more men were waiting inside, mostly gunners and ammunition runners for the cannons up top. Between all of them, they carried Lucas into the wooden tower and through a second door to the secure room at the keep's heart, where a meeting of the cavalry's leadership was already in session.

Being a mere lieutenant, Lucas wasn't normally invited to such august gatherings, but all the commanders rose to help him when he entered. It took the lot of them to do it, for the inner room, though secure, was quite cramped thanks to the large map table taking up most of its floorspace. The room was very bright from the numerous lanterns hanging from the rafters, but the windowless walls and low ceiling still put

Lucas in mind of a coffin. An upsettingly apt comparison, given what he was here to say.

"Finally," the general said, resuming his seat in the far corner, where his back was to the wall and his hooded eyes were free to watch everyone else. "About time you came to your senses, Jean-Jacques. Welcome back."

"Happy to be back, sir," Lucas said, stretching his injured leg into the space below the table that was already crowded with other men's boots. Unable to find a seat with so many present, Townsend made himself comfortable against the door. As the lowest-ranking officer, Lucas should have offered him his stool, but his injuries made that impossible, and Townsend didn't look eager to take a place at the table in any case. He seemed much happier in the back, far away from the ring of commanders staring down Lucas like a firing squad.

"Now that we're all finally in the same place, I believe introductions are in order," the general began. "Even in war, it's important to take time for civilities, for those are what separate us from the savages. Since this is Captain Townsend's first time at our table, I'll go the full around."

He placed a hand on his decorated chest. "I'm General James Cook. I fought the Confederacy in the Army of the Potomac before coming out west to take on the Lakota during Red Cloud's War. Two years ago, I was ordered by President Grant to build a stronghold at Medicine Rocks to protect American citizens and secure our nation's strategic supply of crystal, and here we are."

He gestured next to the commander on his right, an older gentleman with drooping eyebrows and skin that looked like crumpled paper. "This is Colonel Phillip Avery. He commands the colored boys of 10th Cavalry who serve as our garrison."

Colonel Avery, who hadn't looked happy since he'd been pulled off his cushy job guarding the railroads to go deep into Indian territory, glanced up from nervously fiddling with his papers just long enough to acknowledge Townsend. When the captain nodded back, Cook turned to the man on his left, a grandly mustached, middle-aged officer who never seemed to stop scowling.

"This is Lieutenant Colonel George Custer, acting commander of the 7th Cavalry. He and his boys are here on loan from Fort Abraham Lincoln to help us with our Indian problem."

"It's an honor to meet you, Lieutenant Colonel," Townsend said eagerly. "I've heard much about your exploits in the Black Hills."

"Well, I haven't heard anything about you," Custer said, leaning back in his folding camp chair to look Townsend up and down. "They say Washington sent you to reinforce us, but we're packed in like bullets in a box already. My men are bunking in doubles, and Avery's Negroes are sleeping outside in tents. We don't need any more mouths to feed when it's summer and all the redskins are too busy hunting buffalo to give us sport, so you mind telling us why someone thought it was a good idea to send your column of untrained buffoons up to eat our food and crowd my men instead of going somewhere more useful?"

Lucas glanced nervously at the general. For all his talk of civility, Cook seemed content to let Custer make as great an ass of himself as he wished. Fortunately, Townsend was not a man to take offense over matters of fact.

"Our orders sent us here because there is no more useful place for us to be, sir," the new captain replied cheerfully, completely ignoring Custer's blatant antagonism. "I'm certain that you and your men have the Sioux entirely in hand, but we were not sent to reinforce Medicine Rocks against the natives. My unit was ordered here by a special act of Congress. It seems that the crystal shipments, which are the purpose of this position, have not been arriving in Washington due to local criminal activity."

"He means the Whitman Gang," General Cook translated before Custer could wedge his boot any further into his mouth. "And on that score, reinforcements would be most welcome."

"Desperately welcome," Colonel Avery agreed, stopping his nervous fiddling to smile at Townsend with new appreciation. "Last year, the Whitmans were merely one of several highwaymen gangs in the area. A nuisance to commerce and farmers, but nothing that could endanger armed soldiers. Then, this last winter, they got organized, destroying their rivals to become the single most significant threat to our southern and western supply lines. Used to be we could send a wagon full of crystal all the way to the railway depot in Cheyenne with only a dozen soldiers as escort. Now the Whitmans are setting ambushes capable of overpowering entire squadrons. I've lost three crystal shipments and over a hundred men to this nonsense since April."

"I told Congress in my last report that we don't have the manpower to fight the Sioux, guard the mines, *and* root the Whitmans out of the plains," Cook explained angrily. "We've barely been collecting enough crystal for the Whitmans to steal with every Tom, Dick, and greedy Harry dodging the tax table. I could run sweeps to find their smuggling tunnels and flush the cheap bastards out, but then I'd have to take men off guarding our supply lines and horses, so we'd just start losing those. It's all robbing Peter to pay Paul here, which is why I requested another cavalry company. Give me a thousand First Dragoons and we would own this prairie. That's what I told them, and how do they answer? By sending a paper pusher with a pack of barely trained flatfoots who can't even ride!"

"I know my men aren't up to your standards," Townsend agreed, once again unperturbed by this blunt but factually correct statement. "But we didn't come entirely empty-handed."

As he said this, Townsend removed the rifle he'd been carrying all this time. Lucas hadn't bothered looking at it too closely, since it looked like the same trapdoor Springfield as all the cavalry carried. When Townsend laid the gun on the table, however, Lucas saw that this rifle had shards of crystal inset along its breach, barrel, and firing hammer. For what purpose, he had no idea, but the general stood up so fast he knocked over his chair.

"What is that?" he demanded, stabbing his finger at the glittering gun. "And would you care to explain why I'm only seeing it *now*?"

"I tried to show it to you earlier, but you kept saying you were too busy," Townsend reminded him with no small amount of pique, sliding the rifle across the map table to Cook and Custer, who barely avoided knocking their heads together in their rush to get their hands on it. "That's the very first Springfield Crystal-Action. It has twice the range of the original model and is capable of firing standard ammunition as well as a variety of crystal cartridges, including an explosive round that can blow a fist-sized hole in a horse from a hundred feet."

"Poor horse," Lucas said.

"How many of these did you bring?" Cook demanded at the same time.

"Only fifty. We were supposed to manufacture a thousand, but then the crystal stopped coming, so we worked with what we had."

"We?" Cook arched a thick gray eyebrow. "What division of logistics did you say you worked in?"

"I *was* in payroll," Townsend replied smugly. "But since my promotion, I'm now the head field officer of the newly formed Crystal Research and Supply Division."

That was news to Lucas, but news of the new division did make Townsend's sudden arrival in Medicine Rocks far more reasonable. It was hard to run a Crystal Research and Supply Division without crystal.

"Fifty's a start, I suppose," Cook said, passing the crystal rifle to Custer, who'd been waiting impatiently. "Did you bring anything else?"

"Yes!" Townsend said, bubbling over now that he'd finally been given the chance to show off. "In addition to the rifles, I also brought three armored steel wagons built specifically to aid in crystal transport."

Cook looked unimpressed. "You mean those big rolling bank safes taking up all the room in our stables?"

The captain nodded excitedly. "They're the latest design from the Wells Fargo armory in Kansas City! The Defense Secretary oversaw their construction personally. He was *quite* specific that these transports and guns were to be used to ensure that Medicine Rocks resumes its scheduled shipment of crystal without delay."

"We all would love that," the general agreed, picking his chair up off the floor so he could sit back down. "Unfortunately, Captain, shipping crystal isn't our only worry out here. We also have to defend the mines, or there won't be crystal for anybody."

"Defend them from whom?" Townsend asked, looking at Custer. "I thought the Sioux in this area were being managed."

"So did we," Cook said, nodding at Lucas. "Then my lieutenant found out there was an avenue of attack we hadn't considered."

Townsend looked at his old friend in confusion, and Lucas explained, "I heard a report from some miners that they'd seen Sioux in the caves. This was particularly alarming, since, to our knowledge, Medicine Rocks has the only entrance into the mines. It seemed worthy of investigation, so I asked the general's permission to take two dozen men into the mines to see if our enemy had indeed found a back way in."

"That was over a month ago," Cook finished, leaning heavy on the table. "Of the entire company that went down, Lucas and a Negro soldier called Henry Chaucer were the only ones who made it back. I'd about given up hope when one of our tax teams dragged Lucas out this morning, so if you're done pulling crystal guns out of your hat and lecturing us about supply lines, I'd like to hear what my lieutenant found down there."

Townsend raised his hands and backed away to let Lucas have the table, but now that he was finally at the moment he'd fought so hard to reach, Lucas was at a loss for where to start. Even with his two languages, the sights he'd witnessed didn't easily fit into words. All the commanders were staring at him, though, so Lucas took a deep breath and began with the beginning.

"After leaving the fort, we hired one of the miners who said they'd seen the Sioux to take us to the spot. The location was out past where most prospectors have their claims, in a section known as the Deep Caves. The miner claimed to be familiar with the area, so we didn't anticipate difficulty with travel, but before we even reached the Deep Caves, a rockslide killed half our forces. The only other survivor of our mission, Private Chaucer, was one of the rear guard who got buried. The miner was also injured in the collapse and later died of his wounds. Fortunately, I'd had one of my men plying him for details of the journey in case he turned out to be one of Medicine Rocks' many charlatans, so we had enough knowledge of the location to keep going even without our guide. We used that to press into the unexplored frontier of the Deep Caves, where we found the enemy in great number."

"Damnation," Cook said, white beard bristling as he clenched his jaw. "Redskins with crystal! That's all we need."

"Can they even use it, though?" Colonel Avery asked. "It took our best minds in Washington over a year to figure out how to work the stuff into a rifle. What are those savages going to do with it? Bang some rocks together?"

"They seemed quite knowledgeable of its uses," Lucas said, shaking his head. "The group we found was Lakota, and we witnessed them harvesting crystal in copious amounts, though not as our miners do. They were not digging up the crystal but growing it from the rock walls like crops, harvesting the clusters one crystal at a time so that the central formation always remained intact."

"I don't give a damn about their methods," Cook snapped. "What I want to know is how they got down there to begin with. This whole time we've been operating on the assumption that we control the only entrance to the caves. If the Sioux found another way in, that undercuts all our security."

"They could boil out of the ground beneath our feet!" Avery agreed in a panic. "*And* they're stealing our crystal! The Midway Caverns are nearly mined out. If the Lakota are already working the Deep Caves, they could take everything for themselves before we even arrive!"

"So we take it back," Custer spat, looking at his fellow officers with contempt. "Crystal might be valuable, but it doesn't change the calculus of war. These are still savages fighting in small bands with bows and spears. Even if they have found a way into our caves, that just makes them primitives with shiny rocks. We have *guns*! We have cannons and explosives, the education of classical warfare! We are their superiors in every way. If they're in our caves, we'll simply flush them back out."

"It's not that easy," Lucas cautioned. "Even if we use the tunnels to limit their numbers, the Sioux have us badly outmatched. The group we encountered numbered over fifty, and that was just one band. From the runners we observed going back and forth, I'm certain they have more crystal gatherers working in other areas. They're on high alert, too. Even being cautious and watching from a tunnel high above them, we were spotted and fired upon almost immediately."

"And did you shoot back?" Custer asked in a sneering voice.

"Of course we shot back," Lucas said angrily. "It just didn't do any good. One of their holy men, a shaman, was down there with them, and he did something with the crystal that turned our bullets to smoke as soon as they left our guns. Smoke that then turned on *us*."

"How could smoke hurt you?" Colonel Avery asked.

"I... I..." Lucas stopped, groping for the right words, but there were none. Even his beloved mother tongue could not adequately describe how the wafting vapor had been solid but not, like a knife that carved your bones without marring your skin, and all the while a sound galloped through you like a herd of stampeding buffalo.

Just thinking about it set Lucas's heart pounding with the phantom hoofbeats all over again. He still wasn't entirely sure how they'd gotten out of that cavern with so many of his men still alive, not that he'd managed to keep them that way. Once they were discovered, the Lakota had been relentless, chasing the soldiers deeper and deeper into the caves. Only when it was already too late had Lucas realized the Lakota were driving them, forcing them down into the lowest parts of the caverns where even the Indians didn't dare to tread. The Lakota had given up the pursuit shortly after, trusting the caves to take care of the intruders in their stead. And except for Lucas himself, they'd been right.

"Lieutenant?"

Lucas jerked out of the terrifying memories to find the whole room staring at him.

"As I was saying," General Cook continued, "we must now assume the Sioux have access to crystal and at least some knowledge of its uses. This undermines our key advantage of superior firepower, since they already have us outnumbered."

"Not where it counts," Custer argued. "They have more bodies than we do, but buffalo hunters don't make an army. We've no hard evidence that they know how to weaponize crystal or even that they're actually down there. The only proof we have of any of this is one man's word. One *highly questionable* man." The lieutenant colonel turned back to Cook. "Wasn't Lieutenant Lucas jailed for piracy before joining our ranks?"

Lucas turned rigid in his seat, but the general waved the attack away.

"So what if he was? Cavalry's full of lost souls looking to get found through service to their country, and it's bad form to harp on a man's past. You don't see Avery or I holding your court-martial against you, George. Also, last I checked, prison doesn't affect a man's eyesight."

"But the caves do," Custer pressed on, undeterred. "This whole fleabag town is full of miners gone soft in the head from too long in the caves. How do we know Lucas didn't also go mad down there and imagine this entire episode? He was raving about cave angels just this morning."

"I did *not* imagine this, sir," Lucas said furiously. "The only reason I am alive and speaking to you today is because my men sacrificed themselves to get me out of the Lakota's trap so that I could bring word of what is coming. The tribes have crystal. They might even have a better understanding of it than we do. Look, I can prove what I say is true!"

He fumbled into his pockets, reaching inside the lining of his coat for the object he'd hidden there what felt like a lifetime ago. It was a crystal arrowhead, sharp as glass and shining like the moon in the closed-up room. When he placed it on the table for the others to see, the crystal didn't clink or clack against the wood as normal stone would. It landed with the deep beat of a war drum, making them all jump.

"What in God's name does that do?" Avery asked, flinching away.

"I don't know," Lucas said. "But the Lakota have thousands more just like it. Before we were discovered, my soldier stole this from a wall bristling with crystal arrowheads like spines on a cactus. That's why we fought so hard to get a warning back. We had to let everyone know what was coming in time to do something about it!"

The room fell silent as he finished, and then Custer slammed his hand on the table. "Then we've no choice but to beat them to the punch."

Cook sighed. "Is this about that fool plan you were trying to sell me on this morning?"

"Yes," Custer said. "Only it's an even better idea now."

He grabbed one of the maps scattered across the table and turned it so they could all see the huge expanse of the territory the Sioux controlled. "My Crow scouts report the Lakota have a large encampment here." He tapped his finger on an empty stretch of grassland along the banks of the Little Big Horn River. "They say it's the biggest they've ever seen, but since the men are all out hunting buffalo, there are no warriors, making it the perfect target."

Lucas stared at him, dumbstruck. "Are you suggesting we attack a camp of women and children?"

"Spare me the sermon, *Monsieur Lucas,*" Custer drawled in a mocking imitation of Lucas's accent. "Weren't you just howling like a hit dog about the Lakota having crystal? If you really want to stop them, then we have to strike hard and strike fast. It's the only way to get out in front of this disaster, and it's not like the redskins spare our women when they attack our settlements."

"What would such an attack accomplish, though?" Townsend asked. "Not that I disagree with a hard strike, but killing their women and children does nothing to reduce the number of their warriors or their presence in the mines."

"You're missing the point," Custer said, jerking his chin toward Lucas. "Frenchie there already proved we can't face them in the caves. The journey from our side is too long and too dangerous and doesn't let us use any of our advantages. My plan does." He turned back to General Cook. "If we hit their camp hard, it won't matter how dug in they are down there. As soon as they hear the screams of their squaws, those redskins will pop out of their holes like prairie dogs. When that happens, all we gotta do is be ready with our guns and *bam*, problem's solved."

"What makes you think this encampment has anything to do with the caves?" Cook asked, stroking his beard. "It's pretty far away."

"Do you know anything else that could make them gather in such numbers?" Custer said confidently. "I've been hunting Indians out here for years, and I've never seen them camp in groups larger than a handful during buffalo season. A gathering this big *has* to be for something special, and if they really are down there in the numbers Lucas reports, then they'd need an equally large camp up top to keep them supplied. Even if I'm wrong, and this is just an overgrown hunting camp, it's still a rare opportunity to knock the enemy down a peg. The men might hunt the buffalo, but it's the women who process the carcasses and preserve the meat. If we burn this place out, we'll destroy months of supply, greatly hobbling their ability to wage war on us come winter."

Lucas couldn't believe what he was hearing. "You're talking about a massacre!"

"I'm talking about victory!" Custer shouted. "Crystal or no crystal, ain't a man on this planet who can fight without food, and unlike us, those savages don't have a railway to keep them supplied. Best-case scenario, we find their entrance to the caves and shut it down. Worst case, we set them up to starve. Either way, we win."

"You make a strong argument," Cook said, eyeing the crystal arrowhead. "Say I agreed to this plan. How many men would you need?"

"Just my 7th," Custer answered immediately. "We can be ready to ride by first light tomorrow."

"You should take the Gatling gun," Avery suggested. "Even if they're mostly civilians, you'll be dealing with large numbers. The Gatling excels at crowds, and it's doing us no good sitting in the storehouse."

Custer shook his head. "That heavy thing will just slow me down."

"Well, you can't have the crystal rifles," Townsend said, even though no one had asked. "They're to protect the—"

"I don't need any of that!" the lieutenant colonel snapped, keeping his eyes on Cook. "All I need are six hundred brave men with swift horses beneath them. Give me those, and I'll give you victory."

"Very well," Cook said. "But Avery's going with you."

"I am?" Colonel Avery said in alarm.

"I don't need him," Custer insisted. "My men are tried and tested Indian killers. Avery and his Buffalo boys will only get in our way."

"I'm not sending him to fight with you," Cook said. "I'm aiming to hit two birds with one stone."

He grabbed the map Custer had been using and spun it around to face him. "Despite everyone and their mother dodging the tax table, we've still managed to collect enough crystal to justify sending a shipment back to Washington. I've suspected for a while now that the Whitmans have spies in town reporting our movements. That's the only way they can have so many men ready to jump us in the middle of nowhere. But if I give the crystal to Avery's boys and have them slide in behind Custer while he's hooting and hollering about going Indian hunting, everyone will think they're his reserves. We can use the 7th Cavalry's advance as cover to ride the crystal out of town right under the Whitmans' noses."

Custer shrugged. "So long as I don't actually have to bring them with me, I don't care if they eat our dust."

"They might not notice at first," Townsend said. "But I'm sure the enemy will figure out our plan once Avery's troops swing south." He reached over the table to tap the hair-thin line running south out of

Medicine Rocks that marked the road to Wyoming and the train depot in Cheyenne. "According to your reports, everything below us is Whitman territory. We might be able to fool them at the start, but they're bound to realize the plot eventually. Likely when Avery's troops are smack-dab in the middle of their domain."

"Not if they go a different way," Cook said, sliding his finger up the map to a tiny dot hidden in the squiggles of the Missouri River. "After riding out under Custer's cover, I plan to have Avery and his men cut north across the plains to the ferry dock at Fort Buford. We'll send the crystal down by riverboat."

"But that's hundreds of miles in the wrong direction!" Townsend cried. "And there's no road going north! The armored carriages can't drive across open grassland!"

"That's fine," Cook said confidently. "We're not using those things."

"But—"

"You paraded those giant metal boxes right through the center of town when you rode in," Cook reminded him. "That's like walking a safe past a bunch of bank robbers. Mark my words, those things are going to *attract* attacks, not deter them, and all that metal won't matter for beans when the Whitmans steal the entire wagon and take it home to crack at their leisure."

Townsend turned pale. "But, sir!"

"*No,*" Cook said, slamming his fist on the table. "Those wagons stay right where they are, because so long as they're parked inside our walls, everyone's going to think the crystal's still here too. They'll do a much better job being decoys than they ever would driving, and while everyone's watching them, Avery and his colored boys will smuggle the actual crystal north in their saddlebags."

"What if they encounter a Sioux hunting party?" Custer asked.

"Then they'll run," Cook said. "A handful of soldiers can fall back to hold the Indians off while the rest keep riding. The important thing is that we get as much of that shipment as possible on a boat headed back into territory we control. Because if Lucas is right, and the Sioux are arming themselves with crystal, then we're about to be outgunned as well as outnumbered, which means I need two thousand more of *these*"—he stabbed his finger at the crystal rifle on the table—"by yesterday."

"They won't attack us here," Custer said confidently. "Crystal or no crystal, they don't have the guts to ride into cannons."

"Maybe not," Cook said. "But I'd still rather get something out of these mines we're dying to protect than not."

"I see your strategy, sir," Colonel Avery said nervously. "But I still don't understand why *I* have to go personally. Surely one of my lieutenants would be far more suited to—"

"You have to go because I only just thought of this now," Cook explained. "That means I won't have time to warn whoever's running Fort Buford that you're coming, so I'll need someone who can pull enough rank to make sure their barge gets commandeered for our shipment. You know how those river captains get."

"Oh," Avery said, looking more nervous by the second. "I suppose when you put it that way—"

"All I need you to do is ride, old man," Cook said impatiently. "Have you forgotten why we're out here? Our mission, our entire *purpose* is to ensure that crystal makes it to Washington. The president, the cabinet, even Congress all agree that these mines could become America's greatest strategic asset, but all that potential won't amount to anything if we can't get those rocks out of the ground and into their hands. Now I'm sick and tired of taking the heat because your boys can't handle some no-account bandits, so you're going to help me make it right. You're riding that crystal north *personally*, and I don't want to hear another word about it unless it's 'yes, sir.'"

"Yes, sir," Avery whispered, rising shakily from his chair. Custer was already marching out the door, shouting at the top of his lungs for his men to start getting ready to ride out. Townsend was also clearly ready to leave, but when he reached down to help Lucas off his stool, the lieutenant didn't budge.

"Permission to speak freely, General."

Cook heaved a long sigh. "Go ahead."

"This is a terrible idea," Lucas snapped, spitting the pent-up words through clenched teeth. "Even if Custer is right, and that gathering is the Lakota's mining operation, slaughtering a camp of women and children is not a victory. It will enrage the Sioux against us and blacken the name of the US Cavalry. We were stationed here to protect Americans, not to kill innocents who've done nothing but hunt buffalo on the land we promised to let them use for that exact purpose!"

The general gave him a level look. "Are you finished?"

"*No!*" Lucas said angrily. "I warned you about Custer when you called him here from the Black Hills. You knew his bloody reputation, but you told me he was a necessary evil and that you'd keep a leash on him. This is not a leash!"

"Situation's changed," Cook said, nodding at the crystal arrowhead on the table. "*You* changed it, Jean-Jacques."

"All the more reason not to do this," Lucas pleaded. "I just told you that the Sioux's capabilities are beyond what we thought. What if they use that crystal on Custer's men?"

"Then we'll get a look at the enemy's new toys before they use them on *us*," the general said, glaring him down. "I'm not a monster, Jean-Jacques. I hate this situation every bit as much as you do, but I got a war to win. This is the opportunity your men died to give us. Don't waste it getting soft over a bunch of natives who'd shoot you full of arrows in a heartbeat. Dismissed."

"But—"

"*Dismissed.*"

Lucas clamped his jaw. If he could have, he would have stormed out of the meeting room. Alas, his legs were not equal to his ire, leaving him no choice but to limp away angrily on Townsend's shoulder. By the time they left the log keep, the sky was dark, forcing them to go slowly to avoid the now nearly invisible ropes of the tent city that filled the fortress's center.

"I know that didn't go as you wanted," Townsend said gingerly at his friend's furious silence. "But look on the bright side. If both Custer and Avery ride out, there will finally be enough room in the barracks for everyone to sleep in a bed! I'm sure that will raise the men's spirits."

Lucas made a noncommittal noise and scowled at Custer's soldiers pouring eagerly out of the mess, laughing and jeering at one another as they got ready to slaughter women and children.

"This is a mistake."

"I wholeheartedly agree," Townsend assured him. "What the devil is Cook about, sending the crystal to Fort Buford? Even if they make it intact, using the river will take weeks longer than if we'd just put the crystal on the train."

He looked to Lucas for support, and his eager expression dropped. "Oh. You weren't talking about that, were you?"

"We're supposed to be the heroes, Townsend!" Lucas cried. "'Call in the cavalry! Ride to the rescue!' That's what I signed up for. Not *this*! My men didn't die so that cowards like Custer could indulge their taste for murder without punishment."

Townsend rolled his eyes. "Don't be so dramatic. No one wants innocent victims, but this is war. If the Sioux don't want to die, they should stop fighting us. If you think about it logically, you should be cheering for Custer, not doubting him. Unsavory though the lieutenant colonel's tactics might be, if he succeeds in his aims, then this whole awful situation will be over that much sooner."

He finished with a cheerful smile that was not returned, and Townsend sighed. "*Really*, Jean-Jacques, you have to start thinking more strategically. You're part of an army now, not an officer on a single ship. Keep your eyes on the bigger picture, and remember: they're just savages. They can't read or write. They have no inventions, no cities, no great works. If we weren't here, they'd just be killing each other, so try not to work yourself into a snit about it, all right?"

That did *not* make Lucas feel better, but he was too tired to keep bashing himself against the cliff of Townsend's prejudice. He was exhausted in general, his body aching from weeks of terror and abuse. Now that the sun was down, Lucas swore he could hear the whispers that had tormented him in the Dark creeping back into his ears. The malicious voices on the edge of his hearing telling him to let go, to give up and join them.

He never would, *never*. But he was so tired of fighting, and no angel was coming to lift him out of this mess. Just Townsend's patient voice directing him around the ropes as they hobbled together through the growing shadows back to the medical tent.

Chapter 7

Mary crawled out of her hidey-hole in the caves and walked back into town before the dawn had begun turning the night sky green. It was early even for someone who didn't usually have a sun to mind, but the gunman who'd hired her didn't seem the sort to tolerate slack. And anyway, early meant empty, which was just how Mary liked it.

The dark part of the morning was her favorite. It was a clean, quiet, empty time when the drunks were all still passed out, but the miners and shopkeepers hadn't yet started their day's work, which made it just about the only time Mary felt safe in Medicine Rocks. She could walk right down the middle of Main Street, strolling bold as you please toward the looming shadow of the barn-like Price Mining Company.

Mary hopped up the clean-swept wood stairs excitedly. It'd been an age since she'd worked with Price miners. She'd guided their teams only a couple of times since they'd just wanted direction, not crystal finding, which paid a lot less. Still, they'd been honest, respectful men who paid on time and didn't slight her for not being white, which was as good as Mary could ask. It'd be nice to have quality clients again. Not that she saw any signs of such in the building's big dark windows.

Maybe they were sleeping in? Didn't seem likely with that bossy Reiner riding herd, but that weren't her business. As the nuns used to say, "nosy noses get cut off," so Mary made sure to keep hers safely tucked, plopping down on the office's front porch to wait for her employers, whoever they might be.

Her bottom had scarcely hit the boards when Mary heard a commotion up in the cavalry camp. She couldn't see what it was all the way down here, but that ended up not mattering. Not half a minute after she first heard the ruckus, a bugle sounded high and clear, and the wooden fortress gate opened to unleash a river of mounted soldiers thundering down the road.

Between the speed and dust, it was impossible to count their number, but it seemed to Mary that the entire cavalry was riding hell for leather out of town. The white soldiers galloped by first, then came a column of Black ones led by an old man who looked like he'd rather be swallowing horseshoes. They were all heading north, too, which meant they were going Indian killing.

Being of mixed blood, Mary knew she should feel bad over that, but she was mostly just relieved the soldiers were heading away from her. Even when they were riding out, the cavalry caused her trouble, waking everyone up and ruining her peaceful, quiet morning as folks stuck their heads out of tents and windows to see what the commotion was about. By the time the whole column had passed, Medicine Rocks was buzzing like noontime, forcing Mary deeper into the porch's shadow. She pulled her feet up under her oilcloth poncho and hugged her knees, curling herself like an armadillo so the folks standing in the road pointing after the soldiers wouldn't see her.

The last thing she needed was someone accusing her of loitering. Or worse, stalking around Price Mining to rob the place. Poor old building had been burgled so much they wouldn't even need proof to convince the sheriff she was up to no good. Not that anyone had ever needed proof when it came to Mary, but she hated giving them an open shot. She was wondering if she shouldn't move around to the back of the building and avoid the whole thing when she spotted Tyrel Reiner coming out the door of the Wet Whistle.

"Morning, Mr. Reiner!" she yelled, raising her voice so all the would-be-sheriff-callers in the road would know she was here for working, not thieving. That was Mary's logic, anyway, but the gunhand jumped like she'd taken a shot at him instead of a hello, hurrying 'cross the road like a caught cat.

"Not so loud!" he hissed when he got near. "You let everyone know I hired a cave guide and we'll be dodging claim jumpers the whole way down!"

Mary felt that fear was a bit overblown, given his reputation. Just the sight of him walking across the street had been enough to send the gawkers scuttling back to their beds. But he was the boss, so Mary dutifully lowered her voice.

"Sorry, Mr. Reiner."

"And don't call me that," the gunman snapped, looking more cussed than ever. "'Mr. Reiner' was my father, and I ain't answering to no name that still carries the stink of that son of a bitch."

As he said that, one of the three guns he wore at his hips—the sparkly crystal one, not the plain—started shaking like a rattlesnake's warning. A snarl crossed the gunman's face, and he whacked the thing with his palm. This quieted the gun down nicely, but Mary had found the whole situation powerful strange.

Not that he had a crystal gun. The Wet Whistle had more crystal than anyone in town, including the Mining Office. They used it for all manner of oddness, but Mary had never seen this sort before. She was straining her ears to hear if the pistol was the source of his strange sour-note humming when she realized Tyrel was still glaring at her.

"Sorry, Mr. Tyrel."

"Just Rel is fine," he said. "It's quicker, and I'm more likely to answer."

"Yes'sir, Mr. Rel."

"Drop the 'Mister' and you'll have it," Rel said, turning his glare on the dark building. "You're punctual, at least, which is more than I can say for the rest of our company."

"How many more we waiting on?"

"Just one."

That was surprising. Mining companies tended to run the biggest crews in the business. Not that there were many companies left, but two seemed a sorry number for any venture, 'specially given how much Rel had promised to pay. Little groups were quicker and sneakier than big ones, though, so maybe that was his aim. Either way, Mary thought he was being most unfair to their other member, whoever he was.

"You *did* say to be here at dawn," she reminded him timidly, pointing at the dark sky. "The sun ain't over the grass yet, so properly there's still time."

Like most men, Rel looked sour at being corrected, but at least he didn't yell at her for it. He just sat down on the porch steps and settled in to wait, pulling out one of his uncrystaled revolvers to check its chambers. After a few minutes of nervous hovering, Mary sat down next to him. She'd already looked over all her own equipment, but she made a show of inspecting her stuff again to prove how prepared she was. She was playacting checking the lampwick she already knew was perfectly fine when the jingly door of the mining company's office burst open, and a tall figure strode onto the porch behind them.

"Sorry to keep you waiting."

Mary scrambled to her feet, eyes wide as wagon wheels as she turned to face... she wasn't sure, actually. She'd never seen anything like the person in the doorway. Couldn't even rightly say what they were other than beautiful.

If it hadn't been impossible, Mary would've sworn the figure had stepped straight off one of the painted advertisements in the General Store's window. The ones with the faces so pretty they didn't even look real. That was how it was with this person: tall as a man—but definitely not one—yet still unlike any woman Mary had ever seen. There was obviously makeup on that lovely face, but it was an entirely different sort than the thick paint the Wet Whistle girls used. Their hair looked like a pile of golden yarn rolled up atop their head, and while their waist was cinched small by a corset, they wore no skirts. Instead, their long legs were encased in billowy trousers wider and finer than any Mary had ever seen. These huge things were in turn tucked into the tops of shiny leather calf-high boots that had clearly never touched a road.

Everything about the person looked fresh out of the shop, actually, which led Mary to a singular conclusion. This was neither man nor woman. This was a *Lady*.

Mary had never seen a Lady in real life before. She knew they were people who lived in the world's finer places and posed for advertisements, but the figure in front of her might as well've been a mermaid for all Mary knew what to do with her. How did one even address a Lady? Should she tip her hat? Curtsy? How did you do a curtsy, anyway? Was she even allowed to talk to someone that rich?

All these important questions were whirling through her head when the Lady tipped the whole issue on its side by stepping forward and offering her delicate, leather-gloved hand to Mary like a flower.

"How do you do?" she said in the prettiest English ever spoken. "I'm Josephine Price, but you can call me Josie. You're our guide, yes?"

Tongue-tied in bow-hitches, Mary nodded.

"What's your name?"

Oh Lord.

"She's called Mary Good Crow," Rel said when it became clear that Mary wasn't going to answer for herself.

The Lady Josephine Price's perfect eyebrows rose like bird wings. "Ah!" she said, sounding genuinely excited as she turned back to Mary with a dazzling smile. "Are you from the Crow tribe, then?"

That was just wrong enough to snap Mary out of her stupor. "No, Lady Josephine," she squeaked. "My Indian half's Lakota. The Crow hate us."

She regretted the correction at once, 'cause the fancy Lady looked devastated. "Oh no, I'm so sorry! Please forgive my ignorance, and there's no need to be so formal. Just plain old Josie is fine."

Mary nodded silently, praying the terrifying creature would let her be, but the Lady showed no mercy.

"Is Good Crow a Lakota name, then?" she asked, bending over to put herself at eye level with her much shorter victim.

"No… Miss Josie," Mary said, struggling to find a middle ground between what the Lady said she wanted and what experience had taught Mary was actually required. "That was the nuns' idea. I was left on the doorstep of the Dutiful Virgin mission when I was just a baby. Since I was a half-breed, the sisters felt I should have an Indian name. They didn't speak any Lakota, though, so they just made up something what sounded right to them."

"They *made up* your name?" The Lady scowled dreadfully. "Isn't that rather presumptuous?"

Mary didn't know what "presumptuous" meant, but it didn't sound good, and she rushed to the nuns' defense. "They were trying their hardest, Miss. They'd just come down from Quebec following God's call to minister to the Indians, not raise an orphan. I was a great burden to them—that much they made clear—but they still did their best to turn me out well. That's why they named me as they did: 'Crow' on account of my hair"— Mary held up one of her long black braids—"'Good' to remind me how I should act always, and 'Mary' 'cause if there was anyone who needed the Blessed Mother's help, it was me."

That was a lot more answer than Miss Josie had asked for and not even wholly truthful. The actual name the nuns had given her was "Marie Bon Corbeau," but no one had called Mary by that mouthful since her christening. When the nuns wanted her, they just yelled "*Marie!*" or "*Girl!*" and the Sioux hadn't cared about Christian names at all. As a result, Mary had never given much thought to her last name until she'd started working for herself and realized Americans didn't hire people they couldn't pronounce. That was when she'd become "Mary Good Crow" in earnest, but such rambling stories had no place in polite conversation. She'd probably babbled too much already, but if Miss Lady Josie was put off by all the jawing, she was good at hiding it.

"Well, I'm delighted to make your acquaintance, Miss Good Crow," she said, stuffing more politeness into those ten words than Mary normally heard in a year. "I trust you will take good care of us."

"That's what we're paying her for," Rel said. "Or will be, assuming she can actually do what they say."

A chill ran up Mary's spine. That was right. This job depended on her passing some sort of test to prove she could hear crystal. She'd nearly forgotten that detail in the excitement of fancy-Lady money. When it came to the caves, though, Mary felt pretty confident. She'd just turned to head down to 'em when Rel caught her shoulder.

"Not there," the gunman said, pulling Mary back. "I want to know what you can do *before* we go in."

"But how'm I supposed to show you I can hear crystal without the caves?" Mary asked.

Smiling a terrifying smile, Rel shot a pointed look at Josie, who moved around to the front of the porch, blocking them off from the rest of the once again empty space with her height and strange skirt-trousers. "We were hoping you could use this," she said, pulling something out of her pocket.

Mary's eyes went wider than she'd known they could go. There, shining like the moon in the lady's cupped hands, was a crystal. They weren't even close to underground yet, but it was already singing like a flute in the wind. Calling to her with a voice warm as a mother's.

"Can you hear it?" Rel whispered, his narrow blue eyes gleaming like hard glass in the crystal's light.

"I've never heard anything so clear and pure," Mary whispered, her voice shaking in awe.

"Is it saying anything?" Miss Josie asked next, her voice so excited Mary felt rotten about what she had to say next.

"I'm afraid crystal doesn't talk, miss."

"Pointing somewhere, then?" the Lady pressed, grabbing one of Mary's gloved hands to place the glowing treasure in her palm. "Is it like a compass?"

Mary had never used a compass, but the moment the stone was in her grasp, she understood what the Lady was talking about. The glowing

118

crystal was pulling at something inside her like a dog on a rope. Pulling toward what, Mary couldn't say, but the sensation sent pleasant tingles all the way to her toes. She was always excited to head back down into the caves, but she'd never felt the urge as strong as she did now. She had no idea how or where a lady like Miss Josie could have gotten her hands on such a treasure, but it felt like she was holding a solidified note of the cave's song in her hands. A note that was part of something much bigger and wanted desperately to get back to it.

"I can feel it," Mary whispered, clutching the beautiful thing to her chest.

"Can you follow it?" Rel asked.

Mary couldn't *not* follow it. It didn't seem possible to miss a place you'd never been, but the shard's song filled her with a yearning even stronger than yesterday's hunger, pulling her toward the caves so hard, her feet struggled to stay still. She was about to let the crystal drag her away when she realized Tyrel was still waiting for his answer.

"I can get us where it's pointing," she promised, tucking the precious crystal into her pocket before Miss Josie got the idea to take it back. "But it might be a ways."

"How far?"

The pulling hadn't exactly come with a tape measure, but if there was still a crystal this good anywhere closer than the Deep Caves, Mary would eat her hat.

"Deep Caves don't scare us," Rel said when Mary told them this, a grin passing over his boyish face. "Good work, Good Crow." His hand flicked as he finished, tossing Mary a tied-up wad of paper money. "There you go. Thirty dollars up front, as promised. I'll give you the rest when we get back safe."

Mary tucked the billfold into her pack fast as a squirrel hiding food. "Looks like we're in business, then," she said, switching to her guiding voice. "How many days of supplies do we have?"

"Mihir and I could only fit three weeks' worth, I'm afraid," Miss Josie said, lifting her bulging pack. "Is that enough?"

"It should be plenty," Mary assured her, shocked that someone so delicate-looking could heft so much. Clearly, Ladies were a stronger breed than she'd credited. Certainly stronger than Tyrel, who seemed to be having much more difficulty with his pack.

"You can lighten the load by dumping your water," she suggested, opening the bag Miss Josie had packed for her to transfer all the food— including packets of real white sugar, which Mary was definitely saving for a special event—to her own trusty knapsack. "I can find us plenty to drink in the caves."

"That's good, 'cause she only packed us one canteen each," the gunman huffed, finally balancing the weight on his narrow shoulders. "But I'm fine, so if we're all set, let's get moving. We're burning daylight."

Day or night made no difference underground, but Mary was being paid too well to backtalk, and she was also eager to get going. Just turning the caves' direction had made the crystal shard perk up like an excited bird inside Mary's coat, lifting her own heart with delight. She'd never been so excited to start a job, and it showed in her pace, moving her feet as fast as Rel's as the gunman cut a beeline straight toward the gate that marked the mines' entrance, leaving poor narrow-heeled Miss Josie to scramble after.

Chapter 8

After reading about them for so long, walking down the dusty road toward the *actual* Crystal Caverns of Medicine Rocks made Josie feel like the young Arthur must have when he'd first felt Excalibur sliding out of the stone into his hand. Here at last, *here at last*, was the gateway to everything: freedom from the Prices, freedom for herself, freedom to worry about things other than what scandal Miss Josephine would create next and how Josie would get blamed for letting her.

The experience was even more exhilarating than the first time she'd stepped onto the train alone wearing her mistress's clothes. Somewhere past that wooden gate was the glittering fuel of all her hopes. Once she controlled the crystal, the real Josephine would be reliant upon *her* for her fortune! The mere thought of it was enough to put a skip in Josie's step as Miss Good Crow led them through the split-wood fence that separated the boomtown from its fuse.

Even in this starry-eyed state, however, Josie found the entrance to the mines a bit less grand than expected. She'd always imagined the start of the crystal caverns looking like a doorway to another world with a great stone stair leading down into the abyss, but the reality was more like... a cave.

Not even a cave. The dusty hollow below the rock looked like something a dog might dig to escape the heat. If not for the cluster of yawning cavalry soldiers chatting beside it, Josie might have walked right past. The best she could say about it was that at least it had impressive surroundings.

Medicine Rocks was graced with many sandstone boulders but none so huge as the one under which crystal had first been discovered. It was as big as a steamboat! Forty feet tall at least and a good hundred from end to end, though how anyone had ever come up with the idea to dig beneath it for crystal, Josie couldn't imagine. Apart from its size, the boulder must have looked just like all the other Medicine Rocks before its wind-hollowed cliffs had been blackened and cracked by the explosives the original crystal prospectors had used to blast their way down to the treasure beneath.

As was her duty, Mary went under first, shuffling down the dirt slope into the oval-shaped hole that led beneath the giant rock. Josie followed next, though she had to duck a great deal more to avoid knocking her head on the bottom of the boulder. Mercifully, the gap was a great deal larger than it had looked from the outside, dropping them into a wide, sandy hollow big enough for Josie to stand most of the way up. The tan roots of the great rock above them continued farther down on both sides, but the area ahead had been shaped with dynamite and pickaxes into a wide tunnel going down. This passage was blocked, however, by a wide wooden table where four more soldiers sat playing cards around a bright mining lantern.

"Is this the infamous tax table?" Josie whispered to Rel as the black-clad gunhand ducked into the hollow behind them.

"You don't have to pay anything on the way in, miss," Mary assured her, even though she wasn't the one Josie had asked. "The soldiers only mind you when you're leaving."

That made sense. The only taxable asset anyone here cared about was crystal, and no one brought that *into* the mines. Still. "Isn't there something we're supposed to sign? Uncle's letters mentioned a roster keeping track of who went down and when in case you didn't come back up again."

Rel snorted. "You say that like they're going to send someone after you. The cavalry don't give a shit if you go missing down here. I mean, if word got 'round that you'd vanished on the way to a huge strike, then *maybe* folks would put together a search party, but only so they could mine the crystal over your dead body."

Josie scowled. "That's a little harsh, don't you think?"

Rel shrugged. "Welcome to the Crystal Caverns."

Josie glanced at Mary for help, but the girl was already scuttling along the wall past the checkpoint, giving the soldiers—who hadn't even looked up from their game—as wide a berth as Josie would have given a pack of wolves. Rel left less space, but she also didn't acknowledge the soldiers' presence, stalking past their table as silently as a surly cat. Josie, however, found it simply too rude to walk by without at least saying hello.

This turned out to be a terrible idea. It was just supposed to be a casual greeting, but the moment she spoke, all four soldiers jumped out of their chairs and whirled around, staring at her as if she'd dropped down on them from another planet.

"Morning, miss," said the oldest of them, who still wasn't very old. "What are you doing here?"

"Going in," Josie told him cheerfully, nodding at the tunnel ahead. She was about to head on her way when she spotted the dusty ledger the soldiers were using to weigh their cards down so the cool breeze coming up from the caves wouldn't blow them away.

"Is that the roster?"

"Um, yes?" the soldier said nervously, digging it out. "Would you like to sign?"

Josie was about to tell him not to trouble himself when the soldier opened the leather-bound folder to reveal a list of very familiar signatures.

She snatched the ledger from his hands and stared down in wonder. Apparently, her uncle was the only person who used the thing, for his name was signed on nearly every line, along with the date and how far in he planned to go. The few other signatures were also for Price Mining teams, but mostly this was the history of Sam Price as he'd explored deeper and deeper.

There was no record of his exits or crystal. Josie presumed those were listed in the much thicker tax ledger the lead soldier wore on a strap across his chest like a mother carrying an infant. She was sure she'd get to that book, too, in time, but for the moment, Josie was far more interested in the departure ledger's last entry. A line written in a far shakier hand than any of the others.

Sam Price, it read. *December 1, 1875. Deep Caves.*

Her vision grew misty as she ran a finger over the words. They told her nothing she hadn't already known, but seeing the record of that final, deadly venture in his own dear penmanship hurt more than Josie had been prepared for. She touched it one more time then reached into her satchel for a pencil, adding her name to the record directly below that of the man who'd made it possible.

"Thank you, Miss Price," the soldier said, finally snatching off the cap politeness should have required him to remove as soon as he saw her. "Um, have a nice trip?"

"Thank you," Josie said, pulling out a handkerchief to wipe away the stubborn tears it seemed she'd never be done with as she joined Mary and Reliance in the tangled juncture of dynamited tunnels just down the slope from the checkpoint.

The moment she got close, Rel grabbed Josie's arm and yanked her into one of the side passages. "Are you out of your skull? If I'd known you were determined to make a spectacle of yourself, I wouldn't have bothered getting up so early. Those soldiers weren't even paying attention until you fluttered your eyelashes at them. Now they'll be telling the story of the Caving Lady Price to anyone who comes in range!"

"It's not that bad," Josie insisted, face heating. "As you said, it's obvious no one uses the entry ledger, and if the soldiers do gossip, we'll be too far ahead to be troubled by it."

"We still gotta come *back,*" Rel snapped, yanking her black hat down over her eyes.

Feeling rightly foolish, Josie lowered her head and followed the others down the dusty tunnel, scolding herself all the while. This wasn't Boston, where not saying hello to someone when you passed was tantamount to spitting on their shoe. Everyone was rude out here, and while that didn't mean Josie had to become a savage as well, she did need to be smarter about these things. Being daring was all well and good, but if she marched blithely into danger, expecting the world to bow to her expectations, she'd be acting just as self-centered as the real Miss Josephine, a title Josie *never* wanted to earn.

Clearly, it was time for a little less excitement and a little more strategy. But just as Josie was composing a mental checklist of all the ways her impulsive decision to join her uncle in the ledger could come back to bite them, the narrow, chiseled tunnel they'd been following suddenly opened into a great expanse, blowing all the cautious, practical thoughts right out of her head.

"Gracious," Josie breathed, looking around in wonder. "What is *this?*"

The cavern they'd entered was low-ceilinged and wide with curving walls made of a dark substance that was entirely different from the cut sandstone they'd been walking through so far. It looked a little like volcanic glass, but it was dull black rather than shiny, and brittle to the touch. The formations came in a huge variety of shapes, sizes, and configurations from tiny needlelike clusters to giant blocks so perfectly square they looked like masonry. They all shared the same matte-black coloration, though, which seemed wrong. Surely rocks made from the same substance would be more similar in shape?

She was trying to remember if she'd read about anything similar in her uncle's letters or the geological guides she'd purchased when Josie realized that Mary had answered her question.

"I'm sorry, what did you say?"

"I said, 'that's crystal,'" Mary repeated.

"Dead crystal," Rel added, making Josie gasp.

"All of this is dead?" She'd heard that crystal could be ruined if it wasn't mined properly, but she'd never imagined something like this. "*How?*"

"This was where crystal was first discovered," Mary explained, holding her kerosene lantern high to show Josie just how far back the

125

black cavern went. "Story has it that some gold miners got tired of fighting over spots in the Black Hills and decided to try their luck up here. They'd stopped at the Medicine Rocks just for a rest on their way to try panning in the Powder River when they spied something glittering beneath a boulder. When they dug down to see what it was, they hit this place."

She waved her hands dramatically across at the black room, and Rel snorted. "You're saying they blasted a tunnel through a hundred feet of sandstone chasing some sparkles?"

"Well, maybe it didn't happen *precisely* that way," Mary admitted. "This area's been so blasted and picked over by miners it's hard to say what it looked like before. I know this was the first cavern discovered, though. That's why it's in the state it is. Back then, folks thought you could just hit crystal out of the ground like gold or diamonds. They didn't know it had to be tuned first so that the very act of mining didn't destroy what you were trying to remove."

"But how did they ruin *all* of it?" Josie asked, walking through the blackened cavern to tap on the nearest crystal cluster, which didn't even ring back anymore. "Crystal sours when it's struck improperly, yes, but you'd think they would've learned after the first dozen failures. How crystal-mad do you have to be to ruin every single rock the exact same way without realizing you're doing something wrong?"

Mary's shoulders were so buried beneath her piled clothing that Josie only saw her shrug by the bob of her lantern. "'Fraid I don't know, miss. I told you the story just as I heard it. If there's more to it, it's news to me."

"It just seems like such a waste," Josie said, picking her way back to the dusty path their fellow miners had trampled through the brittle, blackened stones. "Imagine discovering the most valuable new resource of the century and then ruining the whole thing through your own incompetence?"

"Never underestimate the potency of ignorance mixed with greed," Rel said, walking through the crack folks had hammered through the rear

126

of the ruined cavern to keep the crystal search going. "And speaking of bad decisions, if we don't want ours catching up with us, let's stop sightseeing and get a move on."

She hadn't been speaking to Josie directly, but that didn't stop her ears from burning. Fortunately, plenty lay ahead to distract her. Mary hadn't been exaggerating the use of dynamite. The next mile beyond the dead cavern was a maze of tunnels carved willy-nilly through the ground in a desperate search for more crystal. Some had clearly gotten lucky, for the walls here were riddled with pockets and holes where crystals had been chiseled out. Properly, this time. They passed a few tired-looking miners headed the other direction back to town, but despite Rel's doomsaying, no one seemed to be following them.

The caves, too, were less of a challenge than Josie had braced for. They were a bit muddy in places, and all the crisscrossing tunnels would have made for a very confusing trip on her own. With Mary's confident guidance, though, Josie was able to relax and focus on not banging her head on the rocks that occasionally protruded from the tunnel's low ceiling. She was starting to wonder if all this hullabaloo about the "deadly crystal caves" might be exaggerated when Mary called an unexpected halt.

"What's the matter?" Josie asked, reaching down to rub her ankles, which were not used to all this walking across uneven surfaces.

"Nothing," Mary said cheerfully, setting her lantern down on the ground. "I just spied Cornbread Yona, so I'm gonna go ask her how the caves are looking."

She said this as if it were obvious, but Josie failed to make sense of the words. "What's a Cornbread Yona?"

"She's a 'who,' not a 'what,'" Mary corrected, pointing down the tunnels, which had been running smaller and straighter as they'd left the man-made warren at the start of the caves and descended into the actual cracks through the ground that made up the crystal tunnel system. "See? She's right there on her bench."

Josie squinted into the darkness. Sure enough, stuck off to the side like a book on a shelf, there was indeed a little old woman sitting on a flat stone with a large box on her lap.

"Is she sitting in the *dark?*" Rel asked, echoing Josie's sentiment.

"Everywhere's dark to Yona," Mary explained with a laugh. "She's blind as a mole, poor thing, but she makes a right fine cornbread. Cooks up a fresh batch every day in the little stone oven she's got tucked off down one of the side tunnels."

"Sounds like quite the businesswoman," Josie said, noting the old woman's gray braids and wrinkled red skin. "Is she Lakota as well?"

"Nope, Cherokee. Got shoved out during the removal and just kept walking. Her cornbread ain't local, either. She told me she learned the recipe cooking for a rancher in Arkansas, but the miners here can't get enough. I don't buy it myself, since she charges miner-gouging prices, but Yona always knows what's going on in the caves ahead, and she'll tell you 'bout it for a nickel."

"Nice racket," Rel observed, pulling a silver coin out of her pocket. "Go on, then."

Mary caught the coin Rel tossed her and hurried over to press it into the blind woman's wrinkled hand. The two of them talked animatedly for a moment, then Yona said something that made Mary go quiet. There was a lot more hushed talking after that, and then Mary trod back up the tunnel with a worried frown on her cave-dirt-smudged face.

"What's wrong?" Rel demanded.

"It's more about what *could* be wrong," Mary said, picking up the lantern she'd left with them. "Yona says the last group she sold to reported good travel: no flooding or collapses or anything like that. Dark's moved around, but that's pretty normal. What I'm worried about are all the folks saying they've had trouble with Whitmans."

"Whitmans?" Josie said as Rel began to curse. "You mean the bandit gang everyone's so petrified of? I thought they were only a problem for travelers."

"Whitmans are a problem anywhere they show up," Mary said. "They've been banned from Medicine Rocks since last summer on account of all the stealing and murder, so I don't know how they got in here, but Yona says people've seen 'em all abouts in the deeper parts, so we'll want to watch our backs."

"How do they know they're Whitmans?" Josie asked, curious. "Everyone's always telling me how full up this place is with thieves and ambushes. What differentiates a Whitman from other criminals?"

"You'll know when you see 'em," Rel promised, checking her guns like she expected a fight right then and there. "They got a look."

Josie waited for her to expound, but all Rel did was slide her readied pistols back into their holsters. "Anything else we oughta watch for?"

"Yeah," Mary said, looking even more nervous now. "She also said that Bear Woman's awake."

"Who's Bear Woman?" Josie asked, too fascinated by all this to feel as frightened as she probably should. "She sounds like a native."

"Bear Woman ain't an Indian," Mary said as she led them down a different tunnel than the one where Cornbread Yona had set up shop. "At least not a living one."

"Is she a ghost?" Rel asked.

"Don't try to scare her," Josie scolded, glaring at her friend. "You know perfectly well there's no such thing as ghosts."

"Oh no, miss," Mary said, shaking her head so fast her pigtails flew. "There's heaps of ghosts down here, but Bear Woman ain't one. She's more of a force of nature, like a rockslide or a flood: dangerous if you get caught unawares but easy enough to get around now that we know she's about." She frowned. "Actually, if the Whitmans are in here, they're probably what riled her up. Bear Woman hates those who disrespect the sanctity of the caves, and ain't no one more disrespectful than a Whitman."

The casual way she said that, as if she were just repeating facts anyone would know, made Josie more nervous than anything else so far.

129

She was about to ask Mary if they could go back so she could question Yona herself. But when Josie looked over her shoulder to check the distance, the tunnel leading to the little old woman's bench—the one they'd *just* turned off not a minute earlier—was gone, leaving only a blank wall streaked with shiny drops of water.

Josie prided herself on maintaining a professional demeanor, but that made her jump like a startled rabbit. It wasn't that she didn't know the caves could move. Uncle Samuel had written pages describing the mysterious way the paths shuffled down here, so she'd long since made peace with the seemingly impossible idea. That said, actually seeing it happen—or rather, *not* seeing—was far more alarming than it had been on paper, enough to make her hair stand on end. She took deep breaths in an attempt to get her heartbeat down to a less terrifying tempo when Rel swaggered up from behind.

"What's the matter?" she asked, resting her thumbs on her belt in the most infuriating fashion. "Having second thoughts?"

"None worth stopping for," Josie replied, forcing her hands to unclench.

"Not too late to turn around. I can follow the guide alone and report back what I find if you'd rather wait in town."

Josie would *rather* fall down a disappearing crack herself than let Reliance Reiner see her turn coward after the bold statements of yesterday.

"I am perfectly capable of continuing," she informed her friend, pulling herself so proud and tall that she bumped her head on the tunnel's wet ceiling. "Especially since we've scarcely begun. If I can't handle this much, I might as well pack up and go back to Boston."

Rel looked a little too pleased at that possibility for Josie's taste, and she crossed her arms over her chest with a huff. "Anyway, what do I have to be scared of? Between your hair trigger and violent temper, I'm sure you'll shoot all the bandits and Bear Women before I even get a chance to see one."

"You can't shoot Bear Woman," Mary piped in helpfully. "It just makes her mad."

"Thank you, Miss Good Crow," Josie said through gritted teeth. "Can we move on, please?"

Mary shrugged and started forward again, but Rel wasn't gracious enough to take the hint.

"You know why everyone's so afraid of the Whitmans, right?" she said in a chilling voice as she dogged Josie's heels down the tunnel. "It's not just because they're killers. Every other mug you see in this town's killed someone over something, but the Whitmans are special. They're corpse stealers. Whenever they raid a wagon train or burn a ranch, they don't just shoot and run away with the valuables like normal highwaymen do. They take everything: horses, wagons, tools, even the bodies of the dead. I've heard from those lucky enough to escape that the Whitmans actually value the corpses most. Some say they'll even kill men who surrender just so they can drag their bodies off to—"

"Rel, *please!*" Josie cried, covering her ears. "What part of this strikes you as a good time to tell scary stories?"

"They're not stories," Rel insisted. "I'm telling you the truth because you need to know what you're getting into. If anyone's been lost in tall tales, it's you thinking you can just waltz into the caves with packets of sugar and that ridiculous getup. Where did you even find something that stupid looking, anyway?"

"You think I wanted to wear this?" Josie hissed, dropping her voice to a whisper as she grabbed a handful of her very fine but absolutely ludicrous linen trousers. "Miss Josephine's not generous enough to fork out for a new wardrobe for anyone other than herself. This was her African explorer costume from last year's Halloween ball, but it was the only remotely suitable caving outfit I could find. I couldn't very well fit a crinoline down here, could I?"

"Or you could've just have worn jeans like the rest of us."

131

"Yes, well, I didn't think of that." Josie huffed, crossing her arms stubbornly. "This is only my second day here. I'm still adjusting to the idea that the rules I was brought up to follow like gospel apparently no longer apply."

"That's probably for the best," Rel said. "No one'd believe you were actually Sam Price's heir if you started running around in overalls."

"The actual Josephine would faint at the sight of overalls," Josie agreed quietly, then she shook her head. "But that's enough of that. I am Josephine Price, and I think we should stop having this conversation."

"Suit yourself," Rel said, striding to catch up with Mary, who'd gotten quite far ahead while they were whispering. "Just remember, there ain't no shame in strategic retreat. I'm happy to take over if this gets to be too much."

Josie scowled at her friend's retreating back. Rel seemed suspiciously eager to leave her behind. Probably because she thought Josie wasn't up to the challenge, but if growing up with the Prices had taught her anything, it was fortitude. She hadn't survived all those dreadful years to crack now when she'd finally reached the precipice of something better. Just like when she'd stepped alone onto that train car back in St. Louis, it was forge ahead or forever hold her peace, so Josie plowed onward, using her long legs to pass Rel and catch up with Mary, who'd just come to another halt.

"What is it *now*?" she asked, desperate to keep her surge of momentum going. "Another vendor?"

"Nothing so nice, I'm afraid," Mary said as she lifted her lamp, which Josie suddenly realized was illuminating only the next few feet of tunnel despite the brightness of its flame. "We've reached the start of the Dark."

That was enough to send Josie's determination squealing off the rails. As with the moving tunnels, she'd read about the Dark several times in Sam's letters. But while "that bit of the caves where lamps don't work" had sounded like a trivial inconvenience on paper, the real thing was something else entirely. It wasn't just that Mary's light was falling short. Josie could actually see the place where the darkness changed, going from normal underground shadows to a tar-thick miasma that lapped at the cave's rough edges like an inky, silent sea.

That just about undid her. She'd been thinking all the worry over the caves was overblown, but just the idea of walking into that darkness that defied all understanding of how light worked turned her bones to jelly. If she hadn't made such a show of charging ahead, Josie would've told Mary to back up a moment so she could recover her nerves.

Alas, she *had* made a show of it, and with Rel so obviously waiting for her to crack, Josie didn't have much choice. It was just a bit of dark, she reminded herself. One every miner down here had to cross to get to their claims. Her uncle had made the trip dozens of times, and he'd been in his sixties and suffered from gout. Josie couldn't call herself worthy of taking over his business if she was too cowardly to step through even once, so she screwed her courage to the sticking point and told Mary to lead the way.

The girl did so by blowing out her lantern. This made sense. There was no point in wasting costly fuel for a light they couldn't see, but Josie still gasped when the blackness fell around them like a curtain. She yelped again when something grabbed her fingers, realizing far too late that it was Mary's gloved hand.

"It's all right," the guide said, her voice oddly muted even though the lack of sight should have made sounds sharper. "I know where we're going. Don't mind anything you hear. Just keep hold of my hand, keep to the path, and everything will be fine."

She sounded so certain that Josie's heart leaped, and she was ashamed to say she nearly crushed the poor girl's fingers in her eagerness. "Sorry," she whispered, but Mary didn't answer. Or maybe she did, and the Dark had eaten her words, for the unnatural blackness suddenly surrounded them.

Josie didn't remember walking forward. She must have, though, or perhaps the Dark had moved farther down the tunnel after the light had gone out, because they were definitely inside it now. Even with the light out and her eyes useless, there was a palpable difference between the earlier tunnels' shadows and what was in front of her now.

It didn't even feel right to label this "darkness." It was more like swimming through a giant vat of tar. Or maybe being spun through one, for while she hadn't moved an inch yet, Josie was suddenly unable to say which direction she was facing. If it weren't for her vise grip on Mary's hand, she wouldn't even have known which way was forward and which was back.

Good *Lord*, no wonder people vanished down here! Forget wandering off the path. If you could lose your sense of direction just by standing still, Josie didn't see how anyone got through the Dark other than by literal blind luck. Thank goodness Mary seemed able to find the way, because this whole undertaking was starting to feel impossible. Even Rel had given in and put a hand on Josie's shoulder, keeping close behind her as the Dark settled in.

This tight arrangement made walking difficult, but it wasn't as if they could have gone quickly when they had to slide their feet along the ground for every step to keep from tripping. Josie was desperate for the contact in any case, because now that all light had been taken from them, her eyes were starting to make up images of their own, conjuring shapes in the blackness that couldn't possibly be there. Her ears were similarly overactive, warping every drip and scrape into a ghostly whisper or threatening step. She was telling herself to stop being a ninny and just get it over with when Rel's hand vanished from her shoulder.

Squeaking in alarm, Josie whirled to see what had happened before remembering that was impossible. "Rel?" she called instead, groping for her friend with the hand that wasn't nailed to Mary's.

"What's the matter?" the guide asked.

"Rel's gone," Josie said, striving not to sound as scared as she felt. They couldn't be more than ten feet inside the Dark. Far too soon for trouble, surely. Rel had probably just stepped back outside to fix something where she could see. But just as Josie was opening her mouth to ask Mary if they could go back, the lower half of her face was covered by the heavy, stinking, unmistakable shape of a man's gloved hand.

Chapter 9

Reliance hated the Dark.

Not for the usual reasons. It wasn't the blindness or oppressiveness she minded. Not that those didn't bother her plenty. She just hated the ghosts more.

There were so damn many of them, and they were so *loud*. All the caves were stuffed with angry, confused souls these days, but the Dark had always been special. Rel didn't know if that was 'cause more people died here than in other places, or if something about the Dark itself caused souls to get stuck, but their voices just about swarmed her under the moment Mary snuffed out the lamp, howling and crying and carrying on like the rowdiest, angriest bunch of no-good drunks any decent barkeep had ever tossed out.

You could make them be quiet, you know.

Like hell was she wasting crystal on that. She'd convinced the Wet Whistle's apothecary to load her up before she left, but the Dark seemed to get longer every time she went through. Even if Rel'd had infinite crystal, she couldn't stay stacked for that many hours together, 'specially not just to make some lousy ghosts shut their yaps.

But it is the repeated use of crystal that makes you better at it, the gun argued. *If you'd just apply yourself more consistently, your reaction to crystal would level out. What's the point of having all that power at your fingertips if you're too afraid of the side effects to use it?*

Big words from a man who'd died with a loaded but unfired gun in his hands. Maybe the great Bernard Reiner should've spent his hours learning how to shoot instead of covering his weapon in gaudy rocks.

Perhaps if you'd been at home where you belonged, you could have disposed of the killer for me with those gun skills you're so proud of. But you weren't there, were you? You were off sulking like a child, kicking snow and feeling sorry for yourself while your mother and brother were—

"Shut *up!*" Rel snarled, letting go of Josie's shoulder to grab the jeweled pistol out of its holster and thwack it against the wall. "You got no right to talk about what I should've done when you were the one who—"

"Rel?"

Rel stopped midthwack, face heating. God damn the sneaky old bastard. She'd thought she was safe under the Dark's cover, but if Josie heard her yelling at her gun, she'd—

Know you're unstable? Her father chuckled. *Don't worry. She might be the help, but she's clever. I'm sure she's already noticed how dangerous and unhinged you've become since—*

A muffled scream drowned out the rest of his poison. Rel shoved the cursed gun back into its holster and whirled around, scanning the Dark even though she damn well knew that hadn't been a ghost. That yelp had come from Josie, who was no longer ahead of her when Rel reached out a groping hand. Mary cried out next, shouting in surprise as the black tunnel they'd been shuffling down came alive with the stomp of boots and the unmistakable click of a gun being cocked.

"Stop your squealin'!" shouted a man—a *living* man—from somewhere on Rel's left. "This here's a robbery! Drop your packs or the loud one gets a bullet in the head!"

"I think it's a girl, Abbot!" another, much more excited voice said on the heels of the first. "Feels like a girl!"

This observation was followed by an indignant squawk from Josie, which was where Rel's patience ended. Mary's, too, apparently, because the next shout came from her.

"There's three on your left, Tyrel!" she cried. "They're clumped up together in the side tunnel with the water flowing down it!"

How the hell did she know that? It was black as pitch in here, but that was about to change as Rel grabbed the flask from her coat pocket. Giving it a quick shake to dislodge the powder that tended to settle at the bottom, Rel popped the stopper and tipped the spout against her lips, dumping a huge swallow of the burning contents straight down her throat.

The shot hit like its namesake. First came the burn of the whiskey, then the crystal dust hit the back of her mouth like a blast of blown-out glass. The shards ripped down her throat, filling her head with noise and her veins with fire. Concussive sound pounded her ears like she was standing in a belfry with all the bells swinging full tilt. Then, quick as it had come on, the chaos ebbed, leaving Rel staring at a whole new world.

She was still in the Dark. The ground and the walls and the tunnels ahead were all still lost in blackness, but the souls wandering through them were now bright as candles. They were *thick* too. Rel had never been dumb enough to take crystal in the Dark before, but it looked just as messed up as she'd imagined: a great mass of ghosts scrabbling over one another like grubs under a rotten log.

Some were little more than hazy clouds, their spirits so twisted by anger and grief that they'd flung themselves apart. Others looked as sharp as the images on photographic plates, their clear eyes staring blankly at Rel like they still hadn't realized they were dead. All of them were talking, mostly to themselves, but Rel hadn't needed crystal to hear that. She'd needed to *see*, because now that she had eyes on the glowing shapes that used to be men, she could also find the ones that still were.

Hands on her guns—her real ones, not her father's crystal monstrosity—Rel spun to the left where Mary had said the men were hiding. Sure enough, she could see them clearly now: three men and the struggling Josie, who was kicking up a storm. They looked muddier than the ghosts 'cause their souls were still inside their bodies, but a glimpse was all Rel needed as she snatched her favorite of her two six-shooters from its holster and fired, pegging the man who'd been attempting to tame Josie's flailing legs with a clean shot through the chest.

The dark waves of death had barely started rippling through his muddy soul when she turned to do the same to his friend, who was groping blindly up the tunnel after Mary. He got a bullet in the back. A coward's shot, but sportsmanship didn't count for beans down here, and the back was a nice big target.

Good thing, too, because a bunch of other ghosts were crowding her shot. If she'd been using the crystal gun, that would've been a problem, but these were normal bullets from a normal pistol, so the dead men didn't even notice. They just kept right on screaming and mumbling and clawing at their glowing faces, completely oblivious to the soon-to-be-dead man crashing through them. Rel finished him off with a shot to the head, leaving herself three bullets in the wheel to deal with the most difficult target: the big fella who was still holding on to Josie.

That one was different. From the way they'd been waving their hands around, the other two bandits had clearly been blind as any normal person in the Dark. The big one must've had some way of knowing what was going on, though, because he turned tail the moment his friends went down, cursing up a vile storm as he dragged Josie back down the side tunnel they'd jumped out of.

At least, that was what Rel assumed. Not being able to see anything but ghosts, she couldn't actually tell if there was a tunnel or not. It *looked* like there was nothing but blank space between her and the glowing man dragging Josie's bright, flailing shape away, but she knew he wouldn't be going that direction if he didn't have cover. If Rel ignored that and took the shot, there was a good chance the bullet would just ricochet off the wall she couldn't see right back into her or Mary. If she tried chasing after him, though, she could fall down a hole or trip over a rock she couldn't see the same as she would without crystal.

It was a damned-either-way situation, but Rel had to do something quick, 'cause the man was getting away with astonishing speed. He must've decided to settle for just Josie and her pack, because he'd dropped whatever weapon he'd been threatening her with and was now using both arms to drag the girl kicking and screaming back the way he'd come. If Rel didn't put a stop to it soon, she'd lose them in the churning swamp of ghosts that filled this place. She couldn't let that happen to Josie, so she holstered her regular pistol and wrapped her hand around the bone-inlaid grip of her father's crystal-covered one.

"Ready?"

Oh, now *you want my help?*

Rel didn't dignify that with an answer. She just pulled the jeweled gun from its holster and took aim down the gaudy, gem-studded barrel, lining up the sight at the end with the final bandit's glowing head but *not* with Josie's or any of the other ghosts flitting past. They might be dead and mad about it, but that didn't mean they deserved what Rel was about to dish out, so she took a deep breath and waited, finger lying still as a stone on the bone-inlaid trigger.

He's going to get away.

"Gimme a moment," Rel whispered, crystal-juiced eyes burning as she waited for a gap in the swirling spirits. Waited. Waited. *There.*

Her finger moved before her brain realized it was done. The thunder came next, the crystal booming through her and into the gun in her hands. Her father moved at the same time, taking the power she'd thrust at him and passing it into the crystal stones that decorated his pistol until they burned like metal in a blacksmith's forge—and not just for Rel. If not for the curtain of the Dark, anyone could've seen her pistol lighting up. But they were in the Dark, which meant no one but her saw the light concentrate itself into a needle, spitting off sparks like a firework as it left the barrel of Rel's gun.

The whole sequence happened in a fraction of an instant. Not as quick as a true gunshot but still fast enough for the glowing needle to thread the gap between the ghosts Rel had been waiting for. It didn't graze a single one as it shot through the stone wall that may or may not have been there and over Josie's bobbing head to land dead center between the eyes of the man who'd grabbed her. Looking down the barrel as she was, Rel was perfectly positioned to see the dart of light flit through the man's flesh to crash into the bright-glowing soul beneath, filling the Dark with a lightning flash as the kidnapper's immortal portion shattered into a million shining pieces.

The sight never failed to shake her. Reliance would've thought she'd grown used to killing by now, but killing wasn't dying. She'd talked to enough ghosts to know there were parts of a person that bullets couldn't touch, but her father's gun was different. She couldn't see her victim anymore without his soul to light him up, but Rel knew there wouldn't be a mark on his flesh to show the injury she'd done him. His lungs would still be breathing, his heart still thumping beneath his ribs, but the light inside of him—the weightless presence that made a person a person—was gone. Blown to bits and scattered to winds none but the dead could feel.

Don't be melodramatic. He was a criminal. It was no more than he deserved.

Rel didn't know about that. She didn't know if *any* crime deserved the punishment she'd just delivered. The people she shot with the crystal gun didn't just die. They got obliterated, robbed of their chance to move on to wherever it was the dead went after.

Nonsense, her father said. *You just spared him from an eternity of being stuck down here. That's a much kinder fate than you meted out for his companions. Just look at those poor souls.*

He nudged her attention to the two men she'd killed with her normal pistol, both of whom were bright new ghosts standing over their bodies with dumbstruck looks on their glowing faces.

See? he said, his superior voice ringing with the richness it always got after Rel used his gun. *You tried to be kind by killing them in the usual way, and now they're stuck like that forever. My gun is so much cleaner, and the corpse is left perfectly intact for later use! A truly superior weapon by all accounts. I don't understand why you don't use it more often.*

Because she hated it, and it hated her. Now that the fight was over and the crystal gun was back to its usual non-lit-up self, the aftershocks were hitting Rel hard. Shooting her father's gun always left her broken and shaking like she'd shot out a part of her own soul. It was an empty, miserable feeling that made her want to curl into a ball and hide. Even if she hadn't been horrified by what it did, Rel couldn't have used the pistol

141

as her main weapon if only because she couldn't fire the damn thing more than twice in a row without collapsing into a pile.

That's only because your mind is still weak and untrained, her father scolded. *If you'd just follow my advice and practice—*

"Rather drink glass, thanks," Rel said, shoving him back in his holster.

The pistol fought her hand the whole way. *There you go again! Refusing to listen to anything that doesn't fit your narrow worldview. You just plug your ears and close your eyes, leaving everyone else to deal with the realities you're too cowardly to face. It's the same thing you did last Christmas when you didn't want to hear the truth I was telling you. Did you know your mother waited up for you the night you ran off? That's why she was standing in the doorway when the killer—*

"Shut up!"

Resonant and powerful with crystal, the command exploded out of her. It vibrated through the jewels and bones of the crystal gun, shocking him to silence like a boot stomped down on his neck. A boot Rel had no compunctions about grinding down even as the crystal she'd taken began slicing in her veins from the filthy effort of acting like him.

"Go to sleep," she ordered, slamming the words down like cudgel blows. "Don't listen, don't look, don't speak. I don't want to hear another word from your useless mouth until I ask for it."

The bone gun fell still in its holster, too crushed even to complain. When Rel was certain he was going to stay that way, she took a moment to enjoy the rare treat of being alone in her head. Then she put her hands on the wet, possibly bloody wall beside her and started feeling her way over to the tunnel where Josie was still thrashing in panic above the dead man's breathing corpse.

"Hang on," Rel called. "We're coming."

"I'm *so* sorry about that," Mary said, hurrying past Rel toward Josie like the Dark weren't dark at all to her. "Stickups usually only happen on the way *out* of the caves. I never dreamed anyone'd be desperate enough to hit a group coming in when they still had all their bullets and wits, so I wasn't listening as sharp as I should've."

Rel cocked an eyebrow. She hadn't realized their guide's crystal listening extended to the Dark, though that would explain how she'd known what was going on. She was about to ask Mary just how much she could hear when Josie did the least Josie thing Rel could imagine.

She began to cry.

"I'm so sorry!" she sobbed, her bright glowing soul fluttering like a paper in a tornado as Mary found her. "He grabbed me, but I couldn't do anything! I couldn't—"

"It's all right, it's all right," Mary said quickly, kneeling to help the larger girl back to her feet. "They're gone. Tyrel shot 'em dead. Or something."

She kicked the still-breathing corpse of the obliterated man away as she said this, and Rel's whole body clenched. She didn't know if Mary hadn't realized yet that the man wasn't dead in the normal sense or if the Injun's crystal-tuned ears had picked up the special shot, but she could feel Mary keeping away both from the soul-dead man and from Rel as she tucked herself under Josie's arm and hobbled them away back toward the Dark's entrance.

The ghosts had certainly noticed. Rel's crystal-granted vision was already slipping, but that didn't keep her from seeing the clots of ghosts shuffling away from the man whose soul Rel had exploded. The tunnel wall—for there *had* been stone between her and the man after all—was perfectly fine, but the ghosts flitting through it were as close to panic as those with nothing to lose could get, fleeing away from Rel through the Dark as fast as their glowing legs could move.

"Good riddance," she whispered, following Mary and Josie as they stumbled the scant ten feet back to the Dark's beginning.

"There," Mary said, letting Josie go to light her lantern the moment they were free of unnatural shadows. "You two stay here and catch your breath. I'm going back for the bodies."

Rel couldn't've heard her right. "Why the *hell* would you do that?"

"'Cause it'll be a problem if I don't," Mary snapped, her voice angrier than Rel had ever heard it. "Corpses can be as dangerous as living men if you let them lie. Not only do they rot and poison the water we all need to survive down here, leaving folks what died in violence without proper burial is how you get more ghosts."

Rel hadn't realized Mary could see the ghosts too. Or maybe she couldn't and was just being superstitious. Either way, her suggestion sounded like an enormous waste of time.

"So what if they turn into ghosts?" she snapped. "That's what they get for trying to rob us, and it ain't like anyone down here's going to notice three more lost souls."

"*I'll* notice," Mary said, glaring at Rel like this was all her fault. "You only have to get through the Dark twice a trip, but me and the other guides are in there all the time. It's bad enough as is, and I ain't making it worse to suit your sense of vengeance." She turned back toward the wavering curtain of the Dark. "Miss Josie needs time to recover, anyway. You sit with her, and I'll deal with this. Shouldn't take me but a moment."

A wasted moment was still a waste, but the half-breed had a point about Josie. The little chatterbox hadn't said a word this whole conversation, which showed how bad a state she was in. A few minutes resting in the lamplight would probably do her good, but Rel didn't like the idea of Mary discovering one of the dead men didn't actually feel dead. Not that there'd be any comforting his soul now, but the idea of having to explain to Mary what she'd done was enough to send Rel lurching back to her feet.

"I'll help."

Mary glanced back skeptically. "Why?"

"'Cause it'll be quicker with two," Rel said. "Quicker and safer. If we lose our guide to the Dark, what was the point of coming in here?"

"I won't get lost," Mary said, looking insulted. Then she gave Rel a little smile. "But I would welcome some help. Men get surprisingly heavy when they kick over."

Rel was all too aware of just how ungainly dead bodies could be, but when Mary put out her hand to guide Rel back into the blackness, she batted it away.

"I'm good on my own," she said stubbornly, marching back into the Dark. "Let's just do this quick. The Dark is long, and I don't want to get stuck making camp in the middle."

That was true enough, but Rel was mostly scurrying because her crystal shot was almost out. She could've taken another little sip to keep her ghost vision going, but she didn't have time for the bellyache that would cause, so she muddled through using her hands, feeling her way past the faint shapes of the still-fleeing spirits to the empty corpse of the big man who'd grabbed Josie.

Sure enough, the bastard was still breathing when Rel reached him. "Sorry about this," she whispered, pulling out her normal six-shooter to plug him in the chest for real. Mary's ears must've been something else, 'cause Rel saw the glowing shape of her living body jerk through the tunnel wall at the gunshot even with the Dark's muting.

Luckily, she didn't come over to investigate, leaving Rel time to grab the now fully dead man and drag him out of the Dark. She did the same for the other two, helping Mary line them up hats to boots along the lantern-lit wall just in time before the last of her crystal vision fizzled.

Now that they were back out in the light, the three dead robbers made for a sorry sight. All of them were bone thin and covered in sores from their filthy clothes. They stank too. An awful, sour stench that had nothing to do with death. They had nothing in their pockets, not even food, so either they were new to robbing or not very good at it. Mary had found the gun their leader had dropped when he'd tried to run, but it was a rusty piece of shit that wasn't even worth stripping for parts. In the end, the only thing of actual value on them was a walnut-sized hunk of crystal stuck into the leader's skull where his right eyeball should've been.

"Why do you think that's in there?" Mary asked, frowning.

"Probably to let him see," Rel said, poking at rough stone. "Crystal doesn't have to be tuned and cut to do things. Sometimes just sticking it into the gap left by something else is enough to get it to take over. I knew a miner who had a crystal finger once. Didn't bend for shit, but he swore he could feel it touching things just like real ones still on his hand."

"Huh," the guide said, frowning. "I was wondering how he got around the Dark so well. Guess the crystal gave him a good look at us, which is why he jumped."

"Not that good if he missed me, probably because this thing's a crude hunk of junk," Rel said, popping out the crystal eye. "Look how rough-cut it is. I bet he couldn't see nothing but—"

"Put it back!" Mary cried, snatching the crystal out of Rel's hand and shoving it back into the dead man's socket.

"What'd you do that for?" Rel snapped. "That crystal's probably worth a hundred bucks, and it ain't like he's got any use for it now."

"That don't mean we can steal it," Mary whispered, closing the dead man's eyes over the lump of rock. "You're a visitor here, so you don't know, but there's rules you gotta follow if you want to survive in the caves, and one of them is don't spite the dead. There's a lot more of them down here than us, and they got less to do with their time. I know you wouldn't want someone stealing your fancy guns off your corpse, so don't do it to them. Let them have their peace."

Rel rolled her eyes at that. She supposed she should've expected a sermon from someone raised by nuns, but it was surprising to see "do unto others" translated to the caves. Still, she supposed if anyone knew whereof she spoke down here, it was Dark-seeing Mary Good Crow.

"Do as you like," she said, turning away. "I'm going to check on Josie."

"Thank you," Mary said, but Rel was already walking down the tunnel toward Josie, who'd been watching them arrange the corpses with a tense look on her pale face. She hadn't made it halfway over before Josie shot up and ran behind the nearest rock, emptying her stomach with a retch. Shaking her head in sympathy, Rel sat down beside the lantern to wait for her to finish, closing her eyes to help her own crystal-abused stomach settle.

It took Josie a long time to come back. When she did, it was with an old lady's hobble, lowering herself to the stone beside Rel like an anchor sinking to the bottom of the sea.

"I'm sorry," she whispered after a long silence.

"'S all right," Rel answered just as quietly. "That was nasty business. Only natural to take it hard your first time."

"I still should have been more prepared," Josie said, clenching her gloved hands. "You warned me it'd be rough down here. I just didn't expect it to happen so soon, and with the Dark, I..." She trailed off with a disgusted sigh. "I'm sorry. I won't be so weak next time."

For some reason, that made Rel mad. "It ain't weakness to be upset over upsetting shit," she snapped. "I'd be upchucking, too, if I'd gotten dragged off into the Dark."

"But you didn't," Josie argued. "You and Miss Good Crow were so professional. You stayed strong and did what was necessary while I went to pieces."

"That says more about us than you," Rel said, giving her old friend a smile. "It's all right to be messed up, Josie. This place will toughen you to leather soon enough. I say enjoy the feelings while you got 'em."

"I assure you, I did not find any of this enjoyable," Josie said, dabbing a damp handkerchief to her lips, which had long since lost the color she liked to paint on them. "But I am relieved it's over. I'm still not sure how you shot those men without being able to see, but your quick action saved us, so thank you. Thank you very much."

Rel shook her head. "Just doing my job."

"I can still thank you for doing it well," Josie said with her usual insistence, which was annoying but at least showed she was getting back to normal. Maybe that meant they could get back on the trail soon, because now that the wooziness and nausea from the crystal were fading to the usual dull throb in her guts, Rel was itchy to get moving.

Josie must have felt the same, because the very next thing she said was "When can we continue?"

"Whenever our guide gets done," Rel said, nodding at Mary, who was on her knees in front of the corpses with her head down.

"What's she doing?"

Rel didn't feel up to repeating the ridiculous conversation, so she summarized. "Cave stuff."

"It sounds like Last Rites," Josie said, cupping a hand to her ear. "Didn't she say she wanted to bury them?"

"Something like that."

"But how is she going to do that down here?" Josie pressed. "I mean, the walls are solid stone."

That was a damn good question Rel didn't care enough to dwell on. She just wanted this to be over. Fortunately, Mary seemed to be wrapping up whatever mumbo jumbo she was doing, brushing the dirt off her already filthy poncho as she rolled back to her feet.

"That's done proper," she said, turning around to face the living people. "Thanks for waiting. Now if you could just help me get these fellows into their final resting place, we can move on with our business."

"Of course," Josie said, grabbing the wall to steady herself as she rose. "But how are we going to do that, exactly? Perhaps I am ignorant, but I didn't think it was possible to dig a grave in a rock face."

"Anything's possible with enough trying," Mary said. "But that won't be necessary. Now that their souls have gone to their rest and are no longer in danger of becoming angry spirits, we got a lot more leeway with the bodies they left behind."

148

Without taking another crystal shot to get her ghost eyes back, Rel couldn't say if that was true or not. One man for certain wasn't coming back, but she was curious if Mary's makeshift funeral had actually worked on the other two. A crystal shot would've shown her for sure, but Rel wasn't going through that again. She didn't hear any ghostly mumbling coming from the corpses, though, so maybe the girl really had found a way to free them from the sticky tar of the Dark.

"All right," she said, relieved despite herself. "Where're we stashing them?"

Mary smiled. "That's the easy part. All we gotta do is shuffle 'em back into the Dark."

Josie recoiled at the notion, but Rel was more fed up than anything. "We just hauled them out of there!" she cried. "What about all that stuff you said about polluting the water and such?"

"That's only if we left them on the ground," Mary explained. "If we stuff 'em up high and dry, shouldn't be no problem. And the Dark's power will mute the smell, so that's not an issue either."

"You seem quite familiar with the practice," Josie observed nervously. "Just how many bodies have you 'shuffled' into the Dark?"

"Me personally? Not many," Mary answered, grabbing hold of the nearest dead man's boots. "But it's the common way down here. People die in the caves all the time, but no one wants to dig a grave in stone or haul a body all the way back to town. Leaving corpses in the corridors normally causes more problems than it solves, but ain't no one can see or smell a dead man in the Dark, so that's what folks here use."

"Probably why there're so many ghosts inside," Rel muttered.

"They sling their night soil in there too," Mary went on without hearing. "The polite ones do, anyway. That's why I always tell people never to drink water collected from the Dark and to keep their hands on the wall beside them. You reach too far up or down in there, you're gonna touch something you don't want."

Josie looked like she was going to be sick all over again by the time Mary finished, but Rel was grateful for the guide's frankness. It was good for Josie to hear all this upfront before they got in too deep. Rel was still on course for finding Samuel's treasure and using it as a lever to force the Wet Whistle into coughing up the murderer's name, but if a blunt discussion of corpses and caca was what made Josie realize mining life wasn't for her and maybe she should sell after all, that worked too.

Rel was really hoping it'd be the latter since that was the option that didn't involve having to walk back into the Dark, but Josie must've been made of sterner stuff than she'd credited, because the girl pushed ahead. She even helped Mary hoist the dead up onto the high shelf of rock Rel had never realized ran along the top of the Dark's walls. She was pretty sure she heard her friend retch a few times through the Dark's strange muting, but Josie didn't speak another word of complaint. She just did that stiff upper lip thing she'd always resorted to whenever the real Miss Josephine tasked her to do something especially hideous and kept at it, completing the grisly task with a servant's efficiency so they could continue at last, moving forward deeper into the caves.

Chapter 10

Mary had never been so furious with herself in all her life. Here she was, on the highest-paying job she'd ever heard of, with an actual decent customer who was letting her carry the prettiest piece of crystal ever plucked, and she'd led them straight into an ambush not two miles from the front door. How could she even call herself a guide after a screwup like that?

Her only defense was that it had been highly unusual. Lying in wait for tired, crystal-addled miners stumbling back to town was a horrible way to make a living, but at least it made sense. Before today, Mary would've said no one was foolhardy enough to try jumping fresh folks with no crystal and all their wits about them. But all three robbers had looked pretty thin and broke, either of which could drive men to desperate acts.

She'd just have to be more careful in the future. Right now, all Mary could say was thank goodness Tyrel Reiner had lived up to the Wet Whistle's deadly reputation. Her usual recourse for such situations was to run, but that would've left Miss Josephine hanging, and it might not've even worked thanks to the crystal eyeball the big one had shoved in his face. If Rel hadn't been so quick with the pistols, they'd all be ghosts moaning in the Dark.

It was enough to shake even the most stoic of cave guides. Fortunately, their second attempt at the Dark was the most uneventful Mary had had in months. In fairness, this was mostly thanks to Rel and his crystal gun. Mary didn't know what manner of monster lived in that thing, but she was now certain it was the source of the gunman's sour-crystal sound. The ghosts certainly seemed wise to it, 'cause they'd kept their distance after that first scuffle, leaving the Dark's tangled tunnels quieter than Mary had ever heard.

It was almost enough to make her like the ugly thing. But Mary hadn't survived this long by involving herself with trouble, and it didn't take an ear for crystal to know Tyrel was haunted by something much worse than your standard Dark ghoulie. She couldn't fathom how a proper lady like Josephine Price had gotten mixed up with someone so dangerous, but Mary also hadn't survived by asking nosy questions. She was just a cave guide doing what cave guides did, shepherding her flock safe through the Dark to the still dangerous, though much less haunted, tunnels beyond.

They exited the unnatural darkness just in time for supper. That was a lot longer than it should've taken even with their false start, but it was common knowledge that the Dark was getting bigger, so at least Mary could claim with a straight face that it wasn't her fault. On the upside, they dumped out right next to one of her favorite places to make camp—a big natural cavern with a seep of fresh water and clean air coming down from a crack in the ceiling—so Mary went ahead and called a halt.

For all their rushing, this turned out to be the right move. She and Rel could've managed another few miles, but poor Miss Josie dropped the moment they stopped moving, yanking off her pretty boots to rub her swollen feet. She kept at this for a good twenty minutes while Rel and Mary set the camp and laid out supper. By the time Mary came over with her food, Miss Josie had moved on to writing, scribbling all over a stack of papers by the light of Mary's lantern. It looked real important, but Mary had already sworn off nosy questions, and she had other worries besides, such as the group of miners who arrived at the campsite right after from the other direction.

She'd been expecting something of the sort. This cavern was everyone's favorite spot to stop coming or going. It was plenty big, though, so Mary didn't mind sharing, 'specially since the men looked too scared of Tyrel to come near.

During her watch later that evening, Mary got one of them to tell her their business. Apparently, they were miners working a decent claim halfway up the Main Gallery, but they'd covered their crystal and were closing up shop. Caves were getting too dangerous, he said. Too many gun-happy idiots who didn't respect the rules. Add in the Whitmans and scalpin' Sioux—no offense to present company—and they'd decided it was time to cash out and head to safer pastures.

It was hard not to take offense at the scalping comment, but there was no point getting mad. She just kept smiling and nodding until the miner moved on to more important matters, such as how the path ahead looked.

Clear seemed to be the answer. As she explained to Miss Josie when they set back out the next morning, they were entering what were known as the "Midway Tunnels." They used to be called the "Back Tunnels" when folks thought the area beyond the Dark was as far as the caves went. That had changed after the discovery of the Deep Caves, though, so a new name had to be invented.

Whatever folks called it, this next section was Mary's bread and butter. The Front Caves had already been mined out by the time she'd started guiding professionally. Before that point, no one had been willing to brave the Dark more than a mile. But greed inspired courage, and it wasn't long before people figured out how to push through the blackness into the treasure trove beyond.

And what a trove it had been! Compared to the blasted-out warren at the entrance or the insanity that was the Deep Caves, the Midway Tunnels were a paradise: a long, tall, underground canyon with a creek of fresh water running down its middle. From this central chasm, hundreds of other tunnels branched off like ribs, allowing prospectors to fan out in all directions without getting lost or stepping on each other's toes. Some folks grumbled that the Midway Tunnels hadn't produced any monster finds like the glittering caverns that had kicked off the crystal rush, but the walls had enough crystal in 'em to keep most miners happy, and when those modest strikes ran out, they paid guides like Mary to find them more.

The arrangement had been good for everyone for over a year now. But with so many new hopefuls pouring into Medicine Rocks every day, even the sprawling branches of the Midway were starting to get picked over. Groups like the one that had stiffed her just before she'd met Miss Josie were becoming more and more common as miners got greedier and crystal got harder to find. Just like the Dark before, the hunger for crystal had driven men into the once "too dangerous" Deep Caves in search of new veins. But those tunnels were a whole different animal than the ones before, and so far, more miners had found death than riches.

"So the Midway Tunnels are safer, then?" Miss Josie asked when Mary explained all this during their walk to the start of the Main Gallery. "I know most of Price Mining's claims are in that section, but I didn't realize it was so choice."

"I wouldn't call it 'safe,'" Mary cautioned. "They might not be as bald-faced terrifying as the Dark or the Deep Caves, but the Midway's still got plenty of dangers. There's cave-ins, loose rocks, gas pockets, not to mention jumpy prospectors with hair-trigger fingers and no trust for their fellow man. And there's the Holes. Can't forget about the Holes."

The lady blinked. "You mean gaps in the trail that you can fall into?"

"More like they *make* you fall," Mary said, poking the stone trail with her boot. "The ground'll look plenty solid, but then a Hole will open like a mouth under your foot just as you're putting it down. They're not normally wide enough to actually swallow you, but they'll take a leg for sure if you ain't quick 'bout jumping."

Miss Josie looked pale at that, but Rel just snorted. "The Holes ain't nothing if you pay attention and watch your feet. I'd take them any day over the real worst horror of the Midway."

"Which is?" Miss Josie asked nervously.

Rel nodded ahead at the wall of shuffling figures Mary could already see ahead of them. "The traffic."

He certainly had a point. It was only natural that so many people swarming down a single narrow canyon would cause backups, but they'd hardly started up the slope leading to the Main Gallery's soaring cavern when they got caught in the glut of people. There were as many miners fighting to get out as in, but naturally, no one was forming lines or moving in an orderly fashion. They just crammed themselves in between the cliffs tight as toothpicks, squishing up against the Main Gallery's wet walls until no one could make headway.

"This is ridiculous," said Miss Josie, peering over Mary's head at the jam. "I saw the overflow tents when I arrived, but I never dreamed the mines would be mobbed as well."

"That's why it's called a 'rush,'" Tyrel replied, shoving his way to the front since Mary's polite 'excuse mes' weren't getting them anywhere. "Just be grateful the ceiling's high or you'd really know what it feels like to be a canned sardine."

He gestured up at the top of the underground canyon, which soared higher than three barns over their heads, but even that was crawling with people. Intrepid miners had put bolts in the stone roof, rigging pulleys to haul themselves up the canyon's sides to get at the little bits of crystal that still glittered at the top of the steep walls. The *tink tink tink* of their hammers and chisels dropped a constant rain of dust and tiny stones on the crowd below, kicking up no small amount of annoyance and even a few drawn pistols.

"They certainly are everywhere," Miss Josie observed, shielding her eyes against the pebble rain. "Where did they all come from?"

"All over, but Deadwood sends the most," Rel replied before Mary could get a word in. "The moment the price of crystal topped gold ounce for ounce, all the greedy idiots who'd been making fools of themselves in the Black Hills stampeded over here to plague us instead."

That last comment was just loud enough and rude enough to get the attention of the biggest glut of miners blocking their way. One of the men even pulled his gun, though he put it right back again when he saw Tyrel's black uniform. Now that Reiner had called attention to himself, a lot of miners noticed, and the crowd in front of them suddenly became much more interested in the walls than the path, moving out the way to let Mary's group slip past.

155

"I'm amazed there's anything left to mine," Miss Josie said, arching her neck to peer down all the side tunnels, many of which were just as crowded as the Main Gallery. "Is the whole Midway packed in like this?"

"Things thin out a lot as you go farther down the offshoots," Mary answered. "But the Main Gallery's always crowded. Unlike the branch tunnels, which like to wiggle, the big canyon rarely moves and always has water. It's the lifeline of this whole area. Folks stick as close to it as they're able—not just for water but also 'cause having so many other miners near means there's usually someone to hear you if you need help."

"I'd say that makes it less safe," Rel said darkly. "Sure, you've got hands close by if something caves in, but with this many crystal-mad fools packed together, it's only a matter of time before some trigger-happy idiot points his gun at an equally trigger-happy idiot and kicks off a riot."

That had already happened, actually. Not while Mary was here, thank goodness, but there'd been three major shoot-outs on the Main Gallery Trail that she'd heard of and probably a lot more she hadn't. Heck, search any wall on this stretch and you were more likely to find bullets than crystal. The branch tunnels weren't nearly so bad, but there were no branches that would take them to the Deep Caves where the glowing crystal's pull was pointing. The only way to get there was to follow the creek, so Mary pressed them on, letting Tyrel take the lead since he was a lot better at getting folks to move out of the way.

This situation lasted for a day and a half. Even with Rel threatening murder at everyone who got in their way, there were just too many folks to move quick, and the Holes were being awful. One almost got Miss Josie's leg to the knee before Tyrel and Mary yanked her out. They also passed a spot of the Slip: a patch of still air that caused things to slip your mind if you breathed it in. It started as little fits of forgetfulness, but it could quickly grow to big things like your family and history, even your name if you didn't get out quick enough.

Fortunately, this was just a small section they could cross by holding their breath, but Mary had met miners who'd been too busy getting crystal to notice the bad air creeping up on them and Slipped hard. It wasn't an end she'd wish on anyone, though it was still preferable to Cave Ash, the black dust that settled on you sometimes if you stayed in one place for too long. Cave Ash wasn't harmful so long as it stayed on your clothes, but get it on bare skin, and it started eating through you like acid. The only way to get it off was by wiping it on someone else or scraping it off with a bit of crystal. A very expensive solution, since it ate the crystal too.

Mary had a chunk missing out of her right arm from the nasty stuff, which was how she'd learned never to take her coat off while she was sleeping no matter how much she sweated. She carried a tarp for the same reason, which she rigged over them when Miss Josie couldn't walk no more, and they were forced to make camp hours before she'd planned. Unlike Tyrel, Mary didn't grouse at the delay. She was having a lovely time, because for all that they seemed to be determined to show her their worst face on this trip, Miss Josie couldn't seem to get enough of the caves.

Having an interested party was a new experience for Mary. Most clients just wanted her to shut up and guide, and those who did want to talk usually only did so trying to prove they knew more about the caves than she did, which made no kinda sense. Why would you waste money on a guide if you already knew everything? And if you knew you *didn't* know, why would you fake like you did to the one person who knew enough to call you out?

Hooey like that was why Mary avoided talky clients as a rule, but Miss Josie was different. She kept Mary up until late asking question after question. Not as a setup for her own pontifications but because she actually wanted to know. Even more amazing, she actually listened to Mary's answers, going so far as to write them down in her notebook like it was real knowledge.

Mary'd never had anyone write down what she said before. She couldn't read what Miss Josie was scribbling in her notebook, but just knowing it was there made her feel ten feet tall. It was so invigorating to be treated like someone who knew what she was talking about for once—and so politely, too! Mary had been "Miss Good Crow"-ed more in the past two days than all the other years of her life put together. It was enough to make a girl puff-headed, which was likely why the universe saw fit to throw a nasty surprise in their way.

Despite Miss Josie's tender feet, they'd actually been making decent time. Nothing near as fast as Mary could've done by herself, of course, but thanks to Tyrel scaring miners out of their way, they'd made enough distance by the third day for Mary to feel safe pushing past her usual stops and skipping right on ahead to the end of the Midway Tunnels. There was a big lake there that fed the creek and was usually pretty safe. Camping on its shore would also give them a fresh morning's start for the much more dangerous Deep Caves that came next.

Mary wasn't looking forward to that part. She'd been to the Deep Caves a mere handful of times, but the few trips she had made had been almost as difficult as getting through the Dark. At least it didn't look like they'd have to go in too deep. Now that they were nearing the end of the Main Gallery Trail, Mary had been checking the beautiful crescent-sharped crystal every chance she got. Its humming had gotten steadily louder over the last few miles, making her think that whatever it was pointing at couldn't be that far.

She'd never followed a crystal, of course, so she might be totally wrong. It *felt* right, though, and Mary'd always had good luck following her feelings. She was pressing the glowing shard into her body beneath her coat just for the pleasure of feeling it hum when a huge noise boomed down the cave ahead of them, followed by a blast of dust so strong it knocked Mary's hat clean off her head.

"What was that?" cried Miss Josie, clinging to a hole some long-gone miner had left in the wall. "An earthquake?"

"Sounded more like blasting," Rel replied, peering down the narrowing V of the underground canyon that marked the Midway's end.

"I hope no one's stupid enough to be blasting," Mary said worriedly, picking her hat up out of the creek and shaking off the water.

Now Miss Josie looked really worried. "Could it cause a collapse?"

"If there was gonna be a cave-in, we'd be buried already," Mary assured her. "But that ain't why folks stopped blasting down here. It's—"

A scream cut her off. Up the trail ahead of them, someone was hollering like a stuck pig. More voices joined a second later, their screams bouncing like bullets down the narrow canyon before cutting off quick as they'd begun. That couldn't be good, so Mary pushed ahead, squeezing around Rel to hurry down the narrow path beside the water.

"Why are you running *toward* the screaming?" the gunman yelled after her.

"'Cause they might need help!" Mary yelled back, hopping back and forth to avoid dunking her boots in the creek. "If I were hollering like that, I know I'd want someone to come running my direction! We can charge 'em for it later if it makes you feel better, but right now, we need to move while there's still something to move to."

She was worried they were already too late. The cut-off screams hadn't started back up again, and the path ahead was deathly quiet. There weren't many turn-offs left this close to the end of the Midway, but the few there were had all led to sizable strikes. That was probably what had tempted whoever it was to try dynamite here despite even the folks what sold the explosives saying it was a bad idea to use 'em. Particularly out here on the threshold of the Deep Caves, where the crystal was thick and the music roared loud as floodwater.

But plenty of things silenced men other than gruesome death, so Mary kept her hopes up, shuffling her feet quicker and quicker along the shrinking rock shelf beside the creek until the canyon grew narrow as a crack, marking the end of the Main Gallery. Beyond that point, the creek slipped under a wall of rocks while the trail went up and over. By the time Mary had scrambled all the way to the top, the trail had grown much wider, opening into a water-filled room bigger than all of Medicine Rocks.

Even after all the times she'd been here, the lake cavern at the Main Gallery's end never failed to make Mary gawk. Its roof went up so high that even her ears couldn't make out how far, and its bottom was filled with water so smooth and black that it looked like glass. The only disturbance was the quiet swirl right beneath the rocks Mary was standing on where the water drained out to begin the Main Gallery's creek. The rest of the lake was as still and quiet as the stone surrounding it, reflecting the light of Mary's lantern like a huge black mirror.

There was a bit of rocky shore around the lake's edge between the dark water and the cavern's dripping walls. This was where the trail continued if you wanted to walk around to the Deep Caves' entrance. How much room you had depended on the lake's level, but experienced miners, or those with guides, knew to stay as far from the black water as possible to avoid the eyeless things that lived beneath it. If not for the explosion, Mary would've chalked the yelling up to them. But there had been a blast, which meant what was waiting was probably worse than lake grabbers. And as usual, when Mary lifted her light, she saw that her gut had led her right.

"*Imbéciles*," she breathed, shining her lantern over the screamers, or what was left of them.

The lake was running high today, but there was still a good fifteen feet of rocky shore between the water and the wall. The carnage had splattered all the way up, staining the muck-coated stones with a different sort of wetness that gleamed dark and sticky in Mary's lamplight. They must have been a big group to leave so much mess, but while the blood was everywhere, Mary didn't see any bodies. Just the dark stain radiating out from an even darker shape sitting like a fallen boulder against the lake-cavern's blast-marked wall.

"Ah, *shit*," Rel whispered behind her.

Mary couldn't have put it better. There, not thirty feet down the rocky shore from them, was a great black bear. Not a normal grizzly, neither. Regular animals never came this far down into the caves, and no bear born in the wild had ever been so large, nor so strange.

The creature blocking their path was as big as a stagecoach, with black fur that rippled like water and eyes that gleamed white as a cave fish's. Despite that seeming blindness, it showed its yellow teeth when Tyrel reached for his pistol, forcing Mary to grab the gunman's surprisingly delicate wrist in her fear-tensed fingers.

"Don't."

"You got a better idea?" Rel growled, yanking out of her grip.

"It doesn't look as if it means to let us pass," Miss Josie added nervously, peering over Mary's head at the splatter with a mix of fascination and terror. "Did it... did the bear do that to those men?"

"No question," Mary said quietly, hooking her lantern onto her pack and raising her empty hands over her head to show the growling shadow that she meant no trouble. "'Cause that ain't a bear. That's Bear Woman, and she hates blasting more than anything."

As if she'd heard them talking 'bout her, the giant bear ceased her snarling and turned around to paw at something lying next to her rearmost haunch. As her giant paws rolled the thing over, Mary saw it was a wooden crate packed with dynamite. Bear Woman smacked the box into the lake next, scattering the red sticks and sawdust over the still water where they sank unnaturally quick, almost as if the lake itself was eager to hide the offending objects from her sight. When the explosives had vanished into the depths, the bear started nosing through what had been the miners, covering her already gory snout in even more wetness. What she was searching for Mary didn't know, but she saw her chance, creeping down the rock pile that covered the creek and onto the lake's rocky shore while motioning for the others to follow.

Rel grabbed her pigtail instead. "Are you out of your red-skinned head? The monster's sitting *right there*!"

"And she might well be doing so until next week," Mary hissed back, yanking her braid out of the gunman's fist. "Bear Woman moves on her own time, and her time runs long. Fortunately for us, we ain't the ones she's mad at. That bear's more dangerous than pretty much anything else down here. But if she ain't growling at you, you can get by, *if* you know what you're doing, and knowing is what you're paying me for, isn't it?"

Rel looked at Miss Josie, who lifted her eyebrows.

"I suppose it is," the gunman said gruffly. "All right then, Miss Expert. What do we do?"

"Exactly as I do," Mary said. "If we run, she'll give chase. If we fight, she'll kill us too. But if we go slow and don't offer challenge, we should be able to walk right past. Just keep your hands up, don't look her in the eyes, and we should be fine."

"Uh-huh," Rel said skeptically. "And if it attacks?"

"Then nothing's gonna save us," Mary replied with a shrug. "I told you back at the start: shooting Bear Woman just makes her mad. Our only chance now she's seen us is flattery."

"Flattery?" Miss Josie repeated skeptically. "How does one flatter a bear?"

Picking her way closer down the rocky shore, Mary showed her, approaching the bear with her face held as low as she could manage without tipping herself forward. She glanced back just once to make sure the others were following her lead, which, to their credit, they were. When she was certain they wouldn't start any trouble, Mary lifted her hands even higher and began to sing.

"Bear Woman," she sang in Lakota. "You protect the sacred places. Your anger is righteous, your claws like endings, but we want to walk on. Have pity on us, Great Bear Woman! Please let us walk on."

It wasn't a real song, just a mix of the music she'd heard in the Lakota camps back before things had gone so wrong. She wasn't even sure if Bear Woman understood human language, but she'd heard from an older guide way back at the beginning that Bear Woman had been a Lakota girl before she'd fallen down a hole full of crystal and lost her soul in its shining, becoming the monster in front of them. Mary didn't know if she believed that story or not, but this wasn't her first time in this situation, and singing had always worked before. 'Specially when she complimented the bear on her valor—and speaking of…

"Bear Woman!" Mary sang loudly, her voice echoing across the lake into something much bigger than itself. "The black paint is always on your face! Running faster than a horse, you win all battles! None can stand before you, Great Bear, but let us walk on. We are so much smaller and weaker, and we mean you no harm. Have mercy and let us walk on."

The song certainly wasn't the prettiest, but it got the job done. So long as Mary kept up the music, the bear kept listening, watching them go by with her bloody snout glistening wetly in the lamplight. They were well past the bloodstain she'd made out of the blasters now, but Bear Woman's white eyes were still on them, which meant Mary didn't dare turn away. She walked backwards instead, singing different versions of the same lyrics over and over with her hands and voice lifted high and her eyes cast low until they'd shuffled all the way 'round to the lake's far edge.

Mary was soaked in sweat at this point, her voice sung raw. When she peeked up to see if they'd made it far enough, though, what looked back across the water at her made the music stick in her throat. Far across the dark lake at the faintest edge of her lamplight, the white eyes were still gleaming, but the giant bear was no more. Its huge black body was gone, and standing in its place was a Lakota woman.

She was as tall as Miss Josie, wearing a fine deerskin dancing dress decorated with a yoke of blue beads similar to, but not the same as, others Mary had seen. These patterns looked much older, like a grandmother's passed-down clothes. The woman's face was as young as Mary's own, though, and still as bloody as the bear's had been. Her eyes, too, were cave-fish white, gleaming like crystal in the distant glow of the kerosene lamp as Mary pushed her group back farther still, retreating down the lakeside until the woman who had been a bear vanished completely into the darkness.

"Good work," Rel said when Mary finally collapsed panting on the rocky shore.

"What was that creature?" Miss Josie asked, breathing just as hard as Mary despite having done none of the singing.

"I bet she's an evil spirit released into the caves by the Sioux to kill us all," Rel said, also sounding a bit less cocky than usual. "You know, like a shaman's curse."

"Shamans don't curse people," Mary said, shaking her head. "And Bear Woman doesn't kill every miner. Just the ones who use dynamite."

"She must hate explosives a lot to do *that*," Miss Josie said with a shudder.

Mary was no longer sure "hate" was the right word. She didn't think the others had seen Bear Woman turn into a real woman 'cause they'd be shouting louder if they had. But while the experience had been bloody, the look on her face had been more sad than angry. It all fit the story about a Lakota girl losing herself to the crystal, but Bear Woman hadn't looked soulless to her. Quite the opposite. She'd looked full up with feelings, enough to make even the cave's music sound mournful.

What it all meant, Mary had no idea, but she made a point in her mind to try talking instead of singing the next time now that she knew "Bear Woman" was true to both parts of her name. For now, though, they'd made it past. That meant it was time for the last leg of their journey, which also happened to be the one Mary was looking forward to least.

"We'll rest the night here," she announced, wiggling out of her pack. "It's been a long day with a big finish, but this lake marks the end of the Midway Tunnels. Once we leave this cavern, we're in the Deep Caves."

"That's a relief," Miss Josie said, looking heartened, which was not the usual reaction to that announcement. "Are the Deep Caves far? I haven't seen any other tunnels."

"It's not under the water, is it?" Rel asked, looking askance at the dark, mirror-still lake.

"No, no, no," Mary said, waving her hands. "You don't touch the lake, *ever*. It's clean as any, but things like to collect under the surface, and you don't want to give them an excuse to come out."

Maybe that wasn't the best way she could've put it, because Josie and Rel both jumped back like the water was fixing to bite them. That was more spooked than she'd intended, but it was always a good idea to steer clear of the black water, so Mary let it lie.

"Contrary to the name, we don't get to the Deep Caves by going down," she said, pointing back at the cavern's wall for distraction as much as direction. "The way through is just beyond those rocks, but it ain't the sort of place you want to go into when you're tired."

"Why not?" Rel asked, sounding more curious than pushy for once.

Mary took a moment figuring how best to explain, but her mind was too thrashed from the Bear Woman incident to come up with something, which was exactly why she didn't want to go in yet. "It's tricky," she said for lack of anything better, opening her pack. "We'll make camp here and start fresh tomorrow. That should set us up pretty."

"Can't we go now?" Josie pressed, nervously fiddling with the silver pocket watch she'd fished out of her split-skirt trousers. "It's only quarter 'til eight. We've plenty of time yet to get another mile in, and whatever's waiting for us in the Deep Caves can't be worse than sleeping in a cavern with a murderous bear."

Mary shook her head. "If Bear Woman wanted to kill us, she'd have done so by now. The fact that we're still breathing proves we're safe here. Safer than anywhere, really, since no one else is gonna dare come in while Bear Woman's sitting at the entrance."

"I'm sure you're not wrong," Miss Josie said, clutching her watch. "It's just... I *can't* sleep here, Miss Good Crow. Not when I know what's on the other shore."

She finished with a pleading look, and Mary sighed. It wasn't that she didn't have sympathy, but she *really* didn't want to start the Deep Caves tonight. It was the sorta place that demanded all your senses be sharp, but if making camp now meant Miss Josie would be awake the whole night jumping at every sound, that wasn't no good neither. Mary didn't know which path would end worse. Both seemed equally terrible, so she decided to go with the choice that at least made the person in charge happy.

"Guess we're doing it now, then," she said, faking a smile to match Miss Josie's as she hauled her pack back onto her shoulders. "Follow me."

Miss Josie did as she asked too well, getting so close up behind Mary she was stepping on her boots. Rel kept near as well, eyeing the lake like something was gonna jump out at them at any moment which, to be fair, it might. But while this ridiculous arrangement wasn't close to the way Mary preferred to do things, it did keep them all together as they climbed up the rocky slope to the actual end of the Main Gallery Trail, which led straight into the wall in front of them.

"Um, Miss Good Crow," Josie said, wringing her hands. "Where is the entrance?"

"All I see is rock," Rel agreed, looking up the curving cavern wall of grayish stone as it rose into the dark. "Did the Deep Caves move on us?"

"No, we're here," Mary said, crouching down to stick her fingers into the crack where the stone cliff met the rocky floor. "This gap's the way through. You wiggle in here and crawl under the wall. There's only a foot of clearance, so it's a squeeze, but if you can tolerate the tightness for twenty feet or so, you'll come out in the Deep Caves on the other side."

She'd thought that explanation was clear enough, but Rel was staring at her cockeyed like Mary was the one toting three guns. "You want us to squeeze through there? Are you shitting me?"

"It does look *very* tight," Miss Josie said nervously, crouching down to stick her hand into the admittedly narrow gap. "Are you sure we can fit? Not all of us are as small as you."

"I've seen bigger folks than you get through safe," Mary assured her. "Even if they do get stuck, a day is usually all it takes to thin a body up enough to wiggle free, so it ain't like you'd be trapped for long."

That was supposed to make them feel better, but Miss Josie looked like death warmed over, and Rel stomped off entirely, cussing up a storm under his breath and whacking that crystal gun of his like he was trying to pummel the poor thing into submission. Gave Mary the crawlies to watch, which was alarming, since this was the first time they'd bothered her this whole trip.

"Is he gonna be all right?" she whispered to Miss Josie.

"Rel's never liked cramped spaces," the lady explained.

Sounded like a problem for someone on a cave trip, but Mary wasn't about to push. "Should we stop for the night after all, then?" she asked hopefully. "See if he feels different tomorrow?"

"No," Miss Josie said, keeping her back firmly to the dark lake and Bear Woman sitting across it. "Let's just get this over with. What do I have to do not to get stuck?"

"First step's making yourself small," Mary said, stripping off her poncho. "You'll want to take off as much as you can, particularly anything with loops or straps that might get caught. I like to take off my shoes as well. Ain't necessary, but I think it's easier to push when you can grab with your foot fingers as well as your hand fingers."

She removed her boots, picking up a rock with her dark-skinned toes to show Miss Josie what she meant.

"We'll need to empty our packs some as well," she went on, turning her backpack around to show the lady how big it was. "If I tried to go through wearing this, I'd get stuck for sure. Can't push the pack ahead of me, neither, on account of how rough the stone gets once you're in. I've hit this problem several trips now, and the best way I've found to get through is to empty everything out, wrap it all up in a tarp so it lies in a big flat rectangle, and then drag the rectangle behind us with a rope. That seems to get everything through with the least amount of disaster, but someone's gotta tie the rope 'round their waist and be the mule. I've done it before, so I don't mind pulling, but I ain't that strong, and we got a lot of stuff. It'll probably take me two trips to get it all."

167

"You shouldn't have to do everything," Miss Josie said, removing her own backpack. "We've got more than one rope and tarp, and Rel and I don't mind pulling our weight. It'll go faster if we all pitch in, and I'd rather pull everything myself than wait another moment in this place."

She must've been really spooked over Bear Woman, 'cause Mary had never had a mine leader offer to help haul baggage before. Miss Josie got right to it, though, digging into her perfectly organized satchel as if she'd been unpacking bags for dragging all her life. They'd gotten pretty much all their gear spread out over two tarps by the time Rel stopped cussing and came back over.

"Sorry 'bout that," the gunman said. A little sheepishly, Mary thought. "I'm ready."

"Let's get your pack flattened, then," Mary said cheerfully, happy the trouble had ended. "You can add your things to one of our sleds or make your own. Once all the gear is ready, I'll go through first to—"

"*I'll* go first," Rel said.

Mary and Miss Josie shared a look.

"Are you sure, Rel?" Miss Josie said timidly. "You seemed very upset about the idea earlier."

"Only 'cause I didn't know it was coming," the gunman replied. "I don't think there's anyone anywhere who'd be happy discovering they were going to have to crawl twenty feet through a crack no wider than their forearm. But if that's the only way"—Rel paused until Mary nodded— "then I'll do what I gotta, and since I'm the only one with a gun, that means going first."

"Why?" Josie pressed. "We're crawling into a cave, not a shoot-out."

"You don't know that," Rel said stubbornly. "Am I the only one who remembers the cornbread woman telling Mary there are Whitmans in the Deep Caves? Bandits normally only bother people with crystal, but we all saw how well that assumption played out in the Dark. We'd be stupid to risk the same mistake twice, so I'll go first and make sure it's safe."

"But what if you get shot?" Miss Josie asked.

"Then I'll shoot back," Rel snapped. "Better me than Mary. If our guide eats a bullet at this point, we're *all* dead. Now stand back and let me get this over with 'fore I lose my nerve."

Miss Josie opened her mouth to say something else, but she was cut off by Rel's duster landing over her head. His vest and black boots followed, leaving the dark-haired gunman looking small as a girl. In the end, the only things Rel kept on were his black jeans, too-big black shirt, and the guns on his belt. Tossing his hat to Miss Josie, he got down on his belly and vanished into the crack, wiggling like a snake and cursing like a sailor as he pushed into the darkness beyond.

"Well," Josie said, adding the gunman's clothes to the pile on her tarp. "I guess I'd better get to work on Mr. Reiner's pack."

Mary nodded, crouching down to make sure Rel was belly-crawling in the right direction, 'cause the crack wasn't the same height all the way through. The best path went right several feet out of the way before swinging back to center, but this information was not well received when she tried to shout it, so Mary left the cursing gunman to find his own way through and went to help Miss Josie instead. The lady was much more pleasant, and by the time Rel shouted the all-clear thirty minutes later, the two of them had everything ready to go.

"You next, miss," Mary said, setting her lantern down on its side to give her as much light as possible. "When you get to the other side, don't go nowhere 'til I reach you, not even a step. The Deep Caves can be mighty confusing, and I'm not sure I'll be able to find you again if you get lost."

"Are you certain what we're looking for is in the Deep Caves?" Josie asked, her pretty face pinched in the lamplight. "I know it's far too late, but now that it's my turn to climb, I just realized I never even asked if this was the right path."

"I would've told you if it weren't," Mary promised, pulling out the crystal shard, which was now singing so loudly she had no idea how the others couldn't hear it. "But the song keeps pointing forward, and this is the only way that gets us there."

She tapped her fingers against the lip of the crack, and Miss Josie, who'd clearly been hoping for any other answer, sighed. "Nothing for it, then," she said, tying the rope lashed to her and Rel's baggage around her waist. "As the bard says, 'if it were done when 'tis done, then 'twere well it were done quickly,' so wish me luck."

"Good luck, miss," Mary said obediently, but Miss Josie was already scrambling into the crack.

She was nothing if not efficient, crawling along even quicker than her gunhand despite the baggage she was dragging behind. Normally, Mary would've waited until after Miss Josie was all the way through before going in herself. But it was so late now, and she was so tired, Mary was worried she'd fall asleep on the wrong side if she dawdled. The crystal shard was bothering her, too, rattling impatiently against her chest now that they were so close to their goal.

Its antsy music mixed with the cave's song, filling her ears with buzzing until Mary couldn't take another minute. She yelled her intention to Miss Josie and shoved herself inside. Once in, she pushed her lamp ahead, dragging the baggage on her belly through the squeeze that separated the dangerous but still understandable closer-in tunnels from the madness beyond.

Chapter 11

Josie had only one goal left in the world at the moment, and that was not to panic. It was a matter of practicality more than pride. The crack she was crawling through was small enough already, so much so that she could only scooch forward while she was breathing out. Whenever she filled her lungs, she got stuck between the ceiling's sharp rock and the floor's jagged stone. Each time it happened, panic began crawling up from her chest like an animal, and each time, Josie fought it back down. Not because she was so very brave—she'd never felt less so—but because Josie knew that if she lost control and started breathing too quickly or flailing her limbs, she'd just be stuck down here that much longer, and that was a situation she'd do anything to avoid.

Think of Uncle Samuel, she told herself as she inched forward. *He was an old man, and he got through this multiple times. You're the one who insisted on dragging everybody down here. The least you can do is not make them wait while you scrabble about. Push, damn you, Josephine Kathleen O'Connor! Push!*

This self-flagellation got Josie through the next several feet. But when she looked up to see how much farther she had left, Rel's face still looked miles away. It seemed an impossible distance, and the baggage rope was so heavy around her waist. Oh, *why* had she brought so many things? And why hadn't she listened to Mary about making camp? Bear Woman might have been scary, but at least she'd been over on the other side of the water. This horrid crack was a much more immediate sort of hell, and while nothing could've made it pleasant, Josie was sure she'd made the crawl a hundred times worse on herself by doing it at the end of a ten-hour walking day. How much faster would she be going if her legs didn't feel like overcooked noodles? At this rate, they wouldn't all be through until midnight.

It would have been slightly more tolerable if Josie had still believed she was crawling toward something worth the effort, but that hope was fading as fast as her strength. Her uncle's letters had always made the Crystal Caverns sound so exciting, a mysterious land of marvels and adventure. So far in Josie's experience, though, she was starting to believe Rel had had the right of it with her horror stories. She wanted to believe it would be worth the effort in the end, for her uncle had loved this place so dearly, but it was hard to stay cheerful when you couldn't even lift your chin without smacking your head on a rock as sharp as an awl.

If Josie hadn't bet her entire future on this venture, she might have tried to turn around. The only reason she didn't was because turning around meant she'd have to crawl back over all that distance *again*. No way in perdition was Josie doing that, so she pressed doggedly onward, nudging forward one breath at a time until, after what felt like a lifetime of lifetimes, her clawing fingers finally caught something that wasn't stone.

"There you are."

She looked up feebly to see Reliance clutching her hand, a worried smile on her too-pale face. "Come on," her friend said, gently tugging Josie forward. "Out you go."

Josie didn't think she could crawl another inch. But freedom was a strong motivator, and somehow, she found the strength, hauling her body out of the crevice into glorious open space.

"Took you long enough," Rel scolded when Josie collapsed at her feet. "You did good at the beginning, but then you crossed the middle and just sort of stopped. Mary was worried we'd have to pull you out, but I told her you'd make it in your own time. You always were a little turtle."

The old nickname brought back old ire. Josie snapped her head up to proclaim that *she* had never been slow. She was just the one who always had to carry everything, and you try being fast when you're hauling the Prices' ridiculous ivory-inlaid folding beach chairs! That was what she'd meant to say anyway, but when Josie's head finally did make it up, the angry words died on her tongue.

"What in the world..."

They were lying in a field. Not a cavern, not a cave, not a tunnel or a burrow. Aside from the cliff they'd climbed out of, which looked much more enormous on this side than it had by the lake, there were no visible walls or ceiling of any sort. Just soft ground and silver grass stretching off into the darkness as far as the eye could see, which admittedly wasn't very far, as their lantern was still in the crack with Mary. Aside from the near-total darkness and the grass's odd silvery color, though, it really did look like they were back up on the Great Plains. The place even smelled like prairie: a dusty, grassy odor that made you thirsty just by entering your nose.

Josie had never beheld anything like it. She almost couldn't believe she was seeing it now, for there seemed no way such a place could exist underground, and yet here it was. She could touch the soil, pluck the grass, and roll it between her fingers. Rel had bits of the silvery stalks stuck to her shirtfront from where she'd lain down on her stomach to pull the rest of Josie's baggage train out of Mary's way. Their food packets and other supplies got dirt on them when Rel sent them rolling out of the way, just as they would in an actual field, leaving Josie no choice but to accept what she was seeing as real. She was still struggling to wrap her poor, exhausted mind around that when Mary popped out of the crack behind her.

"Finally," the girl wheezed, looking a third her usual size with all her coats and ponchos and packs removed. "I hate that part."

"Can't imagine who'd like it," Rel said, grabbing the rope to help haul Mary's towed supplies through as well. "So, where the hell are we? 'Cause it looks like an underground Nebraska."

"I've never been to Nebraska, but that is absolutely some grass." She lifted her lantern to shed more light on the scenery, causing the silvery blades to glitter like mirror shards. "Huh," Mary said, screwing up her face. "Never seen that before."

"What do you mean, you've never seen it?" Josie demanded, having far less success at controlling her panic now that she was no longer in danger of being stuck between two slabs of rock forever. "Haven't you been here?"

"I have and I haven't," Mary said. Most unhelpfully, Josie felt. "As I keep tryin' to tell you, the Deep Caves ain't like the others. The Dark and the Midway have their dangers, but no matter how much they shuffle their tunnels, they never stop being themselves. The Dark is always dark. The Main Gallery is always a tall crack with a stream and branch tunnels, and so on. The Deep Caves ain't so considerate. I've crawled through that crack seven times now, and this side's never looked the same way twice."

"Never looked or never been?" Josie asked, struggling to understand. "Are we in some sort of mirage, or is this field an actual place that moves around?"

"'Fraid I don't know, miss," Mary said, setting her lantern down in the shining grass to free her hands to put back on all the layers she'd shed before going under. "I don't think there's a living person who can explain how the Deep Caves do what they do, but 'shiny field' ain't a bad card to draw. Last time I came through here, we had to jump rocks across a big black pit with a wind that tried to blow you over every time your foot left a stone."

That did sound dreadful, but Josie was too overwhelmed to feel fortunate. "If it's different every time, how does anyone find anything down here?"

"That is the rub, ain't it?" Mary said, putting stuff back into her knapsack. "There's a reason miners stick to the Midway, even though all the easy crystal's long gone. No one's quite figured out how to mine the Deep Caves reliably yet. Stuff down here changes every time you turn your head. There's no landmarks or paths, and distances can be wildly different from one trip to the next. Even I find it easier to get lost than not, and I've got the cave music to guide me. I've been lucky so far, but this ain't a safe place for anyone. That's why I'm happy we've got *this*."

She pulled the crystal crescent out of her shirt, and Josie jumped back. Even Rel flinched, because the stone was no longer just glowing against Mary's palm. It was shining so bright white that the grayish-silver grass around them turned to glittering blue. The effect would have been beautiful if it hadn't looked so alien, and Josie shuddered despite herself.

"Can you please put that away?" she begged. "It's unnerving."

"Really?" Mary looked disappointed. "I think it's lovely. Even the shaking feels soothing now we're through the crack. Kinda like a purring cat."

The crystal *was* vibrating now that Josie looked at it, though she'd never seen a cat purr in a way that could possibly be compared to the knife-sharp crescent rattling against Mary's glove. But the guide did as she asked and put the stone back in her pocket.

"You should be happy it's kicking up a ruckus," Mary said as she tucked it away. "I'm pretty sure that means we're getting close. As I'm sure you can now see, finding anything in the Deep Caves is a frustrating business. Some might say impossible, but with this little thing buzzing like a dowsing rod, I bet I could cut a beeline straight to your uncle's old claim."

"How do you know it's his claim?" Josie asked suspiciously, because she couldn't remember mentioning that detail in Mary's presence.

"What else could it be?" Mary asked. "Everyone in town's heard about Old Sam's final strike. Two of my trips into the Deep Caves was actually guiding groups searching for it. Never did get close to finding the place, but you being his relative and all, it just made sense that's what this was about. I doubt Mr. Reiner'd be throwing around so much money just for sightseeing."

"It'd better be some massive crystal," Rel agreed, tying up the bag she'd repacked while Josie and Mary were talking. "Nothing else is worth that crawl."

Josie very much hoped she was right, but she wasn't as confident as she'd been at the start. Not about her uncle—she still believed as strongly as ever that Sam had left her that shard specifically because he'd wanted her to follow it. But Josie was no longer certain the glowing stone was leading them to something they would find as valuable as he did. You didn't fire all your miners because you'd discovered a big patch of crystal, after all.

She'd gone this whole way expecting some kind of claim or strike, but her uncle had never actually called it such. *She* was the one who'd assumed based off the rumors Reliance had told her. What if Sam Price's "treasure" was nothing but some Deep Cave oddity that changed the world for an explorer like him but couldn't do anything to help Josie meet the hurdles she'd set for herself? What if nothing salable lay down here at all?

It was a chilling thought to have this far in, but Josie was glad she'd had it on this side of the crack. If she'd come to this realization back on the Midway, she'd likely already be talking herself into turning around. Here and now, she had nowhere to go but forward and nothing to hope for but the best.

Or maybe that was just the exhaustion making her melodramatic.

"Shall we make camp?" she asked the others, smiling tiredly. "I don't know about you two, but I think I'm done."

"Never a good idea to bed down next to the only door," Mary said, shaking her head. "I know we're all tired, but let's push on a little farther and see if we can't find somewhere less open."

Josie didn't want to walk another step, but she'd learned her lesson about ignoring Mary's advice, so she kept her mouth shut and repacked her things. When her bag was more or less back together, she fell in behind Mary meek as a lamb, following the smaller girl through the silver grass into what felt like endless dark.

It couldn't *actually* be endless, she knew, but the field was certainly doing a good job of pretending. Despite walking what felt like miles through the rolling plains, they never even glimpsed the other side. There were no columns to hold up the ceiling of rock that must have been above their heads, no fallen boulders, no crystal, nothing. It was extremely unnerving, particularly when what was supposed to be an innocent, time-passing conversation with Mary about Lakota beliefs revealed that their afterlife was a happy hunting ground where space and game were plentiful.

A place, in short, that might look very much like these grasslands, as did the ancient Greeks' idea of the Elysian Fields.

That was two too many afterlives for Josie's comfort. If she hadn't been so sure her feet couldn't possibly hurt this much postmortem, she might have well believed she actually had died in the squeeze and was now wandering the world beyond. That, and they kept finding evidence of other living people passing through, including boot tracks across the grass, several large holes where someone had obviously been digging for crystal, and, most notably, a pile of fresh human excrement, which Josie was *positive* would not exist in the hereafter.

Clearly, then, she could not yet be dead, but that didn't mean they were safe. Despite what Mary had said about miners being too afraid to come down here, they kept passing evidence to the contrary. They did not, however, see any other actual people. It was a big, rolling place, though, so the lack of population didn't bother Josie overly much until they crested a hill and stumbled upon a campsite complete with bedrolls, cook pots, and the still-warm ashes of a campfire but no sign of the people who'd set it up.

"What happened to them?" Josie asked, whispering even though the emptiness was the problem. "Did the cave change and sweep everyone away? Because I can't imagine dragging all this stuff down here only to abandon it."

"Don't know," Mary whispered just as quietly. "But they didn't go peaceably. Look there."

She pointed at a dark stain on one of the bedrolls, and Josie's stomach clenched. "Is that—"

"There's more over here," Rel said, crouching beside a much larger spray of the telltale brownish red that had arced across the stamped-down grass near the fire. "Looks like someone got the wrong end of a fight."

"Then where are they?" Josie asked, looking all around. "I don't see a body or even a blood trail. If they were so injured, where did they go?"

"Maybe back to town?" Mary said with obviously forced hope.

"We'd have seen them if that were the case," Rel pointed out. "Blood ain't that old."

"They probably went farther in," Josie said desperately. "That makes more sense than disappearing into thin air."

"No one said they disappeared," Rel replied, crossing her arms over her chest. "You're both trying your best not to see the obvious, but we already know there's Whitmans down here, and they're famous for taking bodies. Put an empty camp with no tools or crystal on top of that, and I don't think here's much mystery at all to what happened here. On that same note, we should get moving."

"We gotta stop sometime," Mary said, her normally cheerful voice worn to a nubbin.

"We will," Rel promised. "Just not here."

No one was willing to argue that in a dead man's camp, so on they went, pushing farther and farther across the grass until Josie could take no more.

"I don't care!" she cried suddenly, stamping her foot down on top of a grassy rise that looked just like all the others. "There's no point escaping the Whitmans if we walk ourselves to death. I say we stop here and take our chances."

It was a sign of how exhausted everyone was that nobody argued. Even Rel stayed silent, slumping into the grass as if she'd just been waiting for someone to tell her it was okay to stop. Mary had already dug a sachet of dried beef out of her pack and was passing it around. The meat was as tough as old leather without hot water to soften it, but Josie couldn't even contemplate making a fire. She just chewed stubbornly at the fibers and plopped down on the ground, ready to pass out right there without even a blanket when Rel spoke the dreaded words of sense.

"We need to set a watch."

Of course they did. "I'll go first," Josie volunteered, forcing herself to stand back up. "It was my idea not to camp at the lake. You two sleep. I'll poke Rel when I can't take it any longer."

Once again, nobody argued. Josie suspected Mary had fallen asleep before she'd even finished, but who could blame her? Poor girl had done most of the work, as had Rel. Josie had been little better than luggage. She couldn't even claim to be bankrolling the expedition, since, other than providing food, equipment, and access to the finding shard, Rel had been the one paying for everything.

Considering it wasn't her crystal they were in here to find, Rel's quick hand on the coin purse was… not worrisome, exactly, but definitely not to be overlooked. Josie had a few plans for how to deal with that depending on what they found, but none of them would amount to beans if this expedition failed. To keep herself together and make sure she didn't accidentally drift off, Josie pulled out the notebook in which she'd compiled the most pertinent information from her uncle's letters during the long ride to Medicine Rocks. Leaning into the light of Mary's lantern, she flipped through the pages until she found the few words he'd written her about the Deep Caves.

Alas, the passage made as little sense now as it had when Josie had copied it. Uncle Samuel had always had a poetic bent, but not for the first time, Josie wished he'd been a little more specific, because "kaleidoscope of yearnings, wellspring of souls, boundless instrument of the universal choir" was hardly instructive. She was flipping back through her notes to see if they contained anything that might be of actual, practical use for the journey ahead when the world around her suddenly changed.

It happened in the blink of an eye. One moment she was on top of a grassy knoll, struggling to read her own tiny handwriting in the light of Mary's kerosene lantern. The next she was in the exact same position, only the little hill was gone, and so were the empty camp and the rest of the prairie.

Mary and Rel were still there, thank goodness, but they were no longer lying on grass. They were back in a cave but not like the jagged, natural ones they'd walked through yesterday. This tunnel was round like a pipe with walls covered in sharp chips of shiny black stone. It looked like obsidian, but the way the pieces were layered over one another more resembled scales than stone. Add in the roundness and the curving sides, and it looked as if they were standing in the belly of an inside-out snake, which was far too bizarre a notion to be borne alone.

"*Mary!*" Josie cried, dropping down to shake the others. "*Rel! Wake up!*"

"What?" Rel snorted, snapping up with her gun in her hand before Josie had even seen her reach for the weapon. "What's happened?"

"We've only been asleep five minutes," Mary groaned at the same time. "It can't be time to switch yet."

"No, no, it's not that," Josie said, grabbing the lantern and holding it aloft so they could all see. "The cave changed! Look!"

To their credit, Mary and Rel did look. And then they promptly lay back down.

"Are you serious?" Josie demanded. "The whole world changed on us, and you're going back to *sleep?*"

"Why not?" Rel grumbled. "This don't look any worse than the last place."

"The Deep Caves change all the time," Mary agreed, bundling under her blanket like a grub. "If you raise the alarm every time they do something odd, none of us'll ever get to sleep. Just stay close and let the caves do their—" She stopped suddenly, sitting up in her bedroll like a jackknife to dig into her coat. "Hold up."

"If it ain't about to kill us, I don't want to know," Rel said from beneath her hat.

"You'll want to hear about this," Mary promised, pulling out the crystal shard, which was dancing across her palm like a wind-up toy. "Look at it go!" she cried, wide awake now. "The caves must've moved us with 'em when they changed, 'cause we just went from 'in the area' to 'dang close.'"

"How dang close?" Rel asked, sitting up.

"Practically on top," Mary said, pointing down the tunnel. "That way."

There was no more discussion after that. The three of them rolled up their blankets without a word and shot down the cave like an arrow with Mary and the glowing stone as the tip.

"This way," she said, turning right at an intersection to head down another scaled tunnel that looked exactly like the first. They turned right again just a few minutes later, then doubled back, then turned again.

Minutes passed. Josie lost track of how many corners they turned, but despite Mary's insistence that they were almost there, they never actually arrived. They just kept turning and turning until Josie's tired mind suddenly realized what was happening.

"We're going in circles."

"I *know*," Mary said angrily, scowling at the crystal buzzing like a wasp's nest in her palm. "I don't get it. Dang thing should be right next to us, but none of these tunnels seem to get us any closer."

"Perhaps what we're looking for is between the tunnels?" Josie said, placing a hand on the wall only to snatch it right back when the razor-sharp black stones sliced clean through her kid gloves.

Undeterred, she took off her pack to retrieve the small mining pick Mihir had tied to the side for her. "I'm going to give it a few whacks and see if I can't punch through."

Mary backed away to give her space, but just as Josie was hauling back for a good swing, Rel grabbed her arm.

"Don't."

"Why not?" Josie demanded. More sharply than she should have, but she was as short on temper as she was on sleep, and Rel's one-word demands were not helping. "Do you *want* to keep walking in circles?"

"No," Rel said. "But I don't think we should be making noise right now. Look at this."

She crouched down to point at the fine layer of gray dust that had settled on the rounded floor of the circular corridor, but Josie failed to see her meaning. "Would you kindly just tell me what's the matter in normal words for once?"

"There's footprints right there!" Rel hissed. "That's why we need to be quiet! We're not the only ones walking in circles down here."

"I don't see any footprints," Josie said, scowling at the scuffed dust. "And even if I did, they're probably ours. We must've gone around through this tunnel five times already."

"We didn't make these," Rel said, waving for Mary to bring the light closer. "See how big that one is? Looks like someone dropped a damn pumpkin. Even your feet aren't that big, *and* these tracks are on top of ours, which means whoever made them came through after we did."

"Nonsense," Josie huffed, looking up and down the empty corridor. "It's dead silent down here. If there were a man with feet the size of pumpkins following us, we'd surely have heard him, assuming such a person could even exist. If he actually had the body to match those feet, he'd be even taller than the tunnel."

"I don't know," Mary said nervously. "Miners who get in this far tend to stay a while, and crystal does strange things to men's bodies over time. Maybe he grew too big to fit through the squeeze and got trapped?"

"If that's the case, then he likely wants our help, not our lives," Josie pointed out.

"You want to wait and ask him?" Rel challenged. "'Cause if he keeps to his track, he'll be on us in just a minute."

They all went still after that, ears straining in the dark. When absolutely nothing appeared, Josie put her foot down.

"This isn't what we gave up our sleep for," she declared, turning back to Mary. "Can you get me a fixed location in the wall? Somewhere I can strike?"

"I can try," Mary said. "But I can't promise nothing. The song's jumping all over. For all I know, it's above us."

"Can you calm it down?" Rel suggested, glaring at the crystal rattling in Mary's hands. "Sing to it or something? Worked well enough on the bear."

"That was totally different," Mary said. Then she frowned. "Though I don't see how it would do any harm to try. The caves do like to echo."

"And crystal always responds well to music," Josie agreed. "That's the only way you can mine it without destroying the crystalline structure."

Mary didn't look happy about the mining comparison, but Josie was too tired to keep arguing. "Just try," she pleaded. "If it doesn't work, we'll bed down right here and start again fresh in the morning. Maybe we'll get lucky, and the caves will change again to something more open. If not, we'll still get sleep, which is a prize all by itself."

"Amen to that," Mary said, staring hard at the glowing crystal. "All right, I'll give it a shot. You'd better back up a bit. I don't know what's gonna happen."

Josie grabbed Rel's hand and stepped them both away to the edge of the tunnel. This made it difficult to hear what Mary was saying, for while her mouth moved, she didn't seem to make any sound. A spark of hope flared in Josie's chest that Mary was singing the same music as the crystal, music only she could hear. Then Mary's whispering got a little louder, and Josie heard the faint strands of a familiar tune.

"*Frère Jacques, Frère Jacques, dormez-vous? Dormez-vous?*"

"Why are you singing 'Are you sleeping, Brother John?'" Rel asked loudly.

"It was all I could think of!"

"It's fine, Mary," Josie said, digging her heel into Rel's foot. "Sing whatever you like."

"Ain't no point," she groaned. "Rock's not doing nothing."

"Probably 'cause you're whispering," Rel said, ignoring Josie's stomping. "How's the crystal supposed to hear you over all that rattling? You gotta go louder, get its attention."

"But you just said *not* to be loud!"

"If Pumpkin Foot's coming, he can wait like the rest of us," Rel snapped. "Just do it already so we can go to bed."

"And try using the crystal's own tone," Josie suggested, remembering her uncle's notes. "Crystal always responds best to its natural resonance."

"Yeah, when you're cutting it," Mary muttered, scrunching up her face. "I'm trying to follow the shard, not break it."

She must not have been totally closed to the idea, though, for the next thing Mary did was press the buzzing crystal to her ear. She listened for several moments and then moved the rock in front of her mouth. When it was positioned, she took a big breath and sang out strong, combining Mary and Rel's suggestions for one loud note.

Josie didn't know which part was key, the volume or the tone, but *something* must have worked, because the crystal ceased its buzzing and went still, its light shining brighter and brighter as Mary got louder and louder. This went on for nearly a minute until, when Mary's note had gotten so loud it was echoing down the tunnels like a train whistle, the stone in her hands gave a final pulse of blinding light and went out.

"Ow!" Mary cried.

"What happened?" Josie demanded, grabbing the lantern off the floor and lifting it up right next to her head since the flaring crystal had ruined her darksight. "What's wrong?"

"Oh, Miss Josie," Mary wailed, lifting her tear-streaked face to the light. "I'm *so* sorry."

Before Josie could ask what about, the girl opened her clenched fists to show her the dull, broken shards that had been the glowing crescent lying in the bloody palms of her shredded gloves.

"Oh *no*," Josie groaned, pressing her hands over her mouth.

"I didn't mean to!" Mary cried as Josie shoved the lantern at Rel to dig a bandage out of her pack. "I was trying to go up slow, but I got excited 'cause it was working, but then I must've gotten got too loud 'cause it just exploded, and I'm so *sorry*! I broke your crystal!"

"That's not what's important," Josie said, as much for herself as for Mary as she began peeling away the girl's shredded gloves to get at the bloody cuts beneath. "You were just doing as we asked. What matters now is making sure you're not seriously hurt."

"I'll be fine," Mary said with a sniffle. "The shards just sliced me up a little, but what are we gonna do? How're we gonna find what we're looking for in this maze without the crystal singing us the way?"

"We'll figure it out," Josie promised. Again, mostly for her own benefit. "We already know we're close. We just need to keep our—"

She cut off when Rel suddenly pulled her crystal gun. For a horrifying moment, Josie thought her friend was going to shoot poor Mary, then she realized Rel wasn't even facing them. She was looking down the hall, moving to position herself between them and the man who'd just come out of the tunnel at the intersection where they'd taken their last turning. A very, *very* large man with corpse-pale skin and feet that were indeed the size of pumpkins.

Josie's first thought upon seeing him was that he must be a ghost. This was only because of Rel and Mary's ridiculous talk earlier, for aside from his deathly pallor, there was nothing remotely ghostlike about the stomping, huffing figure leering down the corridor at them. Even his odd color turned out not to be ethereal, for as he trod closer, Josie realized he wasn't actually pale at all. He was reflective. His face, thick neck, and bald head were shimmering as if he'd powdered them all over with ground-up pearls like the ones Miss Josephine used on her cheeks for especially lavish parties.

Not that it made any sense for a giant underground man to wear luster dust, but pearls weren't the only things that shimmered. There was another reflective substance that was far more likely, but the costs involved were so astronomical that it took Josie several seconds to accept that the man in front of them was glittering with *crystal*.

185

Not cheap dust either. As her blinded eyes readjusted to the dark, Josie saw that the man was not actually powdered. He reflected the light because all of his exposed flesh—of which there was a lot, since he wore nothing but a pair of too-small trousers—had been covered in flecks of crystal. They were no bigger than confetti squares, each one meticulously sewn into his skin with shimmering thread like the world's most terrifying sequins. The whole thing was so bizarre, Josie didn't realize he was still walking closer until the man stopped barely ten feet away from Rel's raised pistol.

"'ello, 'ello," he said, ducking his bald head so he wouldn't knock his shimmering crown on the cave's curved ceiling. "What we got here?"

Josie hadn't known there was a "we" until the man pulled his massive left arm forward, dragging a second, much smaller... *thing* on a chain to his side. It was too dark for Josie to say more until the creature trotted forward, and she realized it wasn't a creature at all. It was another man. An absolutely filthy one dressed in rotting leather and crawling on all fours beside the giant.

Given the chain, Josie's first assumption was that he must be a prisoner, but he didn't act like one. Quite the opposite. The man seemed perfectly content to sit at the end of his chain, and his hunched body was covered in just as much crystal the other man's.

His sewn-in pieces were larger and denser than the giant's and concentrated mostly on his face, which was so riddled with stitching it no longer looked human. His jaw looked as if it had been broken and rebuilt to hold all the crystal pressing outward on his cheeks, and his eyes were completely ringed in with the stuff, giving his pupils a reflective quality like a cat's or a coyote's. Creatures that saw in the dark, in other words.

"Mary," Josie whispered when she'd found her voice again. "Is this what you meant when you said the crystal does strange things to men's bodies?"

"No, miss," Mary whispered back, her voice hoarse with fear. "I ain't never seen nothing like this before."

"I have," Rel said, aiming her crystal pistol dead at the big one's chest. "They're Whitmans."

Josie nearly choked. *Those* were members of the Whitman gang? No wonder her escort had been so eager to get out of their territory. They looked like crystal monsters.

"Not to be interruptin' your chat," the giant said, ignoring Rel's gun to focus on Mary and Josie behind her. "But're you the ones making all that racket?"

"I'm terribly sorry if we bothered you," Josie said as politely as possible in the desperate hope this situation could still be salvaged with words. "We didn't know it would get so loud."

"Weren't the loudness I minded," the giant said, scratching his crystal-scaled chin. "I just wanted to know if you reckoned that singing just now sounded anything like a bell."

"A bell?" Josie repeated, looking at Mary. "I don't think so."

"I ask 'cause it kinda did to me," the man went on. "But I'm worried that might be wishful thinking. See, me 'n Kip here"—he pulled on the length of chain, which seemed to excite the dog-man enormously—"we been down this hole a long time lookin' for a bell. Ain't we, Kipper?"

The man on the chain growled and snapped in reply, giving Josie an excellent view of the jagged shards of crystal someone had sewn into his gums in place of his teeth.

"Long time," the giant said again, shaking his head. "Weeks, months, hard to say without the sun. But the Shitter said we can't go back 'til we find the bell, so what'cha gonna do?"

He shrugged as if this were all inevitable, and Josie cleared her throat. "Forgive me for prying, but who is the... who is this man you speak of?"

"The Shitter?" The giant laughed a huge laugh. "I suppose I can't be expecting such language from a lady. But I don't mind tellin' you. It's a good story."

187

He leaned down a little and dropped his booming voice to a stage whisper. "The Shitter's the bosses' spyglass into what's coming. Used to be one of them fancy European types, but then he stuck a knob of crystal in his brain, and now he sees the future. Also lost all control of his bowels, but what's a little shit when you *know* shit, eh? Spends all his time in a cell drawing pictures on the walls with his own filth. When he does actually manage to write words, though, they *always* come true, and he wrote a while ago that there'd be a lady named Price who'd appear with a bell and lead us to whatever the bosses are after down here. Didn't tell us what that was, o'course, but I know better than to pry into the bosses' affairs. All that matters to me 'n Kip is that soon as we find what we're after, we get to go home, so I'll ask you again: was that a bell just now?"

He leaned closer as he asked this, and Josie swallowed. "I'm sorry, but I'm afraid there were absolutely no bells involved. None of us have anything like that down here, have we?"

Rel and Mary both shook their heads, and the huge man took a thunderous step forward. "You sure?" he asked, narrowing his bagged eyes. "'Cause you're the first lady I've found down 'ere, and you look mighty Pricey to me."

Josie was opening her mouth to tell him that was ridiculous when light blossomed on her left. For a soaring moment, she thought the guiding crystal had put itself back together somehow, but the light wasn't coming from Mary. It was shining from Reliance. From her crystal gun specifically, which was glowing like a furnace in her hand as she squeezed the trigger and unleashed a thread-thin beam of blinding light straight into the giant's forehead.

It happened so fast that Josie would've missed the whole thing if she'd blinked. Even having seen it, she still wasn't sure what the light was supposed to do. Despite having taken whatever Rel had shot straight to the head, the giant didn't appear pained in the slightest. He did, however, look quite angry.

"What was that?" he shouted, scowling at Rel, who stared at him dumbfounded down the crystal and bone barrel of her gun. "Did you just try 'ta shoot me?"

With a series of the foulest curses to ever assault Josie's ears, Rel shoved the no-longer glowing pistol back in its holster with her right hand while simultaneously drawing one of her normal guns with her left. She'd barely gotten the new weapon up before she fired another shot, into the giant's neck this time. Again, though, nothing happened. The bullet bounced right off the man's crystal scales like rubber off brick, ricocheting back over their heads and down the tunnel behind them. Josie was still coming up from the crouch she'd instinctively fallen into when Rel grabbed her arm.

"*Run!*"

Josie's feet obeyed before her brain could. When she came back to her senses, she was racing down the tunnel after Mary while Rel brought up the rear, firing over her shoulder to land two more perfectly aimed shots in the giant's kneecaps. Once again, however, the bullets bounced off him like pebbles, leaving him laughing as he dropped the dog-man's chain.

"Fetch 'em, Kip!"

With a howl of delight, the released man charged after them on all fours. That would have slowed a normal person, but the crystal-toothed Kip was as swift as an actual dog. He was already nipping at Rel's heels, dodging the shots she fired at his deformed head with the dexterity of a dragonfly. Josie was feeling caught already when Mary suddenly threw herself at the ground in front of them.

That was what it looked like at least, but a second later, Josie realized her mistake. Mary hadn't cast herself down in defeat. She was wiggling through a crack in the floor.

Josie tripped over her own feet in surprise. These were the same black scale-sided tunnels they'd been walking circles through for the past half hour, and *now* there was a crack? How had she not seen it before? How was this even—

"Miss Josie!" Mary cried, waving at her through the hole with one hand while dragging her pack inside with the other. "This way!"

Never one to look a gift horse in the mouth, Josie shoved all her questions aside and dove inside, cramming her much larger body through the tiny hole in the sharp, broken stone. The process tore her clothing and scraped her up quite badly, but she was too terrified to mind the pain. All that mattered was getting to cover before those chomping crystal teeth found her, so Josie pushed with all her might, shoving herself into the crack the same way her mother had crammed cranberry stuffing into the Prices' Christmas goose.

For a horrible moment, it didn't look like she was going to make it. She was cursing herself for not removing her backpack first when Mary's hands shot up, grabbed Josie's straps, and jerked her body through some sort of magical sequence that popped each of her limbs through the opening. Josie was still marveling at it when Mary let go, dropping her face-first into the freezing water of yet another underground creek.

This one was much wider and shallower than the waterway that fed the Main Gallery. It ran beneath the tunnels they'd been circling like a sewer, though luckily, the stone here was not covered in razor-sharp scales. It was, however, very tight, forcing Josie to lie on her stomach in the water to fit. Things got more crowded when Reliance joined them, crashing down through the hole with a string of curses and the unmistakable smell of fresh blood.

The scent turned out to be from a large gash on the girl's leg. Josie couldn't do more than note the injury before Mary came up between them, shoving a large piece of black rock—clearly the bit that had cracked off to form their entry point—into the hole whence it came.

The stone chunk looked much heavier than Josie would've thought the girl capable of lifting by herself. But Mary was clearly running on the power of survival, because she slammed it in tight, wedging the plug into the gap just in time for the pursuing Kip to crash into it.

A yelp of pain followed. Then came a howl of rage as the dog-man began pawing at the barrier. When this failed to dislodge the blockage, there was a moment of silence, and then the air was filled with an even worse sound: the stomach-curdling rasp of crystal scraping through stone.

"He's biting his way through," Mary squeaked.

"*Go!*" Josie yelled, grabbing the groaning Rel with one hand and her pack with the other. "Go, go, *go!*"

Mary obeyed at once, pushing her own pack in front of her up the hidden creek with astonishing speed. Josie hoped to achieve a similar pace, but despite the whipping terror and her earlier practice in the squeeze, she barely managed faster than a crawl. She was just so much bigger than Mary, even when the girl was puffed up with all her coats and layers, and Rel was a dead weight. Probably because of shock from her wound, but Josie couldn't stop to treat her because if she stopped, they'd die. The thin shelf of stone above their heads was already shaking as the giant walked over to see how his dog-man was faring. If he decided to stomp, the floor would crack like candy coating, either crushing them instantly or opening a hole that he could grab them through.

Josie wasn't sure which fate she dreaded more, but she had no intention of meeting either. It didn't matter if Rel was heavy or the way was tight. What were all those years of hauling Miss Josephine's luggage and cursed heavy tea trays for if she couldn't use that strength now to save their lives? She *had* to keep going, so Josie wiggled onward, squirming up the shallow, freezing water like a salmon giving its life to get upstream. She'd thought she was making good progress until she ran into Mary, who'd stopped for some unfathomable reason.

"What are you doing?" she hissed, looking back at the rock plug, which Kipper had already chewed halfway through. "They'll be on us any second!"

"I know, but *look.*"

Mary twisted as she spoke, turning down the flame of the lantern that had miraculously kept burning despite the water running down the inside of its glass chimney. Josie's first thought was that the guide was putting out her light in preparation to hide in the dark, since running was clearly getting them nowhere, but then she realized the light wasn't gone. The lantern was snuffed, but she could still see Mary and the rest of the tunnel quite clearly thanks to the radiant white glow shining up from Mary's bandaged hands.

"It's still here!" she whispered frantically, unwrapping the gauze Josie had hastily tied around her palms to reveal the still-bleeding cuts that glittered like the moon. "Some of the finding crystal's dust must still be in me, 'cause I can hear it clear! We're super close!"

Now hardly seemed the time, but Josie didn't have anything else to suggest, so she nodded for Mary to lead on. The girl did so in a flurry, scrambling through the swift water to a fork in the stream Josie would have sworn before a jury of her peers had *not* been there ten seconds ago. Had things been less dire, she would've asked Mary if the caves always opened doors for her like this. For now, though, she was forced to let the miracle pass unquestioned, scrambling after Mary into the new stream branch.

The moment they were both past the fork, the horrible chewing sound behind them vanished. Terrified this meant Kipper had finished the job, Josie flipped around, thankful this new tunnel was tall enough for her to get up on her knees at least. When she turned to face her doom, however, there was nothing to see. The crack, the crystal-toothed dog-man, the giant stomping overhead, even the fork they'd just taken were gone, leaving nothing but a single-stream creek flowing into the dark behind them and the labored sound of Rel's breathing.

"What was that?" Josie whispered when she could speak again. "What just happened? Where did they go?"

"Nowhere," Mary replied, her voice bright with delight as she looked around the quiet tunnel. "It was us that moved! The caves must've shifted again when we took that fork and shuffled us somewhere different!"

That shouldn't have been such a shock given that Josie had already witnessed the tunnels changing less than an hour ago, but no amount of "should" could stop her collapsing back into the water. "I don't believe it," she choked out. "We're *saved!*"

"The caves take care of those that take care of them," Mary said with a reverence, leaning down to kiss the stone beneath the flowing water.

"Give them my thanks as well," Josie said, glancing nervously at Reliance, who was looking frighteningly blue in the pale light that continued to shine from Mary's palms. "We need to get her out of this water."

"No hope of that here," Mary said, turning around. "Let's try downstream."

"Why downstream?" Josie asked in alarm, because even though everything was different now, the Whitmans had been downstream.

"'Cause it's easier than going upstream," Mary said practically, studying her glowing palm. "Also the light seems stronger going that direction, which makes sense. All this water's gotta be flowing somewhere, right?"

Josie hoped it wasn't to another of those creepy black lakes. Even if it was, she was in no position to complain. Rel was shaking like a newborn rabbit behind her, muttering under her breath in a voice that didn't sound like hers at all. Worried she'd already let the situation get too bad, Josie took off her fitted jacket and tied it around Rel's injured leg, which actually looked less awful than it had at first. Heartened by this stroke of good fortune, Josie slid her arm under her friend's shoulder and started sliding her as quickly as she could downstream after Mary. She was working Rel over a particularly rocky bit when she realized Mary had stopped again.

"What now?"

Mary held up one glowing hand for quiet while cupping the other around her ear. "You hear that?"

Josie held her breath, ears straining over the trickle of water to catch a much deeper, bigger roar in the distance. "It sounds like rapids."

"Or a waterfall," Mary said, resuming her crawl. "Better to hear it before we go over it, I guess, but watch out for strengthening current."

That didn't seem like a worry when the creek they were crawling down was barely an inch deep, but Josie heeded her advice and dug her fingers into the stones, hauling Reliance doggedly behind her.

On and on they went. Josie's pocket watch had long since filled up with water, so she had no idea how long precisely, but she'd never been this tired, soaked, and hungry in all her life. The only reason she was able to keep going was because Reliance would die if she didn't get her out of the freezing water soon. But while the tunnel they were crawling down never seemed to change, the roar ahead of them was getting steadily louder.

The creek was growing swifter as well, the water picking up speed as the channel they'd been following began to tilt inexorably downward. It was still shallow enough that Josie wasn't worried about being swept away, but she had no idea what they'd do when they actually reached the falls that were now definitely ahead.

"I think there's more down there than just falls," Mary said when Josie mentioned this. "Hear how the roar doesn't echo or splatter? That means the water must be falling into somewhere open. There's a breeze, too, so we gotta be coming up on something big."

That was a lot to interpret from sound and air, but Josie knew better than to question Mary's caving skills at this point. She was about to ask how much farther the girl thought it would be when the low tunnel suddenly opened into a much taller space.

"Thank heaven," Josie said, stretching her aching spine. "I never thought I'd miss standing so much. Now I can carry Rel on my back! That should be much easier than crawling, and it'll get her out of the—"

"Uh, Miss Josephine?"

Josie stopped trying to wrangle Rel's limp body onto her back long enough to look at Mary, but the girl wasn't facing her. She was staring straight ahead, eyes wide as eggs in the light of her glowing hands, which were shining brighter than ever.

"You'd better look at this."

Irritated over one more thing when Rel felt as cold as the stone, Josie finished levering her friend's limp body onto her back and shuffled over. "All right, I'm here," she said, huffing the wet strands of her hair out of her face. "What's *so* important that I had to come—"

Her voice cut out with a gasp. The waterfall they'd been chasing was only a few feet ahead, a sharp line in the dark where the shallow creek ended in a spray of mist. Beyond that stretched a great empty space just like Mary had predicted, and shining inside it were thousands of tiny lights.

Josie was about to ask if this was another of the Deep Caves' impossible landscapes when she realized the truth was much simpler. Those weren't stars shining in the darkness. They were reflections. The light shining from Mary's cut-up hands was being bounced back at them by crystal. Thousands and thousands and *thousands* of twinkling crystal clusters coated the walls of a giant cavern for as far as the eye could see.

And on the rock beside the falls that poured into that wondrous sight, sheltered from the spray inside the heavy coils of a long rope ladder, was a letter. Its surface was damp from the constant wetness of the place, the ink gone blurry, but not so blurry that Josie could mistake the familiar, gentlemanly handwriting penned across its front.

My dearest Josephine, it read. *Welcome to the heart of everything.*

Chapter 12

Reliance was not having a good time of it.

There'd been rumors that the Whitmans were shoving crystal where it didn't belong for months now, but she hadn't realized it could get this bad. Hadn't known they could get that *big* nor that tough. Even crystal shattered when you shot it, but the giant hadn't flinched when she'd plugged him with her crystal gun or her normal ones.

She suspected his dog-man wasn't nearly so bulletproof, but she couldn't say for sure 'cause she hadn't been able to land a single shot on the squirrelly bastard. Rel had emptied her pistol's full wheel point-blank into his face—six damn bullets—and hit nothing but air. After that, there'd been nothing for it but to turn heel and run.

The best she could say for herself was that she'd made sure everyone got down that damn rabbit hole before she'd crammed in. It was the least she could do after talking herself up so big to Josie. Security was the pretense under which she'd pinned herself to this venture, so security she had provided. She just wished she hadn't gotten the shit bitten out of her leg for the privilege.

Technically, he bit the fibularis brevis *out of you,* her gun informed her. *Your "shit" remains precisely where you left it.*

Rather than waste precious energy replying to smartass comments, Rel turned her attention to figuring out where she was. Last thing she recalled for sure was kicking the dog-man off her leg and diving into the water after Josie. Stuff got spotty after that. They must've managed something, since she was still here thinking about it rather than off haunting the tunnels, but aside from the pain and the bitter, bitter cold, Rel couldn't remember a thing.

The cold was your body dying, her father said in that damn superior tone. *In addition to removing a chunk of your flesh, the bandit with the crystal teeth ruptured your anterior tibial artery.*

That explained why she felt so lightheaded, but why wasn't she dead?

Because I fixed you, he said proudly. *You forget: restoring corpses to useful function is one of my specialties, and what is a person but a corpse in waiting? Not that I would have minded overmuch if you'd perished after your recent behavior, but I am also tied to your soul, and I have no interest in dying a second time.*

Heaven forbid.

It wasn't easy in my current state and with you too incapacitated to supply me with crystal, the gun went on. *So I improvised by borrowing a few years off the end of your life. This gave me the energy I needed to repair the artery and stop the bleeding as well as restore enough of your muscle and tendons so that you wouldn't be left unable to walk for weeks. You're welcome.*

After witnessing the horrors her father had worked when he'd been alive, Rel didn't find the fact that he'd fixed her leg too surprising. She did, however, find it very suspicious. If he'd had miracles like that in his pocket the whole time, why hadn't he fixed himself when he got murdered?

I absolutely would have repaired my body if I could. But where you lost a mere few ounces of flesh, I was shot nineteen times. Surely even you can grasp the difference in scale.

Rel understood she wouldn't stand around flat-footed while some idiot shot her nineteen times.

Ungrateful child! I save your life, and all you can do is find fault.

If Rel's eyes had been working at that moment, she would have rolled them to the sky.

Your eyes are working just fine. The degenerate bit your leg, not your face. Open them, and you'll see why I worked so hard to keep you ambulatory. I couldn't have you holding me back during a moment like this. Just look at where we are!

It was the most excited Rel had heard him sound since he'd gotten that big packet of crystal from Sam Price. That normally boded bad things for her, but Reliance was also curious, so she decided to take a chance and crack her eyes.

The first thing she noticed was the swaying. Not gentle rocking like a hammock or a boat. This was more like being on a rope swing. A

197

fitting description, Rel found out, because when she finally got her heavy eyelids all the way up, the first thing she saw was the golden mass of Josie's hair tangled around the rope that tied Reliance to her back.

"What the—"

Josie's body stiffened beneath hers. "I'm glad you're finally awake," she said in a strained voice. "But *please* stop moving. This isn't exactly a stable ladder."

Rel froze in place, grabbing onto Josie's back like a baby opossum as she looked around to see where they were.

As stated, Josie was clinging to a rope ladder hanging down in front of what could well be the world's tallest waterfall. It was so high up that the water coming off the top got scattered to mist before it reached the ground, floating off in a cloud rather than gathering into a safe pool to catch them should they slip. And slipping was definitely a danger, because the rope they were clinging to was drenched through. So were their clothes and hair, leaving them both dripping and shivering as the rope twisted in the cold wind pouring down the falls.

"Let me go," Rel demanded, unable to take any more swinging. "I'll climb the rest myself."

"That is absolutely not going to happen," Josie informed her as she resumed their shaky descent. "First, I don't know how to undo the knots Mary used to lash you to my back, and second, your leg is in a splint."

That was news to Rel. Sure enough, though, when she looked down, there it was: a competent splint made from two mining picks and someone's trousers. *Her* trousers, Rel realized belatedly, and her face began to burn.

"You took my damn jeans?"

"We used what was available," Josie said defensively. "We'd removed them already to get at your wound, which looked a lot better than expected, for the record. Anyway, we cleaned and bandaged all the obvious damage, but we couldn't tell if anything was broken since you still hadn't woken up, so we decided to go ahead and tie it up just to be safe."

She went down another rung before adding, "By the way, I'm pretty sure Mary knows you're a girl now. Sorry."

At any other time, that would have been a major issue. Right now, though, Rel barely paid it mind. "Thanks for the effort, but I'm fine," she said, straining her neck in an effort to look behind them, since the way Josie was facing made it impossible to see anything but waterfall spray. "Now can you please tell me what the hell happened? Where are the Whitmans? And for that matter, where are we?"

"That's the good part," Josie assured her, picking up speed. "But it'll be easier to show you than to explain. Hold on, we're nearly at the bottom."

Rel didn't want to wait another damn second, but she couldn't do anything while trussed up like this except hang along for the ride. A decently quick ride at that, which Rel belatedly realized was pretty impressive given that Josie was climbing down a free-swinging ladder carrying the weight of two people.

"You're pretty strong."

"You're pretty light," Josie countered. "Do you eat food now that you live out here, or is it all whiskey?"

"I'm not *that* skinny. Certainly more than a fine lady like yourself should be able to lift."

"Good thing I'm not actually a fine lady, then," Josie said with a smile. "A servant is a beast of burden."

Rel didn't remember Josie doing *that* much heavy lifting. Thinking back, though, she did recall wheelbarrows being employed whenever Josephine decided she wanted to go to the beach. The Prices' beach house had been right on the shore, too, but it still took the servants an hour to schlep all the folding chairs, umbrellas, portable pavilions, and so forth across the dunes, by which point Rel and her brother were already sunburned and ready to go back in. That left Josephine no one to play with except Josie, who didn't have the freedom to say no. She'd had to haul *and* entertain, toting refreshments and building sandcastles while Miss Josephine watched from the shade, finding fault with everything she did.

That she'd never stayed to help, or better still, tell Miss Josephine to get her own damn sandwich, suddenly struck Rel as shameful. Fortunately, she didn't have much time to dwell on far past mistakes before Josie landed them gently on the ground.

"There," she said, getting to work on the knots that held Rel to her back. "I'll have you free in a jiffy."

Rel couldn't wait a jiffy. Now that they were on the ground, the mist was thin enough for her to see what they'd landed on, which looked for all the world like a giant outcropping of crystal. That couldn't possibly be right. A crystal formation big enough to stand on would be the strike of a lifetime. It couldn't be so, and yet there it was, sparkling like tinsel right under her feet.

Wait until you see the rest.

There was no more patience after that. Bracing on her good leg, Rel grabbed Josie by the waist and spun them both around to face the cavern behind them. The giant, glittering, underground palace covered wall to ceiling to wall in thousands—*millions*—of sparkling crystals.

"Holy hell."

"Impressive, isn't it?" Josie said as she finally got the rope free.

This was nothing like. "Impressive" was for big-sky sunsets and bulls-eye trick shots. This was a goddamn miracle.

Just from where she was standing, Rel could see crystals of every known color and structure mixed in with dozens of new sorts that she'd never encountered before. There were sharp crystals and smooth ones, big hunks and little drop-like clusters running in trickles down the walls. All of them took the light from the lantern sitting at the base of the falls and reflected it back a thousandfold, and yet it still wasn't enough to see all the way to the cavern's end.

She could see Mary, though. The half-breed was way out at the light's edge, staring in wonder at a pillar so big that Rel didn't realize it was also crystal until she saw it glitter.

That was enough to make her jaw hit the ground. The crystal pillar was as white as a boiled bone and so thick that the three of them together couldn't have circled their arms around it. It went all the way up to the cavern's crystal-studded ceiling, rising from a thicket of massive crystal outcroppings that would have been wonders by themselves if they hadn't been so dwarfed by the company. Staring up at it, Rel didn't know whether she was seeing the whole thing or if the column was merely the middle section of something even bigger. Either way, it was easily the biggest crystal she'd ever seen. Maybe the biggest ever, a wonder of the world.

Mary certainly seemed to feel that way. Their guide was staring at the giant crystal with an expression normally reserved for acts of God. It was the same way she'd looked at the crescent shard the first time Josie had placed it in her hands. Same strange white color of crystal, too. The big pillar wasn't glowing like the finding crescent had, but it definitely looked to be made of the same rock, which meant...

"We made it," Rel breathed, her face breaking into an enormous smile. "We found Sam Price's final claim!"

Good *Lord,* no wonder Apache Jake had been so eager to get his hands on Josie's inheritance. There was more crystal around where Rel and Josie were standing than all the miners in Medicine Rocks had found in the past year, and who knew how much was in that pillar! It was the strike of the century, fifty times what the dead crystal cavern in the Front Caves must've been before it got ruined. They didn't even know how far back it went yet, but just what she could see already was enough to make Rel grab Josie and whirl her around.

"*You did it!*" she cried, laughing despite the pain as her exuberance nearly tipped them both over, forcing Josie to catch them before they bashed into the sharp crystals at the base of the falls. "But how? Did Mary figure out how to put the guiding crystal back together or something?"

"I'm afraid it was more like dumb luck," Josie said, leading Rel away from slippery rocks before she did something irreversible. "One minute we were crawling through the dark. The next, we saw this place." She waved her hand at the glory shining all around. "I also found *this*."

She hurried over to a hunk of yellow crystal the size of a dining table where her pack was hanging up to dry and pulled out a soggy envelope. Its front had water damage but not so much that Rel couldn't read what was written on it when Josie handed it over.

"Is this a last letter from Sam?" she asked nervously, suddenly bashful at the thought of being handed something so intimate, for the note on the front made it seem highly personal.

"Sadly, no," Josie said. "But it is quite the gift. Go on. Open it."

Rel did as she was instructed, carefully peeling the wet envelope away from the mercifully drier paper inside. Drier and thicker, a heavy sheet of official-looking vellum and bearing the raised seal of the Mining Office notary.

Rel's heart began to pound. "Is this...?"

"The claim deed," Josie finished, her brown eyes flashing. "According to that paper, this whole cavern is Sam Price's legal property. His claim stake's right over there."

She pointed at a modified railway stake hammered into a rare patch of bare stone at the base of the falls. It was too far away for Rel to see if its head was stamped with the same number written on the deed, but she felt no need to double-check. It was obvious what had happened.

"He left it here for you," she whispered, feeling unaccountably jealous that Josie had someone who'd put so much thought into her well-being. "He must've driven in the stake when he first discovered this place and then registered the deed with the Mining Office after he got back to town. He had to know the frenzy he'd kick off once the clerks realized just how big and deep a stretch he'd claimed, so Sam brought the deed back into the caves and left it here to keep it safe. *That's* why no one could find this place even after all of your deeds were stolen. It was never there."

"Precisely," Josie said, grinning from ear to ear. "I'm certain that whoever set fire to the Mining Office records room didn't burn their copy of *this* deed, but the location section only says 'Deep Caves,' and we know firsthand now how useless that is. The crystal was the only way to find this place, which is why Uncle took such great pains to hide it where only I would know to look. He set all of it up!"

"And now it's yours," Rel finished, shaking with the possibilities. "Forget restarting Price Mining. There's enough crystal here to buy the whole damn world! What are you going to do with it all?"

"That's what I wanted to talk to you about, actually," Josie said, her face growing serious as she turned to where Mary was still gaping at the crystal pillar. "Miss Good Crow! May I have a word?"

It took a few tries to break Mary out of her giant-crystal-induced stupor, but eventually, the guide scrambled over, her face breaking into a smile when she saw Rel standing. "Well, look who's awake and about! Welcome back to the land of the living, Miss Tyrella!"

That name was so dumb it wasn't even worth getting mad about. "Just keep calling me Rel," she ordered tiredly. "And don't tell nobody."

"Folks wouldn't believe me if I did," Mary assured her, picking up her lantern and carrying it over to set atop the giant yellow crystal where their bags were resting. "Besides, I like that we're all ladies. Makes being trapped down here feel less threatening."

If Mary thought she was safe just because they were the same gender, she was a fool, but Rel kept her mouth shut. She had nothing to prove to Mary Good Crow, and she was too tired to make a good threat right now in any case. Her dad's spooky hooey always got her that way, the damn parasite.

I'm sorry, who was it that saved our lives?

Rel ignored him and focused on lowering herself down next to the big crystal, which was a far less painful process than she'd expected.

I do quality work.

She did roll her eyes then, casting them up to the glittering ceiling a hundred feet above as she eased her buttocks—which, thanks to the use of her jeans to tie her splint, were covered only by a thin pair of wet, summer-weight long johns—down onto the crystal-studded ground. Mary plopped down next to her, leaning her back against the giant crystal boulder like it was a bench. When they were all settled in, Josie moved to stand in front of them, hands folded over her stomach prim and proper as a schoolteacher.

"Thank you both so much for seeing me safe through this journey," she began. "I know it's late and we're all very tired, but if you'll bear with me a moment, there are a few matters that need to be addressed before we sleep."

"'S no trouble, miss," Mary assured her, smiling over at the giant pillar again. "I don't think none of us could sleep in this place. It feels like a big version of how the Medicine Rocks used to be before they plopped a town down on top of them. You know, a sacred place."

That sounded like Injun nonsense to Rel, but Josie bobbed her head. "My feelings precisely. I understand now why my uncle was so determined to hide this place even from his best friend. The famous strikes that kicked off the crystal rush pale in comparison to the riches we now stand beneath. Riches I am quite certain everyone in Medicine Rocks would happily kill me to obtain once word of this place gets out."

That was putting it mildly. Apache had made Rel hang ghosts out to dry over crystal that wouldn't even scratch the boulder they were leaning against. If the Wet Whistle or anyone else in town even got an inkling this place existed, Josie would be dead before the next sunrise.

Not if you do it first, the pistol suggested. *Two quick shots, that's all it would take, and all of this could be—*

Rel snatched the weapon out of its holster and tossed it over her shoulder, throwing the thing all the way back to the base of the misty falls. The distance pained her as much as it did him, but the strain was worth it to get *five damn minutes* alone in her own head.

"Sorry," she said to the others, who were both looking at her like she was nuts. "You were saying you need to keep this place secret. Just how were you planning on doing that? You gonna give up mining like Old Sam did?"

"Of course not," Josie said, waving her hand to bat the ridiculous notion away. "I came down here looking for crystal to save my business and succeeded beyond my wildest expectations. I'm not quitting now when I'm finally ahead."

"Then you've got a problem," Rel said, leaning back against the crystal to ease the pressure of her father's absence. "Doesn't matter how close to the vest you play it. The moment you hire miners to work this place, everyone's gonna know what you found. Hell, the three of us are too many already if you ask me. You and I got history, but Good Crow's a hire. Even if she swears up and down to keep her mouth shut, you really think she's not going to talk?"

"That ain't fair!" Mary said angrily. "I ain't never squealed on none of the claims I've guided!"

"You've never found anything this big," Rel argued. "You were willing to take this job from me blind for only sixty dollars. How do we know you won't sell us out for a hundred?"

"Rel," Josie said. "Stop it."

"It's a fair question," Rel insisted, pointing a finger at Mary, who flinched like it was a gun. "I ain't faulting anyone for looking out for themselves, but you're an idiot if you think you can trust her to keep her mouth shut."

"I could say the same thing about you," Josie replied stiffly. "As you are so fond of telling me, I know nothing about your new life here. I don't know the people you work for or why a hired gun working at a saloon was willing to pay Miss Good Crow sixty dollars out of her own pocket to guide a mining trip she wasn't even profiting off. There are so many reasons none of us can trust the others with so much crystal on the line, which is why I've decided to split my uncle's claim equally between the three of us."

"Say what?" Mary whispered, brown eyes going huge.

"Have you lost your damn mind?" Rel yelled at the same time.

"I assure you I have not," Josie said, leaning down to rummage through her pack. "I realized this problem was coming our first day in the mines and planned several contingencies depending upon what we found, including one for if we found nothing at all. Given the unprecedented scale of wealth in front of us, however, I've decided to go with the most radical."

She removed an oilcloth dry bag from her backpack as she said this, undoing the leather thong to remove three sheets of paper and laying one in front of each of them. Rel snatched her sheet right out of Josie's fingers and read it in an angry rush that quickly turned to bewilderment.

"I'll be damned," she whispered, looking up at Josie. "You're serious about this nonsense."

"As the plague," Josie said, holding up her own paper. "This is a contract I wrote during my shifts on watch. All three copies are identical, transcribed word for word so that all of us have equal proof. Feel free to read them at your leisure, but to sum up: I am proposing a partnership between the three of us. As the only living people in the world who know about this cavern, we will each be given ownership over an equal third. That way, any one of us who betrays the others will be risking her own fortune as well."

"You don't have to do this," Mary said, cringing away from her copy like it was a poison snake. "I already swore I wasn't going to tell nobody."

"And I'm sure you believe that," Josie said gently. "But given the amount of crystal at stake, I'm afraid oaths are not enough."

"But it's your cavern!" Mary insisted. "We're just here doing the jobs you hired us to do. There ain't no need to—"

"There is *every* need," Josie insisted, waving her hand at stones twinkling all around them. "There's enough crystal just in the circle of this lantern to make us all as rich as Rockefeller. With so much wealth on the line, there's no payment I can offer that can beat what others will be willing to pay for knowledge of this place. It's not that I doubt your integrity, Miss Good Crow, but it's just not practical to expect you to turn down a fortune of your own to save mine. No one but a saint could refuse such an opportunity. That's why I'm asking you to join me instead."

"You mean get shot with you," Rel said.

"That's actually the exact situation I'm hoping to avoid," Josie said with a smile. "I'm sure you've heard the saying 'Three can keep a secret if two of them are dead.' But that only applies if there's one prize for three parties. By splitting the crystal equally, up front, I'm hoping to make us allies rather than enemies, and allies are what we'll need if we're to get through this alive. You're right that everyone in Medicine Rocks would happily kill me to get their hands on this place. I know I can't possibly fight the whole town on my own, but if the three of us work together, we might have a chance. It's not just a matter of survival either. I could never have gotten this far without both of you, and I'm a big believer in fair compensation for labor. Uncle might have left this place to Josephine Price, but you've certainly earned your share, so I think it's not just fair but fantastic to welcome the two of you as my partners going forward."

She finished with a brilliant smile, but for all her talk of equality, Josie's eyes were locked on Rel. That made sense, seeing as Reliance was the one most ready and able to kill them and take everything for herself, but Rel had no interest in being the last one standing or in being part owner of a crystal mine. She had to hand it to Josie. The girl had made a good play. Any sane person would've jumped all over her offer, but Rel hadn't been one of those since accepting her father's cursed soul. She had other priorities now, and if Josie lost this place because of it, that was a price Reliance was willing to pay.

Don't be a fool! her father yelled, his voice diminished by distance but still clear in her mind, which meant he must've been putting in a hell of a lot of effort. *Think for a moment before you throw away a share in the discovery of a lifetime! We still have no proof the Wet Whistle even knows the name they've promised you.*

"I sure as shit know I don't have it," Rel whispered back, making a show of reading the contract so the others wouldn't see her muttering.

"But if I come back with news of this place, they'll give me anything I want whether they have it or not."

And how do you think they'll get it? the gun demanded, rattling furiously against the wet stone. *They get their information by spending* crystal. *That's the fuel for all their fires, and if you take the soft-hearted servant girl's offer, you'll have more of that than anyone! Enough to pay off every soul in the Great Plains if you so choose. Do you think your mother's murderer can stay hidden for long under that sort of barrage? Of course not! You're still dancing like a puppet on their strings, but you don't* need *them, Reliance. The power to do everything you've ever dreamed is right here in front of your nose! If you're too pigheaded to see that, then* you're the one who's failed our family, not I.

Rel was shaking by the time he finished and not just because speaking with him from so far away was draining her dry. Maybe she really was being foolish, because for the first time ever, her father sounded like he was speaking sense. She hadn't even considered Josie's offer because she hadn't seen how crystal mining would help her get revenge—and because Josie wasn't the real Josephine Price. No contract she offered, no matter how meticulously written, would ever hold up in court. But there weren't no courts out here, and with the finding crystal broken, the three of them were the only ones who could find this place. Possession being nine-tenths of the law, that made this place Josie's as much as anyone's, and if she was determined to share it, then maybe Rel *didn't* need the Wet Whistle anymore.

She'd had zero luck finding her family's murderer on her own before, but that was back when she'd been broke. Crystal, especially *this much* crystal, could change everything just like her father said. It also meant she could avoid screwing over one of her oldest friends, a relief Rel wasn't too hard-hearted yet to admit she greatly welcomed.

Just because she'd been ready to do whatever was necessary didn't mean she'd been looking forward to it. She *wanted* to see Josie get one over on the Prices. She just hadn't been willing to trade her family's justice for it. Now, though, it was looking like she might be able to have her cake and eat it too. She still wasn't convinced that splitting the fortune would be enough to keep it. There'd be no stopping the violence once the rest of the world realized just how much crystal was down here, but for once, Rel wouldn't have to face those troubles on her own. She'd have partners—allies just like Josie had said—and who knew? With Josie managing the business side, Mary to keep them from getting lost, and Rel shooting everyone who got close, maybe they *could* make this work after all.

Just sign the contract, for pity's sake, her father groaned. *For once in your life, make something other than the worst possible decision.*

"Screw you," she muttered, but she did take Josie's fancy new fountain pen when it was offered, signing her name—her full real name, just in case the law did get involved—at the bottom of her contract. She did the same for Josie's copy, handing hers over so the other girl could put her name on Rel's copy as well. When they turned to sign Mary's contract, though, the girl hadn't even picked up her paper.

"Thank you for my part, Miss Josie," Mary said quietly, keeping her head down. "But with all respect, I must decline."

"Don't be foolish," Rel scolded, knowing full well how foolish that made *her* sound given the past few minutes. "You were jumping for joy when I offered you thirty measly dollars. You find crystal for a living, so you *know* how much this place is worth. A score like this will change your life!"

"You mean end my life," the guide said, lifting her head with a desperate look. "No offense to either of you, but you don't understand. We might all be women, but you're *white* women. When the law gives you things, you get to keep 'em, but that ain't how it is for me. You point at all this money and claim it'll change my life, but I don't want that kind of changing. I don't want another big fat target nailed to my head. Folks hate me enough already on account of my face, but at least there ain't no profit in killing me. If you get your way, though, that'll change. You said yourself, Miss Josie, that the big reason you're splitting this place is because you know folks'll kill for it, but everyone in town wants to snuff me already. If

I take what you're offering, that'll just make me double dead, and I ain't being double dead for no one!"

She shoved the contract back at Josie, moving it with the tips of her bandaged fingers like she was scared that touching the paper would leave some of it on her. "I know you think you're being kind, but this is a cursed gift I can't accept. I'll swear whatever oath you want that I'll keep this place secret, and I'm fine with staying on as your guide, but I'm not taking anything from you except my payment as agreed. Sorry to be a bother, but that's just how it is."

Rel whistled low between her teeth. She hadn't ever considered what Mary's life must be like when she wasn't guiding, but her skittish behavior on the street made a lot more sense now. She didn't know how to force someone to take money they didn't want, though, so that seemed to be that. If Good Crow was still willing to guide, and if they kept a close eye on her to make sure she didn't squeal, Rel didn't see why she and Josie couldn't split the fortune just fine between the two of them. But while the matter felt settled to her, Josie never had known when to leave well enough alone.

"You *have* to take it."

"But I don't want it," Mary insisted.

"You deserve it!" Josie yelled back, looking far more passionate now than she had when she was trying to convince Rel. "Out of all of us, Mary, you've done the most to earn your piece of this place. My only claim is having a loving uncle, and Rel's only here because we dragged her unconscious body down a stream."

"Hey, I did stuff!" Rel said angrily, but Josie rolled right over her.

"The only reason the three of are here and alive to have this conversation is because of *you*! You're the only person I've met who understands the caves the way Uncle Samuel did, and if I'm ever to live up to his legacy, I need you with me. Not as a guide or an employee, but as a partner."

Rel cocked an eyebrow at that, but she saw Josie's reasoning. With the finding stone shattered, Mary was the only person in the world who could get them back here. Josie could find another gunhand anywhere, but Mary was irreplaceable. She'd already said she was willing to keep guiding, though, so Rel didn't see any cause for all this fawning.

You're just jealous she didn't beg you *to stay.*

Rel shot him a rude gesture behind her back and kept her eyes on Josie, who'd grabbed the Indian's hand with all the melodrama of an opera star. "If other people are what you're worried about, I'll stop them," she promised fiercely. "Just as you've protected us from the Whitmans and Bear Woman, I swear I'll keep anyone in town from harming a hair on your head. If Medicine Rocks is savage, then we shall be stronger, and we shall do it together."

That was laying it on a little thick, but Mary looked truly moved. "You'd really do that for me?"

"Of course," Josie assured her with a brilliant smile. "It's the least I could offer after you sang down a bear for me."

Dang, she was good. Even Rel was starting to feel sold now, but Mary just kept shaking her head.

"I'm sorry, Miss Josephine," she whispered, prying her fingers out of Josie's grip. "I'm touched you'd offer to do so much for me. Truly, I am. But this ain't a risk I can afford. I haven't survived two decades by expecting things to change. I know my score, and what you're asking is too much for this body to take."

Rel could see Josie's hopes fading as Mary spoke. Rel was feeling sore about it as well, because the more she thought about their access to this mother lode depending on a timid little guide beholden only by employment, the less she liked it. If they were going to keep this together, *really* keep it, then they needed Mary tied. But how did you put a leash on someone who'd already turned down riches, could vanish into the caves, and had no family you could threaten? It was looking impossible when a brilliant idea popped into Rel's head.

"What if we gave you the pillar?"

"What?" Mary asked weakly, wiping her eyes.

"Josie's contract says we each get a third of the cavern," Rel said, tapping the paper Mary had shoved away. "But it doesn't specify *which* third we have to take. I saw the way you were gawking at that big crystal earlier, so what if you took that as your share?"

"Could I do that?" Mary asked, her voice filling with wonder as she actually pushed past her fear long enough to contemplate the possibilities. "Would I have to mine it?"

"You don't have to do anything you don't care to," Josie said in a rush, casting an amazed look at Rel. "The pillar would be your property to use as you see—"

"So I could keep it exactly as it is?" Mary asked, turning her gaze up to the soaring spire. "I could let it stay that way forever, no matter what you two did with your portions?"

"That's correct," Josie said. "You wouldn't have the same diversity of crystal we'd get from the walls, but—"

"I don't care," Mary said, shaking her head wildly. "The rest of the place was yours already, but if you're really offering me the pillar, that's what I want."

"Done," Josie said, leaning over to add Mary's stipulation as well as her initials beside the change to each copy of the contract. Rel initialed as well, which left all three contracts in a pile in front of Mary.

"Um," she said nervously, tugging at her braids. "What do I do?"

"Read it and sign," Josie prompted.

Mary's braid-tugging intensified. "I can't read that."

"I can read it for you," Josie offered.

"No, no, I trust you," Mary said. "It's just—"

"You should never sign any contract you haven't read, not even from me," Josie said firmly, passing the papers to Rel. "Here, we'll let Reliance read it. That way you'll know I'm not just slipping things in."

"Reliance doesn't want to read it," Rel groused, but Josie was looking at her so desperately. "*Fine*, here we go."

It took forever. Not only was it a full page of the tiniest handwriting possible, every paragraph was a maze of legal language so dense even Rel struggled to read it aloud, and she'd already been through the blasted thing once. The only good she could say about the experience was that at least Mary was a good listener. She let Rel get all the way to the end before asking questions, mostly about the many words she hadn't understood. Explaining all of those took another eternity, but eventually, they got everything sorted. This left only the signature, but here again, Mary paused, moving Josie's fancy pen from one set of fingers to the other as if she'd never held a writing utensil before in her life.

"What's the matter?" Josie asked gently. "Is there still something you don't understand?"

"No, no," Mary said quickly, clearly as unwilling as Rel to go through that again. "It's just..."

"Just what?"

Mary's ears reddened behind her pigtails. "I, um... I don't know how to write my name."

"Oh," Josie said, looking legitimately shocked before she recovered her composure. "That's fine. I'll write it for you, and then you can just copy my letters. Do you know if your last name is one word or two?"

Mary's blank stare was answer enough, and Josie hurried forward. "Let's go with two," she said, pulling a very well-used leather notebook out of her waterproof document bag and flipping through the pages until she found one that wasn't covered in notes to the margins.

"Here we are," she said, borrowing her pen back to write out Mary's name in big block letters. "'Mary Good Crow.' Now you write it."

Mary did her best, sticking out her tongue with effort as she painstakingly copied each letter Josie had made. The result was a wobbling pile of lines that scarcely resembled English, but it got the job done. Mary even looked proud of herself, at least until Josie told her she still had to sign the other two copies.

"Really?" She groaned. "Ain't it enough just to mark mine?"

"We all need our own copy or it's not official," Josie insisted, placing the papers down in front of her. "It won't take long."

It took a damn hour. Long enough that Rel was able to fetch her gun, unpack all their bags, shake out their wet bedrolls, lay everything out to dry, and get a spread of dinner set out on a busted leg before Mary finished, but what else could you expect from someone with no writing and such a long name? Exhausting as it looked, though, Mary didn't rest until she was done, pressing doggedly on until the last tilting *W* was finished.

"Thank the Virgin that's over," she muttered, shaking out her hands. "Now what?"

"*Sleep,*" Rel moaned, stretching out her throbbing leg on top of her damp blanket.

"You two can sleep," Josie said, rising back to her feet. "Now that I've done my best to make sure we don't all die over this, I'm going to look around."

"You've had the same long day as the rest of us," Rel warned. "You should sleep while you can."

"I agree with the gunwoman, Miss Josie," Mary said in a worried voice. "We don't know what all's back there yet, and it's never a good idea to wander the caves on your own."

"I won't stray from the lantern light," Josie promised, scooping up her notebook. "But I've waited too long for a moment like this to waste another second, not even for sleep. You two rest. I'm going to have a look at just how glorious our futures will be."

She's more ambitious than you are, her father observed as Josie made a beeline for the limit of the kerosene's light. *Perhaps I should be her gun instead.*

"I wouldn't wish you on my worst enemy," Rel muttered, but the insult was automatic. All of her actual attention stayed on Josie as she strolled along the edge of the glittering dark.

Chapter 13

It couldn't rightly be said there was a night underground, but that'd never stopped Mary from waking up in the middle of it.

Mostly it was habit. She'd learned never to sleep too long over any given stretch, since disasters tended to pick up steam the more you let 'em stew, but it wasn't fear that woke her tonight. It was something new, like nerves but happier. If she'd had more experience with the feeling, Mary might have called it excitement.

Whatever the sensation was, it drove her from her bedroll like a fire. She must've gotten some sleep at least, 'cause Miss Josie was back from her wandering, snoozing on top of her blanket with her notebook open on her chest. Rel was passed out right beside her, clutching her guns like a baby with a blanket.

Mary stopped a moment to watch them, partially to make sure they really were sleeping but also just to stare. She wasn't green enough to take Miss Josie's earlier promises at face value. People said all kinds of nonsense when they needed something from you, but still… she'd never had someone swear to protect her before.

There'd been a few like Carlo, who'd been happy to slip her things under the table when his boss wasn't looking. Also Oliver, who'd always greeted her kindly. But neither of them would ever stick their necks out for Mary's sake. Nor would she ask them to. They were scrapers same as her: folks doing whatever they needed to survive. They'd never offer to put their own selves between Mary and her troubles like Miss Josie had.

It was the sorta thing heroes did in stories, not real people. The lady was a fancy talker, so it could be Mary'd gotten played, but that didn't stop her from wanting to believe. Between Miss Josie's promises and the pillar, Mary's life felt flipped like a flapjack. She knew it couldn't actually be what it seemed—nothing this good ever was—but that didn't stop her hands from shaking as she eased around the crystal boulder her friends—

her *friends!*—were sleeping beneath and crept through the glittering dark toward the giant white pillar at the heart of it.

Her pillar.

Grinning like a thief who'd gotten away with something big, Mary ran down the slick dip of water-rounded crystals where the spray from the waterfall drifted back into a stream. The light faded quickly as she left the lantern's circle, but that didn't matter to her. She could've danced through the cavern with her eyes closed thanks to all the music the crystals were throwing up, filling the place with chiming like a whole cart full of bells.

She'd never heard caves sing so rich before! Usually, their music was the thin sort, like listening to someone playing the flute through a window. In this place, though, the music felt as close as Mary's own excited breaths, filling her head with blossoming colors that showed her how to wind through the briar patch of six-foot-tall crystal spikes that guarded the pillar's base. Once inside, the music led her to a less stabby, conical formation of dark-green crystals growing over each other in overlapping sheets like the scales on a pine cone. These made for a perfect ladder, giving Mary purchase for her hands and feet all the way up the rounded stone's eight-foot-tall side until she was standing directly before the white pillar's smooth-polished face.

This was the closest she'd gotten yet. Mary'd thought the soaring column was majestic from afar, but the white crystal was even prettier at this distance. Bigger, too, rising up in front of her so smooth and bright, Mary swore she could see it glowing.

"Ain't you the prettiest thing that ever was?" she cooed, reaching out to pet the pillar's pearly stone. "Don't you worry 'bout nothing, beautiful. You're mine now, and I ain't ever gonna let anyone take a chisel to—"

She cut off with a gasp. The moment her fingers touched the glass-smooth surface, music exploded into her head. Not the wandering cave song that went on forever, beautiful but random as chimes in the wind. This was *actual* music. Music Mary recognized.

Frère Jacques, Frère Jacques...

The crystal didn't sing the words, of course, but it scarcely mattered. The tune was obvious. It was the same old children's song Mary had sung to the finding crystal for lack of anything better, though not the whole thing. Surprise had snatched her hand away before the tune could finish. A real pity, 'cause those eight notes were the loveliest things Mary had ever heard. They'd been more than sound, more even than song. Each one had rung inside her body like a golden bell, filling her soul with leaping joy so giddy and bright, Mary nearly knocked herself off her perch atop the pinecone crystal in her rush to hear more.

"Do it again," she whispered, slapping her hands back against the pillar's oddly warm surface. "Sing to me again!"

The crystal obliged, filling Mary once more with the prettiest music ever to grace human ears. She could've sat in it forever, but even the heartbreaking beauty of having music played *through* you couldn't make up for the fact that something wasn't right. Lovely as the pillar's song was, it was incomplete.

Frère Jacques, Frère Jacques, the notes played just like before. But then, *dormez...*

And nothing. The song would just stop without completing the phrase, and not an accidental break, neither. The crystal was clearly waiting for something, holding the silence like a breath before starting again from the top.

Frère Jacques, Frère Jacques, dormez...
Frère Jacques, Frère Jacques, dormez...

Mary listened to the cycle three more times before pulling her hands off the pillar. The music stopped as soon as she stopped touching the crystal, then started over again when she laid her hands back down. Even one finger was enough to send the music pouring into her, but it never went further than those ten notes, setting Mary back on her heels to think the matter through.

She'd never heard crystal sing a tune before. That could be 'cause she'd never found a crystal as big as this one, but Mary felt there was more

218

to it than size. The way the song kept pausing felt like the crystal was waiting for something, maybe even waiting on her. If that really were the case, though, it'd mean the big crystal was trying to communicate, which was ridiculous. It might sing lovely and bright, but crystal was like the sky or the mountains: a part of nature that just was. It couldn't be alive, right?

Frowning, Mary pressed her pointer finger back against the stone, closing her eyes to *really* listen as the incomplete song rolled through her yet again. It was hard not to get caught up in its prettiness, but if she concentrated, she could tell that each round was a little different. These weren't just echoes of the music she'd put in before. The pillar was singing to *her*, and from the way it kept pausing, it wanted Mary to sing as well.

It wouldn't be a difficult thing. Mary knew the next note in the sequence as well as anybody, but she didn't dare let it out, 'cause that was the same note the finding stone had sung. The one she'd sung back to it in the tunnel that'd made the crystal explode.

Just the memory was enough to make her snatch her hand back. It weren't the pain of getting her hands sliced up that she hated. It was the guilt of breaking something lovely, something irreplaceable. The pillar wasn't shining like the crescent had, but them both being the same pearl-white crystal couldn't be coincidence. Mary didn't see any notches in the big crystal's surface where Sam Price could've knocked out a chunk, but she *knew* this had to be where he'd gotten it. What other voice could've led her to this place?

Mary frowned. If the broken finding crystal was the missing piece of the pillar's song, that explained why it was trying to get her to sing. Poor thing must want its note back. Seeing how she was the reason it was gone, Mary would've been happy to give it, but even the thought of singing into and possibly breaking *another* beautiful, irreplaceable crystal was too much to bear.

"I'm sorry," she said, petting the crystal like it was a nosing horse. "But I can't. The last time I sang that note, you—"

The music in her head doubled as she spoke, drowning out the rest of her apology with the pounding refrain.

Frère Jacques, Frère Jacques, dormez—

The song stopped extra sharp this time, shoving the silence at her like a demanding hand, and Mary scowled. "I get it, all right?" she told the pillar. "I know you want your note, but I've done enough damage already. I can't risk shattering you same as I did your littler piece!"

The music huffed at that, and then the sound shifted again, reaching into her with a softer chiming that was almost like normal cave music—but not quite. It wasn't a song like "Frère Jacques," but it also wasn't the random prettiness the rest of the caves sang. If it hadn't been coming from a giant crystal, Mary would've likened it to the hushing noises people made when they were trying to soothe a spooked animal.

That thought moved her to a new perspective. It was clear now that there was more going on with the pillar's sounds than chance and echoes. Something in there was trying to talk to her, and if that was so, then it was rude to treat them like they didn't know what they were about. Yes, she'd shattered the finding stone, but that chip hadn't talked like its bigger piece, and Mary didn't think the pillar would be coaxing her to sing if doing so would cause it harm. She'd trusted the cave music to guide her feet through the darkness these last two years. Why not trust in this as well?

Like it could hear what she was thinking, the pillar played the tune again, singing each note strong and sweet, like it was cheering her on.

Frère Jacques, Frère Jacques, dormez...

"...*vous*," Mary sang back, heart hammering. "*Dormez vous?*"

An explosion of excited sound filled her head, the notes trilling up and down her bones like little fingers before snapping back to the song as they finished the tune together.

"*Sonnez les matines,*" Mary sang with the pillar, rising to her feet as the music swelled like a sunrise. "*Sonnez les matines! Ding ding dong! Ding ding dong!*"

It was such a simple little song, nothing special or wondrous, but each note filled Mary with greater joy than the last. By the time she reached the last *dong* of the morning bells, she was singing with all her might, eyes sparkling as the white stone began to glow beneath her hands. The light started at her fingers and spread rapidly outward, painting the still-healing cuts on her palms as white as winter moonlight.

Mary gawked in wonder. There must still've been some crystal in the cuts from the broken finding stone even after scrubbing them in the stream, 'cause both her hands were sparkling like stardust. The shining got bigger as she watched, spreading down her wrists and up toward her elbows as the music began to swell. It was still beautiful—so much so it made her want to cry—but there was a pressure to the glory now. A weight that pushed inside her skin as the white light crept up her arms.

Her voice began to falter as fear undercut the joy. The light shining through her skin didn't hurt exactly, but neither was it comfortable, and it was spreading fast. Even after the glow went under her sleeves, the light was so bright she could see it shining through all her layers of clothing, forking up her shoulders and across her chest like bolts of lightning. Or cracks in stone. The same sorta cracks that had appeared all over the surface of the finding crystal right before it—

"*No!*"

Mary tore her hands off the pillar with a gasp. The light vanished as soon as she let go, plunging her and the pillar back into darkness. Her night vision was so ruined, she couldn't even see her fingers in front of her face anymore, but that was a relief in itself, 'cause it meant the all glowing cracks were gone. All she felt when she touched her palms was the dull ache of the cuts from earlier, which seemed no better or worse for the experience. Her skull still throbbed with the echo of the music, but her ears heard nothing but the distant roar of the falls and the clatter of her lantern as someone held it aloft.

"*Good Crow!*" Rel bellowed from back at camp. "What was all that racket just now? You all right?"

221

"I'm fine," Mary called back, faking a cough to hide how bad her voice was shaking. "It's nothing. Sorry to wake you."

She wasn't touching the pillar anymore, but just speaking out loud again was enough to make the music stuck inside echo back at her, filling her ears with a soft trill that almost sounded like an apology.

"It's okay," Mary whispered back, though she didn't dare touch its surface again. "Singing with you was beautiful. Sorry I couldn't handle it."

The pillar chimed back something Mary took to mean "I'm sorry, too," though that was likely just her own guilt talking. Even if she'd stopped it to save herself, Mary couldn't help feeling like she'd failed the crystal somehow. She had no idea what all that music was supposed to do, but she was certain the pillar wasn't malicious. Nothing that joyous or lovely could possibly be evil. She just hadn't been strong enough to give it what it needed, but that wasn't a surprise. Mary had never been good enough for anything in her life. Not for the parents who'd abandoned her, not for the Lakota, and apparently not for the lovely crystal pillar, neither.

That was just about the most crushing thought Mary had ever had. She couldn't even bring herself to look at the white stone as she climbed back down the pinecone crystal, so distraught over her own shortcomings that she didn't notice the broken slivers of crystal were still shimmering inside her cut-up hands until much, much later.

~~~

Tragedy of the pillar notwithstanding, the rest of the day went pretty much as usual for a mining trip. Mary didn't often stay with the miners she guided, but sometimes they'd pay her to stick around if they were going really deep. These long trips were how Mary had learned what little she knew about the actual process of mining crystal. It wasn't her favorite thing to watch, but she was happy for any distraction after this morning, and Miss Josie's approach was nothing if not novel.

As so many new miners had learned to their sorrow, crystal wasn't something you could just whack out of the ground like gold or silver. It was easier to find than other precious stones, since clusters tended to grow on top of the rocks rather than buried inside it. But if you broke those formations any way but the right one, the sparkling stones would go dull as coal and lose the miraculous properties that made crystal crystal.

Seeing as Miss Josie had only just ridden in a few days ago, Mary was dreadful worried the lady would make the same costly mistake, but she should've thought better of Sam Price's kin. Even surrounded by enough crystal to make most miners turn rabid, Miss Josie kept her head nailed down tight, taking a full, stone-by-stone inspection of the claim before she even reached for a tool.

She drew as she walked, sketching out a map with all the cavern's major formations noted in different colors of pencil. Mary hadn't known pencils came in colors until she saw Miss Josie use them. It made for a real pretty picture, but the most interesting thing to Mary's eyes was how Miss Josie's drawing matched what she actually saw.

Maps didn't usually make a lick of sense to Mary. She'd always chalked that up to not being able to read, but she could find stuff on Miss Josie's drawing even without knowing what the writing said, so perhaps it was a problem of size. Most maps tried to paint out bigger distances than any person could walk in a year, like the one showing the whole Montana Territory hanging in Sheriff Brightman's office, which Mary hoped never to see again. By contrast, Miss Josie's sketch was sized so that Mary could mark everything on it with her own eyeballs, 'cept she'd drawn it like she was looking down from on top.

Shown from that bird's-eye vantage, the crystal cavern looked like a rattlesnake egg: longer than it was wide and rounded at the edges. At the top end, you had the waterfall with its hanging rope ladder and big crystal boulders like the one they'd made camp beneath the night before. Past that was a slope packed with smaller crystals where all the misting water from the falls came back together to form a creek that ran straight down the cavern's middle.

The water started as a trickle but got wider as it went, tumbling over a jeweler's case of water-rounded crystals before splitting in two to go around the pillar, which was located smack-dab in the cavern's center on a big mound of thorny crystals. The stream came back together once it got past, racing down the steepening hill to fill the clear pond, which took up the cavern's entire rear third.

The water ran quite deep toward the cave's back wall but so clear that Mary could see straight through to the crystals at the bottom. Most of these were clusters of long, spear-like crystals in a pinkish lavender color Miss Josie claimed never to have seen before. Mary'd never met the like, neither, but she weren't surprised when the long spears turned out to be cutting sharp. When Miss Josie reached under the water to touch one, just brushing the edge was enough to nearly slice a chunk out of her finger.

They both agreed to keep away from the water crystals after that, but it made no matter. There was more than enough wild-colored, easier-to-get-at crystal to keep Miss Josie occupied without having to wade into the spike-filled pond. Mary's biggest concern about the pond was flooding. Water levels could change quick underground, and in an enclosed cavern like this, it was always a good idea to know where your drain was. Since the whole place wasn't underwater already, Mary knew the pond had to have an outlet, but she couldn't see it through all the crystal knives.

It was probably just a crack hidden under the rocks, but not knowing where exactly made her feel like she wasn't doing her job as guide, a slight she couldn't stomach after this morning's failure. She tried putting her ear to the ground, but ever since the pillar's music had filled her near to bursting, Mary's ears had been going haywire, multiplying the cavern's already impressive chiming into a roar she couldn't make heads or tails of.

It felt ungrateful to complain about your head being stuffed with the loveliest sound in creation, but all that glorious music made listening for little things like water trickles practically impossible. There was enough high ground that Mary wasn't too worried, but being unable to hear all the details she was used to made her nervous, 'specially since the caves were no longer all she could hear.

Like most of the upsets in her recent life, it had started with Miss Josie. Mary'd been holding the lantern so Miss Josie could see to draw when the lady had suddenly started talking, and Mary'd realized the sound she'd thought was Miss Josie humming to herself wasn't coming from her throat. The soft music continued whether the lady was talking or silent: a faint, barely audible tune that sang from her body the same way the cave music sang from the rocks.

It was powerful strange, so much so that Mary tried to write the whole thing off as an echo at first. Lord knew there was enough crystal here to cause confusion, and she'd never heard cave-type music coming from a person before. It *had* to be her mistake, but the music didn't stop. The sound actually got more noticeable the more Mary tried to ignore it, and it wasn't just Miss Josie. Rel had a sound ringing off her as well, something bigger and sweeter than the sour crystal note she'd always had.

This wasn't to say the sour note was gone. It was bigger just like everything else, grating on Mary's nerves like a metal file whenever Rel got close. Fortunately for Mary's poor ears, the other sounds were even louder.

Not *loud*—even when she was right next to Miss Josie, the music coming off her was never more than humming—but it was definitely a new development, which made it all the odder that the tune sounded so familiar. It wasn't a known song like the pillar's "Frère Jacques"-ing, but that didn't keep Mary from recognizing it as Miss Josie's. Even blindfolded, she was certain she could've picked the music out of a whole mess of notes, following it like a string right back to her friend.

It was plumb unnerving. Mary was used to the caves being strange. Loved it, even, 'cause their scariness was her safety. So long as she could hear what others couldn't, she would always be one step ahead of anyone

225

who wished her harm. But people making noise was a whole 'nother, spookier matter that was far too close to the ghost noises of the Dark for her liking, and why was it happening *now*? Had that business with the pillar this morning broke her ears, or was this the crystal madness coming home to roost at last?

That last one would explain a lot, actually. But whatever was going on, Mary was determined to ignore it. People found her strange enough as was, and while Miss Josie had always been kind enough to overlook Mary's oddities, that could change in a split. If she and Rel started worrying Mary was off her rocker, all those promises about partnership might well fly out the window.

She couldn't let that happen. Mary had already failed her pillar once. She couldn't risk losing her claim on it altogether because her crystal-finding ears were going screwy, so she set herself to acting as normal as possible, humming every song but "Frère Jacques" to help drown out the new music Miss Josie didn't seem able to stop making.

This served well enough during the map drawing. But when Miss Josie set her notebook aside and pulled out the rolled-up piece of leather containing her mining equipment, things took a turn for the stressful.

"Are you going for that one first?" Mary asked in alarm, looking down at the cluster of wide, flat, leaf-green crystals the lady had stopped in front of.

"Yes," Miss Josie said excitedly, unrolling her bundle to reveal a precisely organized assortment of brand-new silver tuning forks, a gleaming brass hammer, and a diamond-sharp steel chisel. "Aren't they lovely?"

They were. Heartbreakingly lovely, like a jewel version of a bright summer fern. It was one of the prettiest clusters Mary'd seen in the cave that wasn't the pillar, and the sight of Miss Josie's chisel gleaming like a butcher knife right next to it was enough to soak Mary's undershirt in a cold sweat.

"You sure you don't want this one instead?" she asked in a rush, moving over to a big knob of the deep-blue crystal every miner seemed to favor. "The sea-colored stones are always surefire sellers, which is more than I can say for the other. I ain't never seen a crystal like that before."

"Neither have I!" Miss Josie cried, pulling off her gloves to run her fingers all over the crystal's leaf-like fronds. "That's why I picked it. I don't even think there is a list price for *green* crystal, which means it'll probably sell for a fortune."

That didn't make any kinda sense. "How do you know what it'll sell for if you've never seen one?"

"Because novelty always sells," Miss Josie assured her. "Part of the value of crystal is discovering new uses. The blue one's already appeared in the papers back east, which makes it a known commodity, but green is *new*. New is always expensive, and since bag space is limited, efficient choices are a must."

Mary's face fell. When she put it that way, it did sound like a good idea, which was why Miss Josie was the businesswoman and not her. Mary still wished she hadn't picked *this* crystal, but then, the thought of taking a chisel to anyplace in the cavern sat like lead in her stomach, so who was she to complain about this one or that? It weren't like she hadn't known this moment was coming. Miss Josie'd always been up front 'bout her intentions, and she'd already been generous as a saint to share her claim.

Just like the others hadn't demanded Mary chop down her pillar, Mary had no right to tell Rel or Miss Josie what to do with their shares of the cavern. Rel was already hacking at her portion, but at least she was off where Mary couldn't see and seemed to be confining herself to the smaller chunks. Miss Josie *would* be the one who went for the big, fancy stuff, but Mary was determined not to say a word of disfavor. Though that didn't keep her from cringing when Miss Josie reached for her hammer.

Here again, she looked astonishingly practiced for someone who'd supposedly never done this before. She tapped her brass hammer against the crystal all over like a seasoned cutter, listening to the notes it gave back for which would make the cleanest break. When she found the best spot, Josie tapped it several more times to get the sound in her ears before turning to select a silver tuning fork from her spread. The first one she picked rang too low, but the next was a near perfect match, vibrating at the same pitch as the crystal when she struck it.

"Right," she said, picking up her chisel at last. "Here we go."

Mary held her breath as she tapped the still-ringing fork against the chisel's gleaming blade. When it started humming with the same note as its target, Miss Josie smacked the chisel's cutting edge against the crystal's base and gave it a sharp tap with her brass hammer, cracking the joint in a clean line so that the whole crystal leaf fell off into her hand.

"Success!" she cried triumphantly, holding up her prize for Mary to see. "A perfect fracture! Not bad for my first time, wouldn't you say?"

She looked so proud of herself, but Mary could scarcely hear her. The moment Miss Josie had broken the crystal, a screech had cleaved through Mary's head. It was still going even now, spreading out through the cavern like a wave. Everywhere it touched, the cave music went sideways, but the worst was when it reached the pillar. That wail hit Mary like a cannon, filling her again with the pillar's music, but it was not the lovely blossom of joy from before. This was a howl of anger and loss strong enough to knock the air from Mary's lungs, sending her flopping over with a gasp.

"Mary!" Miss Josie cried, dropping the crystal to rush to her side. "What's the matter?"

Mary couldn't answer that 'cause she wasn't sure herself. Normally, the cave music only painted pictures in her head. Feeling it in this physical fashion was new and most unwelcome, particularly over something so small. Miss Josie had taken only one piece. That was nothing compared to other groups she'd guided and certainly no cause for such drama. She knew she was being ridiculous, yet Mary couldn't seem to catch her breath. All she could think about was the crystal on the ground beside Miss Josie going quiet, its voice fading from the cavern's chorus, never to be returned.

It was silly to be so upset over such a small loss when she'd been fretting all morning 'bout the cave being too loud. But even now, when things were calming down, the cry still echoed in her bones, leaving Mary in a panic as she tore herself out of Miss Josie's concerned arms.

"I have to go."

"Yes, of course," Miss Josie said, her face full of well-intentioned concern. "Please go lie down. You look dreadful."

Mary felt like she was about to vomit. She took the escape gladly, stumbling back toward the falls in hopes that the roaring water would drown out the music that had scrambled her mind so. Everywhere she went, though, the pillar's weeping followed. And while no outright blame lay in that sad, sad song, that didn't stop Mary from hearing it, feeling more like a failure than ever as she climbed to the top of the waterfall, as far from the vanishing voices of the crystal as she could get.

Chapter 14

Eight hours later—or perhaps more, her pocket watch had been useless since its soaking, so it was impossible to say for sure—Josie had a tarp the size of the Prices' banquet table covered with crystals on the ground in front of her. She could've collected twice as many if she hadn't roved all over, but getting this much back to town would be challenging enough already, and she was very pleased with the variety she'd managed.

Her treasury consisted of seventy-three stones in thirty-four different colors. Every piece was at least three inches in length, the standard minimum for crystals meant to be used whole rather than ground into powder, but several were much longer. One in particular—a lavender spike from the urchin-like clusters under the pool at the cavern's end that she'd drenched her clothing and risked impalement to retrieve—was almost as long as the pickax she hadn't had to use once. Unlike most miners, who had to follow a glimmer to a vein, all the crystal here was just sitting on top of the rock like flowers in a garden bed. Josie hadn't had to dig an inch to reach any of it, though she had indulged in a somewhat foolhardy climb up the wall to take a sample from a lovely bunch of feathery, blushing crystals that had reminded her of a patch of peonies.

In addition to the wilder, unknown colors, she'd also collected a goodly number of old reliables. These were the crystals they were always talking about in the papers, like the big blue one Mary had pointed out, which gave off enough heat to boil water when resonated in the key of C. She'd also found a whole crevice full of the little star-shaped yellow crystals that exploded with ten times the force of nitroglycerin when given an electrical shock.

The known varieties might not have been as exciting as the new ones, but they were guaranteed sellers at the crystal exchanges that had popped up at every major trading town within a hundred miles of Crystal Bend, and they were everywhere here! With just a few hours' work, Josie had collected enough prime cuts to finance a full rebirth of the Price

Mining Company, and that was just selling the reliables. Who knew what astronomical sums the new colors would fetch at auction?

Just imagining the bidding war had Josie rubbing her hands in anticipation. And to think she'd doubted her uncle's love of the caves! Sure, the journey here had been dark and dreadful, but these last few hours more than made up for it. How could you *not* love a place where money literally grew from the ground? Just the sight of it was so dazzling, Josie didn't even notice Reliance approaching until the girl dropped an enormous sack full of her own crystal practically on top of her.

Josie jumped out of the way with a yelp, scrambling sideways to save her toes from being crushed only to stomp right back over again when she saw what manner of crystal Rel had spent her day collecting.

"What is this?" she cried, digging into Rel's sack of pitifully small grayish-pink rocks. "There's nothing but chips in here, and they're *all* dusky rose? That's the cheapest color!" She looked at her friend in horror. "If you needed assistance with mining, you could have asked."

"I didn't 'need assistance,'" Rel sneered, mimicking the refined accent Josie's mother had drilled into her because it was what the Prices expected, a mockery that ironically made her sound much more like the Miss Reliance Josie remembered. "I mined exactly what I intended to mine."

"But—"

"Did you mean what you said last night or not?" Rel snapped. "'Cause if you're going to nitpick what crystals *I* mine from *my* third, us *partners* are gonna have words."

"Fine," Josie said, putting up her hands. "I was only trying to help."

"Unless you're gonna help me haul all this back, keep it to yourself," Rel said, sitting down to rest her injured leg, which had long since come out of the splint but was still clearly paining her. "I might've gone a little overboard, but I figured we could leave some of the food. We supplied for three weeks, but it only took us four days to get here."

"I was planning to leave almost everything," Josie agreed, pointing at the careful pile of wax-wrapped oil cakes, dried beef, bottled kerosene, and other sundries she'd made in the lee of their camping rock. "There's no point leaving behind crystal for things we can easily replace in town, and this will give us an emergency cache for the next time."

"I'm just ready to get gone," Rel said, cramming the food she'd need for the trip back into the pockets of her duster so she wouldn't have to remove any of the crystal from her backpack. "I got a lot of business waiting for me back in town. Where's our guide?"

"I'm not sure," Josie said, lifting the lamp Mary had left with her to peer around the glittering cavern. "She was helping me with my survey earlier, but then she started feeling poorly and went to lie down."

"I hope she's not sick," Rel said anxiously. "We ain't getting out of here without her."

Josie was about to say she was more concerned about their lack of a doctor when a small figure stepped up beside her as quiet as a ghost.

"Oh, *Mary*," Josie said, clutching her chest. "You gave me a fright!"

"She looks a fright," Rel said, scowling at the girl's ashen face. "What the hell went wrong with you? You looked fine this morning."

"I *am* fine," Mary insisted, rubbing her eyes, which were worrisomely red-rimmed.

"You look as if you've been crying," Josie noted, leaning down for a better look. "What—"

"I'm fine, Miss Josie, really," Mary said, ducking out of her scrutiny. "It's just… mining here's been more stressful than I thought."

"But you didn't mine anything," Rel pointed out.

"I still had to listen to it."

Josie supposed mining would sound different to someone who could hear crystal. That said, Uncle Samuel had also heard the caves, and he'd built a crystal mining empire. Personally, Josie had found the *tink tink* of the tuning forks and chisel unexpectedly delightful, like playing the world's most profitable xylophone. Mary clearly did not feel the same way, however. Josie was about to suggest they rest here a while before beginning the journey back to town when the smaller girl picked up her pack.

"We should get moving," she said, carefully avoiding Josie's lavish crystal display. "I'm sure you're anxious to get those to market."

"Should we not have taken so many?" Josie asked with sudden nervousness, wringing her hands as she started mentally sorting her collection for the crystals she could best tolerate leaving behind. "I don't mind bringing back a smaller load if you—"

"Ain't my place to tell you what you should do with your share, miss," Mary said, giving her one of those obviously fake smiles Josie had put on too many times herself to be fooled by now. "You were kind enough to give me the best part of this place, and it ain't like you sprung the chisels on me. I knew what was coming from the start, so if there's anyone in the wrong here, it's me." She started toward the ladder. "I'll be fine once I get a bit of distance. This place is so loud I can't hear myself think."

"Fine by me, but shouldn't you grab a hunk of something 'fore we go?" Rel asked, pushing herself up. "I understand you don't want cutters near your pillar, but with the finding crystal shattered, won't we need something new to lead us back here?"

"I don't need anything," Mary said with absolute certainty, looking at the pillar glittering behind them in the darkness with a strange sort of melancholy on her face. "My ears got opened wide this trip. Not sure if that's a good thing yet or not, but I could find this place a continent away with my eyes closed."

"If you say so," Rel said, hauling her pack stuffed with cheap crystal onto her shoulders. "Lead on."

Mary grabbed the swinging ladder and shimmied up the soaked rungs with her usual squirrelly grace. Josie was still wringing her hands over how sad the girl had looked when Rel touched her elbow.

"Leave it be."

"But she's upset."

Rel shrugged. "She's a Sioux raised by Catholics. You'd be hard-pressed to find anyone touchier when it comes to sacred shit, and we just spent six hours digging up the crystal she reveres. Of *course* she's not gonna be happy, but so long as she isn't getting in our way about it, it ain't our problem. Just let her be. She already said she'd get over it."

"I don't want her to have to 'get over it,'" Josie snapped. "We're supposed to be doing this *together*. We can't have a good partnership if one-third of us is miserable."

"She just told you she'll be fine," Rel reminded her, walking over to the swinging ladder. "Another part of good partnership is taking your partners at their word."

"But—"

"It ain't your job to fix everyone's problems, Josie," her friend said, using her arms to spare her injured leg as she hauled herself up the falls.

Josie stood clenching her jaw for a good five minutes while Rel hobbled up the rungs. When this ire brought her nothing, she raised the white flag and got back to her own business. Kneeling in the circle of Mary's lantern, Josie pulled the still-damp wad of packing cotton carried from the bottom of her pack and began tearing off chunks, wrapping the crystals one by one. When every jewel had been swaddled to her satisfaction, she stuffed them impatiently—but carefully!—into her backpack, filling the canvas satchel to the seams before the growing feelings of guilt could convince her to leave anything else behind.

~~~

The trip through the Deep Caves was much easier going out than it had been going in. The tunnels had once again changed their guise, replacing the round, black-scaled corridors where the Whitman and his dog-man had attacked them with a lovely passage of multicolored stone that gleamed like a rainbow in the light of Mary's lantern. It was the sort of wonder her uncle's letters had been full of, and if everyone hadn't been in such a dark mood, Josie might have actually enjoyed the walk. It was nice to see that the caves could be something other than damp and terrifying, and there wasn't a Whitman to be seen! Alas, even cheery colors couldn't lift the pall hanging over Mary as she led them silently through the maze back to the squeeze.

That part was *exactly* as awful as Josie remembered. Worse, actually, because unlike packed food, crystal did not squish down to fit through the crack in the cliff that was their only way back. They ended up having to make trips to get everything through, dragging the blanket-wrapped crystal like tails behind them as they crawled on their bellies through the crevice.

The process took so long they were forced to make camp when they finished, which meant they ended up sleeping by the black lake after all. Not that Josie raised a word of complaint. She'd learned her lesson about putting off sleep, and after their run-in with the Whitmans, Bear Woman no longer seemed so terrifying. At least she attacked for understandable reasons like hating dynamite, not bells and excrement prophesies and all the rest of the bandit's madness.

It probably should have been worrisome that the bar had fallen so low, but at least now Josie understood how everyone in Medicine Rocks had gotten so blasé. It was hard to get worked up over any one specific thing when you were assaulted by existential threats on an hourly basis. But numbness could be just as important a survival mechanism as alertness, so Josie embraced hers wholeheartedly, keeping her eyes on her feet this time and not the black water or the old dark blood that was still visible on the rocks as they walked back to the gap in the cliff that would return them to the Main Gallery.

At least Mary was starting to perk up again. As soon as they reentered the familiar Midway Tunnels, her cheerful demeanor returned just like she'd said. It was such a relief, especially since Reliance seemed to be going downhill.

Not that she'd ever been chatty, but Josie had thought her old friend was warming up. Once they started running into other miners on the Main Gallery Trail again, though, Rel had slid back into the worst of her new behavior, speaking only in monosyllabic grunts, snarling at everyone they passed, and muttering to herself with her hand locked onto the grip of her crystal gun. If she hadn't been the one pushing hardest on them to make good time, Josie would have said the girl was terrified to go back to town.

Her demeanor did wonders for their pace, at least. Josie had been worried the heavy packs of crystal would slow them down and make them targets, but the crowds on the Main Gallery Trail scarcely looked at Rel before jumping out of her way. They still had to camp in the middle, but the next day, they made it to the start of the Dark with hours yet to spare before evening. But while Rel seemed intent on pushing through, Mary put her foot down.

"Absolutely not," she said, crossing her arms over her chest. "The Dark takes the better part of a day even when nothing goes wrong. If we go in now, we'll end up having to make camp inside, and ain't no one thinks that's a good idea."

"I can get us through," Rel growled, clutching her gun like a cliff edge. "We can walk overnight and sleep in a bed back in town tomorrow. I know Josie would prefer that."

"I absolutely would *not*," Josie said, moving to stand next to Mary. "I know you don't think much of my grit, but I've spent a week of nights sleeping on stone already. I'll happily weather one more if it means we don't have to trudge through the worst bit of this entire journey exhausted."

"Why are you in such a durn hurry anyway?" Mary asked suspiciously. "No one's stupid enough to try robbing us after the way you've been terrifying everyone. Medicine Rocks'll still be there whether we make it by morning or afternoon, so why don't we take a breather?" She pointed at a blackened crack in the roof of the wide cavern where

236

they'd stopped. "This is one of the only camps this far in with a smoke draw, and I've still got a little wood left. We could have a fire and eat a hot meal for once. Wouldn't that be nice?"

"'Nice' ain't a word that applies down here," Rel snapped. But for all her talk of pushing on, she must not have been willing to do so alone, because when Mary started placing her few sticks of cherished firewood in the sooty ring of stones, Rel plopped herself down, stretching her leg out in front of her with a grimace.

"You really should take it easier," Josie advised, sitting down beside her. "I don't know how you managed such a miraculous recovery, but it won't keep up if you keep abusing your leg like that."

"My leg's my own business."

"It's all of our business if you lame yourself and we have to carry you out," Josie argued, passing Rel her canteen. "What are you in such a rush to get back to, anyway? When we left Medicine Rocks a week ago, you couldn't wait to leave."

"Things are different now," Rel said when she'd finished chugging Josie's water. "Being in the mining business is old hat for you, but it's a big change for the rest of us. I got a lot of people who ain't going to be happy 'bout my change in profession. I've already figured out what I'm gonna tell 'em, but it'll be a hard sell, and every hour I make them wait only makes it harder."

"I see," Josie said with a smile. "You're nervous."

"Damn straight I'm nervous," Rel said, looking much more like the uncertain girl Josie remembered as she handed the canteen back. "But I'll get it done. This is just more of the same thing I've been doing since the day Momma and Chase died."

"What's that?"

"Whatever I have to," Reliance replied, tipping her hat down over her eyes as she lay back to get some sleep.

Per Rel's insistence, they got moving again the moment everyone was awake. In a stroke of luck—good or bad, Josie wasn't sure—a large group that had passed them by while they were setting up camp the night before came back out of the Dark just as Mary was preparing to lead them in. Apparently, they'd been trying to do as Rel had wanted and push through the night when they'd been ambushed by Whitmans.

"Whitmans?" Rel said, her already pale face turning the color of new cheese. "What the hell are Whitmans doing in the Dark? That's practically in town!"

"Dunno," said one of the miners, who was nursing a broken ankle from the mad dash back through the darkness. "But there're heaps of the bastards."

"They weren't heading for town," another put in. "The ones I heard moving were crawling all over the side tunnels like they were looking for something."

Josie's blood ran cold as she remembered the bodies that she'd helped Mary lift onto the shelf running along the top of the Dark's tunnels. "Could it be corpses?"

"Could well be, miss," the miner said, looking as spooked as Josie felt. "Those mad-eyed Whitmans do like their dead, and a lotta stiffs get dumped in the Dark."

"I never thought of them being taken," Mary whispered, crossing herself with an expression of pure guilt. "Did you see them taking bodies down?"

"'Course not!" the man spat, his voice taking on an entirely different tone than when he'd been addressing Josie. "It's the goddamn Dark! We didn't see shit."

"Don't yell at her," Josie snapped. "Mary's the one who bandaged your ankle, remember?"

The miner was already opening his mouth to defend his right to yell at other races, so Josie glared at him harder until he thought better of it.

"Whatever," he grumbled, looking away. "Don't make no difference what those madmen are doing. Can't nobody get through the Dark until they're finished. They even chased the robbers out."

"Guess even a Whitman's good for something, then," Rel said, checking her guns. "But we can't sit around waiting on them."

"You're dead if you go in there, son," warned one of the miners who hadn't spoken yet, keeping a wary eye on Rel as he wiped the blood off his shirtfront with a shaking hand. "Even the cavalry runs when they see Whitmans."

"Good thing I ain't cavalry, then," Rel said, picking up her pack and digging out the flask Josie strongly suspected contained crystal. "I know a thing or two about the Dark, and we got us a good guide. We can avoid them."

"You sure?" Mary whispered, looking nervously at the wall of blackness a dozen feet down the tunnel that marked the beginning of the Dark. "I appreciate the vote of confidence, but—"

"We don't have any more time to waste," Rel said sternly, pocketing her flask before sliding the backpack back onto her shoulders. "The moment you're done patching up these fools to appease your cave code, we're going."

That shouldn't have been her call to make, but neither Mary nor Josie was willing to argue when Rel looked that determined. Josie was also desperate to get back to the sunlight in any case. They'd been down here a full week now, and since she'd prioritized crystal over food, they didn't have enough supplies to wait another day. Surely the Dark could hide them from the Whitmans as well as it hid everything else.

That was her hope, anyway. Josie was confident in her friends' skills, but of all the horrors of the caves, the Whitmans were the one she felt least confident facing again. She still hadn't forgotten the terror from her first trip into the Dark, and those had been rank amateurs. The Whitmans were a whole different species of criminal.

Thinking about that would only make her more nervous, though. Time was slipping fast through their fingers, so Josie assisted Mary in getting the injured miners back to the camping spot to fulfill the girl's compulsion to help. When that was settled, she grabbed her pack and hurried back to Rel, who was already swigging from her flask as she led the way into the Dark.

Like the squeeze, this part of the journey was also just as awful as Josie remembered. The Dark remained blinding and terrible, full of horrifying sounds and flickering phantom images conjured up by her blinded eyes, but at least her fears of Whitmans didn't materialize. Josie didn't know how Rel was doing it, but the girl cut them a bandit-free path, even advising Mary where to turn when the guide would have taken the straight.

The roundabout trail made the journey even longer than usual, and Josie was worried about how often she smelled whiskey on Rel's breath even through the numbing effect of the Dark. Still, she couldn't argue with the result when, nearly ten hours after they'd started, Rel led them unmolested and unrobbed back into the perfectly normal darkness of the Front Caves.

"Well, that was exhausting," Josie said, flopping against the wall as Mary relit her lantern. "Shall we take a breather before we tackle the final leg back to town?"

"You two can," Rel said, turning away from Josie to wipe something off her mouth that looked worrisomely like blood. "I gotta keep moving."

"Are you all right?"

"I will be," Rel said, dropping her now obviously empty flask back into the pocket of her duster. "And the sooner I get this done, the more all right I'll be. I'll meet you back at Price Mining when I'm finished. Just do me a favor and watch out at the tax table."

"Okay, but what am I watching out for?"

"Taxes."

Josie had a good laugh at that before she realized her friend wasn't joking.

"I'm not committing tax fraud, Rel."

"Everyone else does," Rel argued, crossing her arms over her chest. "It's just greed for most, but in our case, it's a tactical issue. If you roll up to that table with a bursting bag full of crystal no one's ever seen, the whole town's gonna know you hit it big."

"That's inevitable," Josie argued. "The secret's going to be out the moment I start spending crystal, and not paying my taxes will give those who don't like my presence here a legal avenue of attack."

"The law don't matter out here."

"It matters to me," Josie said angrily. "You might not respect it, but the law has been my greatest weapon. Everything I am in this place is due solely to the fact that Samuel bequeathed his property to Josephine Price. My position is not yet so sturdy that I can afford to undermine myself by breaking the very laws that lifted me up. I'm sure Sheriff Brightman would love nothing more than to arrest me for tax fraud and seize my assets, so I'll be paying what I owe down to the penny. And seeing as you're also part owner of a long-term asset now, I strongly suggest that you do the same."

"Suggestion noted," Rel said, turning her back on Josie to haul her pack of cheap crystal down the tunnel only to stop again a few steps later. "One more question."

Josie rolled her eyes. "Does this also involve lawbreaking?"

Rel chuckled and beckoned her over. Confused, Josie approached. Mary tried to join them as well but backed off instantly when Rel glared.

"That was uncalled for," Josie whispered as Rel pulled her farther down the tunnel. "Mary's part of our team, too. She's also the one holding the lantern."

"I got a light of my own," Rel said, striking a match to light a tiny candle box she'd pulled from somewhere in her too-big coat. "And I thought you'd prefer if I asked this away from prying ears."

Now Josie was deeply curious. "Asked what?"

Given that she'd been the one in the hurry, it took Reliance a remarkably long time to get to the next part.

"All those letters Josephine used to send us like clockwork after we left Boston," she said at last, her blue eyes looking strangely timid in the flickering light. "You wrote them, didn't you?"

Josie went still. "What makes you say that?"

"I recognized your handwriting from the contracts."

"Oh," she said, shoulders slumping. "I suppose my secret's out, then."

"I should've known it was you from the start," Rel said. "Even my mother used to comment how much nicer Miss Josephine was in writing than in person."

"I never intended to deceive you," Josie said in a rush. "But I hated the thought of you being all alone out there, and Miss Price was always so busy that—"

Rel snorted. "Busy doing what? Buying every godawful dress in Boston just so no one else could wear them?"

Josie shrugged helplessly at the harsh truth of that, but Rel waved it away.

"You don't have to defend her to me. I also grew up with Josephine, and I'm not going to rat you out for sending letters in her name. I just wanted to know if the things you wrote us were your own words or stuff the Prices told you to say."

"They were mine," Josie said, twisting her fingers. "I know it was presumptuous, but I didn't want you to feel forgotten."

"I didn't," Rel said, reaching out to squeeze Josie's shoulder before turning back down the tunnel. "That's all I wanted to know. Have fun getting your stuff searched."

Josie was desperate to say something, but Rel vanished around the corner before she could think of what. She was still staring after her when Mary came over with the lantern, looking more nervous than ever.

"I hope you won't take this the wrong way, miss," she whispered. "But mean as she was being about it, Miss Rel did have a point. Even if we lie and say they're from one of Price Mining's other claims, if you dump a bag of never-before-seen crystals on the tax table, we're gonna have a scene."

"Don't worry, I already have a plan to deal with that," Josie said confidently, delighted to move on to a less personal topic. "I will simply open my bag and pay what they ask, and if anyone challenges me on where the crystal came from, I'll tell them the claim's on file at the Mining Office. If they say they can't check because the office burned down, I'll remind them that the only reason I don't have proof of that is because our company was robbed, and since Sheriff Brightman has so far failed to recover our stolen items, they may direct all complaints to him."

Mary looked impressed. "Can you really do that? Shovel it off on the sheriff, I mean?"

"I have no idea," Josie said blithely. "But as Uncle Samuel liked to say, 'if you can't be fair, be frightening.' My aim is to make my situation appear so vastly complicated no one will want to prod it, especially since we're going to be *paying* our taxes. My bet is that the cavalry will be so thrilled they're actually getting crystal without a fight for once, they'll let us go through, no questions asked. And if that doesn't work, I'll appeal the whole thing and kick the can down the bureaucratic road to a time when I can deal with it with more resources, such as the money from selling all this crystal."

That plan sounded marvelous to Josie. Mary looked less convinced, but she didn't take the argument further as they made their way back through the labyrinth of blasted sandstone tunnels. Josie was silently rehearsing the final version of precisely what she meant to say to the soldiers when they turned the final corner and came upon the tax table at last.

The very empty tax table.

"Where is everyone?" Josie said, looking around in confusion. "There should be at least two soldiers posted here at all times, shouldn't there?"

"They must've gotten called off," Mary said, looking *much* happier now that the whole tax problem appeared to be moot. "That happens sometimes when they're moving troops around. Remember the big army that rode out the morning we left? Maybe they called for reinforcements."

The explanation seemed as plausible as any, but the unmanned table gave Josie a bad feeling. One that only got worse as they ducked under the stone lip that marked the caves' exit and stepped out into the cool breeze of a beautiful summer evening filled with hordes of men running toward the mines as if fleeing for their lives.

"What in the world is going on?" Josie demanded, pulling Mary quickly to the side before the mob trampled them. When no one in the rushing crowd stopped to answer, Josie reached out and snagged one of the running men by the sleeve.

"The hell you doing, woman?" he demanded, snatching his coat out of her hand.

"*Trying* to ask you a question," Josie said back just as angrily. "What's happened here? First the tax table was empty, and now you lot are running into the caves like rats off a sinking ship. Whatever is the matter? Is the town burning down?"

"It's worse than that," the man said, taking off his hat to wipe his profusely sweating brow. "A cavalry soldier just rode his horse to death in the middle of Main Street shouting 'bout how the Sioux done slaughtered our entire army! All the other soldiers ran off to carry him to the fort, so there must be some truth to it. Now everyone with sense is getting down to the tunnels to mine what they can 'fore the redskins arrive to kill us all."

That explained the stampede, but "Why would the Sioux be coming here?"

"'Cause here's where the crystal is!" the man shouted, too flustered to notice Mary hiding in Josie's shadow. "From what the soldier was shouting when they carried him off, crystal's how the savages did it. Seems the Injuns got crystal arrows and a whole mess of other bullshit now. Medicine Rocks is the only place where crystal's mined, so o'course they'd come at us. That's why I'm doing like everyone else and getting my share 'fore they get here. Now get outta my way!"

Sensing that she clearly wouldn't get any more blood from this stone, Josie stepped aside to let the red-faced man resume his panicked race into the tunnel. When he'd vanished back into the stream of such fear-driven foolery, Josie turned back to Mary.

"Do you think he's right?"

"I can't begin to say, miss," the guide replied in a tiny voice, sticking so close to Josie that she could feel the girl shaking even through Mary's multiple layers of coats. "But if you're all right from here, I'd best be getting back into the caves myself. I don't think it's safe for someone with my skin to be in Medicine Rocks right now."

"I think it'd be far less safe in the caves," Josie countered, nodding at the mob pouring past them. "That's where everyone's going."

"Yeah, but I know how to hide in there," Mary said, though she sounded much less sure of herself than usual, and Josie smiled.

"Mary," she said gently, crouching down to look the cowering girl in the face. "How would you feel about staying with me?"

"With you?" Mary said, wide-eyed. "Oh no, miss, I couldn't. I wouldn't want to impose."

"It'd be no imposition," Josie assured her. "I'd actually feel better if you came back with me as my guest. The Price Mining office is much too big for just Mihir and me, and it'll be easier to keep my promises from under my own roof."

If Mary's eyes were big before, they were absolutely huge now. "You mean you really meant that stuff from before? About not letting people get at me?"

"Like gospel."

"Even with folks so riled?"

"That's the most important time," Josie told her solemnly. "A promise that's only good when things are easy is worthless, but I meant every word I said to you in that cave. Even if you don't believe me, you signed my contract, which makes you so much more than my friend. You're my business partner now, Miss Mary Good Crow, and a Price *always* takes care of her business."

She finished with her very best smile, but Mary didn't reply. She just stood there with her shoulders hunching farther and farther up toward her ears, staring at Josie as if she were afraid the world would end if she said yes.

"Come on," Josie said, putting out her hand. "Let's go home."

Timid as a newborn kitten, Mary took her scarred, trembling hand out of the folds of her poncho. Josie waited until the girl's fingers reached all the way around her palm before closing her own around them, giving Mary every chance to escape as she led her up the hill toward the Price Mining building where Mihir was already coming down the steps to welcome them home.

Chapter 15

"The *entire* 7th Cavalry?"

Lucas set aside the cane he'd been using since Dr. Pendleton had taken out the crystal pins, ignoring the pain shooting up his only mostly-healed leg as he crouched down to speak with the exhausted soldier face-to-face. "You are the only survivor of Custer's entire company?"

"Yes, Lieutenant," the rifleman panted, attempting to wipe the dried blood from his face with his equally bloody sleeve. "Rode my poor horse to death to bring the word. They got us, sir. They got us all."

"How is that possible?" General Cook demanded, still in his shirtsleeves with a napkin tucked into his collar after being rousted so suddenly from dinner. "Custer led six hundred and eighty experienced soldiers against an encampment of squaws and babies. How the devil did he *lose*?"

"That's what the scouts reported, sir, but it ain't what was there," the soldier said. "The lieutenant colonel had us riding hell for leather to get to Little Big Horn 'fore the redskins caught wind of our intent. Lot of our horses went lame in the process, so my troop fell back to secure 'em. By the time we caught back up with the main army, the whole plains was boiling with Sioux. There were *thousands* of 'em, sir! My troop couldn't even get close, so Major Reno ordered us up to a nearby hill to see if we could offer cover fire. By the time we got in position, the whole 7th Cavalry was already being massacred. The Indians just swarmed 'em under."

"So it was numbers that did us in?" Cook asked.

The rifleman shook his head violently. "It weren't just that, General, sir. It's true there were a lot more redskins than the scouts said there'd be, particularly warriors. But they weren't the biggest problem."

"Then what was?"

It was the obvious question, but it still took the rattled soldier a long while to answer. "They weren't normal Indians, sir," he said at last, his eyes getting that long, empty stare you saw only after truly awful battles.

"I've shot plenty of Sioux in my time, but these weren't savages with bows and a few old rifles. This was an army, and they had…. *things.*"

"What things?" Lucas prompted gently.

"Unnatural things," the soldier said, his voice shaking like the grass. "They had arrows with crystal points that hit like cannons, and the warriors had crystal paint all over their bodies that made 'em damn near bulletproof. I got one of 'em straight in the chest—I *know* I did—but the shot bounced right off. And they had wolves!"

Cook looked dubious. "You mean like the animals?"

The man nodded frantically. "Aye, sir! Great huge bastards bigger than any wild wolf I've ever seen, and they spoke like men. I swear I heard 'em talking Indian to each other as they drove our boys into a knot so the bows could pelt 'em better, but the worst were the gray hairs in the back. I didn't spy 'em proper until we got on the hill, but there was all these old men singing and drumming 'cross the river from our position. Major Reno told us not to bother with 'em. Native superstition, he said. Focus on the warriors. But then all the old men finished their singing and raised their hands together, and a wind like a twister blew across the battlefield. It didn't touch the Sioux, but our troops got flattened right off their horses. Once they were down, the Sioux rode in and trampled our boys under. The gust hit our position next. Blew me into a tree half a mile away. By the time I climbed down and ran back, everyone else was dead."

"Damn," the general muttered, pulling the napkin off his neck at last. "And you're *certain* this is what happened?"

"I swear to God, sir!" the soldier cried. "I know it sounds crazy, but I swear that's what I saw! Custer's army didn't die just 'cause we were outnumbered. They had us out-everything-ed! We could've fielded every man in this fort, and I still don't think we'd have survived."

He was sobbing by the time he finished, his exhausted body falling to pieces now that he'd finally done his duty and delivered the message. Lucas knew the feeling well, and since the general had already turned away to glower at the map table, he went ahead and rose creaking back to his feet, calling in a soldier from the room outside to take the weeping rifleman to the infirmary.

"That damn cocky fool," Cook said the moment the door was shut again. "Why the hell didn't he turn back when he saw their numbers?"

There was only one person the general could be talking about, and it wasn't the rifleman. "I think you just answered your own question, sir," Lucas said, taking a seat to rest his throbbing leg, which hadn't been nearly as ready for all that crouching down as he'd hoped. "Custer didn't turn back *because* he's a cocky fool. He must have still thought he could win."

"Then he's an even bigger idiot than I gave him credit for," the general said, sinking onto his own stool. "But the biggest idiot is me for letting him go. I knew there was a chance the Sioux were already using the weapons you saw in the caves, but I figured we could get ahead of it with a surprise attack. That, and I was so damn *tired* of listening to him rant about redskins. I thought if I let him get the killing out of his system, he'd get off my back for a spell and kick the Sioux down a few pegs in the process. I never imagined he'd lose a whole damn company!"

There was nothing Lucas could say at this point that wouldn't sound like "I told you so," which was not a wise position to take with your commanding officer. Cook already knew in any case, which explained what happened next.

"All right, Jean-Jacques," he said with a sigh. "What do you think we should do from here?"

Lucas blinked in surprise. "Me, sir?"

"You were the one who pegged this crystal mess from the start," Cook said with a shrug. "If I'd listened to you, the 7th Cavalry would still be alive. I'm not a man who looks to make the same mistakes twice, so how do you read the situation?"

Lucas frowned. He'd been under the general's direct command for more than a year now, but Cook had never said anything like this before. Strategic decisions weren't usually a lieutenant's business, but since he'd asked...

"I'd say our next move depends on the Sioux," he said, scooting his stool over to the table to grab the map of eastern Montana and the one of western Dakota that together showed their current theatre of war. "We don't yet know if Custer rode into a trap or if he really did catch them by surprise and simply couldn't handle what he caught. Either way, the Lakota will be emboldened by this victory. I am certain they will go on the attack and soon, before we can reinforce. My only question is where."

"Normally, I'd say the Black Hills," the general said, circling his finger around the dense cluster of gold mining settlements covering that portion of Dakota. "That's always been the Lakota's biggest bone of contention. It's supposedly some kind of sacred place, their 'center of the world' or some such. The Department of the Interior's been trying to buy the land from them ever since gold was discovered there, but the red bastards won't sell for love or money. They won't stop killing our miners and settlers who've moved in chasing the rush, either, which is the whole reason we're in these Indian Wars. We've stayed on top thus far through superior arms, but now that they know they can beat us, they'll beeline straight for Deadwood."

Those were Lucas's thoughts as well, but even though the general was the one who'd put it forward, Cook didn't look settled on the idea.

"That's what I would've said two weeks ago, anyway," the old man muttered. "But I'm no longer so sure. Crystal is changing things faster than any of us can keep up, and we *still* don't know how they're getting into the mines."

"My guess is they have an entrance somewhere around here," Lucas said, running his hand in a wide sweep east of Medicine Rocks. "That's the direction most agree the caves run in, though who can say for certain with ground that moves itself? The only way to know for sure is to track them through the caves, which we don't have the manpower for. That said, I don't think we'll have to go looking for them. If crystal really is to be the deciding factor in this war, then the enemy's best move is to cut off our supply before we can acquire crystal weapons of our own. That's what I'd do."

"I was thinking the same thing," the general agreed, tapping his finger on the little illustration of a mining pick that marked their own position. "I'll send riders to Fort Abraham Lincoln and the gold mining towns just in case, but Sitting Bull would be a fool not to turn this momentum at us. We're America's only source of crystal, *and* he knows we just lost a good chunk of our soldiers. He's never had a better time or reason to attack."

"But he might not have the means to pursue it," Lucas said hopefully. "The Lakota make up the largest share of the Sioux, but they are still just a confederation of tribes who did not always get along before this conflict forced them together."

"They seem to be getting along well enough now," Cook said, rising from his seat. "Until we hear otherwise, we have to assume that army is headed our way, so I'm calling everyone in, even the scouts."

Lucas scowled. "How will we know the enemy's position without scouts?"

"If they are as many redskins as we think, it should be pretty obvious," Cook replied grimly. "I don't like it anymore than you do, but we *cannot* lose this position. If the Sioux take the mines, everything we came out here for is lost, which is why I want every able body we've got defending them. I just hope Avery hasn't gotten too far north with the crystal yet."

"You're calling back the shipment?" Lucas grimaced. "Captain Townsend won't like that."

"Captain Townsend can stuff his hat," Cook said with a snort. "I need those men more than Washington needs fancy rocks. Custer's loss has put us in a tight position, but if we can get Avery and his boys back here, we should have just enough soldiers to hold under our cannons until reinforcements arrive from Fort Lincoln."

Lucas saw the logic, but this plan of Cook's still didn't sit well with him. The general's strategy made good use of Fort Grant's fortified position, but no defense lasted forever. He especially didn't like their odds if the rifleman was right about the Sioux using crystal to bounce bullets. There *had* to be something else they could do besides just defending—a way to shift the situation closer to their favor. He was still chewing on the matter when someone knocked frantically on the meeting room door.

Cook was opening his mouth to bid them enter when Captain Townsend burst into the room. "The crystal shipment's been ambushed!"

"Say again?" the general demanded.

"A rider just came in from Colonel Avery's detachment," Townsend reported in a pinched, too-high voice. "They were attacked on the plains four days north of us."

"Was it the Sioux?" Lucas asked.

Townsend shook his head. "Bandits. Whitmans, specifically."

"Like hell it was!" General Cook shouted. "We've never had whisper of a Whitman that far north, and I sent Avery with a hundred men. There's no way those thieves could've had something ready. Where's your witness?"

"Fainted in the infirmary," Townsend said. "You're welcome to question him again when he wakes up, but it won't make a difference. The crystal's gone, Colonel Avery's dead, and his detachment was decimated. The survivors continued to Fort Buford since it was less distance to carry on than turn around. Only one rider was sent back to bring us the news."

General Cook stared at Townsend for a long moment. Then he began to curse in a foul and creative manner that Lucas had never heard the old soldier driven to before.

"All right," he said when his tirade was finished. "How many men have we got who *aren't* dead?"

"Five hundred from the 10th plus Townsend's infantry for a total of thirteen hundred," Lucas answered promptly. "We've also got another hundred horse-hands, cooks, and other base workers who can be armed in a pinch."

"I'd say we're pinched," Cook replied, rubbing a hand over his face. "Give them guns and get them into the training yard. I want every man in this fortress ready to defend the walls at a moment's notice."

"You can't do that!" Townsend cried, his fear-paled cheeks turning scarlet. "Those criminals took our crystal! We have to go after them!"

"Not possible," the general said. "I don't know if you've heard the panic, but it's likely we're about to be up to our ears in Sioux. If you ever want to see crystal again, I suggest you forget about what's already lost and start whipping your infantry into a shape that can hold this position."

"But we can't just let them take it," Townsend pleaded, looking truly desperate now. "I was sent here specifically to make sure the crystal got through! If I can't even manage one shipment, my career is over!"

"That's not my problem."

"What about the town?" Townsend asked, trying another angle. "The miners never seem to have crystal when they're at the tax table, but I've seen how they spend when they get to the bars and bawdy houses. Their constant and blatant tax dodging has left us bankrupt, but I'm sure the local businesses have crystal in plenty. We can commandeer some of that and try again! With the armored wagons, this time."

"*I am never using those idiot wagons!*" Cook yelled. "And I'm not taking crystal from the townsfolk, either. The citizens of Medicine Rocks are violent, greedy, gun-toting menaces who outnumber us ten to one. I can't protect this place if I've got to worry about my own people shooting me in the back, particularly since the townsfolk are better at crystal than we are. Have you seen the stuff the Wet Whistle gunhands are packing? Puts those crystal rifles you're so proud of to shame. Frankly, I'd rather fight the Sioux's giant wolves."

Townsend's furious face grew bewildered. "Giant wolves?"

"You're just going to have to wait," Cook told him. "It's not like a few more weeks will make any difference in the long run. Even if I got a cart of crystal on the train tomorrow, we wouldn't see any more guns or whatever else your boys in Washington are cooking up until next Christmas at the earliest. That's the reality out here, so stop trying to move mountains and go roust your infantry, because they're joining the colored boys of the 10th for defense drills starting tonight."

Joint drills were a move Lucas had been pushing for months, but he was too upset to enjoy the victory. He was certain his men would mount a valiant defense with or without the general's training, but what was the point if their guns were useless? Even the general's rant about the Wet Whistle reminded Lucas of how powerless he'd felt the last time he'd been called in to help keep the peace in town. Tyrel Reiner and that bastard Apache Jake had gunned down eight of his soldiers before he could blink. That was what happened when those with crystal met those without, and the more he thought about that, the more frustrated he became.

"I think Townsend may be right."

"What?" Cook said.

"You do?" Townsend asked at the same time.

"Not about chasing after the stolen crystal," Lucas clarified. "It's far too late for that. But I agree we should look into other means of obtaining crystal for ourselves. Custer lost because he was outnumbered and because the enemy had crystal that rendered his attacks useless and destroyed his defenses. That's no different from our situation right now, so why should we expect a different outcome?"

"Because we have cannons," Cook reminded him angrily.

"We have *twenty-two* cannons," Lucas corrected. "And they can only shoot when the enemy is inside their firing range. That's not going to be enough to hold this place if the Sioux are using crystal to bounce our bullets. They're just going to get in under the guns and bring down our walls while we waste our ammunition firing shots that don't work!"

"What would you have us do, then?" the general demanded. "Shoot ourselves and save them the trouble?"

"I'm *saying* we can't just hide behind our walls and hope for the best. If we're going to have a real chance at winning, we need to fight crystal with crystal."

The general looked appalled at that idea, but he must have been serious about listening, because all he said was, "And how do you suggest we do that?"

"By making crystal weapons of our own," Lucas answered, smiling at Townsend. "We already have proof of concept. Townsend's crystal rifles are based on standard-issue trapdoor Springfields. If we can get the crystal, what's stopping us from modifying the guns we already have in the same fashion?"

"We can't make crystal rifles *here*," Townsend cried. "This is a frontier outpost! We don't have the proper tools or facilities—"

"Neither do the Sioux, and they managed well enough," Lucas reminded him. "The same goes for the gunmen here in town. Last I heard, the Wet Whistle whorehouse didn't have a weapons factory, but they still managed to arm their people so well that even General Cook does not wish to fight them. Why can't we do the same for ourselves? We've got a smithy and a quartermaster who repairs our guns all the time. Their work might not be as fancy as the stuff from the factories, but it *has* to be better than going into battle with weapons we already know are not sufficient."

"Be that as it may," Townsend said stiffly, "it still won't work because the cavalry is forbidden from keeping crystal for its own purposes. All crystal collected under the Mining Office's tax is property of the federal government and *must* be sent back to Washington. It's the law!"

"I'm aware of my legal responsibilities, Captain," General Cook told him peevishly. "But I also know that President Grant would shoot me personally if I lost this base because I was following the law, so I'm game to take my chances." He turned back to Lucas. "How do you propose we get this crystal?"

"It's not going to be popular," Lucas warned. "If Custer's rifleman hadn't just ridden his horse to death in the middle of town screaming about Indians, I don't think it'd even be possible. With everyone so scared, though, we may have a chance."

"Oh *no*," Townsend groaned. "You're going to suggest something illegal, aren't you?"

"You're welcome to leave the room if you don't want to be party," Cook offered, waving the nervous man away as he sat back down on his stool and leaned toward Lucas. "What've you got in mind?"

Chapter 16

Unlike everything else in the crystal warren, the entrance to the Wet Whistle's smuggling tunnel was always right where Rel remembered. It wasn't even hard to find thanks to all the footprints making a trail through the dust into what was supposed to be a dead-end cavern one turn ahead of the damn tax table. That it hadn't been blocked up yet was plain stupid, but if the cavalry didn't care enough to look under their own noses—or had been too well paid off, more likely—that wasn't Rel's business. She was just happy it didn't require any more squeezing or darkness. All she had to do was push aside the stiff sheet of burlap covered in mud to make it look like another piece of the wall, and she was walking into a rough-cut tunnel wide enough to push a cart down, which they did on occasion.

Have you figured out what you're going to say yet?

Rel had something in mind. Whether they'd buy it was another question.

Would you like me to help?

"Not in a million years," she said with a snort. "Every time you offer to 'help,' I end up with another hook in my mouth."

What a charming metaphor.

"Just hush up and let me work," Rel ordered, double-checking her bulging backpack to make sure all the tiny crystal chips were still inside. "This is liable to get dicey."

The crystal gun settled grumpily into its holster as Rel came to a stop in front of the water-stained wood door that connected the smuggling tunnel to the lowest level of the Wet Whistle Saloon. She hadn't even gotten her fist up to knock when the door was opened by Felix, the Wet Whistle's counting man. And behind him, looming like a grinning specter, was Apache.

"Rel Reiner," he said, giving her the most charming smile the Devil ever put on a man's face. "Just the someone I was hoping to see."

257

Rel didn't bother asking how he knew she was coming. She just ducked her head and hurried inside, remembering to slouch at the last second. Being around Josie had brought back all her old habits of good posture and such, which was dangerous. Being five foot five made it hard enough to pass as a grown man already. If she started high-stepping like a show pony, the jig was gonna be up quick. Even if this was her final turn into the Wet Whistle, Rel intended to keep her cover to the end, lurching inside with a tilt and a swagger she hoped was the picture of a man who'd worked himself haggard.

Not much of a stretch. You always look haggard.

"You wanna do this here or upstairs?" Rel asked as Apache closed the door behind her. "'Cause I'd like to get the reporting portion over as soon as possible. The Dark was rotten with Whitmans. I had to chug crystal every step to sneak by, and now my stomach's cut to scraps."

She hacked up a little blood to prove her story, which wasn't actually a story at all. She truly was done to death on that score, but the bleeding was a small price to pay for avoiding the army of flickering shapes she'd spied through the Dark's twisting walls. It'd taken her whole flask plus some homemade dust she'd ground while Josie and Mary were yakking to keep her eyes bright all the way through. Rel was certain that choice was gonna have very real lasting effects, but despite her sob story and pitiable display, Apache shook his head.

"I'm not the one whose ears you'll be bending tonight," he said, handing Rel his handkerchief. "Boss wants to see you personally."

He put a hand on Rel's shoulder as he finished, just in case she was stupid enough to run. She must've been a little, 'cause the thought of bolting did occur. But Rel held the deadly impulse at bay, flashing him a big, fake smile of her own.

"Then show me to her."

He smiled back and pushed her forward, steering Rel ahead of him as they climbed the ladder up from the deep basement to the still-underground floor where she'd interrogated the dead miner what felt like years ago. This was where the Wet Whistle did most of its dirty business, so Rel hoped that would be the end, but Apache kept pushing, directing her down the long, smoky hallway to the cellar stair that led up to the saloon.

The place was in fine form tonight. Whatever panic had sent all those men scurrying into the caves clearly wasn't dinging business at the Wet Whistle. The tables were packed with miners playing cards while rouged-up women hung on their shoulders, encouraging them to bet high. The bar was similarly crammed in, though Rel couldn't fathom why. Everyone knew the booze here was overpriced and watered to shit. Not even miners were desperate enough to waste crystal on that slop, but the bar had the best view of the stage, which was the real reason most of these men were here.

Miss Shandy was up there right now, singing her conniving little heart out while removing her lace gloves so slowly you'd need a ruler to see the progress. The con was obvious, but that didn't stop the men at the bar from hollering and throwing crystal into the bucket at her feet. This was partially because they were horny idiots, but they also weren't entirely in their right minds. In addition to Miss Shandy's beckoning, Clink was also up there playing his piano like he was trying to beat it to death.

Rel winced when she spied him, stepping as far away from the stage as she could without looking like she was trying to duck Apache's grip. Of all the dangerous things in the room, the skinny pianist was hands down the scariest. Officially, he was nothing but a part-time ivory tickler. But while Apache doled out everyone else's crystal in tiny sachets, the bottle on top of Clink's piano was always full of shimmering, crystal-mixed spirits.

He was flying high on the stuff tonight, pounding the keys in a raucous melody that contained more than just music. It bubbled into Rel's brain like champagne, driving her toward all sorts of reckless, dangerous thoughts. Fortunately, she knew what he was doing, so she was able to resist, but the rest of the room had no such protection. They were deep in his spell, betting higher and spending more than they ever would without Clink's crystal-fueled tune egging them on. Even the girls weren't spared, driven by the music into promising wilder delights at higher prices than they'd ever have dared in silence.

What an elegant and sophisticated establishment you've joined, her father observed, turning in his holster. *Look over there! I do believe that woman is sticking a shot of crystal up her—*

Rel gave the crystal gun a smack, earning herself a warning *tsk* from Apache, which was unnerving 'cause he typically gave you just one. Luckily, they were already at the next set of stairs leading up to the building's second floor. This staircase was much wider and grander than the basement's wooden ladders, but it was harder to ascend since it was crammed full of men anxiously waiting their turn for the Wet Whistle's actual main attraction: prostitution.

I'm just glad your mother isn't alive to see this, her father said as Rel shoved her way through the eager crowd. *Her heart would break if she knew how low you'd sunk.*

Gritting her teeth at the presumption of a man who'd abandoned his wife and children in a stranger's house for over a decade daring to put words in her mother's mouth, Rel slapped the gun again, silencing his voice so she could focus on not tripping over stairs she could barely see in the red lantern light. At the top was a landing where a pair of black-clad gunmen were letting men through one at a time into a garishly papered hallway filled with closed doors and theatrical moans. The gunmen tipped their hats to Apache as he came up, shoving the horny crowd aside to make room for their boss as he walked Rel around the corner and up a final, much narrower flight to their final destination: the iron-banded door that guarded the Wet Whistle's topmost story.

"And here we are," Apache said, opening the door with a key from his pocket to release a blast of smoky, furnace-hot air straight into Rel's face.

She covered her mouth at the assault, hacking more blood into her palms as Apache pushed her inside. Good Lord, she'd forgotten how choking it was up here. Even in high summer, the madam of the Wet Whistle kept her potbelly stove going full blast. This plus her distrust of windows and preference for living at the top of a giant, crowded building meant her rooms were always an inferno, and her decorative choices didn't help.

The parlor Apache walked Rel into looked like a storage room from an insane old lady's European castle. There were rugs piled on top of rugs under velvet sofas and gold-tacked settees crammed in so close together, you couldn't actually sit on them. The walls were papered in an eye-bleeding red, purple, and gold *fleur de lis* pattern, which was fortunately visible only in slivers between the rest of the decorations, which mostly consisted of taxidermy heads.

Every savage animal in the Americas was on display. They had moose, boar, mountain lion, even a full-sized bear, all stuffed with their claws up and their sharp-toothed mouths open. All those fangs hanging so close together made for an intimidating sight, but the most worrisome thing in the room by far was the man guarding the door at the parlor's opposite end.

"Evening, Casper," Apache said cheerfully, inclining his head a fraction.

The other man nodded back but said nothing, which was typical. Rel didn't know if Casper *could* speak, for his face was covered neck to scalp in bandages. His hands and neck were similarly wrapped, giving him the appearance of a leper. He didn't stink like a leper, at least, but it was still unnerving to be trapped in the stuffy parlor with the likes of him, and that wasn't even counting the old elephant gun he wore strapped across his back like a spear.

Rel didn't know why he carried such a useless antique. The gun was a slow muzzleloader and way too big to use in close quarters, but it was pointless to ask since Casper wouldn't answer. Rel wasn't even sure he could see her through all the bandages until Casper pointed straight at her face and then the door behind him, indicating impatiently that she was to go inside.

"Have fun," Apache said, walking back to the stairs so fast, it could've been argued he was running. "Remember not to be an idiot."

Rel flashed him an annoyed look and slouched forward, doing her best not to flinch as Casper removed the two normal pistols from her belt, though not the crystal one. She was curious why he didn't touch her father's weapon, but again, no point in asking. All she could do was stand there, tapping her boot impatiently as he placed her weapons on the ivory-inlaid table beside him and motioned for her to go ahead.

She did so with difficulty. The office door was made of the same heavy logs as the building's exterior. Pushing it open took the whole of her strength. Casper closed it behind her with one hand, leaving Rel alone with the woman she'd met only once before. The head of the Wet Whistle empire, the one they all called "boss." Rel had never heard anyone use her proper name, but the people who didn't work for her called her Volchitsa, which Rel's no-good father had condescendingly explained was Russian for "she-wolf."

Rel didn't know if that was the whole of it or if the word had other, less flattering connotations, but Volchitsa had clearly embraced the name. Her attic office—windowless, of course, because why would Volchitsa ever give her enemies an open shot?—was a vaulted wooden fortress dripping with gold plate, crystal, and the stuffed heads of wolves.

There must've been twenty of the poor animals hanging all the way up the walls to the peaked ceiling. Volchitsa also had a full-body specimen on the dresser behind her desk. That one was the most lifelike, its stuffed head turned so that its yellow-glass eyes stared down whoever was foolish enough to enter the abode of its killer, for Volchitsa loved to hunt. Rumor had it she'd personally shot every animal on display in her rooms plus countless more besides and slept in a nest of their pelts.

Rel didn't know about that last part, but there was no question Volchitsa had enough furs to cover every bed in the building if she wanted.

They were everywhere up here, stacked in piles in the corners or lying across the furniture. She had a big white one draped across the back of her throne-like chair, framing her sharp, scowling face in a halo of predatory fur.

Just looking at all that hair sent sweat rolling down Rel's cheeks. The heat was even worse in here from the iron stove going like a broiler in the corner. But despite being buried in animal skins, Volchitsa didn't look flushed in the slightest. Her skin was pale and powdery and her brow free of sweat, all while she was buttoned up to the chin in a man's full hunter-green suit and wool overcoat—fur-lined, of course.

Her braided hair had long since lost its color, turning that flat pewter color that happened when blonds lost their shine. Her face was still sharp with only the faintest hint of crow's feet, though, making her actual age difficult to guess. Her watchful eyes were blue and narrow, the left one drooping slightly thanks to a pale knife scar that ran all the way down that side of her face. Her fingers, wrists, and neck were decorated with what had to be pounds of jewelry rumored to be her inheritance as the disgraced daughter of a Russian prince, though Reliance had also heard she was a Cossack who'd fled to America after murdering her local lord.

Honestly, both stories sounded equally implausible, but it didn't really mater. Whatever she'd been before, she was Volchitsa now. The wealthiest, most dangerous person in Medicine Rocks and the one Rel would have to fool if she ever hoped to see another sunrise.

"Ah, Reiner," Volchitsa said in an accented voice so sharp and cold, it cut clean through the suffocating hell she'd made of her rooms. "You look filthy."

"I just came out of the caves ten minutes ago, ma'am," Rel reported, holding her mud-caked duster still to keep from shedding any more dirt on the gold-stitched carpet. "I could go back down and bathe if you'd rather—"

"It was an observation, not an order," Volchitsa said, steepling her fingers as she leaned back into her throne of fur. "Sit."

That *was* an order, and it got Rel's back up something fierce, but now was not the time for pride. She needed to play this carefuller than anything else in her life, so she forced a smile and removed her heavy pack to lower herself onto the intricately carved wooden chair with the even more intricately embroidered cushion.

"Not that one."

Rel's head snapped up to see the She-Wolf glowering at her. "You'll get it filthy too," Volchitsa explained. "Do you know how difficult it is to clean needlework in this wilderness? Use the stool in the corner. That's what it's for."

Biting her tongue against everything she so desperately wanted to say to that, Rel fetched the wooden folding stool, snapping it open and setting it down in front of the hard-to-clean masterpiece. This put her knees practically inside Volchitsa's desk, but Rel wasn't totally cowed. If the wolf woman had a problem, she could damn well not set fancy chairs no one in Medicine Rocks was clean enough to sit on in the middle of her damn office.

"So," Volchitsa said, packing a wad of tobacco as well as a pinch of crystal into the bowl of her long-handled ivory pipe. "Did you accomplish what was asked?"

"Yes and no," Rel said, clutching the stool to steady her nerves. Here went nothing. "As I'm sure Apache told you already, I couldn't convince Miss Price to sell here in town. She'd gotten it into her head that Sam Price really had left her a treasure in those mines, and she weren't letting go of it for any sum. I couldn't get her to listen to any sort of reason, so I played along with her delusions and took her down into the mines thinking they'd scare the stupid out of her."

"That much I know already," Volchitsa said, blowing a plume of smoke into the air as if the room wasn't suffocating enough already. "But it doesn't take eight days to frighten a fresh-wooled lamb. You *did* find something, didn't you? Tell me, and be specific."

264

"I can do better than telling," Rel said, reaching for the pack she'd been carrying on her back like a snail shell. She tipped it out on top of Volchitsa's desk, pouring the crystal chips from on high so that they went spilling over the edges onto the carpet.

"*That's* what we found," she said when the bag was empty. "A giant strike of the shittiest crystal you can mine."

Volchitsa picked up one of the larger pink stones, which was still smaller than a dime. "You're saying it was all rose?"

"Every bit," Rel said, plopping back down on her stool. "Don't get me wrong, there's an impressive amount of it, but the whole vein's locked up in these tiny petal formations. That pile's all first picks, but you still won't find a crystal in there that's bigger than your thumbnail."

"I see," Volchitsa said, sweeping the stones away to clear a spot to rest her elbows. "And how did Price's heir react? Was she disappointed?"

Rel snorted. "No. Josephine has a virtuoso talent for sucking up to rich relatives, but she doesn't know crystal from crab apples. She was jumping around clapping her hands at how much there was without a glimmer of understanding that not all pretty rocks are worth the same."

"And did you educate her?"

"Of course not. I got myself hired to bodyguard, not guide. Why should I ruin her fun? 'Specially since she was paying me so much for it."

The lies rolled easily off her tongue, but Rel was sweating harder than ever, and this time, it had nothing to do with the heat. There'd be no supporting this story once Josie started spending her crystal, but Rel didn't need the fib to hold forever. She just needed Volchitsa to believe that Sam Price's legendary final find was nothing but a larger-than-normal rose vein long enough for the three of them to get established. Once Price Mining had gunmen and money of their own, the Wet Whistle wouldn't be a threat to them, or at least not an unmanageable one.

And free yourself, the gun reminded her. *We can't adequately exploit our newfound crystal if you're still leashed to this place.*

Rel was getting to that, but there was a pace to these things. The Wet Whistle had taught her the best way to lose a mark was to rush them, so Rel bided her time, doing her best to look tired and put out—neither of which required much acting—as Volchitsa threaded her long fingers through the pile of low-grade stones.

"This is most unfortunate," she said at last, taking a long draw off her pipe as she looked Rel over. "But why did you feel it necessary to bring this pile of worthless crystal to me? Why not just tell me the claim was poor and save yourself the effort of hauling it? Unless you were afraid I wouldn't believe you."

"That didn't cross my mind at all," Rel lied, keeping her breathing steady as a drum. "I brought this to give to you as compensation, because I intend to leave your employment."

Volchitsa's silver eyebrows shot up to her hair. "And why would you want to do that?"

"Because I'm tired," Rel said, slumping into the stool in an effort to look like someone who'd hit her end. "I came into Medicine Rocks on fire to catch my family's killer, but that was nearly half a year ago now. Getting back together with Josephine reminded me there's more to life than getting even. For example, the king's ransom she's offering to pay me if I help her play miner. Babysitting a rich girl ain't the most glorious gig, but it's a damn sight better than killing myself chasing down a murderer who could be anywhere on the continent by now. I know you've already laid down a good bit of crystal on my behalf. I like to think I've given you good work in return for that, but I'm not any closer to catching my man, and I'm tired of shitting glass. My only aim now is to humor Miss Price enough that she gives me a ride back east in her fancy carriage when she finally realizes what a crap claim she's got. But I didn't want to leave you hanging after you invested so much in me, so I brought you as much of her crystal as I could. I know it ain't great quality, but there's thirty pounds of it, so I figure that makes us even."

That sounded like a believable burnout story. Rel had thought long and hard to make it so, but she wasn't sure if it had worked. Volchitsa's face was hard to read, her long, pale nails tapping against the mountain of low-grade crystal on her table.

"Let me be sure I have this straight," she said at last. "You're bribing me to leave my employment so you can go and swindle Josephine Price instead?"

"I wouldn't have said 'swindle,'" Rel hedged. "But that's the gist of it, yes."

Volchitsa leaned on her elbows, pipe dangling from her colorless lips. "And you expect me to believe that?"

"It's the truth! What's so hard to believe about me not wanting to risk my neck doing your dirty business when Price'll pay me four times as much to sit on my ass?"

"Oh, I believe you are greedy," Volchitsa said. "It's everything else that I don't buy. You might be familiar with the Price family, but I knew Sam. Not as a living man. He wanted nothing to do with me then. But I've become quite well acquainted with his business methods since his death, and I know he wouldn't deign to look at a rose vein like the one you describe, let alone stop and claim it, so try me again."

Rage washed over Rel like a grass fire. "It was you," she said, clenching her fists. "*You're* the ones who smashed up the Price Mining Office. You stole all their deeds!"

"You say this as if you expect a confession," Volchitsa said idly, blowing a puff of smoke in Rel's face. "But I've said nothing anyone with ears wouldn't be able to piece together. All of Price Mining knew Sam was a fool for his niece. He used to set company policy using her letters, and since I pay attention to what men say when they're drunk, I feel confident that the Josephine Price who sent her uncle formulas predicting which color of crystal would become the next best seller based off stock reports from the *New York Times* is not an ignorant ninny who'd celebrate a low-value strike no matter how big it was. My only question to you, Rel

267

Reiner, is just how much crystal did you find down there that you were willing to come here and lie about it to my face?"

"It ain't a lie," Rel said stubbornly, sticking to her story because what else could she do? "Maybe I overstated how little it was worth, but there really ain't anything down there that's worth fighting over. You've got all of Sam Price's other claims. Leave us this one. If nothing else, it'll keep Josephine out of your hair."

"I'm not worried about a too-smart rich girl being 'in my hair,'" Volchitsa said, poking her pipe at Rel. "But I do begin to worry about you. I never would have thought you'd give up avenging your family for crystal. What happened to your dedication?"

"Ain't a person allowed to change their mind?" Rel cried, wrapping herself in self-righteousness. "You sent me to convince Miss Price because our families were friends, but being around her is what reminded me I didn't always live like this! I don't have to be… to be…"

"Like us?" Volchitsa supplied.

"Yes," Rel said, going on the offensive. "You're right that Josephine's no fool, but she *did* offer me a job, and she *is* my friend. Enough of one to remind me that my family wouldn't want me to kill myself avenging them. They'd want me to live and be happy, so that's what I plan to do, and you got no right to stop me. Even if it's only rose, that's still enough crystal to pay back what I drank from your stash twice over. Not that I should have to pay back anything since I took it doing your work, but I didn't want you saying I cheated you. Hell, if anyone's getting cheated here, it's me! I slaved for you for months, and you never even gave me a lead. But I'm done dancing on your string. I'm done with it all!"

That was supposed to be the final word, but Volchitsa just chuckled, sending long ribbons of pipe smoke up to join the haze as she shook her head.

"See, that's the part of all of this I believe least," she said. "You will never be done with me, because I don't buy for a moment that you've given up on your revenge, and I still have what you want."

268

Rel wasn't falling for that line again. "Sorry," she said, standing up. "But unless you're ready to cough up a name right now, we got nothing to—"

"His first name is Victor."

Rel froze. The gun at her side went still as well, an odd sensation since Rel hadn't realized how much he'd been moving in his holster until he stopped.

"What did you say?"

"You heard me," Volchitsa replied with a toothy smile, looking more and more like her namesake animal with every second. "I know who killed your family. I know where he is. I can even take you to him if you like."

Rel's hands began to shake. "You're bluffing."

"I don't bluff," she said, settling more comfortably into her chair just in time for Rel to lurch forward, sending crystal flying as she slammed her hands on the desk.

"You're saying you knew where that murderer was this whole time, and you didn't *tell me?*"

"Why would I do that?" Volchitsa asked, blowing smoke at Rel's face until she backed off with a cough. "Finding that man is what kept you working for me. If I told you what I knew, you'd go kill him, and I'd lose my ghost talker."

Rel couldn't believe what she was hearing. "You led me on!"

Volchitsa laughed at her good for that one. "Oh, child, what business do you think I'm in?"

"I ain't one of your whores!"

"Of course not. They're much more reasonable. But it is time for you to stop lying, Reliance Reiner."

Rel froze again. "How do you know that name?"

"The same way I know the name of your murderer," Volchitsa replied. "Because knowing is my business. The business *you* came to me seeking, so I suggest you think long and hard about what you can offer, because this name isn't going cheap."

Rel dropped back onto her stool as the gun at her hip started vibrating.

Don't even think about it, her father snapped. *She's just playing you again.*

"I can't not think about it," Rel whispered, not even caring if Volchitsa overheard. "She's got me."

She's got nothing! It was a lucky guess.

"How do you know she guessed it right?"

The gun had nothing to say to that, and Rel's fists clenched to bloodless balls. "You told me you didn't know who shot you! You said he was a stranger! *How do you know she's right about his name?*"

That doesn't matter now! The only thing you should care about is how this harpy is exploiting your anger to steal our crystal!

"It ain't your crystal!" Rel shouted, whipping her head back to Volchitsa, who was watching the one-sided exchange with great interest. "What do you want?"

"Same thing I've always wanted," she replied. "Price Mining. All of it, including legal ownership of Sam Price's final claim, which means the deed."

Rel shook her head. "I can't. Josie'll never give it up."

"So it's 'Josie' now?" Volchitsa said with a bloodless smile. "Well, then, I suggest you use that camaraderie to convince her otherwise."

Rel was opening her mouth to say it wasn't that simple when Volchitsa raised her finger.

"Think about your next words carefully," she advised, setting down her pipe. "I used to wonder why you were so obsessed with finding the man who shot your family. I've met plenty of revenge-mad killers in my time, but you didn't fit the type. Plenty self-destructive, you had that, but on the whole, you were too pragmatic for someone intent on throwing their life away over something that couldn't be changed. Then I figured it out. Your father was a necromancer, wasn't he?"

I don't answer to that ignorant name.

"Filthy business, necromancy," Volchitsa went on. "Say what you will about whoring. At least it serves a natural drive. But there's nothing natural about what Bernard Reiner did, is there? Raising the dead. Making them dance like puppets."

Volchitsa paused to see if her words got a reaction, but Rel just clung to her stool tighter than ever, so the She-Wolf continued.

"They say the place where a necromancer practices becomes poisoned over time. Crops fail, water fouls, animals miscarry and die. People die, too, but they don't move on. Just like in the Dark, their souls get stuck. With no body to support it and no way to move on, the spirit collapses in on itself, becoming little more than a mad shadow. Suffering, tortured echoes of their former selves, screaming forever for a salvation that will never come." She leaned across the crystal-covered table, getting so close that Rel could smell the smoke on her breath. "Tell me, Reliance. How many souls are screaming for you?"

Rel jerked back so fast the stool went flying. She didn't want to remember, but there was no stopping it now. Their voices were still in her head. Always in her head, even when she shoved them away. She hadn't even touched a piece of crystal yet back then, but that didn't stop her from seeing them bright as candles: Mama and Chase, floating over their dead bodies, screaming for her to help them. Fix them. *Save* them.

But Rel couldn't. She'd tried and tried for days. She'd even listened to her father and helped bind him inside that thrice-cursed gun in the hope that he could do something from there, but he couldn't. Nothing could unstick them. Nothing but this.

"I need that bastard in my hands," Rel told Volchitsa through clenched teeth. "The only way to free a fettered soul is to give them justice, so I'm going to drag that murdering son of a bitch back to what he did and slit his throat over their graves. Only then will my family be at peace. You have to *give me that name.*"

"I will give it to you when you've earned it," Volchitsa said, waving her away. "The man you seek is a powerful and useful ally. If I'm going to betray him, you're going to have to make it *very* worth my while. We'll start with full ownership of Price Mining and Josephine Price on a carriage back to Boston, and I think I want the one who led you to the claim as well. Even if we know where we're heading, the Deep Caves can be vexing. It'll be much easier to move my people if we have someone who already knows the way. What guide were you using?"

Rel took a shaking breath. Betraying Josie was bad enough, but she didn't know if she had it in her to throw Mary to the wolf as well. Before she could make up her mind, though, Volchitsa rose to her feet.

"Never mind the name," she said, checking her gold-and-crystal pocket watch. "Just bring the guide and everything else to me. Once I've assessed the value of this claim for myself, we'll discuss if it's enough to earn your reward. Now get out of my office. I have other business to attend to tonight."

Rel tried to get another word in, but Casper had already opened the door behind her. Unwilling to fight two monsters at once, Rel stumbled out of the office, leaving the pink crystals scattered all over Volchitsa's desk like a wagonload of rose petals. She was so numb from what had just happened that she didn't even notice her father yelling at her until she was halfway down the stairs.

You can't do this! he roared through her skull. *That cavern is priceless! It's not just a vast hoard of wealth and power. It's a unique formation that could be the key to understanding the mechanisms that created crystal in the first place! I will not let you trade all that potential to save two people who are already* dead!

"You don't get to tell me what to do anymore," Rel whispered, gripping her aching stomach. "You're dead, too, old man. I'm the only Reiner still alive enough to get a say, and I swore I'd do whatever it took to end the hell you trapped us in."

But this won't do what you want! Reiner cried. *That's what I've been trying to tell you since we left that gaudy office! Killing a murderer to free his victims only works on vengeful souls who cling to this world out of their own*

272

misguided anger, but your mother was the sweetest little fool to ever draw breath, and her son was just as bad. If you were the one he'd murdered, it'd be another matter, but do you really think those two innocents would delay their eternal reward for petty revenge?

"Of course not," Rel snapped. "I told you that at the time, and *you* said there wasn't any other way!"

I said what you needed to hear. You'd been starving yourself moping over their graves for nearly a week. If I hadn't given you a goal, something concrete you could work toward, you'd have joined them, and then we'd all be stuck screaming in the middle of nowhere.

Rel stopped midstep. "So you lied to me."

Everything I told you was factually accurate. It's not my fault you were too emotionally distraught to realize the difference between a soul holding on out of anger and one that's been trapped against its will. Seeing as the mistake was actively saving you from guilting yourself into an early grave, I saw no reason to correct the error, but that's no longer true. It's time to stop being a fool and accept reality.

"For what?" Rel shouted, not even caring who heard her screaming at her pistol. "If killing that man won't free their souls, what was all this even for?"

Crystal, he replied, his ghostly voice trembling with want. *That cavern of Sam's is worth more than that greedy serving girl could ever imagine. Letting her mine it for cash would be like stripping the Sistine Chapel for the marble. The third she already gave us is a good start, but we should be planning how we can get control of all of it, not taking orders from a glorified pimp. There is a power trapped inside those caves greater than any this world has ever known. We can make it ours together, but you have to let go of the past. Stop living beneath the yoke of what cannot be changed and start looking forward to what* can!

By the time he finished, his voice was loud enough to shake Rel's skull. She hadn't known he had the strength to do something like that, but it didn't change her answer in the slightest.

"No."
What?

"No," Rel said again, squeezing the gun's bone-inlaid handle until the pins squeaked. "I'm not listening to another thing you say, you lying *bastard.*"

I expected that, he said with a sigh. *You always were a slave to your emotions. But if you can stop playing the victim for two seconds and* think, *you'll realize what I'm saying works in your favor. If killing that man won't free your family, then Volchitsa has nothing she can hold over you. You can leave this place without betraying anyone, walk right back to your little servant friend, and—*

"What part of 'no' did you not understand?" Rel snarled. "You talk a lot of bullshit for a man with no mouth, but I'm not being your patsy anymore. You've never said anything that didn't serve you first. I should've realized that from the start, but it doesn't matter now. I've got my assignment. I'm going to get the She-Wolf what she wants, and then I'm going to drag that murdering bastard back to Momma and Chase so they can rest in justice."

But I already told you that won't work!

"You also told me you were lying. You think I'm going to believe you're spitting straight now, when you're so hungry for crystal you'd even stoop to sweet-talking me?"

I was attempting to reason *with—*

"I don't care," Rel snapped, slamming the gun back in its holster. "Killing that murderer to set their souls free is the only story you've ever told me that has a happy ending, so that's the truth I'm choosing to believe. I'd rather screw up and die trying for their sake than live a hundred years serving yours."

But at what cost? If you do this, you'll be handing Volchitsa everything your precious little fake Price has worked for.

"Josie'll get over it," Rel said coldly. "She can do that 'cause she's still alive. Momma and Chase don't have that luxury. You took that from them when you bound all of us up in your cursed work! It weren't enough to ruin our lives. You had to go and ruin their deaths as well! But I'm through letting you hurt them. I'll jump through whatever hoops Volchitsa sets for me until I get my hands on their killer. And if murdering him doesn't work, I'll try something else. I'll do whatever I have to to set us all free, so make like the dead are supposed to for once and *shut your damn mouth!*"

She shoved the words more than said them, packing them full of the resonance that made ghosts do what she said. Such efforts normally required crystal, but Rel had never needed help to boss her dad. He'd been hers ever since the night she'd agreed to shelter his soul in the light of her life. But something must have changed in the months they'd spent here, because he didn't fall silent as he should have. Even with her laying down the law, he just kept going.

This is your final warning, he said, his angry voice grating like a metal rasp inside her skull. *I have done my best to be patient with you, Reliance, but this time you go too far. I will not let you throw away the opportunity of ten lifetimes on a childish hope I've already told you is false. If you proceed with this doomed plan, we are finished! There will be no more help, no more patching up the damage inflicted by your own willful ignorance. There is so much more I could offer you, so much more I could teach, but if you will not listen to experience, logic, or factual evidence, then I have nothing left to say except die on your own, you stupid, headstrong child!*

"Fine with me," Rel snarled, starting down the stairs again. "Good riddance, you pompous old shit stain."

The gun gave a final, furious rattle in its holster, and then, for the first time since the night she'd let his soul into hers, Bernard Reiner's presence went quiet in her head. His pistol went still as well, sitting lifeless as any other lump of metal in her empty gun belt, which was when Rel realized she'd never retrieved her pistols from Casper.

Turning with a curse, Rel tried to go back upstairs to get them, but her feet refused to move. She'd been pushing herself to the limit all day. Now, after that final cathartic scream at her hateful father, she had nothing left to give, not even to climb a single stair. The best she could manage was a controlled fall all the way back to her tiny cell in the basement. But even as she collapsed fully clothed on top of her bunk, a little spark was quickening in the emptiness her father's absence had left behind. A little warmth that almost felt like hope.

For the first time in six months, the end was actually in sight. The old asshole had tried to tell her it was a lie, but her father would say anything to get his hands on Josie's crystal. That didn't mean what he'd told her before was true, of course, but killing a murderer to free their victims was a common solution in ghost stories, and most of those had a bigger grain of truth to 'em than Bernard Reiner possessed in his entire body.

Volchitsa had already told her more tonight than in all her previous months at the Wet Whistle put together. If Rel got that deed she wanted and held it over, she was certain she could make the She-Dog cough up the rest. Rel just had to hold out a little longer, push a little further, and her mother and brother could *finally* move on to the beautiful hereafter they were the only Reiners to deserve.

With that happy thought, sleep slammed into Rel like an express locomotive, sending her tumbling blissfully into the quiet, empty, dreamless dark.

Chapter 17

Mary woke to the strangest feeling. She was lying on something soft, white, and poofy as a summer cloud. Just like a cloud, it was also high off the ground. Enough to make her startle before she remembered Miss Josie had put her up for the night.

Mystery solved, Mary flopped back into the wonderful softness. Apparently, rich people didn't stop at putting feathers in their pillows. They slept on giant bags of them, cramming their mattresses full of goose and duck down. Mary couldn't deny the comfort of such, but it felt so wasteful, and why did it need to be so *high*? The big wooden frame would've made sense if the floor was dirt, but the attic bedroom was made from the same saw-milled boards as the rest of the Price Mining building. Mary could've eaten off that wood without batting an eye, so why wasn't it good enough to sleep on?

It made no kinda sense, but she wasn't about to look a gift bed in the mouth. She was too busy kicking her bare feet just for the joy of feeling the smooth sheets slide over her calloused toes. Her *clean* toes, for Miss Josie had also been kind enough to prepare her a bath after they'd gotten in last night. Not no splash off in the water barrel neither. This was a *real* bath with *real* hot water.

Wasting all that wood heating water in the summer was plumb ridiculous, but Miss Josie had been so insistent, and the steamy bath had felt *so* nice after the caves' mud and damp. It weren't like the fire could be put back in the logs, so Mary had given in and lingered until she went all pruney, scrubbing every inch of herself double-over with Miss Josie's fancy flower-smelling soap. The result had left her cleaner than she could ever remember being. Miss Josie had even helped her wash her hair, which Mary hadn't done since the spring on account of how long it took to dry.

Her hair was still down now, falling all around her like a black waterfall. Between that and her scrubbed face, Mary barely recognized herself in the scrap of mirror nailed to the back of the bedroom's door, another ridiculous luxury Miss Josie treated as commonplace.

She'd actually apologized for the mirror being so small when she'd shown Mary up here last night. Mary hadn't had the heart to tell her that she'd never stayed in a bedroom with a mirror of any size before, or a bedroom at all for that matter. She'd slept in the barn when she'd lived with the nuns at the mission, and the year she'd spent with the Lakota, she'd slept in a buffalo-hide tepee same as everyone else. Since coming to Medicine Rocks, she'd pretty much lived in the caves, so this whole featherbed-wood-floors-mirror thing was a fairyland Christmas so far as Mary was concerned. She was still squishing her face into the pillow just for the fun of watching the imprint poof back out when someone knocked on the door.

They had to knock again before Mary remembered she needed to say "come in." She did so in a fluster, blushing up to her wild hair, which was flying all over without the grime that usually weighed it down. She was twisting the stuff between her fingers to get it into some kind of order when Miss Josie burst into the room, carrying an armful of bright-pink cloth.

"Good morning, Mary!" she said cheerfully, closing the door with a kick of her pretty boot that had been dyed the same rich blue as her fancy dress. Mary didn't know if something was happening or if fine ladies always wore stuff like that around the house, but Miss Josie looked like she'd wrapped herself in a midsummer sky.

She sounded sunny too. To Mary's great relief, the thundering song of the Mother Lode had fallen off after they'd left the cavern. But while the caves had gone back to sounding like always, just a little louder, the new people sounds hadn't faded a bit. Even after a full night outside the caves, which should've been enough to clear any crystal madness, Mary could hear Miss Josie's familiar melody tittering bright as the morning sunlight. It was such a strange new factor to consider that Mary didn't realize Miss Josie was also still talking with her actual voice until she stopped.

"Sorry, what was that?"

"I said, 'I hope it was warm enough for you last night,'" Miss Josie repeated, setting down her lovely armful of rose-colored cloth on the little desk beneath the window. "This room belonged to our senior clerk, Mr. Spencer. It's supposed to be the nicest in the building after Uncle Samuel's and Mihir's, but now that I'm standing in it, I realize the stovepipe doesn't carry nearly as much heat up from the second floor as I thought. I'm dreadfully sorry about that. I hope I didn't freeze you."

Mary had no idea what she was talking about. She'd been surprised they even bothered with heating in summer, though she'd figured that was because Sam Price's headman, Mihir, was from a hotter place than Montana. When Mary'd asked if that meant Mexico, he'd explained to her most patiently that he wasn't that sort of Indian. He was called such because he'd grown up in India, which was different from Indiana and had nothing to do with the tribes.

Honestly, Mary wasn't totally clear on the subject yet. She was just happy Mihir liked a fire, 'cause that meant she got to enjoy being toasty guilt-free. She'd been less happy when she'd gotten out of the bath to discover Miss Josie had taken all her clothes, proclaiming them "too filthy" to bring inside. Not that that wasn't true, but those were the only clothes Mary owned. From that point she'd been afraid all the fires were because rich people liked to go around naked in the evenings, but then Miss Josie had brought her a lovely white cotton dress she'd called a "shift."

Apparently, a shift was something you wore under your clothes or to bed, which was ridiculous, since both the fabric and stitching were finer than any dress Mary had ever owned. If it hadn't shown her bare arms so indecently, she would've worn it on Sundays and felt the prettiest thing. Sleeping in it seemed a criminal waste, but at least Mary felt like a princess when she hauled herself out of the cloudlike bed to ask what Miss Josie wanted so early.

"We're going out," the lady said excitedly, tossing open the curtains. "I've actually been up for hours thinking about how we're going to mine the Mother Lode without getting it stolen out from under us, and I believe I've come up with a solution. First, though, I need to take a good look around town, and since you know far more about Medicine Rocks than I, I'd like you to come with me."

Mary wasn't nearly as sure of herself in town as she was in the caves, but guiding was guiding. "I'll get ready, then," she said, moving quickly now that she had a job. "Where did you put my clothes?"

"They're not dry yet, I'm afraid," Miss Josie said. "I thought I'd just give them a quick brushing, but they were so dirty I had to soak them in lye and then have a go with the washboard."

Mary blinked. "You washed my clothes?"

"Yes."

"*You?*" she repeated, still not comprehending. "Washed *my* clothes?"

"I had to do my own as well, so it was no trouble," Miss Josie assured her. "I just hope I wasn't too rough. I've heard you're not supposed to wash denim, but it was so dirty I figured I couldn't make it worse. It was quite a surprise when your trousers turned out blue. I'd assumed they were black like Rel's, but they're actually a lovely bright color when they're clean."

She smiled at Mary, but when the girl didn't answer right away, Miss Josie's face fell into a frown. "I hope I didn't upset you," she said nervously. "I realize I should have asked first, but you were already asleep, and I wanted to get everything finished up as fast as possible."

"No, no!" Mary said, waving her hands. "Thank you very much for the trouble! I'm just shocked is all. I just didn't think someone like you knew how to do laundry."

That was about the worst way she could've blurted that out. Luckily, Miss Josie didn't take offense.

"It's wise when traveling on your own to cultivate a repertoire of practical skills," she said. "I can also sew, cook, and tend a hearth if necessary."

That didn't sound very fancy-ladylike to Mary, but Miss Josie had been the one who'd built all those unnecessary fires now she thought back on it, so Mary nodded her head like a turnip on a string and moved on to the next problem in the line.

"If my clothes are still drying, what am I gonna wear?" She looked down at the sleeveless dress she'd worn to bed. "This shift-thing is a beauty, but I think I'd start a commotion if I wore it outside."

Miss Josie paled at the idea. "Absolutely not!" she said, picking up the pink cloth parcel she'd brought with her into the room. "You'll be wearing this."

"What is it?" Mary asked, too nervous to touch the finery even with her cleaner-than-ever hands.

"It's a dress," Miss Josie said, unfolding the pretty pink cloth to reveal it was actually a pretty pink skirt. "It was supposed to be mine, but the hem was always too short no matter how much I let it out. That should make it perfect for you, though, and I'm sure the color will be lovely with your dark hair."

She spoke everything nice and clear, but Mary was still having trouble understanding. "You want me to wear one of your dresses?"

"You can't very well go naked," Miss Josie said with a laugh, unfurling the fabric like a flag onto the bed. "I've also brought you a corset, petticoats, stockings, and gloves. I would have boots as well, but I've feet like gunboats, so I'm afraid you'll have to make do with your own for now. We'll just keep the skirt low so no one will see until we can order up a wardrobe of your own."

"What would I do with a wardrobe?" Mary asked, confused. "Where would I even put such a thing?"

"No, no, I mean a collection of clothing, not a piece of furniture."

That made a lot more sense. Even so, "I feel the question still stands," Mary said, eyeing the dress like it was a pretty but deadly snake. "I got no call for clothing like that."

"Of course you do," Miss Josie said triumphantly. "You're a part owner of the largest crystal mine in the world, Miss Good Crow. You can wear anything you like!"

That sounded more like a threat than a benefit. Mary had a hard enough time keeping one set of clothes mended, and that was cotton and wool. She didn't even know how to work with the shimmery fabrics Miss Josie had piled on the bed. But the lady looked so happy about the notion that Mary couldn't bring herself to fight. She just held out her arms and let the older girl move her around like she was a doll, a feat Miss Josie was surprisingly good at for someone who was surely more used to being dressed than dressing.

The corset went on first, sliding directly over the shift with hooks in the front and lacing in the back. Being made for the stately Miss Josie, it was a bit long, but the undergarment wasn't nearly as awful as Mary had feared. From the way the Wet Whistle ladies used them to completely change their figures, she'd assumed corsets squished you like bread dough, but this thing didn't feel half bad. Sure, it kept her from bending over like she was used to, but the metal pieces made standing up straight a breeze, and it'd probably help with holding the weight of a pack as well.

Mary was starting to think there might really be something to this corset idea when Miss Josie yanked the laces, changing her mind. It still wasn't unbearable, but the extra tightness was *much* less comfortable than before. It made her waist look frighteningly scrawny in the mirror too, leaving Mary feeling like a skeleton until Miss Josie came in with the padding.

There was an awful lot. Apparently, fancy dresses needed more supports than a bridge to hold themselves up. First came a wire and wool contraption over Mary's rear that Miss Josie called a bustle cage. On top of that went the petticoat, which was a whole bunch of skirts sewn together into a huge ruffle that went all the way to the floor. Then came the actual pink skirt, which was separate from the top of the dress and had a whole bunch of swoopy bits Miss Josie tied all over with ribbon so that the skirt ended up in piles and gathers, letting Mary move about without dragging too much on the ground.

Miss Josie still had to hem the bottom to make up the difference in their heights. Again, though, she did so with aplomb, sewing up the extra inches quick as lightning. It didn't seem right that a rich lady who got waited on hand and foot should be so good with a needle, but Mary was glad of it. By the time Miss Josie finished, the dress hit just above Mary's toes, leaving her room to walk without revealing her boots, which she was sure would look ugly as mud on a painting under this pretty thing.

Once the skirt was set to her liking, Miss Josie moved on to the dress's top, which went over Mary's arms like a coat but was called a bodice. It was even prettier than the skirt with all manner of lace and ribbons and mother-of-pearl buttons so tiny that Mary's fingers could barely grasp them. Fortunately for her, Miss Josie was an expert in this as well, buttoning up the whole line faster than Mary had failed to fasten the first.

"There," Miss Josie said when she was finished, turning Mary 'round to face the mirror. "How do you like it?"

It was impossible to say. Mary didn't even recognize the elegant, dark-haired lady standing next to Miss Josephine. The feeling only got worse when Miss Josie started braiding her hair with those whip-quick fingers, fashioning Mary's horse-thick mane into shiny plaits that hung around her face in decorative loops. A bonnet lined with matching pink ribbons topped the look off, leaving Mary prodding her own cheeks just to make sure the girl in the mirror really was her.

"You look lovely," Miss Josie said proudly, circling Mary like a rancher admiring a pony he'd just finished grooming for the fair. "I *knew* you would. Pink always looked dreadful on me, but it is absolutely your color." She nodded then, as if she'd just decided something. "This shall be your dress henceforth."

"You'd never," Mary said, terrified to move lest she knock loose one of the shiny buttons. "I can't accept this."

"I insist."

"But where will I put it?" she asked desperately. "I can't store something this nice in the caves!"

"You won't need to," Miss Josie said, pinning a bonnet over her own hair, which she wore in a pile of golden curls. "This is your room now. You're welcome to stay as long as you like."

Mary's eyes went big as eggs. "Me? Stay here? With *you?*"

"I wouldn't have it any other way. I can move you to a different room if this one is not to your liking, but—"

"No, no, I love it," Mary insisted, twisting her hands, which now looked like big flapping bird wings under the white gloves Miss Josie had shoved over her scraped-up, though at least no longer glowing, fingers. "But… are you sure *you* want to do this? Medicine Rocks doesn't exactly take kindly to me."

"They haven't taken kindly to me, either," Miss Josie said, putting on her own gloves. "But they'll just have to adjust, because we're here to stay." She checked herself in the mirror scrap one last time and opened the door. "Ready to go?"

Mary'd been so overwhelmed by all the puttings on that it took her several moments to remember the point of being lashed into this dress was so that she could wear it out.

The prospect nearly had her climbing the papered walls. "I can't go out like this!" she cried, clutching the giant skirt. "Everyone'll laugh at me!"

"You mean admire you. No one laughs at a well-dressed lady."

"I ain't one of those!"

"You could walk into any garden party in Boston right now and be welcome," Miss Josie assured her with a beaming smile. "I may not be as skilled as a true lady's maid, but I know how to dress a woman to maximum effect, and I assure you that outfit will be most sufficient for walking down Main Street in Medicine Rocks. People won't even recognize you."

Mary hoped they didn't, for Miss Josie's sake. If folks here thought she was elevating Mary above her place, they'd drag them both down. Mary didn't want anything like that to happen to someone who'd been so kind to her, but Miss Josie wouldn't listen to reason. She just handed Mary her boots and floated down the stairs, waiting impatiently on the office's front porch like Mary was the strange one for holding them up.

"This is gonna end in tears," Mary moaned as they stepped onto the boardwalk, which was mercifully not muddy for once, thanks to the midsummer dryness. "Why do you need me to walk through town with you? Surely Mihir would've been a better choice?"

"I was actually planning on him being with us," Miss Josie said, setting off. "Unfortunately, I was too excited and kept the dear man up late running numbers. He's still sleeping it off, so I'm afraid it's just the two of us."

Mary had no idea how you stayed up half the night with numbers, but businesspeople got their heads spinning over all sorts of things, so who was she to say? Mary was much more worried about the crowded street, for it was now prime morning, and the whole town looked to be out.

That was bad news for her. Mary had never done well in crowds, but things were always worse after a battle, and she'd never heard of the cavalry suffering a bigger defeat than that noise about Custer last night. Going by the fear she could hear quaking through the townspeople's low humming sounds, it'd be a miracle if she didn't end the day tarred and feathered. But while there were a lot of eyeballs drifting toward Mary's direction, no one looked like they were getting ready for a lynching. Quite the opposite. Folks were actually smiling at her for once, tipping their hats like gentlemen as the ladies walked by.

It was the strangest thing Mary had ever witnessed. Sure, the pink dress was pretty, but it wasn't as if the bonnet covered her entire head. Her face—the exact same red-skinned, half-breed face the town had made a sport out of hating for the last two years—was bare for all to see, and yet no one seemed to notice. They'd been blinded by the dress and the wealth it proclaimed, stepping out of the way and bidding Mary good morning like she and Miss Josie were cut from the same silk cloth.

Miss Josie, of course, didn't seem to notice at all. She was too busy staring at the placard signs hanging from the false-fronted buildings to offer the throngs of men more than a distracted nod. For Mary, though, it was an utterly new experience. One that was about to be put to the ultimate test when she spotted a pack of miners coming down the way.

She flinched closer to Miss Josephine. They'd lost a lot of weight, but Mary still knew those grimy faces. It was the group she'd guided right before Rel had snatched her off the street. The ones she'd left in the dark after they'd stiffed her.

Given the threats they'd hollered back then, Mary's first instinct was to turn and run. That was easier said than done in a dress the size of a horse, but while the men had absolutely spotted her, they weren't reaching for their guns. Like everyone else, they seemed too distracted by the pretty ribbons and shiny braids to notice her half-Injun face sitting in the middle. They just gawked at her corset-assisted bosoms and walked right on by, leaving Mary feeling like she'd just gotten away with something twice.

She looked down at the dress in awe. She'd thought Miss Josie was talking out the other side of her face about folks not recognizing her, but the lady had been dead on. This dress was magic! A dazzling distraction that tricked men into seeing ladies rather than what was actually in front of their noses. She was about to suggest they step into the General Store just to see if the shopkeeper who'd pulled that gun on her last time would kick a *lady* out of his establishment when Miss Josie stopped walking with an angry huff.

"Where the devil are they?"

"Where are who?" Mary asked, knocked out of her fancy-dress dreamland.

"The other mining companies!" Miss Josie said, waving her gloved hand at the business signs hanging in a line above their heads. "Uncle used to complain about them all the time, and Mihir said that even though he hasn't really left the building since Sam died, he felt certain they'd still be in business. That's why I wanted you with me this morning. I thought since you were a guide, you'd be able to tell me which companies had the best practices, but I haven't seen a single one since we stepped out! With the exception of the General Store, every shop we've passed has been some variation of saloon, flophouse, or gun shop. Oh, and crystal. Crystal exchanges, crystal cutting, mining tools for crystal. You get the picture."

"Crystal is what folks come out here for," Mary reminded her timidly.

"But where are they getting it?" Miss Josie demanded. "It can't all be individual prospectors. No one was ever as big as Price Mining, but there used to be dozens of smaller companies running mining teams. They should be booming now that Uncle's no longer snapping up all the good workers and claims, but I don't see a single one."

"Lot of places went out of business after Price Mining closed," Mary said with a shrug. "Not sure why precisely, but I know there was harassment going on. Claim jumping, back shooting, that sort of thing."

"I can't say I'm surprised," Miss Josie said darkly. "There seem to be lots of people in this town who care about nothing except how much crystal they can cram into their own pockets, and law enforcement here is clearly a joke."

"Don't forget about the Whitmans," Mary added. "They've been hitting everyone leaving town with anything larger than a two-wheel buggy for months. I'm sure that's hurt the other mining companies."

"I'm sure it did," Miss Josie agreed, looking around in dismay. "But I never imagined they'd *all* be gone. What are we going to do?"

"Does something need to be done?" Mary asked, still not understanding what this was about. "You've already got one mining company. Surely you don't need more."

"What I need is *help*," Josie said, lowering her voice to a whisper. "We've succeeded beyond my wildest dreams in finding the treasure that's going to turn everything around, but it's all for nothing if we can't get that crystal out of the ground. Even if it only takes us an hour to fill our packs each time, the three of us can't make the trip quickly enough to generate the income I need on our own. Even if we could, I can't run a company if I'm constantly underground. We need *people*: miners, clerks, cooks, guides, all the functionaries of a proper business. We'll also need to hire a small army to get past the Whitman blockade so we can actually sell the crystal after we mine it. This is the problem I was up all night trying to solve! My initial plan was to use the crystal from this first trip to hire workers for the second, but now that I've been down to the caves myself, I realize it won't be that simple. Even if my uncle's odd decision to fire everyone hadn't muddied our reputation, there's no telling whom we can trust. If we hire the wrong people and show them to our cavern, we could end up shot in the back and thrown down a hole while they steal our claim!"

"Spoken like a Medicine Rocks native," Mary said sadly.

"That's why I decided to team up with another established company," Miss Josie went on, glaring up the street. "It'll be more expensive than doing things ourselves, since we'd have to give them a cut of the profits rather than just paying a wage, but at least I could negotiate those terms at a table rather than at gunpoint. That was my hope, anyway, but it never occurred to me they'd *all* be gone. It looks like the only miners left in Medicine Rocks are small teams and single operators, which means we're right back where we started!"

"You could always wait," Mary suggested, trying not to sound too happy about the delay. "Make smaller trips with just the three of us while we figure out who to trust."

"That would just make us even more vulnerable! Every time we go into the caves, there's a chance someone will follow, especially if we keep bringing back, and paying taxes on, bulging bags of crystal."

288

Mary bit her lip. "I know this might sound crazy, but do we *need* bulging bags of crystal? You've already brought back a fortune in new colors. Surely that's enough to keep your building up and the three of us fed for a while yet?"

"But not enough for me," Miss Josie said desperately, her face pinched. "I can't explain the whys and hows of my situation at present, but trust me when I say that I *need* crystal. I need lots of it, I need to be able to get it back to civilization, and I need to sell it for buckets of money. If I can't manage that, I might as well close up shop."

That amount of pressure sounded ridiculous for a lady who was already rich, but Miss Josie looked so determined that Mary didn't dare contradict her. As she'd already told herself a million times now, it weren't her place to dictate what the others did with their shares. Miss Josie had already given Mary the best part of her claim. If she wanted to mine her third down to the rock, that was her right. The pillar could wail all it wanted, but unless Mary was ready to claim jump the only person in Medicine Rocks who'd ever been nice to her—which she absolutely wasn't—she couldn't do anything about it. Like so many awful things in this world, it was how it was. They'd both just have to accept that, though Mary wasn't above a sigh of relief when Miss Josie turned around and started stomping back toward Price Mining.

"We'll just have to think of something else," she muttered, chewing nervously on the finger of her glove as she hurried down the boardwalk. "We got lucky there was no one at the tax table, and I'm sure Rel won't be foolish enough to flash her crystal around, so we shouldn't have to worry about our secret getting out just yet. And with the Whitmans running rampant, I couldn't send a crystal shipment even if I had one, so that buys us some time as well. Surely even *she* won't be able to spend the entire balance of the remaining railroad fortune in one year."

"Who won't spend what?" Mary asked.

"Never mind," Miss Josie said, waving the words away. "Returning to the topic at hand, even if all the companies are out of business, there has to be some power left in Medicine Rocks. A reliable business partner who can help protect our crystal *without* turning on us. Do you know anyone like that?"

Mary couldn't think of a one. Plenty of folks in town would happily sell them protection, but she knew of no one who wouldn't turncoat the moment they saw how big a claim they'd been hired to guard. She wasn't nearly as upset over that as Miss Josie, since, again, she didn't want the place mined at all. But she hated seeing her friend so distraught. Miss Josie had tried so hard and welcomed her so warmly even before the Mother Lode turned out to be a mother lode. Mary wanted her to succeed—she really did—but there seemed no way around this problem.

She was going to suggest they wait and talk to Rel about it—she worked for the Wet Whistle, which was basically the cook pot for all of Medicine Rocks' seedy business, so if anyone knew who they could cut a deal with, it'd be her—when a sudden burst of bugling made them both jump.

The horn call stirred up an old terror in Mary's chest. She was still getting her shakes under control when Miss Josie grabbed her hand and started dragging her toward the sound. They'd barely started when the wooden gate of Fort Grant swung open so that riders in cavalry blue could gallop down the street, blowing their horns and yelling out notice that the general was calling a town meeting. Right now.

"The general?" Miss Josephine said in a voice that was equal parts worried and excited. "Is it usual for the general to address the town like this?"

"First time I've seen it happen," Mary said, shuffling her feet in an attempt to weigh down Miss Josie, who was plowing up the hill at full speed. "I didn't even know we had a general here 'til now."

"Do you think it has to do with what that man said last night?" Josie asked, hauling Mary with surprising strength.

"You meant how we're all 'bout to be murdered by Sioux?" She shook her head. "Don't think so. If there was really an attack coming, they'd be locking that gate, not opening it up to the likes of us." Mary looked at the backs of the crowd that'd already gathered in front of the fortress, and her body began to shake all over. "Can we *please* go back?"

"In a moment," Miss Josie promised. "I just want to see what this is about."

Mary was sure they'd find out whether they wanted to or not, but Miss Josie was already tapping on shoulders and fluttering her lashes, abusing her power as a lady to get them a coveted spot in the front row.

This put them closer to the cavalry fortress than Mary had ever been. Close enough to see the faces of the mounted soldiers forming a wall across the front entrance. There were also two officers standing up above on the fortress's wooden walls. One was a white-bearded grandpa wearing a blue coat covered in all manner of important-looking nonsense. Mary assumed he must be the general, but the man standing with him also had a gold braid sewn onto his coat.

That seemed more impressive to Mary given how he was so much younger. Handsomer, too, with a sharp, clean-shaven jaw and thick dark hair that he wore pulled back in a ponytail. Mary thought he looked just like the picture of the dashing cavalry soldier from the 3-cent stamp, only instead of sitting on a white horse, this man was leaning hard on a wooden cane. She was going up on her tiptoes to see what his injury was when the bugles trumpeted again, and the general raised his hand.

"Citizens of Medicine Rocks," he said in a booming voice that had clearly been bossing soldiers around for decades. "For those of you who don't know me, I'm General James Cook, head of Fort Grant and field commander for the Eastern Montana Defense. I've called you out this morning to address the rumors that have been circulating since last night. As I'm sure you're already aware, the 7th Cavalry under Lieutenant Colonel George Custer was defeated by Sioux forces at Little Big Horn a few days ago."

A wave of whispering kicked up at this, causing the general to bang his fist on the wooden wall. "Stop that and listen! The deaths of these fine soldiers are indeed a great loss for our nation, but it is no cause for panic. Despite the unpatriotic fearmongering I've heard spreading throughout our community, Medicine Rocks is in no immediate danger of attack. But that doesn't mean we can relax our vigilance! The Sioux have always been a dangerous and deceitful enemy, and with the 7th Cavalry gone, our ability to secure the local area has indeed been diminished.

"I've already sent for reinforcements to alleviate this, but as I'm sure you've heard, our enemy now possesses crystal. Unless we get some of our own, we are in danger of being outgunned as well as outnumbered. To bridge this gap and ensure a greater supply of crystal for our mutual defense, I am changing the way taxes are collected. In addition to the usual tax table, soldiers will now patrol the entirety of the Front Caves from the tunnel entrance to the beginning of the Dark. If one of these patrols stops you, you will be expected to submit to a full inspection and pay your taxes on the spot. Any discrepancies between the crystal you report and the crystal we find will result in *all* crystal being confiscated. Repeat offenders will receive a lifetime ban from the mines."

The whispers turned into a roar. Miners began yelling and throwing things, calling the general all manner of vile names. It was a terrifying thing to be at the front of, 'specially with the wall of soldiers standing not five feet away, but Miss Josie refused to move when Mary tugged on her arm. Mary was about to try again, harder, when the handsome officer at the general's side lifted his hand, and a cannon went off inside the fortress, sending a cannonball screaming over the crowd and out into the grasslands.

That got everyone's attention. The angry mob ceased its screaming, and the miners from the tent camps who hadn't yet gathered started pouring out of the side alleys to join the rest. This doubled the crowd's size, but the mood was far more timid after the display of the big gun's power, and the general nodded.

"As I was saying, these new measures might sound extreme, but if y'all had just paid your taxes in the first place, we wouldn't be in this situation. You've left your defenders starved, but never forget that without this fortress, Medicine Rocks would still belong to the Indians! It's because of the bravery and sacrifice of these soldiers that you have the freedom to mine crystal at all, so I suggest you find your sense of civic responsibility. If everyone does their part and pays what they owe, we can see about returning to a more civil state of affairs. That's all I have to say except to remind you that all of these new policies are effective immediately. Anyone who has questions can address them to my aide, Lieutenant Lucas."

He gestured at the handsome man beside him, and Mary jerked back with a squeak. Did he say *Lucas*? She squinted up at the top of the wooden wall, pushing her bonnet off her forehead to get a better look.

This was silly in hindsight. The cave music was good at showing her big things like rocks and holes, but it fell flat when it came to details, and since all her interactions with the downed officer had been done without a lamp, Mary had never seen his face to recognize it now.

He did look about the size she remembered, but the dashing soldier couldn't possibly be the same bony, bedraggled man she'd pulled out of the Dark. That he was standing proved it, 'cause there was no way his broken leg could've healed enough for him to walk around on with only a cane just yet. That said, his thick, curling hair *did* look like the soft stuff she'd touched back in the pit, and she *had* heard rumors about a doctor who used crystal to perform miracles, and it *did* seem unlikely there'd be two lieutenants here with the same name, so perhaps...

To the devil with this! It didn't matter whether he was or wasn't. Mary hadn't done all that work covering her trail to mess it up now. Her policy of staying away from the cavalry had worked perfectly for two years. All she needed to keep that streak was to turn around and walk away, which was exactly what she was doing when Miss Josie suddenly started marching in the opposite direction, straight toward the line of soldiers.

A sheet of ice formed over Mary's stomach. "What are you doing?" she whispered frantically, darting back to grab the crazy woman's arm.

"Seizing an opportunity," Miss Josie replied, her brown eyes gleaming with a light Mary was learning to fear. "I think we've just been handed the solution to our problem."

That made no sorta sense. Not even Miss Josie's strange sort of sense. "How does a cavalry crackdown on tax dodgers solve anything for us?"

"It doesn't directly, but it tells me a great deal about *them*."

She pointed at Lieutenant Lucas, who was climbing down from the wall with some difficulty, presumably to answer questions like the general had ordered. "They tried to make it sound like this was about everyone doing their part, but what *I* heard is that the cavalry—the strongest military force in this area—is so desperate for crystal that they're willing to risk a riot." She wiggled her eyebrows at Mary. "See where I'm going?"

Mary did. Heaven help her, she saw the whole disaster that was about to unfold, but it was too late. Miss Josie was already hurrying toward the lieutenant, leaving Mary in the dust.

Chapter 18

Josie rushed forward so quickly that she almost fell. Her delicate boots—which were treacherously small already, since they were actually Miss Josephine's boots and not cut for Josie's feet—struggled in the rutted dirt of the road, sending her tripping and teetering until she was forced to slow down. Only her legs, though. Josie's mind was still spinning as wildly as ever, whirling pieces into place as her brilliant idea took form.

"Lieutenant Lucas!" she said urgently, seizing his sleeve the moment she was in reach. "May I have a word?"

He must not have anticipated being accosted in such a manner, for the poor man jumped like a jackrabbit. Being a military officer, though, he recovered at once, his face breaking into a dazzling smile when he'd saw that he'd been grabbed by a lady.

"Good morning to you, *mademoiselle*. How may I be of—"

"I need to speak to General Cook," Josie blurted, too impatient for niceties.

"I'm sorry, but the general is a busy man," Lucas replied in the faux-disappointed tone all attachés adopted when defending their superiors from unwanted appointments. "But I am at your disposal. If you would care to speak your concerns to me instead, it would be my honor to—"

"It must be him," Josie insisted. "This is a matter of some delicacy, but one I think he'll be happy to hear." She leaned in closer, dropping her voice to a whisper. "I may be able to get your outpost a great deal of crystal."

That got his attention. "Crystal, you say?" Lieutenant Lucas leaned heavily on his cane, dropping the dazzling smile for a much less polite but far more sincere scowl. "You must forgive my bluntness, but this had better not be a scam. We've had to deal with a great many swindlers since arriving in this town. You've already heard the situation we're in, so if you're running a scheme, I suggest that you walk away right now."

"It's nothing of the sort, I promise," Josie said, doing her best to look legitimate. "I'm Josephine Price of the Price Mining Company, and I've a proposition that could be of great strategic benefit to all. I'd explain right now if I could, but this isn't something that should be discussed in the street. Particularly not *this* street."

They both glanced at the shouting crowd, which the line of soldiers at the base's gate was already riding out to disperse.

"All I'm asking is a few minutes of the general's time," Josie pleaded. "I assure you, it'll be worth his while."

The lieutenant didn't look sold, but something she'd said must have gotten through, because he turned back toward the gate. "Wait here," he ordered, walking off with impressive speed for a man with a cane.

Smiling in triumph, Josie spun around to share the good news with Mary, only to find the girl wasn't there. She was cowering five feet back, staring at Josie like a deer on the tracks.

"What's the matter?" she asked, hurrying back to her side. "Did someone say something to you?"

A great many angry miners thronged the street, but they'd seemed too busy hurling profanity at the cavalry to bother a lady. Josie supposed it was possible to do both at once, but Mary shook her head. Greatly relieved her friend hadn't been harassed, Josie took her hand and tried to move them closer to the gate so they'd be ready when the general arrived, but Mary refused to budge.

"I can't," she said.

"Can't what?" Josie asked, confused.

Mary dropped her eyes and pointed at the wooden fortress. "I can't go in there."

"Of course you can. We're—"

"*You're* a lady," Mary said desperately. "But I ain't you. The pretty costume might've tricked a few miners what were happy to be fooled, but the soldiers in there got friends who died fightin' people who looked like me."

"This is different," Josie insisted. "We'll be speaking to the officers, educated men. They won't—"

"Don't matter," Mary said, backing away like a spooked cat. "I've learned my lesson about the cavalry enough times already. I ain't risking another."

Josie gritted her teeth. She'd expect this sort of stubbornness from Rel, but Mary was normally so obliging. When Josie stopped trying to haul them into the fortress long enough to actually look at her friend, though, Mary's face held no defiance. Quite the opposite. The girl looked terrified, literally quaking in her boots. And the longer Josie thought about that, the more she felt like a villain.

"I'm sorry," she said, letting Mary go at once. "Of course you don't have to come with me. I can handle this perfectly well on my own. You go back to the office. Mihir probably has breakfast ready by now. Go on and help yourself. I should be back in half an hour."

Mary's whole body sagged in relief. But even with her escape secure, she still had the kindness to ask, "You sure you'll be good by yourself?"

"Absolutely," Josie said, pushing her friend down the road. "You've done enough of my work for one day."

Mary still looked worried, but she didn't press the matter. As soon as Josie insisted it was all right, she turned tail and fled, hiking her pink skirt up to show the mud-stained deerskin boots beneath as she ran full speed down the hill toward the peaked roof of the Price Mining building.

Josie watched her all the way to the door to make sure she got back safely before returning her attention to the fortress, turning around just in time to see Lucas hobbling through the gate with the general close on his heels.

"Pleasure to meet you, Miss Price," General Cook said, tipping his hat out of what must have been habit, for his tone made it clear he was not actually pleased in the slightest. "My lieutenant says you had something you wanted to tell me about crystal?"

"Yes, sir," Josie said brightly, plastering a beaming businesswoman's smile over the bad taste the conversation with Mary had left in her mouth. "It'll only take fifteen minutes."

"You've got five," the general said, looking over her shoulder at the mess still going on in the street. "I'll see you in the meeting room once we've reestablished public order. Jean-Jacques will escort you there."

Lieutenant Lucas gallantly offered Josie his arm, which she took out of self-defense. Just like her blindness with Mary, she'd been too excited over her own plans to notice that the miners screaming about the new tax still hadn't backed off despite the soldiers' advance. There were quite a lot of them, too, enough that Josie was very happy when Cook ordered the gates closed behind them.

The inside of the cavalry fort was very different than she'd imagined. It looked like a wooden castle from the street, but once you passed under the log palisade, the fortress wasn't that much different from the rest of town. Just a bunch of temporary tent housing and cheaply constructed wooden cabins built up against the boulders to save on timber.

Thanks to their position on top of the hill, the cavalry actually had more of the titular Medicine Rocks than anywhere else in town. The hunks of grooved and pitted sandstone were everywhere in the camp, some going up three stories, a feature the fortress used to its advantage. Every boulder tall enough to see over the walls had a wooden ladder and pulley system bolted into its side. These led to wooden platforms where clusters of big black iron cannons had been aimed in all directions. From the demonstration earlier, Josie knew the elevated position gave the guns range to fire outside of town, turning this place into a formidable holding despite the canvas tents pitched all over the yard.

The area had quite a lot of tents, actually. The walls and central tower looked to be legitimate constructions, but the rest of the fort had clearly been built using the fastest, cheapest methods available. The barracks and mess hall were built from pine boards milled as thin as matchsticks to make the logs stretch, and all the smithies and outbuildings were little more than roofed sheds. The outpost was still impressively large, but the ramshackle state of the interior did not inspire confidence, though what really shocked Josie were the soldiers.

She'd known there were Black soldiers in the cavalry, of course. The papers loved hand-wringing about the infamous "Buffalo Soldiers" and the risks of arming Negro men. Josie didn't buy a word of that rot, but she was surprised to see so many here inside the fortress, since, before this moment, the vast majority of soldiers she'd seen in Medicine Rocks had been white.

"That's not by accident," Lucas said when she mentioned this. "Washington doesn't like risking white soldiers on dangerous outposts, so most of our garrison comes from the colored 10th Cavalry. Before General Cook took me under his direct command, I was a sergeant in the 10th. My men built this fortress and have guarded it ever since. They are the backbone of our defense, but unfortunately the townsfolk of Medicine Rocks don't see it that way. The miners especially have proved most unkind to Black soldiers, particularly when said soldiers are trying to make them pay their taxes. After several incidents, General Cook decided it would be best for everyone if the 10th was confined to base duties while in town."

"He locked them up?" Josie said, aghast.

"Nothing so cruel," the lieutenant said quickly. "They're allowed out for leave and such. We just no longer assign them duties that might put them in conflict with the townsfolk. The 10th fights hard enough against the bandits and the Sioux. The last thing they need to worry about is getting shot in the back by the very people they're supposed to be protecting."

Josie supposed she could see the logic, but it still sounded grossly unfair, especially since it was the miners' problem, not the soldiers'.

"It won't last, though," Lucas went on grimly. "Now that Custer's gone and led his men to their deaths, the 10th will have to resume mine work to make up for the lost manpower. I'm not looking forward to the trouble that will bring, especially with the new taxes and sweeps, but it's not all storm clouds. My soldiers have been camping in the yard all summer since Custer's men declared the barracks were for whites only. Now the 7th is gone, my men can return to their beds. So you see, life is not without its small mercies."

He said this with malicious cheer, and Josie scowled. "I take it you did not agree with Custer's decisions?"

"I did not agree with anything the late lieutenant colonel did, may he rest in peace." Lucas crossed himself then added, "But we are not here to talk about the past. What matters is the future and how we may yet survive it." His charming smile snapped back into place as he looked over at her. "I have great hopes for this proposition of yours, Mademoiselle Price."

Josie couldn't tell if that was sincere or if he was just paying her lip service, but she had a good feeling as Lucas led her into the wooden tower at the fortress's center.

This building was by far the best constructed. The logs of its walls were as big around as her leg, and the gaps between them had been sealed with a solid foot of mud daubing. The darkness this created made Josie feel as if she were back in the caves again, though without the underground's coolness. It was actually beastly hot once Lucas showed her into the second inner chamber at the tower's heart, but at least they had no chance of being overheard through such thick walls, so Josie took a seat on a folding stool beside the map-strewn table to sweat it out.

"Will the general be long?" she asked, taking out a handkerchief to dab her already damp brow.

Lucas peeked out the door. Then he smiled and stepped aside as General Cook stomped in.

"My condolences on the death of your uncle," the general said, not looking sorry or even at Josie as he plopped down in the wooden camp chair Lucas had hastily placed across from hers. "Sam and I had our differences, but he was a good man who cared deeply for the future of this country, and I respected him for that."

"He is very much missed," Josie agreed with far more emotion than she'd expected. It was surprisingly moving to meet someone who'd interacted with her uncle outside the bounds of friendship or family. She wanted to hear more about the Sam Price Cook had known, but the general was already tapping his polished boot, so Josie pushed down the loss that would apparently never stop stinging and got on with her business.

"My uncle is the reason I'm here, actually," she said, lowering her voice, even though no sound could possibly escape this vault of a room. "I don't know how much heed you pay to town gossip, but I'm sure you've heard the rumors that Sam Price found something on his last trip into the caves before he died."

"I've kept abreast," the general said, looking at her more keenly now. "But if you're searching for investors, you're barking up the wrong tree. Our orders expressly forbid us from getting involved in the crystal business."

Josie hadn't been aware of that, actually, but it didn't change her plans. "I'm not here looking for money," she said. "You see, the rumors were correct. Thanks to my uncle's efforts, I've recently found myself in possession of a great deal of crystal."

"How much crystal?" Lucas asked, pulling over a stool of his own.

"Enough to get me murdered if the wrong person catches wind of it," Josie said bluntly, crumpling her handkerchief in her fist. "That's why I came to you. With a claim this rich, there's no amount I can pay men to mine it for me that can beat what they'll earn by selling the location to someone else or taking over the claim for themselves. All the workers my uncle trusted have moved on, and there are no longer any other mining companies big enough to partner with. But the cavalry is different. You're the greatest power in the area by an order of magnitude. If you joined forces with Price Mining, no one would dare raise a finger against us."

301

"Oh, I get what's in it for you," the general said. "But you still haven't mentioned what we get out of this arrangement."

"Crystal," Josie answered. "If you supply me with honest men who'll mine my claim without betraying its location, I will pay all my taxes to the ounce."

"So what?" Cook said. "You're supposed to be doing that already."

"Yes, but no one is," she reminded him. "You said yourself just now at the gate that the reason we're in this situation is because people have been dodging their responsibilities, but raising the tax rate isn't going to change that. Nor will running sweeps. Yes, you'll catch more people trying to scam the system, but men who were already aiming to break the law aren't just going to hand over their crystal quietly because they got caught. They *will* fight back, which will likely cost you even more men."

"I don't need you to tell me that," the general said testily. "I'm well aware of the difficulties we've invited with this decision, but we don't have much choice. We need crystal if we're to hold this fortress against what's coming, and I've yet to find a way to make greedy miners cough that up which doesn't involve gunpoint."

"I have one," Josie said, smiling wide. "Don't use them at all. Those miners you're complaining about came here to get rich. Of course they're not going to happily hand over the crystal they risked their lives to collect for something as vague as protection against an enemy they can't even see, particularly not when you're being so draconian about it. You can't threaten a lifetime ban on miners who've already risked everything to come out here."

"They wouldn't have to worry if they'd just pay what they owe," the general snapped, then he sighed. "But very well, Miss Price. Say we go along with this plan and supply you with labor. Even if you were true to your word and paid all your taxes, that's still seventy-five percent in your pocket and only twenty-five in ours. Seems a measly price for the risks you're asking us to shoulder."

"We could ask the Mining Office to temporarily adjust Price Mining's tax rate," Josie suggested. "I'm sure they'd have no problem with me volunteering to pay *more* than my legal share, say forty percent of crystal recovered?"

"Sixty," the general said.

"Fifty," Josie countered, lifting her chin. "I still have to pay income taxes on my profits, don't forget."

Cook considered that for a moment. "Fifty might be sufficient to justify an expedition," he said at last. "Though it really depends on the size of the pie. At the risk of looking a gift horse in the mouth, just how much crystal could we expect from participating in this arrangement?"

"As much as you can carry," Josie said grandly, spreading her arms like a circus man. "This is the richest strike my uncle ever found, possibly the biggest ever. A true Mother Lode with crystal just lying on the ground, waiting to be picked up. A few trips should be all it takes to fill your coffers with whatever color crystal you desire, *and* you'll have it quickly! I'm ready to go right now. All I need are hands that won't stab me in the back. Provide me those and I'll smother your men in so much crystal, the Sioux won't dare attack!"

"You truly are Sam's relation," the general said, shaking his head. "He was a salesman, too, and just as unbelievable. But the proof of the pudding is in the eating, and seeing as I can't make my men work doubles to keep these new crackdowns going for more than a couple weeks, we don't exactly have the luxury of turning you down."

"Then it's a yes?" Josie asked excitedly.

The general raised his finger. "I'll give you one run. If this strike's really as rich as you say, that should be enough to see us through this current crisis. And if you're playing us false to draw off soldiers in a time of war, I'll have you shot for treason."

"I am *not* lying," Josie said, more insulted than afraid. "What possible benefit could I gain by leading your men into the mines unless I had something for them to do there?"

"I don't know, but I'm not in a position where I can afford to take anything at face value," Cook said. "I'm sorry if that makes me come off as unreasonable, but the businesspeople of Medicine Rocks don't exactly have a reputation for straight shooting. For all I know, you're working for the Whitmans, and this is all a plot to get even more of my men killed."

Josie recoiled at the thought, but the general wasn't finished. "I didn't say I wasn't going to do it. Just know that the only reason I'm biting on your too-good-to-be-true offer is because your uncle was one of the only honest men I knew in this town, and he was always singing your praises. That, and I really need the crystal. How long do you think it'll take to get it back here?"

"Um," Josie said, scrambling the numbers in her head. "We made the first trip down and back in eight days. It should be quicker now that we know where we're going, but bigger groups move slower, and we'll need time for mining, so... ten days? Give or take?"

The general scowled. "Not as fast as I was hoping, but better than nothing." He stuck out his hand. "You've got yourself a deal, Miss Price. I'll have fifty men at your doorstep first thing tomorrow, plus my own lieutenant to lead them."

From the look on his face, this was news to Lucas. He didn't seem happy about the assignment in the slightest, but he must have been used to the general's snap decisions, because the only thing he said was, "Where in the mines is your claim located?"

"The Deep Caves," Josie admitted with a wince. "But only just! I made it there with nothing but a guide and a guard, so I'm sure a troop of professional soldiers will have no trouble."

"I'm sure they won't," Cook agreed, blocking Lucas's furious scowl with his body as he went to open the door for her. "Thank you for bringing this opportunity to our attention, Miss Price. I hope for all our sakes that everything goes smoothly. I'd love to chat longer, but you've given me much to do, so I'm afraid I must bid you farewell. One of the boys outside will be happy to walk you back to your office."

Josie's head was still spinning from how quickly everything had come together, but trying to stall such a clear dismissal was clearly pointless. She had a lot to take care of as well if she was going to lead a troop of fifty soldiers to her mine by tomorrow morning, so Josie bid the officers good day and marched out of the tower, taking care to avoid any of the "boys" the general had offered lest she frighten Mary to death by bringing a soldier to her door.

~~~

"I don't think this is wise, sir," Lucas said the moment General Cook shut the door behind Miss Price. "Even if she is telling the truth, the Deep Caves are not a place to be taken lightly."

"That's a fine bit of opinion from a man who was so hot for crystal last night he convinced me to risk a riot," the general replied, turning around with his arms crossed over his chest.

"Pressing the miners was a gamble," Lucas admitted. "But it was one we knew how to manage. We've dealt with greedy, gun-happy miners before, but no one understands the Deep Caves!"

"She seemed to," Cook said, sticking a thumb over his shoulder in the direction Miss Price had gone. "If Pretty Missy Price can get down and back without mussing her hair, I'm sure you can survive."

"But…" Lucas dropped his face and raked his hands through his hair. "Does it have to be *me*?"

"Ah," the general said. "There's the rub."

Lucas closed his eyes in shame as Cook's hand landed on his shoulder. "I know you had some trauma in there, but there's no one else I can trust with this. If Miss Price is telling the truth, there's enough crystal down there to make an ordinary soldier forget his duty, but no one who clawed his way out of the Dark on a broken leg to warn us about the Sioux could ever be counted among the common run. You've earned my trust above and beyond, Jean-Jacques. It can only be you."

305

Lucas closed his eyes again. He couldn't say how long he'd been waiting for someone to say those words. But, "I'm not sure I can, sir," he whispered. "I know I'm the one who argued for crystal, but the Deep Caves are where I lost my men, and I don't… I'm not certain I *can* go back in there."

"You'll be fine," the general assured him. "This trip's not nearly so deep as your last, and Miss Price said—"

"Price wants our free labor," Lucas said angrily, head snapping up at last. "She's downplaying the dangers so we'll agree to let our men die for her profits!"

Cook shrugged. "What did you expect? She's a capitalist. But unlike her windbag uncle, this Price understands that she needs us as much as we need her. This is our chance to get the crystal we need on our own terms, *without* relying on miners who'd rather shoot us than pay their share. I'd love not to have to risk our boys doing those sweeps, and I know you would, too."

"That part of the plan was always a necessary evil," Lucas admitted, rubbing the bridge of his nose. "All right, I'll do it."

"Of course you will," the general said confidently. "I ordered you to. I just hope you can do it quicker than ten days."

Lucas actually thought ten days was ridiculously optimistic for a mining trip of this size, but what else could he say? He had his orders.

"I'm still going to push the tax and the sweeps until you get back," Cook informed him, straightening back up. "The workshop Townsend's setting up will be ready to start adding crystal to our guns faster than you can get it to us, and like hell am I going back on my word after a speech like that. But you and I both know we can't keep this kind of pressure up for long without risking a real rebellion, so get down there and bring me a miracle."

"I'll do my best, sir," Lucas said, looking at the leg he'd unconsciously stretched out in front of him. "I just hope I'm able to walk by tomorrow."

"Given how fast Dr. Pendleton fixed everything else, I'm sure you'll be fine," Cook said cheerfully, grabbing a clean sheet of paper to write out his orders. "I'm giving you Townsend's infantry. They're slops compared to real cavalry, but they shoot straight enough. I know you'd prefer your own men, but I need the 10th here in case the Sioux show up, and we can't send a pack of Black men down into a cave with a white woman."

Lucas found that remark patently offensive. He trusted his soldiers over Townsend's untrained throw-togethers in every matter, including women. But he'd been insubordinate enough for one day, and the general was right about leaving the better troops to defend. Even so.

"May I bring Chaucer?" he asked. "He's the only other one of us who's been to the Deep Caves, and he's the cleverest man I know. I'd love to have him along to watch my back."

"Fine, but you're responsible," Cook said. "And if Miss Price objects, he's out. We need to stay in her good graces, and speaking of." He gave Lucas a calculating smile. "Assuming she's not lying through her teeth about all this, that girl has just outed herself as a valuable military asset. While you're down in the caves with her, I'd like it if you could... *inspire* her loyalty, if you take my meaning."

"I'm afraid I don't, sir."

"You know," the general said, rolling his hand. "French at her. Do whatever it is you do that earned all those letters I see addressed to you in pretty handwriting."

Lucas reeled back. "You want me to *seduce* Miss Price?"

"Who said anything about seduction?" the general chided, as if he hadn't just suggested exactly that, but Lucas wasn't having it.

"With respect, sir," he said through clenched teeth, "I am no longer that type of man."

"Of course you aren't," Cook said. "You're an officer of the US Cavalry, expected to conduct yourself as a gentleman at all times. I'd never ask you to do anything untoward. All I'm saying is that if you see an opportunity to secure Miss Price's dedication to our cause, you take it. And if she *does* happen to get other ideas, well, she's young, handsome, and probably the richest person in Montana. What more could you ask?"

Lucas lowered his eyes. "I'll see what I can do."

"Good man," Cook said, scribbling his signature onto the orders and handing the paper to Lucas. "Give this to the quartermaster so he can start packing your supplies, then go tell Townsend to pick fifty of his best walkers and have them report to Price Mining first thing tomorrow. The clock's ticking on the Sioux, so I want you to get in there, get as much crystal as you can, and get it back here lickety-split. Make that girl run if you have to. Just get it done. I'm pinning a lot of hopes on you, Jean-Jacques. Don't let me down."

"I won't, sir," Lucas promised, taking the paper. "You have my word."

The general nodded and strode out of the room to talk to the other officers who were already lining up outside. As the heavy door swung shut, Lucas doubled back over on his stool and pressed his palms into his eyes, steeling his panicking nerves for the whispering horror he'd just agreed to walk back into.

Chapter 19

Rel woke to a boot nudging her in the ribs.

"Rise and shine, princess," said a deep, mocking voice.

She rolled over with a curse, damning whoever it was thrice over for waking her just when she'd finally gotten to sleep. She damned the crystal, too. She'd been too exhausted to feel it for the first few hours, but once her body had gotten a smidgen of life back, her guts had filed a mountain of complaints, most of them needle-sharp. Never, *never* again was she taking that much at once, but the cruel waker didn't seem to care how she was feeling. He was still looming over her with that damn boot prodding her poor abused middle. But when Rel reached down to teach him a lesson about letting sick dogs lie, her hands found nothing in her holsters.

That got her awake. Rel sat up like a shot, fumbling all over for her weapons. But while she found her dad's cursed crystal gun lying under her left shoulder, her other two pistols were nowhere to be felt.

"Looking for these?" Apache Jake said, dangling a pair of scuffed six-shooters in front of her nose.

Rel snatched her guns to her chest while Apache chuckled.

"Your meeting with the boss must've left you in quite the state if you forgot your iron," he said. "Or maybe you barfed out your good sense along with all the rest?"

"You ain't funny," Rel muttered, returning her workhorses to their holsters along with her father's crystal Colt, which was just as still and silent now as it'd been when she'd fallen into bed, though not *this* bed.

"Where am I?" she asked, looking all around the tiny wooden room that definitely wasn't her bunk in the basement. "The hell did you do?"

"Moved you upstairs," Apache replied casually, as if that were an acceptable thing to do to a body while she was reeling from crystal. "You're up on the second story now."

"You put me on the whoring floor?" Rel was more shocked than offended. The whoring floor was prime real estate, not the sort of space that was wasted on gunhands. "I didn't realize I ranked."

"You don't," he said, crouching down beside her. "But we had a spare closet, and as the manager of this here operation, I felt it prudent to shove you into it. Got a lot of unmannerly louts in the lower levels. Didn't seem smart leaving a delicate flower such as yourself down there unconscious and alone now that we've dropped the pretense of you being a boy."

Rel went still. "Volchitsa told you?"

"Weren't no need," he said with a mocking smile. "This here's a fleshhouse, darlin'. Takes more than a bad haircut and some baggy clothes to fool the likes of us. The girls had you pegged months ago. Fellas downstairs are a little denser and more afraid of your guns, but they were starting to catch on, which is why I took this opportunity. I run a tight ship here, Miss Reiner. That means fixing things *before* they become problems."

Rel supposed that was thoughtful of him in a high-handed, condescending sort of way, but she refused to be grateful. "Well, if you're finished making sure I don't disrupt the smooth operation of your money mill, I'll be getting back to bed. I've been emptying myself of crystal from both ends all night."

"Actually, you've been at it for two nights and the whole day in between," Jake said, pointing at the few streams of sunlight that had fought through the thick layer of dust on the tiny room's equally tiny window. "This here's your second morning under my tender care."

Rel didn't believe it. "You're saying I've been puking my guts out for thirty-six hours?"

"That's not unusual, given how much crystal you chugged," he said, standing back up. "But it's time to buck up and get back to work. There's a commotion at Price Mining, and the boss wants you on it pronto."

Rel remembered feeling happy about the notion when she'd gone to sleep. In the sober light of day, though, the thought of facing Josie after what she'd promised Volchitsa set her abused innards clenching all over again.

"Do I gotta?"

"Boss says so."

"Do you always do what your master says?"

The surly words had scarcely left her mouth before Rel felt the sharp edge of Apache's pistol stabbing into the hollow under her jaw. She hadn't heard him move, hadn't seen it, hadn't felt it. One second he was standing beside her bedroll. The next, he was crouching on top of her, his fist yanking her head back by her short hair and his gun set to blow her brains out.

"You don't get to use that word with me," he said, his pleasant smile gone as he looked down at her with eyes turned hard as gunmetal. "I work for the She-Wolf because she's the only person in this shithole who can give me what I want. The second that changes, I take my gun somewhere else. I got that freedom now, and Volchitsa knows I'll kill her if she tries to step on it. That's our understanding. You'd best make sure you understand it, too, before you open your mouth to me again."

"All right, all right, jeez," Rel said, putting her hands up. "It was just an expression."

The gun didn't budge, forcing her to swallow as she choked out, "I'm sorry."

"That's more like it," Apache said, his signature smile snapping back into place as he returned his well-used pistol to its holster. "Now get your lazy carcass out of bed."

Not stupid enough to press her luck twice, Rel did as she was told, ignoring the stabbing in her middle as she hauled herself to her feet. "Can you at least tell me what sort of commotion I'm walking into?"

"Not sure yet," he said, walking back to the window to check the street below. "My man on watch said they looked like miners, but it's no

311

one we recognize, and their guns are cavalry issue. I also know Miss Price paid the cavalry a visit yesterday."

"She did what?"

"Went to the general," Apache clarified. "For what precisely, I haven't found out yet, but I don't have to tell you how much getting the cavalry involved will complicate matters."

Rel didn't give a damn about their matters, but she was pissed as all get-out that Josie had gone to the soldiers behind her back. Of all the outsiders she could've brought in, the government was the worst possible choice! They made the laws, which meant if they decided something of yours should be theirs, you couldn't do shit. The army could take everything the three of them had worked for, including Rel's portion. Not that Rel had a portion anymore after last night's deal with the devil, but Josie didn't know that.

"What the hell was that idiot thinking?"

"Who knows?" Jake said, smiling over his shoulder. "But her opinions ain't our worry anymore. We're through trying to convince Price to sell. All we want now is the paper proving ownership over Sam Price's final claim. Get that for us, and we'll count it a job well done."

"That wasn't what Volchitsa said last night," Rel told him. "She wanted all of it. What changed her mind?"

"I did," Apache replied, much to Rel's surprise. "I told you, the boss is my *boss*, not my master. I ain't a rabbit under her paw like the rest of you. She pays me because I know how to get shit done, which includes telling her when she's holding on to a carcass longer than it's worth. We already got the goods outta Price Mining. Other than getting one up on a man who's already dead, that deed's the only thing of value left in the place."

"Why do you care so much about deeds, anyway?" Rel asked, genuinely curious. "It ain't like y'all do anything else legally."

"Actually, we do most things legally," Apache informed her proudly. "That's how we get away with so much. If we jumped that claim like a bunch of idiot bandits, Price could complain to the government and bring down heat that we can't match. But if we take the only proof she has that it was hers to start with, she'll be left without a paddle, and we'll get all that crystal without having to lift a finger."

"And you foist all the actual risks off on me."

"Now you're getting it," he said cheerfully. "It's called working smarter, darlin'."

Smarter for him, maybe. He wasn't the one being coerced into robbing his oldest friend. Then again, perhaps it was better this way.

She'd always known Josie wasn't cut out for life in Medicine Rocks, and her making a deal with the cavalry proved it. It was only a matter of time before the army came up with a justification for why all that crystal should belong to them. But if Rel stole the deed before they even set out, she'd defuse the situation before Josie's bad decisions came home to roost. Volchitsa had already said she wanted Price on a carriage back to Boston. That might not be what Josie wanted, but it was a hell of a lot better than dead or stranded out here because the cavalry seized her assets. When you looked at things that way, it scarcely counted as betrayal at all.

That was such a leap of logic that Rel subconsciously paused for her father's biting comeback, but none came. Despite the obvious opening, the crystal gun at her hip remained quiet and still as her other weapons, sending a nervous tremor through Rel's abused body as she turned to the door.

"I'll be back with the deed before noon."

"I'm counting on it," Apache said cheerfully. "And as soon as you do, we'll have a nice little meeting about bringing in the man who murdered your family."

That was all Rel could've asked for, but her heart was still pounding like a nervous steel driver as she slipped into the purple-papered hallway. She tiptoed past the sleeping whores' closed doors downstairs to grab a bit of corn porridge, the only food her stomach could handle right now. Once she'd shoved down as much as she could tolerate, Rel slapped her dusty black hat on her head and headed out the front toward Josie's.

Just like Apache had said, the place was hopping. The doors of the barnlike half of the building—where the mining teams had lived back when Price Mining still had such things—were thrown wide open, showing off an army of men carrying stuffed packs for what would clearly be a serious crystal-mining expedition. They were dressed like any other miners in ragtag coats and patched-up denim, but their identical Spencer rifles and shiny silver six-shooters made it clear as a bugle call that they were cavalry.

Even after Apache's warning, seeing the proof with her own eyes made Rel furious all over again. Not that she had any right to such feelings anymore, but *dammit*. What was the point of all that partnership talk if Josie was just going to go over their heads? She was stomping into the front office to confront her about it when Rel came face-to-face with a dark-haired girl she didn't recognize.

She froze in the doorway, clutching her still-aching stomach as she tried to figure out who the hell was looking at her so familiar. Not until the girl said her name did Rel realize her mistake. This wasn't some threatening new stranger. It was Mary Good Crow, and she looked different because she was *clean*.

Her clothes, hat, and pack had all been washed, brushed, and mended. Her hair had been scrubbed shiny as well, the thick black braids glossy as onyx rather than dull like charcoal, but the biggest change was her face. It had a whole different structure now that the layers of grime had been scraped away. Higher-cheeked and more obviously red-skinned, but prettier too, allowing Rel to see the rich gray-brown color of her eyes for the first time now that they were no longer shadowed by dark smudges.

"I'll be," she said, smiling despite everything. "They cleaned you up like a fairground pig."

Mary did not look amused. "Where in tarnation have you been?" she demanded, scurrying to Rel's side. "Miss Josie's been looking all over for you since yesterday! We even went to the Wet Whistle, but they claimed you were sleepin'."

"Why're you asking where I was, then? Sounds like you already knew."

"I didn't know they were telling the truth!" Mary cried. "Who sleeps for a night, a day, and then a night again?"

"Tired people," Rel said, looking through the glass at the mob waiting on the street. "But it seems you two got on fine in my absence. Mind filling me in on why there's a company of soldiers dressed like miners waiting outside our door?"

The question was just meant to test the water, but Mary started shaking like Rel had invoked the devil. "They're gonna mine for us," she whispered, huddling under her hat. "Miss Josie couldn't find anyone else to hire, so she cut a deal with the general that if he gave us men to mine, she'd give him half the crystal they pulled out."

"*Half?*" Rel roared. "That's robbery! I thought the tax was only twenty-five?"

"Yeah, well, things've changed," Mary grumbled. "The town's hopping mad about it, but ain't no one gonna fight the cavalry, which is why Miss Josie picked 'em to partner with."

"I'd say that's every reason *not* to." Rel scowled at her. "And you agreed to this?"

Mary answered by cringing farther into the folds of her poncho, and Rel's jaw clenched. "She didn't ask, did she?"

"Not as such," the guide whispered.

The look on her face said there was more to the matter, but Rel had already thrown back her head. "*Josie!*"

"I'm up here," came the cross reply. "There's no need to bellow."

Pushing Mary aside, Rel stomped up the stairs to the office's second floor to a sunny corner room that must've been Sam Price's private office. Josie was seated under the window, scribbling furiously at a once-broken, now-mended desk overflowing with papers.

Not surprisingly given the men outside, she was dressed for caving. Sensibly this time in a man's denims, boots, and jacket, not the ridiculous costume she'd worn for their first trip, but she didn't look ready to go just yet. Her hair was still up in the same frivolous ringlets she used to drape across the real Miss Josephine's shoulders, and her scowling face was still pinched and powdered, making her look like a disapproving debutante who'd just been stood up.

"*Really*, Reliance," she scolded. "You can't just storm in like this if you're going to keep pretending to be a man. People will make assumptions, and I don't think the real Miss Price would enjoy hearing rumors about herself having a wild affair with Tyrel the height-challenged gunhand."

"You're the one who ought to be worrying what other people think," Rel told her, slamming her hands down on the desk. "You wanna tell me what fifty cavalry soldiers are doing standing in front of your ready room?"

"Getting ready, I hope," Josie said, retrieving the papers scattered by Rel's outburst. "They're going to be working with us from here on."

"And who told them they could do that?"

"I did," Josie said, fixing Rel with a steely glare. "Look, I'm sorry you found out this way. I tried my best to get your permission, but we couldn't reach you in time."

"Then you shouldn't have done anything!" Rel yelled at her with a fury that had nothing to do with the crystal or Volchitsa's orders. "You went behind my back!"

"I did nothing of the sort! I *would* have happily asked permission if someone had told me *where she was.* What was I supposed to do? Barge into the Wet Whistle and demand they produce you so we could discuss the details of our super-secret crystal mine?"

"You could've waited!" Rel snapped.

"No, I couldn't," Josie snapped back. "Did you forget why we had to split the claim in the first place? It's because everyone in town was going to turn against us the moment they realized what we'd found! Did you think those threats would go on hiatus just because you weren't at leisure to face them?"

"That don't give you the right to ignore my say!"

"I wasn't trying to ignore you!" Josie pleaded. "If I erred, it was assuming you would be reachable like a normal person. Something had to be done to protect our investments. You weren't available, so I made the decision I felt would be best for everyone."

"Not for Mary!" Rel said, pointing back down the stairs at the girl who was already fleeing out the front door. "Maybe you couldn't find me, but she was right here the whole time. Did you even think about how *she'd* feel before you cut a deal with those Sioux-shooting horse-humpers? 'Cause I don't believe for a second she was a willing participant in this marriage of convenience. She's terrified of soldiers, probably because most of them say hello by pretending to shoot her."

Josie had the decency to look ashamed, at least. "I have already apologized to Mary," she said, twisting her hands. "I know this arrangement makes her uncomfortable, but it was the only way I could think of to mine the crystal without losing it. By signing a contract with General Cook, I've secured a future for all—"

Rel snorted. "You really think the cavalry will honor their word just because they signed your damn paper? Why don't you ask the Indians how well that worked out for them?"

"Why are you being so difficult?" Josie cried. "You didn't even want Mary to have a share at the start!"

"This ain't about Mary," Rel said. "It's about you and how you're still treating us like we're your damn employees! You swore up and down in the caves that we'd all be equal partners, so why does it seem like you're the only one who gets a say the moment we get back to town?"

"*Me?*" Josie roared. "All I've done since returning is work for *you*! While you were off hibernating, I've been toiling day and night to make sure we actually have a chance at keeping the fortune we all worked so hard for! If you cared so blam-jam much, you should have been here helping, but you *weren't*. You ran off and left everything for me to clean up like I'm still your dratted maid! Well, I'm *not*, and I don't see how you have any grounds to criticize how I managed our affairs!"

Rel had plenty left to say, but it wouldn't do any good. Little or grown, no member of the Price family would hear reason once they got their hackles up. Josie might not be their actual blood, but she'd been stewed in that same rotten pot, and right now, Rel was hard-pressed to tell the difference between the fuming girl in front of her and the real thing.

"You make a damn good Josephine Price," she said coldly, knowing full well how much those words would hurt. "Go on and do as you please. You will anyway, so I'm done wasting my breath except to say that you'd better make sure the cavalry doesn't touch a crumb of my crystal."

The angry flush had left Josie's face completely by the time Rel finished, leaving her pale as a soap carving.

"Are you..." She stopped to swallow. "Does this mean you're not coming with us?"

Rel shook her head. "I gave it a good shot, Josephine," she said, turning to open the office door. "But if this is how you treat your partners, I'm done. I got better places to be stepped on than here."

"*Reliance!*" Josie called, but Rel was already walking down the hall as fast as her feet could carry her.

It was running, plain and simple, but in a crooked, perverse way, Rel was glad of it. A hard break like this would make what was about to happen easier for them both. Rel'd much rather Josie hate her for being right than for what she did now, which was to slip down the stairs to the clerk's office where Mihir was still working.

"Mr. Reiner!" he said, rising from his chair the moment Rel opened the door. "How may I help you?"

318

Rel stopped, caught off guard by the cheery greeting, which was a far cry from the open hostility she'd received the first time they met.

"I'm looking for some paperwork," she said when she'd recovered. "I've got my copy of the contract Josie had us sign, but there's something I need to check against the original deed. Josie said you'd know where it was."

The lie slid so easily off her lips she was ashamed. No matter how badly she'd acted today, screwing over someone who'd given you a piece of their kingdom should've been harder than this. Rel was still trying to decide if she should pull her gun and rob Mihir the moment he produced the deed or wait to see what drawer he took it from and come back later after Josie and the cavalry had left for the mines. Both left an equally terrible taste in her mouth, but before she could decide anything, Mihir shook his head.

"I don't know why she told you that, because when I spoke to Miss Price last, she was insistent that I *not* have it."

A new cramp settled in Rel's stomach. "Say what?"

"She said it would be too dangerous for me to have the deed in the building, given all the break-ins we've suffered," Mihir explained with a touched expression. "She didn't want to risk me becoming the victim of another attack."

Of all the damn times for Josie to be thoughtful. "If the original deed's not with you, then where is it?"

"With her," Mihir said. "I was worried when she first suggested keeping it on her person, but now that the cavalry's here, I feel *much* better. I had dinner with General Cook and his lieutenant several times while Samuel was alive, and while we didn't always agree, I'm certain they'll keep our Josephine safe. Not that you weren't doing a magnificent job of that on your own, of course."

"Of course," Rel muttered, eager to get away now that she knew her target wasn't here. Damn Josie and her thinking ahead. Robbing Mihir in an empty office was one thing, but pickpocketing the head of Price

Mining in the middle of a cavalry company was a whole other kettle of fish. How the hell was Rel supposed to—

"Mr. Reiner?"

Rel looked over her shoulder to find Mihir standing just behind her.

"I owe you an apology, sir," he said, inclining his head. "The first time we met, I treated you most rudely. I had not had good experiences with Wet Whistle employees in the past, and I faulted you for that before you'd even said a word. As someone who is often judged by his appearance rather than by his character, it was particularly wrong of me, and I am most sorry for it. I was also most incorrect. Ever since returning from the caves, Miss Price has had nothing but praise for your valor, integrity, and swift action in the face of danger. She even said you saved her life, so on behalf of one who considers her family, thank you from the bottom of my heart."

"Uh… you're welcome," Rel said, feeling ready to hurl again, but Mihir wasn't finished.

"I must also thank you on my own behalf," he continued excitedly. "Ever since you joined our team, my relationship with the Wet Whistle improved enormously. The foreman there, Mr. Apache, came over personally to say that since you and Miss Josephine were such old, good friends, he would henceforth consider our organization like a sibling to his. I didn't know what to say at the time, but since that day, we haven't had a single bit of trouble! No more robberies, no more vagrants trying to sleep in our bunks or lighting fires in the kitchen. I can even spend nights in my own bed again rather than sleeping on the couch holding a shotgun! It's been marvelous, and I owe it all to you."

He bowed his head even lower. "Thank you very, very much, sir. You are indeed a gentleman. I hope greatly that you and Miss Price will remain close friends, and I look forward to working with you more closely in the future."

The onslaught of praise left Rel reeling. She had no idea what Apache was thinking, if he was just flexing his power or if there was yet another, larger game at play, but Rel had never felt so called out in all her life. If her father had still been listening, he'd have laughed himself to misfiring at the irony. He must have meant it when he'd said he was done, though, because the crystal gun at her hip didn't even wiggle.

Rel almost wished it would. Being pissed at her dad would've been easier than dealing with the flood of emotions Mihir had just unleashed on top of her. If she didn't get away from his damn thankful face soon, she'd drown, so Rel muttered something polite-ish and bolted, running for the exit as fast as she could. When she grabbed the knob on the door she'd come in, though, she heard the thump of Josie's heels coming down the stairs.

Panicked, Rel spun the other direction, tearing across the clerk's office and out a broken window into the empty yard by the stable to regain her composure and figure out what the hell to do now.

Chapter 20

Mary huddled in the shadows of Price Mining's front porch, peeking around the pole at the cavalry like a deer watching a pack of wolves. She'd run out here when Miss Josie and Rel started yelling upstairs, a decision she was sore regretting. The fancy parlor might've made her too nervous to move lest she break something worth more than all the money she'd made in her life, but at least it was shelter. Out here in the open, there was nothing to protect her from the pack of soldiers jawing in the road while they waited for things to get moving.

Blessed Lady, but there were a lot of them. Men in groups were always worse than men alone, and these were big, rough-looking sorts who carried their guns far too comfortably. They'd had the good sense not to wear their uniforms, since a suited-up company marching into the caves would've had every prospector in the territory trailing after to see what the fuss was. But while they probably looked enough like hired miners to fool most, every one of them was eyeing Mary like she was a rabid animal that needed to be put down, which was enough to mark them as cavalry from fifty paces no matter how they dressed.

Shaking in her boots, Mary ducked behind the porch pole and sank down to the floor with her arms wrapped around her knees to make herself as small as possible. She understood why Miss Josie had done it, but knowing these were "good" cavalry who were "working for them" didn't make the men any less scary. It weren't like soldiers followed orders all the time. She'd seen packs of 'em going into the Wet Whistle despite their officers yelling all over about that place being off-limits, usually just before those same officers headed in as well.

Seeing how easily the men ignored orders when they pleased made it hard to trust the general's word to Miss Josie that Mary would be safe. If the old graybeard couldn't keep his men out of the bawdy houses here in town, how was he going to make them do anything down in the caves? Given the nasty way some of them were already looking at her, Mary wouldn't be surprised if she ate a bullet before they cleared the Midway. And while it was gratifying to think that Miss Josie would be furious on her behalf, no one would punish a soldier for shooting an Indian, and Mary'd still be dead, so that wasn't much comfort, was it?

All these awful thoughts were stampeding in a circle 'round Mary's mind when a new problem swung in to send the rest flying. It started with a sudden silence as all the soldiers stopped loafing and snapped to attention. When Mary peeked her head up to see why, she spotted two new men coming down the road from Fort Grant. One was a Buffalo Soldier who looked far too happy for the easy way he carried his gun to mean any good. The man beside him, though...

Mary shrank back into the shadow of the porch. Unlike the rest of the terrifying company, the man walking next to the Black soldier was one she knew by heart. He wasn't using a cane anymore, but there was no mistaking the handsome dark-haired officer who'd stood beside the general during the tax announcement. The one who'd clung to her in the Dark and spoken to her in French. Lieutenant Lucas.

Just like yesterday, the sight of him sent her into a panic. Mary couldn't even rightly say what she feared so much. The only thing she'd ever done to this man was save his life. Surely that would temper the violent behavior she'd come to expect from soldiers, yet for some reason, he felt more dangerous than any of the others. She was seriously contemplating going back inside to take her chances with the yelling when Miss Josie burst through the door behind her.

Mary jumped so high she knocked her hat on the lantern hanging from the porch's ceiling. She was struggling to keep the huge thing from falling on top of her when she caught sight of Miss Josie's face.

"What's the matter?" she cried, forgetting all about the metal swinging wildly over their heads.

Poor thing looked like someone had just shot her horse in front of her. Her music sounded just as distraught, scratching up and down inside Mary's ears like a terrified animal.

"Oh, Mary," the lady whispered, grabbing her hands so tight it hurt. "I'm *so* sorry! I've handled this all wrong!"

"What've you done wrong?" Mary asked, her brows pulling into a scowl. "What did Rel say to you?"

"Nothing I didn't deserve."

"Horse apples," Mary scoffed. "I heard the way she was yelling at you. No one deserves that sorta meanness."

"But she was *right*," Miss Josie wailed, squeezing Mary's fingers even harder. "I knew you were afraid of the cavalry—I *knew* I shouldn't have acted without asking—but I just wanted everything to work out so badly! I got so swept up in my own plans, I didn't think of anyone but myself. I acted just like Miss... like a selfish person I don't admire. A person I *never* want to be! I see that now, and I'm so very, very sorry. Can you ever forgive me?"

"Of course I do," Mary said without hesitation. "Though I'm not sure precisely what sin I'm supposed to be pardoning. You say you've been selfish, but all I've seen you do is give. You gave me work and my pillar and one of your fine dresses, none of which were things I had any claim to. Really, Miss Josie, I don't think—"

"*Please* just call me Josie," the lady begged, bowing her head. "This is exactly what I'm talking about! I didn't give you anything, Mary. You earned all of those things, and I don't ever want you to feel that you owe me for them. You are not my employee nor my servant. You are my partner and trusted friend. I deeply regret ignoring your feelings and bringing in the cavalry. It's too late to go back on a contract that's already been signed, but I promise I won't do anything like this ever again! You don't even have to come with us this time if you don't want to. I'll find another way to navigate to the—"

"Hey, hey, *Josie*," Mary said, using the name she'd said she wanted despite how unnatural it felt. "When did I say I didn't want to go with you?"

She was actually dying to get back to the caves. As thrilling as it'd been to put on the dress-mask and walk around town like a respectable sort, it wasn't ever going to feel natural. Just living in the fancy Price building with its hot baths and private bedrooms and having food served to her with no one ever mentioning the cost had Mary walking on pins. Heading back underground in her normal clothes felt like letting out a long-held breath even with the cavalry plotting murder behind her. And while this certainly wasn't the company she preferred, Mary hated seeing Miss J—seeing *Josie* looking guilty as a grave robber over it.

"It's gonna be all right," she said, turning her hands around so that she was holding Josie's instead of just being squeezed.

"It's *not* all right," Josie said fiercely, pulling out of Mary's grasp to grab a handkerchief for her runny eyes and nose. "You had to lie down just from me mining one crystal. How are you going to handle fifty men doing the same?"

Mary had been wondering the same thing. They weren't even underground yet, but she swore she could already hear the crystal crying. It was only gonna get worse as they went deeper, but there weren't nothing for it. Things were always bound to turn out this way, and she'd learned a long time ago there was no point fighting what couldn't be changed. Better to focus on the good parts she could still salvage, such as the desperate friend in front of her.

"How I handle myself is my business," she said gently, giving Josie a smile. "But if you meant that stuff about being partners, then you gotta trust me when I tell you I'm not mad. I won't lie and say you haven't been pushy, but that's not always a bad thing. I was petrified to wear that dress, but it ended up being great. Same goes for my third of the cavern. I never would've signed that contract on my own, but you didn't let me balk, and now I've got a wonder of the world that's mine to hold forever. That's two good things you've pushed me to despite my fretting, so maybe I'm the one who should stop being scared and digging in her feet all the time."

"You've done nothing wrong," Josie insisted.

Mary shook her head. "I never claimed I did. All I'm saying is neither have *you*. Rel can toss whatever blame she wants, but from where I'm standing, you've never tried to do anything but right by us. And while I agree that you shouldn't go making promises without talking to us first, that's an easy thing to fix. I'm certainly not going to punish both of us for it by sitting out a trip. I *like* going into the caves with you, Josie Price."

"Even with the soldiers?" she asked nervously. "I swear on my life I won't let them harm you."

That was a foolish promise. Lady or no, there wasn't a thing Josie could do to stop that many men from acting however they pleased, but hearing her say so still made Mary's heart float up in her chest. No one had ever sworn on their life to protect her before. Never welcomed her into their home or mended her clothes or acted like they genuinely wanted her around. She'd always been a stranger and a threat, an unwanted burden even to those who'd brought her up. But Josie had called Mary friend and partner without caring who overheard. That was a treasure worth more than any crystal to Mary's thinking, and her greed for it overcame even her fear of the soldiers as she looked her friend in the face.

"I'll be good if you are," she promised. "Like you keep saying, we're in this together. So if this is what you need to do, then I'm with you. It's simple as that."

Her cheeks were burning by the time she finished. That sorta stuff always sounded so noble when Josie said it, but the words felt childish and stupid on Mary's lips. It must've been good enough, though, 'cause Josie lurched herself forward, throwing her long arms all the way around Mary's poncho-covered, backpack-wearing body for a hug that lifted her off the ground.

"Thank you," she whispered, her music fluttering like happy larks. "Thank you, thank you a thousand times! I'm so lucky to have a friend like you."

Mary was too shocked to move at first. But after a moment, she wrapped her arms around Josie as well, pressing her face hard into her friend's warm shoulder. Others would surely think it foolish, getting so worked up over such a little thing. But small noises made big sounds in empty rooms, and Mary had been alone for so, so long. She couldn't even remember the last time someone had hugged her like this, but while the jumping in her insides was mostly due to joy, there was also an equal measure of terror. Not because she didn't believe Josie was sincere, but because this was too much good.

Mary'd learned from experience that life didn't work out like this for her. Every time something happened to get her hopes up, suffering always came right after to smack them back down, and the bigger the rise, the bigger the fall. Josie hadn't even let her go yet, but Mary could already feel the doom blowing in like a storm front, leaving her shaking even harder than before as her friend broke away to go greet the approaching lieutenant.

Chapter 21

"Thank you again for coming with me, Chaucer," Lucas said, struggling to find a place for his beloved officer's saber among the miner's clothes Townsend had provided for their mission. "Really, truly, *merci beaucoup*."

"What else could I do?" Chaucer teased. "You begged me so pathetically only a monster could've turned you down."

"One does what one must, and this was a must. If I didn't have at least one other soldier along who knew what he was doing down there, I'd go mad."

"They did stick us with a bunch of know-nothings, didn't they?" his companion said, eyeing the knot of infantry waiting for them in front of Price Mining. "Just look at those game-eyed bastards! They know as much about caving as they do about horses, which is less than none. No wonder you came crawling to me."

"Desperate times, desperate measures," Lucas said, pressing a distraught hand over his heart before breaking back into a smile. "But I am truly happy to have you with me, my friend. I know how great an ask it was to go back into that hell. I wouldn't have ordered you if you'd refused, but I am very, *very* glad you said yes."

"I certainly approve of your bribery," Chaucer replied happily, lifting his arm to wiggle the freshly-stitched chevron on his sleeve. "'Sergeant Chaucer' has a right nice ring. Can't believe you got the general to approve it."

Lucas's expression turned smug. "The general wants his crystal."

"See, see?" Chaucer said. "*This* is why I agreed! Palling around with Cook's new favorite is crackers for my career. If I survive this mission, maybe they'll make *me* a lieutenant!"

"The day they make you a lieutenant is the day I become general, which will be Judgment Day."

"Or next week if things go the way the gossip's pointing," Chaucer said, looking back over his shoulder at the solders scrambling on the fort's western wall, the last direction the Sioux were known to be gathering. "If we come back and discover Sitting Bull's killed everyone, does that make us ranking officers?"

"That's not funny."

"Wasn't meant to be. The patrols they called back say they've seen wolf prints the size of wagon wheels in the grass all around town. If that ain't a sign of the end times, what is?"

"All the more reason to finish this mining expedition *quickly*," Lucas said, picking up his pace. "The only way to fight crystal is with crystal."

"To do what with, though?" Chaucer asked, hurrying to catch up. "Make our own giant livestock?"

"That's not our worry. We're just the collectors. Figuring out how to use the stuff is Townsend's job."

"So we're all going to be armed with crystal account books and handkerchiefs, then?"

That was an awful thing to joke about, but Lucas couldn't help but laugh. This was the other reason he'd fought to bring Chaucer. It was hard to be afraid when you were with someone whose first reaction to danger was to insult it. Not that his good humor had saved them last time, but it made Lucas feel slightly better about this mission as he came to a halt in front of his new company.

They truly were a sorry bunch, though that wasn't necessarily their fault. Between the Civil War and the endless demands of the Western frontier, there weren't many good soldiers left to recruit. Infantry were the quickest to muster, since they required the least training and equipment, which was probably why they'd been assigned to Townsend.

It was certainly why they'd been given to Lucas. It was hard to get worse than the literal criminals he'd worked with in his youth, though. They might not be what he would wish, but at least Lucas knew how to handle such a situation, placing one hand on his pistol and the other on the handle of his saber as he turned to address the tattered soldiers.

"Men of the Temporary Underground Special Detachment," he announced, using the name Talmadge had come up with to keep his paperwork tidy for lack of anything better. "I am Lieutenant Jean-Jacques Lucas, and I will be your commander for the duration of this mission." He gestured at Chaucer next to him, who gave a royal wave. "This is Sergeant Henry Chaucer, my second-in-command. Yes, I know he is Black. Yes, I know he is British. Yes, I know he is rude. If you have a problem with any of those, keep it to yourself."

As expected, the all-white infantry looked terminally insulted by the concept of a Black officer, let alone the knowledge that they'd be serving beneath one. But Lucas wasn't here to coddle prejudice, so he just moved on.

"We're here to do a job and do it fast. I'm sure you've heard all kinds of rumors about the caves. I'm also sure you've heard that Chaucer and I are the only survivors of the last unit we sent down. If you don't want history to repeat itself, you'll follow every order we give the second it is given, no matter how strange it might seem. Additionally, we will be working with civilians, including a lady. You will treat her as such, or you will answer to me. Unless you are witnessing her about to step off a cliff, you are not to touch her person or speak to her unless spoken to. Now get your packs and get in line. We're leaving as soon as Miss Price gives the word."

The men didn't look happy with any of this. But untrained though they were, they'd been soldiers long enough to at least not backtalk him to his face. This didn't stop a few of them from casting Chaucer nasty looks, but while Lucas took careful note of the offenders, he wasn't too worried. No one with a mouth as big as Chaucer's survived this long without being able to look after himself. He'd be fine, and if he wasn't, Lucas would be there to help.

Satisfied the matter was settled for the moment, Lucas put the soldiers out of his mind and focused on looking as gentlemanly as possible, smoothing back his hair and straightening his rough miner's coat as he turned to greet Miss Price, who was already running down the stairs.

He was glad he'd taken the time to compose himself, for the sight of her was shocking. He supposed she couldn't be expected to wear petticoats and a bustle into the mines, but he hadn't expected *trousers*. They were the same denim jeans that every miner wore, including himself at the moment, but they looked entirely different on a lady. The same went for her buttoned wool shirt, canvas jacket, and long boots clinging to her calves, which were distractingly visible because of her lack of a skirt.

Lucas had never seen anything like it. But rich people were known for being odd, and the outfit wasn't overly alluring. At least, Lucas didn't find it so, but then he was French and a former sailor. It was hard to be excited over trousers when you'd seen Polynesian girls swimming through the sky-blue sea in nothing but their hair. The Americans were far less jaded, gawking like gulls despite there being nothing to see aside from the general idea of a leg beneath the shapeless, heavy fabric.

He supposed he should have expected that in hindsight. Soldiers and women were always a bad mix, even if the lady was dressed in a steel curtain. He was sure the terror of the caves would put a damper on any rude ideas, but he made a note to stay close to Miss Price at all times, just in case.

At least she didn't seem the sort to encourage any nonsense. Just like when she'd approached him at the gate yesterday, Miss Price's expression was all business as she marched straight over and held out her hand.

"Lieutenant Lucas! Splendid timing. Are your men ready to go?"

"As ready as they can be," he said, looking over her shoulder at the figures standing huddled on the porch. "Are these your men?"

There were two of them: a small figure who looked to be little more than a hat resting upon a pile of ponchos, and a gunman dressed in

331

the Wet Whistle's trademark black, who was just now coming out from around the side of the building.

That was going to be a problem. Sheriff Brightman was supposed to handle crime in town, but Lucas's soldiers had been called in to restore peace enough times that he instantly recognized the pale, eternally scowling Tyrel Reiner. Strangely, Miss Price looked just as surprised to see the gunman as Lucas was. He was hoping this meant Reiner's presence was a mistake when the fool woman's face suddenly lit up like a sunrise.

"Rel!" she cried in inexplicable delight. "Did you change your mind about coming?"

The gunman gave a surly shrug. "Couldn't let you go off and die without me."

That seemed a horrid thing to say, but there must have been more going on than met the eye, because Miss Price looked as giddy as a prisoner receiving a stay of execution. "One moment," she said, hurrying over to talk to the villain while Chaucer moved just as quickly to pull on Lucas's sleeve.

"*Lieutenant*," he hissed. "That's—"

"I know," Lucas whispered back. "I don't know what he's doing here, but I want you to stick to him like glue. If the Wet Whistle is involved, we've got more to worry about than just the caves."

Chaucer's eyes went huge. "*Me?* Stick to creepy Tyrel Reiner? I thought you wanted me to survive this trip!"

"If he does anything, I'll back you up," Lucas promised. "I just need you to keep an eye on him in case he tries anything funny."

"How funny is funny? 'Cause I've seen him sitting at the Wet Whistle bar talking to his gun like it could talk back on at least three occasions."

Lucas scowled. "What were *you* doing at the Wet Whistle?"

"Come on, sir," Chaucer pleaded. "It ain't like there's much choice for ladies out here, 'specially for men of my complexion. The Wet Whistle might be an overpriced den of criminality, but at least they rip me off the same as they would a white man. That makes them positively egalitarian, and where else am I supposed to spend my pay?"

Lucas sighed. He didn't begrudge a man his paid company, but the Wet Whistle was a place no one should go. He couldn't count how many fights he'd broken up over the women there or how many soldiers he'd caught stealing cavalry property to pay debts they'd racked up in that pit of a place. But as bad as their business practices were, the Wet Whistle's gunhands were even worse. They were well trained, well armed, and well protected enough to murder in broad daylight without consequence. He'd lost a dozen good men to their guns and never seen anyone brought to justice for it.

He wouldn't be comfortable going into the caves with any of their number but particularly not with Reiner, who never seemed to do anything without corpses being somehow involved. Asking Miss Price to leave him behind was clearly a fool's errand, however. She looked absolutely delighted Tyrel was coming, leading him over by the hand to introduce him to Lucas as her personal guard, family friend, and business partner.

That last one made him do a double take. He was about to ask what manner of business she could possibly be involved with that included a known criminal when he remembered the other part of his mission. He was supposed to be getting in good with Josephine Price, not probing her apparently *highly questionable* judgment.

No matter. He'd let General Cook deal with the politics of having a Wet Whistle agent on their mission when they got back. Getting the crystal was the only thing that really mattered, and the nice part about having fifty soldiers was that you didn't have to worry too much about a single gunman. He was about to dismiss Miss Price's employees entirely when the lady coaxed the other member of her team off the porch. The poncho-wrapped figure came down timidly and pulled off their huge hat to reveal—not a boy as Lucas had presumed—but a lovely young Lakota woman with wide brown eyes and night-black hair bound in two braids that fell like velvet ropes across her shoulders.

The sight of her made Lucas go still. He couldn't say where, but some deep part of him was convinced he'd met this lovely creature before. She looked a little like the bashful woman in the pink dress who'd been standing behind Miss Price at the gate yesterday, but Lucas didn't think that was it. He'd barely taken note of that lady, but this girl he *knew*. He was certain of it. Miss Price was introducing her as their guide, so perhaps that was it? The cavalry had employed several native guides over their time here, though Lucas didn't remember any who looked like this. He was racking his brain to try to recall when Miss Price finally got the girl to speak.

"My name is Mary Good Crow," she said in a trembling voice that struck his heart like a bell. "I've been to this claim before, so make sure you follow what I do and step where I step, and you should do just fine."

That was all she had to say. Just a brief few words, but each one hit Lucas harder than the last, and he grabbed hold of Chaucer's arm.

"It's her!"

"I was thinking the same thing," Chaucer whispered as Miss Price ducked back inside the building to collect her own backpack. "A Wet Whistle thug *and* a Sioux traitor? This thing's got the She-Wolf written all over it."

"No, I mean it's *her*," Lucas said, heart beating so fast he felt lightheaded. "I'd know that voice anywhere. That's the woman who saved me in the Dark!"

Chaucer gave him a sideways look. "You mean the cave angel?"

Lucas nodded.

"You sure?"

How could anyone be sure of a dream? His memories of that awful time were a broken mess of fears and illusions. He couldn't even say for certain how long he'd wandered lost before falling down that hole. But while everything else about the Dark was an incoherent smear of pain and hopelessness, that sweet, whispering voice was carved into his soul. Even if he lived for a thousand years, he would never not know her. Mary Good Crow was his angel. He'd bet his life upon it.

"I'm going to talk to her."

"Didn't you *just* order us not to talk to the ladies unless they spoke to us first?" Chaucer said, but Lucas was already striding away, walking as quickly as his still-twinging leg could manage after the lovely figure who'd already run ahead toward the mouth of the caves.

Chapter 22

Mary was cursing herself for a fool. She hadn't intended to say anything, but then Josie had pulled her forward. Since Mary couldn't well snub the men depending on her to show them the way just because she'd saved their lieutenant's life and didn't want him to know, she'd had no choice but to play along. She'd tried her best to talk different than usual, but it clearly hadn't worked. The moment she'd opened her mouth, Lucas had gone from looking at everything but her to honing in on Mary like a hawk.

He'd practically run her down coming up to the caves, only to be foiled by his own men. The extra soldiers General Cook had stationed at the entrance to run his new sweeps hadn't given Mary more than a sneering look, but the moment they spotted Lucas, they'd snapped to attention and started talking all manner of "good morning, sir," and "look at us doing our job, sir." By the time he'd dutifully acknowledged everything they wanted to show him, the rest of the group had caught up, spurring more talking as Josie insisted on signing the whole party into the ledger book.

From there, it had been easy to stick Lucas to Josie's side. All Mary'd had to do was drop a word in Josie's ear that Lucas had been to the caves before, and her friend's chatty nature had taken over, forcing the lieutenant to choose between being rude to the owner of the crystal they so desperately needed and chasing after Mary.

Not a bad escape considering how bad she'd bungled the start, and it was good for Josie too. Mary didn't like how quickly she'd forgiven Rel even though the surly gunhand hadn't said a word close to "sorry." Reliance seemed unwilling to get near the lieutenant, though, so this arrangement worked for everyone.

All in all, Mary was feeling quite clever as she led the soldiers through the black crystal cavern, but her cockiness faded quickly when she got to the same-y tunnels beyond. The Front Caves' blasted-out warren was always confusing with its dead ends and double backs, but the turns seemed particularly bad today. She chalked it up to nerves for the first half, but after working through more forks than Miss Josie'd put on the table at dinner, Mary was forced to admit that the caves here had done a full shuffle since they'd come through the day before yesterday.

That was very unusual this close to the surface. Enough to make Mary stop paying attention to who was talking to who and actually focus on her job. She was way up ahead of the pack, standing at a fork with her ear to the wall and her lantern turned down to a flicker so the light wouldn't put off the crystal, when Lucas suddenly spoke right behind her.

"Do you always work in the dark?"

Mary nearly jumped out of her skin. Much as she fretted about the change in her ears, one thing she did like about the new people music was that it let her hear when folks were sneaking. But she'd been too focused on the cave song to catch the lieutenant's sound this time. She was about to tell him off for scaring her like that when Mary realized he'd asked his question in French.

Furious she'd almost let herself be fooled again, Mary pushed away from the wall and slapped her hat back on her head, pulling the brim all the way to her nose so he couldn't see her face. "Sorry," she told him gruffly. "I don't speak whatever that is."

"You spoke it well enough before," Lucas replied in English, bending down to peer under the barrier she'd made.

Mary jerked her face away. "We've never met."

"Are you certain?" he asked, following the motion quick as a kingfisher. "Because I was saved from certain death in these very caves by a marvelous woman with a lovely voice that sounded very much like yours."

"The echoes down here make everyone sound the same," Mary dodged, turning back to the fork. "Pardon me, I gotta find our path."

"But there's only one way forward."

Mary's head shot up in surprise. Sure enough, the fork she'd just been contemplating was gone, replaced by a single straight tunnel running dead ahead as far as the eye could see.

Furious at the caves for betraying her like this, Mary cranked her lantern back to full and stomped back toward the main group. She made it a grand total of two paces when the lieutenant caught the hem of her poncho.

"I'm sorry," he said. "I don't mean to be a nuisance, but I must know. Are you the one who saved me?"

Mary ground her teeth. It would've been easy enough to tell him no, but Lieutenant Lucas was obviously a persistent man, and she wasn't much of a liar. If she gave in and told him the truth, though, he'd just stick to her that much harder, which would make her even more of a target, since Lucas seemed like an officer who actually did his duty. Soldiers hated that, she knew, but what was she supposed to do? She couldn't put him off forever.

This was why she didn't truck with cavalry. They were always trouble, always! She'd bent her rules for Josie because Josie needed her, but she didn't owe Lucas spit. She'd already saved his life once. What more did he want? This wasn't her burden, and like beans was she gonna carry it. But when she turned around to tell Lucas it was none of his business whether she knew him or not, the lieutenant wasn't even looking at her anymore. He was watching the tunnel ahead, staring at darkness just outside her lantern glow like he was falling down it.

No, Mary realized too late. Not just darkness. That was the start of the Dark up there.

Well, at least she knew now why the tunnels had changed so much. The Dark had made another of its jumps. It was still moving, actually. Now that she knew what to watch for, Mary could see the wavering line of the tar-thick Dark creeping toward them down the tunnel, eating up the light of her lantern as it went.

Even for someone who loved the caves as much as Mary, it was an unnerving sight. The Dark moved all the time, but she'd never actually seen it traveling 'til just now. It really did look like the world was vanishing inch by inch, but while the other soldiers who were finally catching up behind them gasped and cursed at the sight, Lucas didn't say a word. He didn't twitch, didn't blink, didn't run or shake. It reminded Mary of the time she'd fallen through the pond ice when she was little. Even as she'd sunk into the dark water knowing she was going to drown, she hadn't been able to move her limbs and swim back to safety. Her body just wouldn't work.

Later, she'd learned that was from the shock of the cold, not cowardice, but at the time, it'd felt like she was already dead. If the nuns hadn't come running to pull her out, she would've been, because there was no getting out of a choke hold like that without help. That was what Mary had learned back then, and it was what she did now, reaching out to wrap her fingers around the lieutenant's death-stiff ones.

"All right," she said loudly, waving her lantern at the group to distract from what her other hand was doing. "This is the start of the Dark. We've hit it a bit earlier than usual, but that just means we'll be getting out all the sooner. Lights of any sort don't work inside, so everyone needs to put one hand on the person in front of you and one on the wall to your right. That way no one gets lost. I'm going to stand here with the light to make sure everyone's following directions. Once the last person's inside, I'll snuff the lantern and guide you using my voice 'til we reach the other side. Keep one foot on the floor at all times, and do *not* let go of the wall. Rel Reiner, you're good at this, so you go first."

Mary wasn't even sure where Rel was, but the girl shoved her way to the front the moment Mary said her name. Oddly, Lucas's Black sergeant was right beside her, sticking to the gunhand like a burr on a horse no matter how many death stares she shot him. Mary wasn't sure if that was bravery or stupidity on the sergeant's part, but she was happy to wave the pair through. Rel was almost as good at the Dark as she was, and no one'd be stupid enough to attack a group this size, so Mary was confident all would be well. Having another person who knew what they were about also made it easier for her to actually wait to the end like she'd said instead of charging forward like she usually did. This turned out to be important, because even after the last soldier vanished into the wall of the Dark, Lucas still hadn't budged.

"It's okay," she whispered, raising their joined hands in front of his terrified eyes. "See? I've got you. You're not getting lost."

She finished with an encouraging smile, but Lucas still wasn't moving, and she *really* needed him to. Even assuming nothing went wrong, it was going to take a dangerously long time to shuffle so many through the Dark. She didn't fault the lieutenant for being afraid after how his last trip here had ended, but if he didn't start walking soon, they were going to be marching through the night in there, and no one wanted that. Nothing she did was getting through to him, though, not even pushing, so Mary decided to try a different approach.

"This isn't like the last time," she whispered, giving up and switching to French since nothing else was working, and she hadn't really wanted to keep dodging his questions all the way to the Deep Caves anyway. "I'm here. You're not alone. Just keep hold of my hand and I'll lead you safe to the other side, I promise."

For a horrible moment, it didn't look like that was gonna work either. Then, like a rockslide coming loose, Lucas began to move. It was just shaking at first, then he took a step, his eyes shut tight like a child preparing for a whipping. But no blow came. Mary made sure of it, holding his hand and easing him forward, keeping the warmth of her lamp close to his face even after all light vanished.

"You see?" she whispered when they were in. "You did it! Now you just gotta keep walking."

He broke a little then, curling forward into a silent sob he probably thought she couldn't see. If this'd happened before the pillar had opened her ears, Mary might not've, but the caves' song these days was too rich and bright to be stifled by anything. Even with the Dark doing its best to muddy the sound, the crystal's music painted everything clear as a picture in Mary's mind, including the shadow of Lucas's shaking body bent over her hand like a pilgrim.

She stayed perfectly still until he was finished, keeping her silence to spare him his pride. When he finally straightened up, Mary tugged him gently forward toward the rest of the group, who were waiting up the tunnel just like she'd told them. She'd been planning to put Lucas's hand on the last man's shoulder so he could join the train, but she realized at the last moment that letting go would break her promise. She couldn't do that, so Mary took him with her instead, keeping her fingers locked tight through his as she called cheerfully for the others to start walking, raising her voice like a torch to lead them down the tangled path that only she could see.

Chapter 23

From a business perspective at least, this venture was so far a wild success. Josie had expected traveling with so many people would be delay-ridden and slow, but the lieutenant kept his men snappy and organized. The soldiers were also far better walkers than she'd been at the start, and they had none of the ambushes, fights, crowding, or other human problems that had stymied their original expedition, since no one seemed willing to provoke a pack of fifty armed men. Their numbers even seemed to scare away the Holes that had nearly eaten her leg the first time through.

No single element made that much of a difference, but put together, they were a wonder. Josie had told Lieutenant Lucas that she planned to make camp as soon as they cleared the Dark, but they managed to plow well into the Midway Tunnels before they were finally forced to stop for the night. This should have made Josie ecstatic—faster trips with fewer complications meant less expense and more profit—but the whole day, all she could think about was how she and Reliance still hadn't made up.

When she'd first appeared out of nowhere on the porch, Josie had been ecstatic. She wasn't foolish enough to think that meant everything was well again, but the fact that Rel had come back at all proved that she cared. So long as those feelings were present, Josie was sure there was no rift the two of them couldn't mend! But after a full day of silent, angry glares, that confidence was starting to wane.

The simplest solution would have been to ask Rel directly, but she never got the chance. Managing a troop was much more taxing than she'd expected, and whenever she did get a moment, Lucas would invariably show up with some matter that desperately needed her immediate attention. Even when she tried just to catch her friend's eye, Sergeant Chaucer always seemed to be in the way, distracting Rel's attention at the back of the line. If the idea hadn't been ridiculous, Josie would have sworn the two officers were working together to keep them apart.

"It's just so *frustrating*," she whispered to Mary as the cavalry laid out their bedrolls in the hollowed-out old claim just off the Main Gallery Trail that Mary had chosen to be their shelter for the night. "I keep thinking that if I could only talk to her, we could work this out, but I can't seem to get a spare moment."

"I don't think you could work it out with a hundred spare moments," Mary whispered back, tilting her head at Rel, who was sitting across the cavern cleaning her guns with a murderous scowl while Chaucer set up his bedroll right beside hers. "She's still mad as a bee in a bonnet, and there's no use talking to mad people."

"But if I could just—"

"You can't make someone listen by throwin' more words at 'em," Mary said tiredly, taking off her pack and leaning it against the chisel-scraped wall. "Rel will come to you when she's ready."

"But what if she... doesn't?" Josie asked, biting her lip.

"Nonsense," Mary said. "Ain't neither of you the sort to let things go. She'll come back to make sure she has the final say, if nothing else. And probably much more nicely if you let her have her space."

That observation was depressingly astute, and Josie slumped in defeat. "You're right," she muttered, sliding a frustrated hand through her cave-damp hair. "And it's not as if we could have a proper conversation with all these strangers around, anyway. I'll try again once we reach the Mother Lode and everyone spreads out. I'm sure we'll both be in a much better mood once we're not being constantly badgered by soldiers."

"Sounds as likely as anything," Mary agreed, but her attention was no longer on Josie. Her eyes had drifted to the pile of lanterns the soldiers had made at the cavern's center and the downtrodden-looking lieutenant sitting slumped beside them.

343

"Are you all right?" Josie asked, suddenly petrified that something had happened while she'd been distracted. "Did he say anything inappropriate?"

"I'm fine," Mary said quickly. "It's just… I'm not comfortable sleeping near so many soldiers, so I'm going to find my own spot to bunk for the night. I'll be back 'fore you wake up, so don't worry none."

"Of course," Josie said, determined to be maximally supportive. "Do whatever you feel you need to. We'll stay right here and wait for your return."

The girl flashed her a grateful smile and darted back toward the main tunnel, vanishing so quickly and completely around the corner, Josie worried she'd fallen into the creek. She hadn't, of course. That was just how Mary moved: quick and silent as a deer in the forest. She was wondering where the girl hid herself at times like these, if she simply went to another cave or if there was some secret crack in the stone known only to her, when Josie heard the scrape of boots on the stone and turned to find Lieutenant Lucas standing just a few feet behind her.

"Forgive me," he said, removing his cap. "I didn't mean to startle you. I was just curious, does Miss Good Crow often go off alone at night?"

"Not normally," Josie said, moving to block his view of where Mary had gone. "But she doesn't care for soldiers. There's no need for concern, though. Mary is the soul of responsibility, and she knows these caves better than any. She'll be back in plenty of time for us to move on tomorrow."

"I wasn't worried about that," the lieutenant said, leaning to the side in an attempt to see around Josie's blockade. "But I was hoping I could speak with her a little—"

"Well, she clearly doesn't want to speak with you," Josie said, lifting her chin. "I'm sorry to be rude, Lieutenant, but I must ask you not to harass my friend. I've imposed on her enough already, asking her to guide men she fears. I won't pile insult on top of injury by forcing her to socialize with you as well."

"Of course," Lucas said, backing away at once. "I would never wish to do anything that might trouble her, it's just... I wanted to tell her I was sorry."

It was none of her business, but Josie couldn't help herself. "Sorry for what?"

"Everything," he said with a self-deprecating chuckle. "I'm an officer of the US Cavalry. We are supposed to be the heroes who ride to the rescue, but she's saved me twice now, and I can't even get her to look at me long enough to thank her for it. To be honest, it's making me feel less of a man. But that's my problem, not hers. You are absolutely right. I'll leave her be."

Josie wasn't sure what to make of that, but the lieutenant was doing what she'd asked, so she nodded. He nodded back, returning his cap to his head so he could tip the brim to her. "Excuse me, Miss Price. It's been a long and humbling day, so I'm going to get some sleep. Sergeant Chaucer has the first watch. He'll be happy to assist you should you need anything."

"Good night," she said, but Lucas was already walking away to his spot in the middle of the cavern, falling onto his bedroll like a felled tree.

Josie knew she should follow his example. It had been an exhausting day, and her own blanket was already set up next to the wall where the sergeant was keeping watch, eating his dry ration in tiny bites to make it last. Everyone else had already bedded down. Including Reliance, who was lying off by herself at the cavern's far end with her back to the others.

Despite what Mary had *just* said, it looked like a perfect opportunity to finally have that conversation. But as Josie turned to tiptoe toward her sleeping friend, an unfamiliar voice spoke softly in the silence.

"I wouldn't if I were you."

Josie jumped and whirled to see Sergeant Chaucer smiling at her.

"Sorry to speak uninvited, miss," he said in a hushed voice. "But I can see what you're thinking, and if you'd take some friendly advice from someone who's tangled with Tyrel Reiner before, that's not a bear you should go poking."

Josie was getting *very* tired of hearing other people's opinions about her business, but that didn't stop her from recognizing the opportunity that had just been presented. Reliance never talked about her life in Medicine Rocks. Josie knew she worked as a hired gun at the Wet Whistle, but nothing beyond. Talking to someone who knew her only as Tyrel was a rare chance to learn how the rest of town saw her, which would be useful to know since, if everything went according to plan, this would be their home for the foreseeable future. Josie was sure it wouldn't be a flattering portrait, but as ever, curiosity got the better of her.

"How did you 'tangle' with Tyrel?" she asked, tiptoeing over to join the sergeant against the wall. "What was he like?"

"Scary," Chaucer said with a dramatic shudder. "I don't know how he came to work for you, but the first time I encountered Tyrel Reiner was about a month after this last Christmas. My squad got sent down the hill to help the sheriff with an incident involving two Wet Whistlers stealing corpses from Boot Hill."

"*Corpses?*" Josie cringed. "What on earth did they want with those?"

"I'm sure I don't know," the sergeant said. "But Tyrel Reiner and the Wet Whistle's head killer, the beanpole bloke what calls himself Apache Jake, had a whole cart of the poor dead bastards piled up by the time we arrived. We told 'em to stop, which of course meant they started shooting. Killed three of us before we knew what was what, including my old sergeant. Naturally, the lieutenant was furious. Unlike a lot of officers, Lucas actually gives a damn about our lives, and he went after the Wet Whistle hard. Anyone else would've swung for shooting soldiers, but as always with those blighters, it all came to nothing. Even with a half dozen witnesses, Reiner and his boss got away scot-free. He's shot plenty more people since and never had to answer to no one. That's not too unusual for a frontier town, but there's no denying Tyrel Reiner's a stone-cold killer who does whatever the Wet Whistle tells him. He's deep in the She-Wolf's tits, that one."

The entire story was disturbing, but the last sentence was what made Josie go still. Uncle Samuel's final note had also mentioned a she-wolf. She'd thought he was just being cryptic to keep anyone but her from guessing his true intent, but the way Chaucer said the words now made her wonder if he hadn't been referring to a specific person.

"Who is the 'She-Wolf'?"

Chaucer's face turned sheepish. "That's what the madam of the Wet Whistle calls herself. Not that *I've* ever been to that place, of course. We cavalry officers are far too gentlemanly for such vulgarity, but it's our duty to keep an eye on all the local criminals, and she's at the top of every list. There's not a bit of dirty dealing that goes down in Medicine Rocks without the She-Wolf's say-so. Opium, gambling, crystal smuggling, bootlegging, bribery, she's got her paws in all of it."

"What about burglary?" Josie asked, curling her hands into fists on the denim trousers she'd borrowed from her late uncle's dresser. "Does she steal?"

"Most certainly," Chaucer said. "Her people act as thieves and fences. I heard she even had a hand in the fire that destroyed the Mining Office records building last winter. Can't prove it, of course, but if it wasn't her work, she's slacking."

He gave Josie a measuring look. "I'm surprised she hasn't approached you yet, Miss Price. Not that you'd ever be involved in such unsavoriness, but the She-Wolf doesn't normally allow anyone to run a business here without nosing in for her cut. That's why I wanted to warn you about Reiner. He might act like he's your man, but the only ex-Wet Whistlers are dead ones, and I'd hate to see you get taken for a ride just because you're new and no one's had the guts to tell you the truth yet."

Josie's fists were clenched bloodless by the time he finished. "Thank you, Sergeant Chaucer," she said in a tight voice. "This has been most enlightening."

"I hope I didn't offend, miss," the soldier said nervously, glancing at the sleeping Lucas, who hadn't moved a hair. "I'm not normally one to tell a person their business, but we need this crystal something fierce. Everyone's survival is counting on this mission being a success, and I'd be a sorry excuse for a soldier if I didn't at least call attention to the spy in our midst."

"No, no, you did well," Josie said, forcing herself to smile. "I appreciate the warning, Sergeant Chaucer. I'll think carefully on it."

"Of course, Miss Price," he said, tipping his hat several more times as Josie walked stiffly to her blanket and lay down.

Lay down but didn't sleep.

Chapter 24

Rel felt like she'd been falling down a well for three days straight.

It wasn't supposed to go like this. After discovering her plan to take the deed from Mihir was a bust, she'd chased Josie into the caves out of desperation. She hadn't had any real strategy, but how hard could it be to get a piece of paper from someone who kept their backpack more organized than a banker's vault? She'd figured she'd just wait for her turn on watch, nab the deed, and hightail it back to the Wet Whistle with no one the wiser. At least, that was her thinking until she'd found out who the cavalry had sent over to lead the expedition.

Of all the bad cards she could've drawn, she had to get the damn Frenchman. Most of the cavalry was willing to look the other way when it came to Volchitsa's business and got paid well for the privilege, but even the She-Wolf hadn't figured out Lucas's price yet, and he had a particular bone to pick with Rel. He'd been on her like a rash from the moment she'd stepped off the porch, and his Negro sergeant was even worse.

Between the two of them, Rel hadn't been able to get within ten feet of Josie waking or sleeping. She'd hoped to have this over the first night so she'd have the Dark to run to in case she got caught. Yet two nights later, here she was: belly crawling through the squeeze into the Deep Caves with some idiot infantryman's boots kicking half a foot from her face and not a thing to show for it.

If her father had been up to his usual tricks, Rel was certain he would've been full of belittling commentary, but the crystal gun hadn't spoken to her in days now. Considering how much effort it normally took to get him to shut up for even a few minutes, that should've been a relief, but with everything else that was going on, the unnatural silence just felt like another bad omen. Particularly after day two, which was the day Josie had suddenly stopped smiling.

Here again, you'd think that'd be a blessing. Planning a robbery had been so much easier when she'd been pissed, but Josie had looked so damn gleeful when she'd come back after their fight, it'd given Rel second thoughts about the whole venture. So much so that she'd actually considered telling Josie the truth in hopes the girl would understand.

But then, the morning after they cleared the Dark, something had changed. Rel didn't know what, why, or how, but from the moment Josie woke up that next day, she hadn't looked at Rel once. And, oh God, had it stung.

Rel had never realized how much she'd started looking forward to Josie's smiles until they were gone. They'd reminded her of the time before everything had gone to hell, back when she'd had family and friends and things to live for that weren't murder and ghosts. She kept telling herself it was better this way, that stealing from a Josie who hated her would be easier than having to crush that hopeful smile, but the logic didn't do a damn thing. She just kept falling farther and farther behind, stumbling after the soldiers like she was just another shade.

At least she didn't have to stumble far. They'd barely gotten all the soldiers through the squeeze when Mary announced they were only half a mile from their destination. The news caused a sigh of relief all 'round, and even with her head stuck in her troubles, Rel could see why. This incarnation of the Deep Caves was her least favorite yet: a silent forest of rocks shaped like giant lodgepole pines with black rubble for bark and gray needles sharp as cracked flint.

They'd grown *thick*, too, crowding in so dense that Rel couldn't see more than a few feet in no matter which way she turned her head. That huge Whitman and his freaky dog-man could've been within arm's reach, and she would'nt've known 'til they grabbed her. She told herself to take comfort in knowing that her own group would also be hidden, but it was hard to feel secure with fifty idiots pointing at every little thing like they'd never seen a magical underground forest made of stone before.

At least the Frenchman had the good sense to tell them to shut up, deferring to Mary, who led them straight through the maze of slicing branches like a dog after a scent. Rel still had her doubts about the girl's ability to find their way without the crescent finding stone, but she should've had more faith in Mary's obsession with that pillar. After barely half an hour's beelining, she pulled them up short at what looked like a rabbit hole nestled in one of the solemn trees' stony roots.

"Here we are," she announced, holding up her big lantern to illuminate the soldiers' skeptical faces. "Hop on down."

"You heard Miss Good Crow," Lucas said, hand resting on his shiny officer's saber. "Down you go."

Like she wanted to show them how simple it was, Josie went first, taking off her pack to make herself small enough to fit down the hole. The lieutenant followed next, then all the other soldiers one by one. When Rel reached to remove her own pack, though, Mary caught her by the sleeve.

Rel's head snapped up like a spring. For a breath-snatching moment, she was petrified the girl knew everything and was about to tell Rel to go get lost in the woods. That was just her own guilt talking, though, because what Mary actually said was, "Are you the one making that racket?"

"Making what, now?" Rel asked with a confused blink.

"That dinging sound," Mary said, breaking a stone needle off the tree above them and tapping it against the glass of her lantern. "*Ding ding ding,* like that."

Rel would've called that more of a *ting* or a *clink*, but it didn't make no difference. "I ain't heard anything but us since we left the gaggle back on the Midway," she said. "You're the one with the cave ears."

"Don't treat me like I'm stupid," Mary warned. "I know you hear plenty, and this ain't a cave sound. It's a voice, like someone trying to imitate a dinner bell." She gave Rel the side-eye. "You *sure* you're not doing anything? 'Cause I've been hearing it since we stopped, and it's definitely coming from a your-ish direction."

"It's not me," Rel said sternly. "All I've done is walk."

Mary looked at her for a long moment, but on this one point at least, Rel was telling the truth. She really hadn't made any sound except

351

footsteps for miles. Even that fool Chaucer had given up trying to drag her into conversation. It was clear from the way her eyes were darting that Mary still heard something, but she must've decided it wasn't Rel, 'cause a few moments later, she gave up and started checking the treetops.

"Maybe it's a crystal woodpecker," she muttered, waving her lantern around. "Can't be too dangerous, whatever it is, seeing as we ain't dead yet."

"Let's get a move on 'fore that changes," Rel urged as she shrugged out of her pack. "The others are probably already at the cave."

Her guess turned out to be more accurate than Rel expected. In a group as large as theirs, folks other than Mary had lamps. The stream tunnel was as dark as ever when the two of them dropped down the hole, but just a few bends later, Rel's night vision was blinded by the reflected light of a half dozen kerosene flames glittering off a night's sky worth of crystal.

"*Hey!*" Mary shouted, splashing ahead. "Be careful! There's a waterfall!"

Rel couldn't even hear the falls over all the shouting. Not that she blamed the soldiers—the Mother Lode was worth shouting about—but the noise of all their voices bouncing off the tunnel was deafening. Fortunately, someone had already found the rope ladder old Sam Price had left tied to the rock above the falls and was sending the loudmouths down one by one.

Lucas was already at the bottom, shouting orders about only mining crystal from Josie's left wall, since Rel and Mary had refused to take part in this agreement. Rel acknowledged the effort, but it was hard to take the lieutenant's calls for restraint seriously when his own voice was so gleefully greedy. All the cavalry sounded that way: like wild children set loose in a candy shop as they raced to get their hands on the glittering treasure. Even shy, scared Mary found the courage to cut in line for the ladder so she could get down to her pillar and protect it from the ravaging that was so obviously about to take place.

The whole scene was so chaotic, Rel had to stand back to keep from getting shoved off the falls. She was contemplating just staying up here until the mining was finished when she realized she wasn't alone.

"Reliance."

Josie's voice was soft as a prayer, but that didn't stop Rel from startling so violently, she nearly slipped over the edge. She caught herself at the last second, bracing her boot against the largest of the rocks breaking up the stream water before it went over the falls. Even with certain death below her, though, it was remarkably difficult to turn and face the person she no longer deserved to call friend.

Josie had stepped into the stream right next to her by the time Rel managed it, her face an unreadable mask in the dancing light of the lanterns below. It was the first time they'd been alone since their fight in the office. Better than alone, for Mary and the soldiers were way down at the bottom of the falls. This was the best place for a holdup Rel could've asked for, and yet she couldn't make her body do anything but shake as Josie looked straight at her, practically through her, and asked the question Rel really should have seen coming.

"Do you work for the She-Wolf?"

Aw, shit. "Who told you that name?"

"It doesn't matter," Josie said angrily. "Do you work for her or not?"

"It ain't like it's a secret," Rel snapped, shoving the truth at her, since there was no point in lying. "I work for the Wet Whistle. She's the owner. I thought you were smart?"

Josie must've been truly furious, because she let the misdirecting insult fly by without so much as a blink. "Were you with the She-Wolf when her men invaded my uncle's house?"

"Sam Price ain't *your* uncle, and no. I wasn't in town yet when that happened."

"But you knew the She-Wolf was behind it?"

"I never said that."

"Don't treat me like I'm an idiot, Reliance Reiner!" Josie yelled, her anger echoing across the flowing water. "You think I didn't know you were involved in shady dealings? From the very first day I arrived in Medicine Rocks, everyone warned me against you! I chose not to listen because I wanted to believe you were still the Reliance I'd grown up with. I told myself you'd been twisted to bad deeds by this corrupting place, but if I gave you a better path, you'd revert to the brave, honest girl I remembered. That's why I split this place with you! It wasn't just so you'd keep my secret. I wanted my friend back! I wanted to give you a future where you could be yourself again, and we could move on to a better life together! But you were never my friend, were you? You *knew* the Wet Whistle was the one who'd stolen our deeds the whole time, and you didn't tell me!"

That wasn't precisely true. Rel hadn't known Volchitsa was behind the Price Mining break-in until the meeting in her office, but that was only because she hadn't tried. If she'd cared enough to spare a thought on the matter, she could've pinned it as the Wet Whistle's work the first time Josie told her, but she hadn't cared. The only thing she'd been thinking about was how she could use Josie's arrival to her advantage, which made her even more of a villain than her friend believed.

"All those times you tried to convince me to sell the company and go home, you weren't looking out for my well-being at all, were you?" Josie said, clenching her fists. "You just were trying to get Sam Price's last claim for your mistress! It wasn't enough to steal everything else he'd worked for. She wanted the complete set, and it was your job to get me to hand it over!"

There were a lot of clever things Rel could've said to that. A lot of assumptions she could've kicked over and doubt she could've sown. Even Josie looked like she wanted Rel to deny it, to yell with as much fury as she had back in the office that Josie was being ridiculous and none of this was true. But the only word that actually made it out of Rel's mouth was "Yes."

"You played me for a fool!"

"Yes."

It was a stupid, stupid thing to say. Even Volchitsa had never actually admitted guilt, but Rel couldn't stop herself. Even after throwing away every other decency, a stubborn part of her still believed that Josie deserved the truth, and in a backwards sort of way, confessing made things simpler. With all the bridges burning before her eyes, Rel no longer had to worry about what might have been. There was only one way this ended now, so Rel pulled her pistol—one of her trustworthy iron Colts, not her father's crystal curse—and pointed the barrel at her friend's chest.

"Give me the deed to the Mother Lode."

Josie stared at the six-shooter like she'd never seen one before. "I can't believe it," she whispered. "After everything I did, saving your life and giving you enough crystal to make you richer than she'll ever be, you're *still* working for her?"

"The deed, Price," Rel said, tightening her finger on the trigger lest Josie think she was bluffing. "The real one Samuel registered with the Mining Office, not that fake crap you gave us."

"It wasn't fake!" Josie cried, looked more betrayed than frightened despite the gun aimed at her heart. "I gave you a third of my future so you wouldn't have to do things like this anymore! I gave you *everything* you could ever want!"

"You don't know a damn thing about what I want."

"Then *tell me!*" her friend screamed. "It doesn't have to be this way! We used to help each other out of every trouble. We can do that again! Now that I'm contracted with the cavalry, I've got the strongest force in Medicine Rocks behind me and enough crystal to keep it that way. I can break you out of whatever trap she's put you in, I promise, just tell me why you're doing this!"

Rel was desperate to tell her. She'd wrestled with the dream of confessing constantly over the last two days, because Josie was the only person still alive who'd loved her mother and baby brother as much as Rel did. If anyone could understand the corner she'd been driven into, it was

Josephine O'Connor. But even knowing she might still be forgiven, Rel couldn't risk it, because she knew Josie.

She *knew* that the moment she explained her predicament, her friend would start coming up with all manner of convoluted Josie-plans that would take forever and probably not work. Seeing as Rel was about to cost her everything, she couldn't blame the girl for trying. But if Rel didn't do exactly as Volchitsa said, her best shot at freeing her mother and Chase would slip away forever.

Rel couldn't afford to take that risk, and honestly, Josie couldn't either. It was easy for her to say they'd figure it out when Rel was the one pointing a gun at her, but if she set herself against the She-Wolf, she'd end up destroyed, not just crystalless. No one survived a head-on fight with the Wet Whistle, so for the good of all involved, Rel threw herself into her chosen role, pulling back the hammer on her pistol with all the drama of a penny-novel villain.

"*Fine!*" Josie shouted, eyes flashing with defiance as she spread her arms to give Rel a clear shot at her chest. "Go ahead and do it, *if* you can. But if you're counting on me to blink, you're barking up the wrong tree. You of all people should know I'd rather die than go crawling back to Josephine Price! I put everything I had into this, and I will not be intimidated into giving it up by a scared little girl like you. So go ahead and shoot me if you're really so heartless. I can't believe I put my trust in you!"

She lifted her chin, daring Rel to do it, and for a horrible second, Rel almost did. If Josie cared more about a crystal mine than her own life, then she could damn well die for it! But despite the emotions overriding her senses, some part of her body must've still remembered itself, because Rel's finger didn't budge on the trigger. She was trying to decide if that was a good turn or a bad one when the *crack* of a gunshot echoed down the tunnel.

Rel panicked at the sound, terrified she'd really gone and done it. Then another bullet whizzed by her ear, and she realized the shot hadn't come from her gun. It'd come from farther up the tunnel where, now that she was no longer locked in a battle of wills with Josie, Rel realized she could see shapes walking toward them through the stream.

There were dozens of them: big figures, little figures, bent-over figures and straight. It was too dark to make out more than outlines yet, but one of the shadowy figures was instantly recognizable, even though she couldn't see his face. A mountain of man with a bald head and crystal specks glimmering all over his exposed chest.

"*Rel*," Josie hissed, jumping closer despite the gun Rel was still pointing in her direction. "That's—"

Rel shushed her with a hiss, swinging her pistol toward the new threat. A move that made the giant's body shake with laughter.

"You're hard to find, little rabbits," boomed the huge voice she'd hoped to never hear again. "But we always catch 'em in the end. Don't we, Kipper?"

Rel's healed leg twinged as a new figure crawled out of the shadows near the man's huge feet, opening its hinge-like mouth to reveal a twisted forest of crystal spikes she knew all too well. But it wasn't just the two Whitmans this time. The tunnel was full of shuffling figures now, and while the crystal giant with his dog-man on a chain looked just as awful as they had before, the rest were a complete surprise.

The underground stream was packed to the walls with unwashed, unshaven, slack-jawed men. Most were wearing rags and carrying rusty guns that looked like they'd been dug out of the scrap pile, but while they looked like vagrants, every single one of them had crystal stitched into their skin. Not near so much as the giant or the dog but enough that Rel could see it shining in the lamplight from down below, which struck her as very bad news indeed.

"What do we do?" Josie whispered, pressing herself into Rel's side.

Eyes on the enemy, Rel slowly slid her pistol back into its holster to free her arm, which she wrapped around Josie's waist. "Hang on."

That was all the warning Rel had time to give before she hurled them both over the edge of the falls. Bullets whizzed above their heads as they fell, followed by the giant's booming laughter as he called for his men not to waste shots on idiots who'd already killed themselves. But despite the seeming desperation of their escape, Rel wasn't near to giving up. When she'd pulled Josie off the ledge, she'd taken care to lean to the right, aiming them toward the ladder dangling down the falls. As soon as they were out of sight of the shooters on the falls, Rel whipped her free arm sideways to grab the swinging ladder.

Rel had been shot several times in her life, but nothing had ever hurt like the burn of that rope on her hand. The rough hemp ate through her glove in less than a second. The rope ate through her skin next, but Rel forced her fist to stay closed through pure cussedness, gritting her teeth against the fire until she'd slowed their descent long enough to catch hold of a rung with her boot.

They stopped falling with a jerk that nearly knocked them off again. She'd forgotten how heavy Josie was, and the miscalculation had almost ripped her foot clean off the step. Rel overcorrected by looping her other leg around the rope that formed the side of the ladder, sending them spinning. She was curling her body over Josie's to keep either of them from bashing their heads into the wet cliff wall when the wave of Whitmans made it to the edge of the falls and started shooting down at them.

"Climb down!" she screamed, letting go of Josie to grab the ladder with both hands.

She didn't have to tell the girl twice. Her friend was already flying down the ropes so fast, it looked like she was falling. Rel scurried after her as quick as quick could, swinging her body from side to side to make herself a harder target for the gunmen overhead. Fortunately, the bandits' shots were as crazy as they were. Even with a firing line hailing down bullets, not a single one found Rel's flesh. Josie also seemed uninjured, though much more panicked than before.

"How did they find us?" she cried, taking her eyes off the perilously swinging rope just long enough to glare at Rel. "Was this part of your scheme?"

"Of course not!" Rel yelled back. "What kind of idiot comes up with a plan that gets them shot?"

"You haven't been shot yet," Josie pointed out.

"Only 'cause they're terrible!" Rel replied, letting go to fall the rest of the way to the bottom.

The drop was longer than she could really take, but the hand she'd burned up catching their fall was giving out, so there wasn't much of a choice. Luckily, nothing snapped when she landed, and someone was already there to help her back to her feet. When Rel looked up to see who, Lieutenant Lucas shoved her head back down, keeping her against the cliff as he and his soldiers fired back up at the Whitmans.

"Get Miss Price to safety!" he yelled over the deafening racket. "*Go! Go! Go!*"

Rel went, dragging Josie off the ladder and running them both over to the cover of the big crystal boulder where they'd signed the contract their first night here. Mary was already crouching in its shadow, waving frantically at Rel and Josie as they dove onto the ground behind her.

"Where'd they come from?" the guide squeaked as she helped the other two up. "I know they weren't following us in the stone forest 'cause the trees told me, and you saw the stream tunnel when we dropped down. It was empty as a dead log, so how are we suddenly up to our necks in Whitmans?"

Rel was opening her mouth to say she had no idea when the crystal gun at her hip gave its first twitch in days.

I called them.

Feeling like the ground was giving way beneath her, Rel grabbed the gun and whirled around, leaving Josie and Mary watching the gunfight between the cavalry and the bandits streaming down the ladder as she bent over the pistol with a snarl.

"What the hell did you do?"

Nothing you didn't bring upon yourself, her father replied smugly. *You were going to give this cavern to that harlot queen for nothing, so I was forced to take matters into my own hands.*

"With the Whitmans?" Rel hissed, shaking the gun in fury. "When did you even have time to make a deal with them?"

The gun rattled in disgust. *I made no deals with bandits. They were merely the tool that was available. I already knew from our previous encounter that they'd be in the area, and they'd even been so kind as to tell me how to summon them. Pretty basic stuff, really.*

Rel swore so vilely Josie actually scowled over her shoulder. "The dinging Mary was talking 'bout earlier," she said, ignoring the censure. "That was *you.*"

Ding, ding, ding, the pistol said, making a noise that did indeed sound very much like the one Mary made tapping on her lantern. *Not quite the bell they were searching for, but their standards seemed low enough that I was sure it would work. My greatest worry was that I wouldn't be able to make myself heard. I can actually cast my voice quite far in this form without you noticing, but reaching ears capable of hearing me is another matter. Fortunately, the big one has so much crystal stuffed under his skin that I was able to resonate with it quite effectively. From there it was a simple matter of ringing the dinner bell and waiting for the livestock to come, though I didn't expect to catch so many.*

"Well, you did, and now we're screwed!" Rel yelled at him, no longer caring if the others heard. "I understand you being mad at me, but you're not getting the crystal, either, if the Whitmans slaughter us all!"

That's not nearly as big an issue as you make out, the gun said. *As you're fond of reminding me, I'm already dead.*

"Not as dead as you'll be without me. Our souls are tied, remember? If I kick off, you're out a body."

That's a gamble I'm willing to take, the gun informed her in a cold voice. *But you're not defeated yet. Take another look at the Whitmans' foot soldiers. See anything familiar?*

Rel was so sick of his professor bullshit, but she didn't have any other ideas, and it was easy enough to look up at the Whitmans coming down the ladder. She didn't see anything she hadn't noticed before, though. Just a bunch of filthy bandits with crystal shoved where it shouldn't be.

Look again, her father suggested. *The proper way, this time.*

"No," she growled. "I told you, I'm done playing your stupid—"

For God's sake, Reliance! Do you want to live or not? Just drink the damn crystal, and everything will make sense.

Cursing under her breath, Rel dug into her coat for her flask. Nothing was left inside but dregs, but she was pretty tuned to crystal at this point, and the little drops at the bottom were still enough to flare her sight, letting her see the bright souls shining in Josie and Mary and the cavalry soldiers who'd formed a defensive ring at the bottom of the ladder. The light was also glaring from the giant Whitman and his dog, but their new lackeys swarming down the ladder remained dark, which didn't make sense.

"What the devil?"

At last she begins to see, her father chuckled, his presence reaching through her mind to lock her attention on the Whitmans' goons, none of which had so much as a flicker of a soul inside them.

"How is this possible?" she whispered, eyes wide. "Those are dead bodies! Corpses! How the hell are they climbing?"

Don't waste time asking questions you already know the answers to, her father scolded. *You've seen genius like this before. It's what caused you to throw a tantrum and run away from home the day our family met its end. That's my work on corpse animation up there, which means—*

"Whoever did this is the one who stole your research," Rel finished breathlessly, heart hammering. "Our murderer's a *Whitman!*"

Goddamn, she was an idiot. Why hadn't she realized this before? The corpse taking, the crystal stealing, even the timing of the Whitmans' rise this spring—it all lined up. Her father had been toying with puppeting dead bodies forever, but he'd never made any real progress until Sam Price had sent him that first packet of crystal. The crystal was what had turned all her father's theories into horrible reality, which was why he'd gotten so obsessed with the stuff, but what the hell were they going to do about it now?

You are in quite the corner, her father agreed. *These shambling amalgams are nowhere near* my *level of sophistication, but with that much crystal to fill the gaps, it doesn't really matter. As I'm sure the cavalry is already discovering, they're quite resistant to bullets. Human flesh is so much stronger without pain or fear to hold it back. Unless those boys are good enough to shoot off the head or break a major bone, nothing's going to stop the Whitmans' dead from overwhelming your little band. Nothing, that is, except me.*

Rel's blood ran cold. There it was.

Don't act so surprised. I told you I wouldn't let you ruin this for us. I am now your only salvation, so if you don't want everyone here to end up a crystal-powered corpse, I suggest you be an obedient child for once and do exactly as I say.

Rel could give no argument to that. Lucas and his men were dumping their ammunition into the corpse-men, knocking them off the ladder like apples off a tree, but it hadn't done a bit of good. The dead men got right back up just like her father said they would, crystal gleaming from their waxy flesh as they charged the semicircle firing ring Lucas had ordered his soldiers into. They weren't even using the rusty weapons they'd been given except as clubs to beat the panicked soldiers down, swarming over them in a wave of broken, clawing fingers and stomping, ragged boots.

Tick-tock, Reliance, her father whispered. *It's not my life you're wasting.*

With another foul curse, Rel lowered her head. "All right," she muttered. "But only if you tell me how you're planning to fix this problem first."

Her father didn't usually respond to bargaining. He must've really wanted to brag this time, though, because he didn't even bother insulting her before he explained.

The crystal men are puppets, sacks of flesh enlivened by crystal vibrations channeled through their bones. Even with their living souls vacated, their brains still contain enough base knowledge from when they were human to follow simple commands, which is how that giant lummox up top is controlling them. That said, I find it highly unlikely that either of the two living Whitmans present was the one who inserted the crystals and animated these men. They're too stupid for such complexity, but that works to our advantage. If the necromancer who stole my work isn't present, then these corpses are being commanded by unskilled operators who likely have no clue what they are doing, which means it should be no trouble at all for me to take control.

"You can stop this?" Rel asked, peeking back at the fight, which seemed to be going very badly for the cavalry. Lucas and Chaucer were screaming at the men to spread out and aim for the heads, but the other soldiers were lost in their panic, running screaming for the walls while the dead jumped on top of them like grisly crickets.

Of course I can, her father said. *They're my invention! Even working remotely through your idiot mind, it should be nothing for me to assume command. With proper amplification, of course.*

Rel's stomach sank again. "You mean crystal."

It is what makes the world go 'round, he said cheerily, his voice practically humming in anticipation. Too bad Rel had drunk all of hers already.

You don't have to drink it, he said, answering the question before she could ask. *Just getting it into your bloodstream should be sufficient.*

That didn't sound safe.

It's not going to be. But you're the one who's always going on about doing whatever she has to. Well, my dear, here's your chance. His soul moved inside hers, forcing Rel's attention to Josie and Mary's terrified faces.

People are dying because they were stupid enough to trust you, he whispered. *I can save them, but only if you give me what I need. Fortunately for you, crystal is everywhere in this place. All you have to do is figure out how to get that*—he flicked her eyes down to the crystal-covered ground—*into me. Just mind you do it quickly. You're running low on soldiers.*

The cavalry was going down at an alarming rate, but Rel didn't care about them. She didn't even care about herself anymore, but the thought of Josie and Mary dying because of her father's treachery was more than she could stand. She'd have gladly drunk a barrel of crystal to

363

make this stop, but she didn't have a barrel or whiskey, so Rel did the only other thing she could think of. She grabbed one of the crystal spikes growing off the bottom of the boulder they were using as cover and slid her rope-burned hand down it, pressing her palm into the stone's knife-sharp edge until she'd cut to the bone.

Excellent, her father said, his voice growing rich as the crystal scream roared into her. *Keep it up!*

"Rel!" Josie cried at the same time, staring at her bloody hand in horror. "What in the world are you—"

A chorus of shouts cut her off. Down at the bottom of the falls, the pile of Whitmans the cavalry had shot off the ladder—those too broken from the fall to get back up and come after them, anyway—started quivering like a bubbling pot. The attacking corpses had stopped as well, sagging over the soldiers they'd been beating down like finger puppets with the finger removed. They stayed that way for a good ten seconds, their limp bodies quivering and jerking like the last spasms of a headless fish. Then, all at once, the dead men pulled themselves straight up in lockstep and turned their faces toward Rel.

Good, Reiner's ghost told them, speaking to them through the crystal storm that was ripping apart Rel's brain. *Now, my children, let's reestablish some order.*

The dead jumped at his command, throwing themselves back up the rope ladder like their legs were made of springs. They were even faster and more coordinated now than they'd been earlier, flying up the rungs like racing dogs toward the two bright-glowing Whitmans at the top.

Rel was holding her breath to see what would happen when they collided, but she never got to see. When the corpses were less than five feet from reaching the top of the falls, the big Whitman sneered and grabbed his partner, using the dog-man's crystal teeth to cut the rope ladder off the rock and send the wave of dead men surging up it tumbling into free fall.

Huh, Reiner said as his corpses plummeted to the rocky ground below, smashing into pieces so small, no amount of crystal would get them up again. *Seems the big one's not so stupid after all.*

"At least he's trapped up there now," Rel said hopefully, releasing her hold on the crystal. "Maybe with all his lackeys dead, he'll—"

As if he'd been waiting for his cue, the giant she'd thought was stuck at the top of the falls suddenly leaped out into thin air. For a heart-stopping moment, Rel was certain he'd just leaped to his death, but the Whitman didn't look scared in the slightest. He just rolled himself into a ball and plummeted, crashing like a comet into the bloody mess that had been his minions.

The shock of his impact knocked everyone off their feet. The surviving soldiers Lucas had been rallying fell on top of one another, and then everyone started scrambling to get out of the way as the giant stood up from his crater, stretching like he was just waking up from a good nap.

"There you go, Kip-Kip," he said affectionately, placing the dog-man he'd protected inside the shield of his body onto the ground. "Seems we got us one o' them fancy crystal types about. You go sniff 'em out. I'll play with the soldiers. Oh, and try to find that Pricey lady and the bell while you're at it. The Shitter said they'd be 'round here somewhere."

Josie's face went bleak with fear as he said that, but before Rel could even think about doing something, her father grabbed control of her hands.

Don't you dare, he snapped, moving her bloody palm back onto the crystal. *Now is not the time to lose focus, not unless you want everyone to die.*

It looked like that was going to happen anyway. She'd fought these two before. Not even the crystal gun had had any effect. Without the corpses, what were they going to do?

You think that puppetry was the extent of my power? Her father scoffed. *I have not yet begun to fight.*

That was too bad, 'cause Rel already felt defeated. Her whole body throbbed with crystal like never before, and the spear she'd grabbed hold of was starting to turn black in her hands, coal black and dead like the crystals in the Front Caves. Rel could feel the death inside her, too, a rot that was eating her body and soul. She couldn't hear anything except his voice over the crystal roar, but she could see Mary's and Josie's mouths moving as they screamed at her, trying desperately to pry her bloody fingers off the—

Ignore them, her father ordered, his ghostly hands forcing hers harder onto the crystal like they were his body now. *Power never comes without cost, and since you never bothered learning to master the techniques you're now reliant upon, your price is higher than most. I have the skill to make up for your incompetence, but you must give me more. Unless you want all these people to die like* they *did.*

A vision filled Rel's mind, one she'd seen too many times. An image of her mother and brother, but not the happy, loving people they'd been in life. These were the horrors their spoiled death had twisted them into, screaming wraiths trapped forever in agony. Then, suddenly, the familiar image flickered, and the tortured faces of her family blurred to become Josie and Mary's, trapped like that forever because of—

"No!" Rel shouted, turning away.

Yes, her father said, shoving the vision at her until it was all she could see. *There's no mystery to what will happen if you fail. You're going to have blood on your hands one way or another, Reliance. Yours or theirs, but choose fast. The dog is almost upon us.*

He was already there, actually, crouched on top of the crystal boulder with his crooked teeth gleaming in the light of the dropped lamps. The jagged grin got wider when he spotted Reliance, and he leaped at her, misshapen jaw opening wide to rip out her throat.

Do it now!

Rel obeyed with a roar, shooting her bloody hands up to grab the monster by his gleaming crystal teeth. The fangs sliced through her fingers as easily as they'd cut through her leg. Except this time, Rel wasn't the only one who got hurt. She could bite back now, and she did so with a vengeance, sucking the sound she could hear vibrating through each crystal into the mad cacophony that was already inside her. She'd never heard the roar so clearly before, never felt its flow shift under her fingers like water changing direction. She wasn't even entirely sure what she'd done, but the moment she took his sound, the dog-man's teeth began to turn black.

Not that the monster seemed to notice. Even after Rel had made a stain across the entire front of his mouth, he just kept biting, stabbing his blackened teeth anywhere they'd go. He'd practically chewed through her arms when her father shoved her.

Grab the boulder!

The blow sent them both flying, landing Rel on top of the boulder with the dog underneath. She hadn't known her dad had the strength to do something like that, but there was no time to worry about petty details. She was already fighting past the snapping dog's jaws to the boulder underneath, the thousands of pounds of crystal waiting just under her fingertips.

Do it! her father ordered, his voice louder than ever, almost like a real sound in her ears. *Finish this, Reliance!*

She was no longer certain what she was doing anymore. The only things left in her mind were his voice and the crystal roar, but she couldn't afford to lose herself just yet. Blackened or no, the dog-man's teeth were still sharp, and they were nearly at her throat. If she let him get even an inch closer, she'd die like a fool and take her father down with her, and then the Whitmans would kill everybody. What was the point of shoving her gun at Josie if Rel didn't even make it out of here to free her family? She couldn't let all that pain be for nothing, so Rel grit her teeth and pushed with all the strength she had left, slamming her bloody hands—and the dog-man's head—down onto the boulder.

Yes!

The reaction was immediate. The moment her blood—not even her fingers, just the blood dripping off them—touched the stone's surface, the whole boulder began to turn black. The stain spread through the pastel-colored crystal like ink dripped on tissue, blossoming and expanding until it was all she could see.

A moment later, Rel realized that wasn't hyperbole. Darkness was *literally* all she could see. She was floating in an infinite blackness that went on every way she turned her head. She was terrified this meant she'd just bled out and died for real when her father appeared beside her.

Not the fading shade she'd made her Devil's bargain with all those months ago. This was Bernard Reiner as he'd looked the day he'd died: dark-haired and severe with never-pleased features and blue eyes that matched Rel's own. He was even still sporting bloody gunshot wounds across the front of his dove-gray vest, but he didn't look like a sad, dead man. He looked victorious, and the longer he grinned at Rel, the more certain she became that she was the one he'd beaten.

What did you do?

Rel slapped a hand over her mouth. That sad little whisper wasn't her father's. That had been *her* voice from *her* mouth, or what should have been her mouth. Looking down, Rel saw in horror that the place where her body should have been was now as empty and dark as everything else here. She was gone. *Gone!*

"Your body's not gone, stupid girl," her father said in his own deep, living voice. "It's just undergone a… change in management."

She stared at him, shocked, and his smile grew wider still. "Do you know why I put up with your foolishness at the Wet Whistle for so long? It's because they fed you crystal. That pretty rock's not just good for boiling water or exploding or whatever other party tricks idiots have come up with to waste it. It's the precipitate of the soul, the music of the universe condensed into physical form. For those who know how to control it, it can do almost anything, including give a dead soul enough strength to overpower a living one and take her corpse for his own."

You can't! Rel yelled. *That's* my *body!*

"What are you going to do about it? Haunt me?" He threw back his head with a mocking laugh. "Please, you wouldn't even still be here if ripping out souls didn't leave behind such stickiness." He rubbed his glowing fingers through the darkness around them with a grimace. "I'd planned to get around it by sublimating your music completely into mine, but your bargain with the She-Wolf forced me to accelerate my timeline. I needed a play that would trick you into giving me enough crystal to wrest control before you traded away the find of the century for a name I already knew."

Rel would've choked if she'd still had a throat. *You're saying you knew this whole time who—*

"Of course I know who Victor is," her father said dismissively. "He killed me, and he was *most* rude about it. But I could have dealt with him at any point. *You* were the one who was intent on destroying everything I've worked for, so I pulled back, let you think you'd won, and then I used the Whitmans to force your hand. You've always been so sentimental, I knew you'd give me everything the moment your little friends were in danger, and that's exactly what you did."

Rel couldn't even speak to that. She just felt like such a fool. Even after her father had admitted to luring the Whitmans, she'd done what he'd said, too scared of losing even to question his intentions.

"Don't be too hard on yourself," her father chided. "A parent always knows how to manage his children. But just because I tricked you so easily doesn't mean you're free from responsibility. Believe it or not, you actually had far more natural ability for our family art than your brother ever possessed. With practice and proper training, you could have been one of the greats, possibly even as skilled as myself. Alas, your bad attitude and constant poor judgment ruined any will I had to pass on my skills to you while I was alive, and you wouldn't listen to a word I said after I was dead. You thought you knew better, that you were too *good* for the knowledge our family has collected over centuries. You just kept charging blindly forward, relying entirely upon a power that you steadfastly refused to understand. Are you really so surprised that *this* is how it ended?"

Rel had built up armor to her father's cruelty over the years, but the truth of those words ripped straight through it, sending her to her knees. Or it would've if she'd still had knees. As she was now, Rel just sort of collapsed into a puddle of nothing, making her father chuckle.

"Good to see you finally understand. Accepting one's weaknesses is the first step toward growth. A little past the fact on your part, I'm afraid, but better late than never."

He bent over as he spoke, picking up the crystal gun Rel hadn't realized was lying next to her in the nothingness. "I'm sure you know what comes next," he said, turning the bone-inlaid handle toward her. "In you go."

I'll never.

"Of course you will," he said, his voice pounding like hers used to do. "Go to sleep, Reliance. You're no longer needed."

Just like when she'd hammered him with orders in the past, Rel found she couldn't disobey. No matter how she screamed and fought and cursed him to the devil, his words were absolute, dropping her like a stone into the bottomless dark.

Chapter 25

"Reliance!"

Mary was clinging to Josie with all her might, holding her back from the many faces of death on display above them.

They were still lying at the foot of the giant crystal boulder, which now looked more like a giant lump of coal. The horrible dead color seemed to be coming from Rel's blood, of which there was an *awful* lot. More than Mary'd realized there could be in such a small person, and yet somehow Rel was still on top, pinning the dog-Whitman to the rock with her torn-up arms.

Both of them were moving sluggishly now, the dog-man panting around his broken crystal teeth, which were now as black as the stone beneath them. The rot had spread to his skin as well, turning his whole body dark and shiny like dead-log fungus. The farther the discolor spread, the less he struggled, gnawing slower and slower at Rel's arms until he fell totally still, his last breath wheezing out of him in a sad little whine.

Wishing death on another was a sin, but Mary wasn't above a sigh of relief when the bandit who'd done them so much harm finally quit this world. She let go of Josie next, freeing her friend to scramble up to Rel while Mary knelt down to check on the boulder. It was a pointless gesture. She could already see the crystal was gone, but she wasn't ready to give all the way up until she pressed her ear against the stone.

Nothing. What had once been a crystal big enough to send all of Medicine Rocks at each other's throats was now just another piece of dead rock. It had the same overcooked color as the crystal in the Front Caves' cavern, only this hadn't been the fault of ignorant miners. This crystal had been killed by blood. *Rel's* blood.

Mary wouldn't have believed it if she hadn't seen it with her own eyes. She'd watched plenty of blood get spilled over crystal, including no small amount of her own, but she'd never seen anything like this. Drops of it were still leaking off the boulder onto the ground as she watched, leaving little dead spots on the still-bright smaller crystals of the floor below.

Moving in a panic, Mary whipped off her poncho and shoved it against the boulder's base to catch the poison drips. Her overcoat went down next, then her inner coat, then the gray wool sweater she'd been wearing pretty much nonstop since she'd found it in an abandoned cabin four years ago. One by one, every bit of Mary's extra clothing came off and went 'round the boulder, ringing the giant stone in sops so that no bit of the poison blood could do more damage. She was checking to make sure the dam would hold when Rel suddenly rolled to her feet.

This was a shock for everyone. The whole time Mary had been fussing with the crystal, Josie had been up top tending to their friend. She'd pulled the monster man's teeth out of Rel's arms and bound her gnawed-up skin back together with strips of cloth torn from the cleaner bits of Rel's duster.

From the little attention Mary had paid these ministrations, Rel had borne everything in dumb stillness, probably on account of the bleeding out. But then, like someone had pulled a lever inside her, she'd shot bolt upright, yanking her arm out of Josie's grasp while her friend was still tying the final knot on the bandages.

"Reliance!" Josie gasped, startlement turning to joy. "Thank heaven you're all right! I was so—"

She was still gushing when Rel put a bloody hand on Josie's face and shoved her off the boulder. She would've bashed her skull open if Mary hadn't jumped so quick, catching hold of Josie's arm just before she crashed into the crystal-sharp stone floor.

"What the devil, Rel?" Mary shouted, clutching her stunned friend as she glared up at the blood-soaked gunhand. "You could've killed..."

The angry words died on her tongue as the person standing on the rock turned and looked at her. A person who was most definitely *not* Reliance Reiner. It was her body, to be sure, but the sneer on its face was nothing like the Rel Mary knew. Even at her meanest, Rel had never looked that cruel. It was enough to set Mary's crawlies scrambling, but the worst of it all was the *sound*.

Even before the pillar had opened her ears to the music people made, Rel Reiner had always carried a sour note. That offness had persisted even after Mary had learned to hear her truly, though it had never been loud enough to overtake the determined melody that was Rel's true song. At least, not until now.

The Rel looking down on her at this moment was all wrong notes. They sawed away at her like out-of-tune fiddles, filling Mary's head and lungs and heart with wrongness so sharp, she wasn't even surprised when Rel's body spoke in a voice that sounded nothing like her.

"Run along, young ladies," it said, looking down at them with blue eyes that belonged to someone else. "There's nothing here for you anymore."

"Did you hit your head?" Josie yelled, fighting her way out of Mary's arms. "Darn it, Rel! What in the world is—"

"Josie, *no!*" Mary cried, snatching her friend back as the thing wearing Rel's skin hopped off the boulder. "That ain't Reliance!"

"Don't be ridiculous! Of course it's her. Just look at..."

Her voice trailed off as Not-Rel walked past them as bold as you please, dragging the dead dog-Whitman behind by his scrawny legs as she walked up the little rise of crystal that separated the boulder-strewn part of the cavern from the battle raging at the foot of the falls.

"Massacre" might've been a better word. Just like he'd said, the giant Whitman was taking on the cavalry singlehanded, and he was winning. The soldiers were trying their best, shooting the monster with everything they'd brought. But just like Rel's shots before, the bullets bounced right off the Whitman's crystal-spangled skin. Meanwhile, the giant was smashing everything unlucky enough to come into reach.

He stomped a man while Mary watched, grabbing another in his huge hand and flinging him at the wall so hard he stuck, his flesh skewered onto the sharp crystals like wool on a carding brush. The wet sound he made when he landed sent a numbness all through her, a horrified helplessness in the face of such certain death. She didn't see how anything could stand against him, which made it all the more amazing that Lucas and the few cavalry he had left still were.

The lieutenant was running like a charging horse, reloading his rifle as he bellowed for his men to stay in a circle to keep the Whitman from charging more than one of them at a time. Sergeant Chaucer had climbed up the wall and was sitting on a big spike of crystal, aiming steady down the barrel of his rifle as he struggled to land a shot in the giant's unprotected eyes. He must have gotten close enough, because the giant closed his crystal-stitched eyelids and charged his position, forcing the sergeant to leap off his perch before he got crushed. The Whitman trampled another soldier on his way, crushing the poor man into ground that was already sloppy with blood and broken crystal.

The scene was the grisliest Mary had ever beheld, including that mess with Bear Woman back by the lake. Even Josie looked hopeless, staring at the bloody wreckage with panic in her eyes. There didn't seem to be anything left to do now except to run for it, but where? The rope ladder up the falls was gone, and Mary had yet to find another way out of the cavern. She was beating the heel of her palm against her head to try to knock her terror-slowed brain into thinking of something when the thing inside Rel raised her obviously-not-Rel's voice to bellow across the cavern.

"*Whitman!*"

The giant paused midway through stomping down another soldier and turned his bald head. "Oy," he said testily. "That ain't my name. The Whitman brothers are my bosses. *My* name is—"

"I don't care," said Not-Rel, lifting the dog-man's carcass. "Missing something?"

"Kipper," the big man whispered, his cave-pale skin going gray beneath all the sewn-in crystal chips. "That's my dog. *You killed my dog!*"

With a roar of loss, the giant kicked the dead cavalryman he'd been stomping out of his way and charged up the slope. Even in her fear-dumb state, it was enough to send Mary scrambling out of the way, dragging Josie with her, but Not-Rel didn't move a muscle. She just tossed the dog-man's body aside and drew Rel's crystal gun, leveling the gem-and-bone-studded barrel at the charging giant's chest with an arm that—Mary realized with a start—was no longer a chewed-bloody mess. She had no idea how or when it had happened, but the shredded skin Josie had worked so hard to tie up was suddenly whole and smooth again, allowing Not-Rel to take level aim as she pulled the trigger.

Rel's crystal gun had never behaved as a normal weapon should, but Mary hadn't ever seen—or heard—anything like what happened next. The moment the thing wearing Rel's skin fired, the gun lit up with a whine like nails on a chalkboard. The sound stabbed through Mary's skull, forcing her to cover her ears as an arrow of sickly yellow light exploded out the end of Rel's pistol to strike the charging giant.

Up 'til this point, the crystal sewn into the giant's skin had bounced everything they'd thrown at it. Mary would've gone so far as to call him invincible. But the awful light from Rel's crystal gun went through him like a hot poker through paper, leaving a smoking hole the size of a wagon wheel through the middle of his torso.

The attack still wasn't quite enough to stop him. Even with a brand-new window through his ribs, that kind of momentum didn't just quit. Despite being dead on his feet, he still made it nearly to the top of the rise 'fore finally pitching onto his face, grinding to a bloody stop inches from Rel's blood-shined boots.

Silence fell over the cavern. Down in the wreckage at the bottom of the falls, Chaucer and Lucas emerged from the broken mound of crystal they'd taken cover behind and started frantically checking their downed men. Rel's body also doubled over, collapsing on top of the dead giant's as she slammed the crystal gun back into its holster.

"Fool, *weak* girl," the thing inside Rel snarled, spitting out a mouthful of blood as she wiped the sweat from Rel's death-pale face. "That should never have taken so much. I *told* her to practice!"

More cursing followed, leaving Mary an opening to scoot away while the gunslinger was distracted. She was tapping Josie's arm to get her to follow when the taller girl grabbed her by the shoulders.

"Did you see that?" she cried, shaking Mary like a rag doll. "Reliance saved us! I *knew* she wasn't bad!" She ran to Rel next, pulling the still-cursing girl into her arms before Mary could stop her.

"I knew you'd come through!" she said in a rapture, clutching her friend tight. "That was incredible! But why didn't you shoot your gun like that before?"

"Because it wasn't her gun," the thing in Rel said, removing Josie's limbs from its person. "It's mine, and now that the invaders have been dealt with, so is the rest of this place."

"What are you talking about?" Josie asked, her smile starting to slip.

"Poor girl," it said, clucking Josie on the chin. "You really should have run when I gave you the chance."

With an apologetic smile, as if it just couldn't be helped, the thing in Reliance pulled one of Rel's normal pistols and shot Josie point-blank in the stomach. The sound of it cracked through the quiet cave like breaking ice. Mary certainly felt like she'd been dropped back into that freezing water, for her lungs, heart, and limbs had all stopped working, leaving her staring helplessly as Josie brought her hands up to touch the bright-red bloodstain rapidly spreading across her shirtfront. That was all the motion she managed before she crumpled, falling like a dropped glove at her murderer's feet.

"*No!*"

The word exploded as feeling rushed back into Mary's body, whipping her forward to grab the convulsing Josie and drag her back behind the blackened crystal boulder. Another bullet whistled over her head as she ran, blowing a chunk out of the stone she was fleeing toward, but this Rel didn't seem to be a tenth as good as the original when it came to shooting. Despite firing off four more bullets at Mary before she finally dragged Josie to cover, not one of them came close to hitting. The impostor was reloading the wheel to come 'round the boulder and finish the job when another gunshot cracked from down by the falls.

"You back-shooting traitor!" Lucas shouted, firing his silver Colt as he charged up the hill. "I'll see you burn in a thousand hells for this, *Reiner!*"

The thing in Rel's body paid no mind to the shooting or the threats, but the moment the lieutenant said "Reiner," it paused. Only for a moment, but the brief hesitation gave Lucas the chance he needed to land a bullet in Rel's shooting arm.

The impostor dropped its gun with a string of angry words in a guttural language Mary didn't know. But while Lucas's shot had definitely struck true, Mary could already see the mangled flesh of Rel's arm pulling itself back together through the chewed-up strips of her sleeves. The same must've gone for the next two bullets Lucas landed in Rel's legs. Again, Mary saw the shots hit clear as day, but again, the monster called Reiner didn't go down. It just drew the second of Rel's normal guns and fired back.

Some of the shots actually came close to hitting this time, since the lieutenant was running straight at the pistol. But everything changed when Lucas leaped forward, ignoring Reiner's wild-flying shooting as he launched himself over the giant Whitman's still-smoking corpse and tackled his enemy to the ground.

That did the trick. Mary didn't know what kind of black magic Reiner was using to heal bullet holes, but it couldn't do a thing about Rel's stature. Her voice might've changed to a cruel old geezer's, but her body was still that of a short, underfed girl. Lucas wasn't a huge man, but he was still much bigger than Reliance, and he used every ounce to his advantage, slamming Reiner into the ground with his boot stomped down on her neck.

"Good show, Lieutenant!" Chaucer called, running up to join them.

Chest heaving, Lucas bent down to yank Rel's pistol out of Reiner's hand, keeping his gun aimed at Rel's face as he flung the weapon out into the darkness. "Are you hurt?"

It took Mary several seconds to realize the lieutenant was talking to her. "No," she said belatedly. "But Josie's shot!"

"On it," said Chaucer as he scrambled to Mary's side. After one look at the red stain soaking nearly all of Josie's chest, though, he shot right back up.

"Get some pressure on that," he told Mary, spinning on his heel back toward the falls. "I'll go find the medical bag!"

Mary nodded and slapped her hands over Josie's wound, feeling murderously stupid for not having done so sooner. Josie's face was the color of old paper in the light of the toppled lanterns, and her shirtfront was cold and claggy with blood. Mary was encouraging her to keep breathing when Chaucer came back carrying a leather satchel with a red cross painted on its side.

"I'll take it from here."

Mary scooted over to give him room. "I didn't know you were a medic."

"Me neither," Chaucer said as he shoved a wad of gauze into Josie's wound. "Higgins was supposed to be our sawbones, but he went and got himself crushed, so I'm afraid you're stuck with the leftovers. I have seen this done a lot, though, so I'm pretty sure I've got the gist."

That wasn't reassuring, but the cotton bandage Chaucer was wrapping around Josie's middle did seem to be stopping the blood a lot better than Mary's hands. She still didn't look anything close to good, but at least she'd started breathing a bit less deathly slow by the time Chaucer secured the bandage with a lopsided square knot.

"There," he said, wiping his bloody hands on his trousers. "Lieutenant will have words about my knotwork, I'm sure, but that should stem the worst of it. We still need to get her to a real doctor, though."

"I'll take her," Mary volunteered. "No one's faster getting through the caves than me."

"That won't work," Lucas said, keeping his eyes on Reiner. "Not that I doubt your abilities, Miss Good Crow, but you can't carry her all that way on your own. None of us can safely. We'll need a stretcher, and we should keep checking for survivors. Miss Price might not be the only one who needs doctoring."

"Wouldn't get my hopes up, sir," Chaucer said grimly, looking toward the falls. "I'm not seeing any movement down there."

"We have to be certain," the lieutenant insisted. "I'm not leaving anyone behind this time. Go check our men, Sergeant. Miss Good Crow, you take care of Miss Price."

Mary nodded and wrapped her arms around Josie. Meanwhile, Chaucer grabbed the medical bag and jogged back down the slope toward the mess that had been the rest of the cavalry. Lucas kept position atop Reiner while reloading his pistol, filling the six-shooter's wheel with what appeared to be the last of his ammunition. He was still slotting bullets when Reiner chuckled beneath him.

"Quiet, you whorehouse traitor," Lucas ordered, digging his heel harder into the back of Reiner's neck.

"Now, see, that's inaccurate," Reiner choked out, turning Rel's head unnaturally far around to flash Lucas a menacing grin. "Betrayal implies loyalty, and I owe no allegiance to any of you blind fools. None of you have any concept of the wonder you stand within, which is why I'll be taking my cavern back now."

"I'd like to see you try," Lucas said, aiming his freshly loaded pistol at the spot above Rel's ear. "I was considering taking you in for questioning, but you've convinced me that killing you here will be far less trouble and much more satisfying. Let's see if you can heal a hole through your brains, you miserable, soldier-killing son of a—"

The execution was interrupted by Chaucer's terrified shriek as the sergeant came tearing back up the hill.

"Lieutenantlieutenantlieutenant!" he cried, pointing frantically over his shoulder. "The men! They're standing!"

"Really?" A smile shot across Lucas's blood-smattered face. "That's wonderful!"

"No, it's not!" Chaucer yelled. "Because they're still in *bits*! It's just like what happened with the bandits before, only it's *our* soldiers this time, and they're coming this way!"

The lieutenant's shock at that must've been what Reiner was waiting for, for the moment Lucas turned to see what Chaucer was talking about, Reiner shoved Rel's body up, knocking Lucas off-balance and fleeing down the hill. The lieutenant fired after them a split second later, but his shots were blocked by a line of shambling figures.

Their bodies were so twisted and broken that they scarcely looked like men anymore. But while Mary had done her best to stay away when they were alive, she couldn't miss that these were no dead bandits. They were cavalry soldiers, or what was left of them, and they'd formed a protective ring around Reiner, who was strutting cocky as a jaybird.

"That's more like it," Reiner said, voice booming with the rotten dissonance Mary normally only heard in her head. "Go on, my children. Remove them from my sight. Your master has more pressing matters to attend."

Rel's eyes went to the pillar, filling Mary with a horrible sinking dread she had no time to suffer. The moment Reiner had spoken, every dead thing in the room jerked like bells on a string. Even the giant Whitman hauled himself back up, lifting his head out of the ditch he'd plowed in the floor to stare at their group with filmy, empty eyes.

"To hell with this," Chaucer said, dropping the heavy med-bag on the ground. "*Run!*"

No one argued. Mary hauled Miss Josie into her arms and bolted, stumbling over gun-shattered crystal as she struggled with the weight. She'd barely made it five feet when Lucas swooped in and took the lady, freeing Mary to run full tilt.

380

"Is there another way out?" he yelled as they charged down the stream toward the back of the cavern.

Mary shook her head. "Just the falls!"

"That's not going to work, is it?" Chaucer said, firing over his shoulder at the corpses charging after them until his gun clicked empty. "You're the bloody guide! Don't you have anything else?"

"*Chaucer!*" Lucas barked, but while Mary appreciated him coming to her defense, his sergeant wasn't wrong. Guiding them to safety *was* Mary's job. Everyone else was fighting and dying and doing their part, but all she'd done so far was watch in horror as everything she'd come to care about got stomped to bits.

It was her fault for getting her hopes up. She'd *known* things were going too good for disaster not to be right around the corner. She'd *known* it was all bound to end in tears. Well, here were the tears and likely the end, but for once in her life, Mary wasn't willing to take them.

All her days, she'd accepted what couldn't be changed, going when folks said get and hiding from anything bigger than her. She'd always told herself there was nothing for it, that this was just the way life was. But the costs felt so much higher this time, 'cause it weren't just her life on the line. It was Josie's and Lucas's and Chaucer's. It was the pillar Reiner was walking toward and the crystal screaming all around. Its music banged inside her head, wordless as always, but that didn't stop Mary from understanding. Everything living knew that sound. It was a cry of terror. A cry for help.

Answering that call was the first rule she'd learned down here, so Mary did something she'd never done before. She stopped running, digging in her heels so hard the water-rounded crystals in the stream bed rolled under her soft boots like marbles.

Lucas must've been watching her, because he pulled up short at the same time. "What is it?" he asked, shifting Josie to his left arm so he could draw his saber. "Did you think of a plan?"

"Something like that," Mary said, turning around. "Follow me."

"But that's back toward the enemy!" Chaucer cried, which was true, but his lieutenant was already chasing after Mary, following her upstream to the outcropping of giant, spiny crystals ringing the pillar's base.

"Take cover under there," Mary ordered, pointing at the gap between crystal spines and the cavern's floor. "I'm gonna try something. Watch Josie for me!"

"We will keep Miss Price safe," Lucas promised, handing Josie to Chaucer so he could give Mary a boost onto the giant pinecone-shaped crystal. "Be careful, Marie!"

The familiar name made her do a double take, but the cavalrymen were already doing like she'd said, hunkering down below the crystals that surrounded the pillar like a hedge of prickers.

The corpses caught up right after, throwing themselves into the thorny stones with no care for what got stuck. But while the dead clearly didn't feel pain from the points running them through, they couldn't control their jerking bodies well enough to slide between the spines. This led to a pileup with the dead soldiers pushing themselves as far onto the crystal as their lifeless bodies would go while Lucas circled underneath, chopping off anything that came in range with his saber.

The situation wasn't ideal by any measure, but it seemed a stable enough standoff for the moment, and Mary didn't have time to wait for better. This high up, she could see Reiner again over the dead soldiers. The thing in Rel's body seemed to have stopped its march on the pillar once Mary doubled back, but the pause had given it time to retrieve Rel's gun from the darkness where Lucas had tossed it. That wasn't too big a worry given the impostor's lousy aim, but it only took one good shot, so Mary hied herself along, scrambling up the sharp ridges of the pinecone crystal until she was standing once again in front of the pillar.

The giant crystal was every bit as beautiful as she remembered: a soaring column of moon-white stone so smooth, Mary could see the whole room reflected in its surface despite all the lanterns having been dropped way back at the falls. It still sang when she touched it, too, but the beautiful song was panicked this time, a pillar-sized version of the terrified screaming that had called her over in the first place.

"It's okay, I'm here," she told it, wrapping her arms around the warm stone. "I'm sorry I ran away before. I'm ready now!"

The music trilled in reply, the notes running up and down her bones like scrambling fingers. She didn't even wait for the pillar to start singing "Frère Jacques." She just jumped straight to the note it wanted, singing the finding crystal's tone out loud and true as she could.

Just like last time, the reaction was immediate. No sooner had the music started to vibrate in her chest than the stone under her body lit up like the full moon on snow. Her hands flared as well, the sparkling scars left by the exploding finding crystal shining like forked lighting that spidered up her arms as the pillar's thundering music burst into her skull.

The flood of sound was just as terrifying now as it had been the first time. Worse, actually, because the whole cavern was panicking, its music screaming as its crystals were blackened and broken all around. Even the pillar's voice was jumpy, its music coming in fits and starts like it was trying desperately not to overwhelm her, but Mary wasn't having it.

She was done with being timid. She was always running and hiding, and what had it gotten her? Another day of being scared. Another day of giving up everything *she* cared about 'cause she couldn't fight back, but not anymore. She'd seen what crystal could do now. If the Whitmans and Reiner could use it to put everything Mary loved in danger, why couldn't she do the same to save it?

That was the long-shot notion that had sent her running up here. It weren't much of a plan, but knowing that Reiner had been heading for the pillar told Mary there had to be something useful. Anything was better than running away, knowing she'd let that killer take Josie and her crystal, so Mary held on tight, throwing her voice into the cavern's chorus as the pillar's light grew brighter and brighter and brighter.

At least she made sure not to go out of tune this time. Not that she'd given it much thought 'fore she'd scrambled up here, but Mary was pretty sure losing the note was where things had gone sideways last time. She knew what to expect now, and her opened ears were a lot sharper, letting her follow the crystal's music like a pin on a line.

A bullet whizzed by her ear, clipping the side of the pillar. Another followed right behind it, then another and another as Reiner tried to shoot her off the stone. The dead took heed as well, climbing up the pinecone crystal she was sitting on. One broken corpse actually got close enough to knock off her hat before Lucas sliced its legs out with his sword.

Any other point in her life, that would've been Mary's sign to hightail it out. Now, though, the near miss just made her all the more determined 'cause it proved she was on the right path. Reiner wouldn't be spending all those bullets and corpses on someone who was wasting their time, so Mary sang though the gunfire, lifting her voice in a chorus that was now much bigger than just her cavern. It came from all over, from the crystals in Deep Caves and bigger clusters even farther away, buried deep in the roots of the Earth.

Their combined voices rang through the ground like a great bell, their songs twining together into the pillar, who fed it all into Mary. They were well past the point where she'd bailed the first time, her skin so riddled with shining cracks that her body was shining almost as bright at the pillar. If ever she was going to break, now was the time, and yet, despite being full beyond bursting, Mary did not shatter.

Like the pillar she clung to, she just kept getting brighter and brighter, louder and louder, bigger and bigger until she could no longer tell what was crystal and what was her. It was all just a big wash of sparkling light and roaring music, though not panicked anymore. This was the glorious, joyful, leaping music she'd heard the first time, but even better now 'cause it was running through her blood and bones, not just her ears.

Her whole self was inside the music now, singing with the crystal body and soul as the brightness finally faded from her eyes, and she realized she was no longer standing on the pinecone crystal. She was somewhere entirely new, standing in her dirty boots on a seemingly endless whiteness as sparkly and radiant as a snow of pearls. She was gawking at it in wonder when something else appeared in the strange brightness with her. A huge, ferocious, familiar shape of a giant bear with a bloodstained muzzle and milky, cave-blind eyes.

"So," Bear Woman growled in Lakota. Very, *very* old-sounding Lakota. "You're the one she chose."

"I—what?" Mary asked in the same language, her glory-addled brain woefully confused. "She who?"

For some reason, this innocent question angered the bear. "You gave yourself to something eternal, and *you don't even know what you did?*"

Mary's first instinct was to say sorry, but she wasn't. She was proud of herself for finally taking a stand on something, and while she saw no sign of the crystal powers she'd hoped for, Mary would never be sorry for trying.

"Don't look so pleased with yourself," the bear growled. "You have no idea the trouble you've started."

"I answered a call for help," Mary replied stubbornly. "Reiner was gonna destroy everything, so the pillar and I worked together. How's that trouble?"

"If she'd actually needed help, she could have called me," Bear Woman snapped. "But I heard nothing until the two of you started howling, which can only mean one thing: she used this crisis to trick you into singing with her."

"I wasn't tricked!" Mary cried. "I'm honored the pillar gave me another chance. It had no reason to share its music with me again. I'm the one who brought disaster into the cavern! I still don't rightly know what I'm supposed to be doing or where I am, but I did this 'cause we needed help, and here you are, so I'd say I made the right choice."

The bear looked insulted. "I'm not here to help you."

"Then why are you here?" Mary asked, emboldened by the music that continued to bubble inside her. "And why do you keep talking about the pillar like it's a person?"

"She's not a pillar or a person," Bear Woman said. "She's a Song. The Last Song that must never be sung, but *you* sang her, and now we're all off the cliff."

That did sound dreadful, but Mary couldn't make herself be afraid. The pillar's music had been too lovely for that. The joyful song was still running through her even now, bubbling like a creek all through Mary's body, which no longer showed any signs of cracking. The old scars on her hands were still glowing, but the rest of her looked perfectly fine. Better than fine! Her body felt healthier than ever, her joints freed of a hard life's worth of aches and pains. Even the chunk of skin she'd lost to the Cave Ash was back like it had never been gone, leaving Mary peering under her clothes to see what other miracles the song had wrought.

When it was obvious Mary wasn't taking her warnings to heart, the bear heaved a long sigh and changed her shape, melting back into the young Lakota woman Mary had seen beside the lake. "Everything the power does, it does in a circle," she said tiredly, holding out her hands to Mary. "Someone also yelled at me when I first sang my Song. But there's no putting spilled water back in the pot, so come. Let's have a look at you."

That struck Mary as an odd thing for a blind woman to say, but she far preferred this to being growled at, so Mary did as she was told, stepping forward to let Bear Woman tap her all over the face and limbs like she were testing to see which parts of Mary were hollow.

"Your voice isn't much for a Singer," Bear Woman muttered, tapping Mary's throat. "But I knew that already from the times you sang for me, and yet..." She pressed her ear to Mary's chest. "Your heart rings a good tone." She pulled her head back, smiling for the first time Mary had ever seen. "I see why she worked so hard to court you."

"Who is she?" Mary asked, fascinated. "What's her name?"

"That's for her to tell," Bear Woman said, her expression growing serious again. "You're her Singer now. The others will call it a calamity, the Last Song choosing a Singer whose feet are in two worlds, but those blind old fools couldn't see the real calamity when I shoved it up their noses, so who's to say she didn't choose wisely? You might yet turn out to be just what we need."

She ran her hands over Mary's face and hair again as she finished, and Bear Woman's lips split into a sharp, bear-toothed grin. "*Just* what we need," she said, letting Mary go as she walked away. "Wait there. I'm going to fetch someone who can help you."

"Wait?" Mary repeated desperately. "Oh no, ma'am, I can't do that! My friends are still trapped with that monster. He's going to kill them and turn all the crystal in the cavern dark if I don't go back and do something! Please, you're strong. You gotta help me—"

But Bear Woman was already gone, vanishing from the empty whiteness like a popped soap bubble.

"Tarnation," Mary muttered, looking around the dazzling nothing, which now felt more like a prison than a wonder. The whole reason she'd done this was to fix things, but all Bear Woman had offered was a bunch of talk that made no sense. The one part she had cottoned was that she and Bear Woman were alike now, but if Mary really had been chosen by a Song or whatever, shouldn't she have crazy powers too? Maybe not turning into a bear, but there had to be *something* she could do that wasn't waiting around here. What was the point of telling Lucas and the others to hunker if she was just gonna trap herself in some white nothing?

Mary was getting good and panicked over that when something trilled in her mind, something that wasn't her. It was the music that had settled to a hum in her bones, strange but still as warm and lovely as fresh bread on a cold day.

"Is that you?" she whispered, poking at her wrists where she could feel the vibrating clearest. "You gotta take me back! That thing in Rel has terrible plans. It's already ruined a bunch of your crystal, and it'll do far worse if we don't stop it. Please, I'll swear I'll sing you 'Frère Jacques' every day if you'll just help—"

The music pulsed, insulted. Mary couldn't say for sure how she knew that, but while the feelings flooding through her definitely weren't her own, nor even in words, they were just as bright and clear as her own thoughts, leaving no doubt about their meaning.

There was no need for bargaining. They were two forks of one river now. If Mary wanted something, Calamity would help. All she had to do was sing.

"Calamity," Mary repeated to herself, addressing her glowing hands since that made as much logic as anything. "Is that your name?"

It was what the others called her.

"Well, I don't want to call you that," Mary said angrily. "'The Last Song Calamity' is a name for something dreadful. You're lovely."

This observation delighted the music enormously, sending it swirling through Mary's mind like petals in a stream. See, *this* was why Mary was her Singer. She'd never feared the crystal or the caves, and the crystal and the caves were her.

"I'm very glad to hear that," Mary said, and she was! She'd never known anyone, disembodied or otherwise, who was this happy to be partnered with her. Any other time, she would've sat for hours talking to the new soul who seemed to have set up residence in her skeleton, but, "I really gotta go," she said, pointing at the whiteness. "You brought me into this place. How do I get out?"

The question wasn't even fully out when an image appeared in Mary's head like someone had shoved a painting in her ear. A picture of herself, stepping backward.

"It can't be that simple."

The image reappeared more aggressively, and Mary waved her hands. "Fine, fine! Here we go. I just hope you've got a plan for what happens when we come out, 'cause I don't."

The Song filled her mind with calming music, soothing her worries away as Mary stepped backwards, but she had nothing to step on. The floor of the whiteness that had seemed to go on forever wasn't there when her heel came down, leaving Mary falling backwards through the radiant light and into a scene she recognized.

At least, Mary thought she recognized it. The cave looked just like the Mother Lode she'd left, but every inch of it was shining like Christmas. The crystals were all glowing as bright as the guiding stone used to but in their own colors rather than white. Together, they lit up the cavern like sunrise through a stained glass window, but the pillar was brightest of all. It stood in the middle of everything, shining an iridescent white of every color put together, and floating in the middle of all that gloriousness was Mary.

It was such a staggering change to come back to that Mary didn't realize she *was* back until she saw the others. Lucas, Chaucer, and Josie were all below her, peeking out of the glowing thicket of crystal spikes that surrounded the pillar's base with expressions of wonder. The dead had all pulled back to Reiner, who was crouching in their midst, staring up at Mary from beneath the giant Whitman with a jealous sort of fear splashed all over Rel's bloodless face.

The Song inside her cried out at the sight, her bright music turning mournful and afraid. Mary absolutely agreed, for now that the cave song was in her flesh and bones instead of just her ears, she could hear what Reiner's sour noise was actually doing. This wasn't just dissonance. It was a different song entirely. *Reiner's* song was inside Rel's body just as Calamity was inside Mary's, only theirs didn't look like an equal partnership. Reiner's dissonance had drowned out Rel's sound completely, but it didn't stop there. The sour notes were also ringing inside the dead soldiers, smothering the voices of their ghosts and the music of the caves until the only sound was Reiner's, leaving their corpses no choice but to dance to its tune.

Just hearing it was enough to make Mary's stomach clench in disgust, or it would've if she'd had one. Despite the falling, it didn't seem that her body had made it out of the whiteness with her, for she saw nothing but crystal below her when she looked down. The Song was there, though, and she was madder than Mary had known music could get, pounding so hard with sound that Mary could scarcely think straight, which perversely gave her an idea.

Moving quickly as only someone with no body to worry about could, Mary flitted over to the dead soldiers and hummed a bit of the pounding song at them. It worked even better than she'd hoped, drowning Reiner's dissonance straight out of the corpses, who then flopped over just like dead bodies should. But while Mary's strategy worked aces on the dead, it wasn't so good for the living.

Light as she tried to be, even that small hum was enough to make Josie, Chaucer, and Lucas cry out in pain, and she hadn't even been aiming their direction. Reiner, on the other hand, got blasted head-on. For a wildly hopeful moment, Mary thought maybe it'd blast the corruption out of Rel's body just as it had for the corpses, but Reiner's claws must've been dug deeper into her, 'cause the only thing that went flying was Rel.

If she hadn't had the good fortune to land in the pond at the cavern's far end, the fall would've killed her. Just knowing it might've happened was enough to make Mary snatch her music back. She didn't care what happened to Reiner, but that was Rel's body gasping for air and dodging the glowing crystal spears that lined the pond's bottom like spikes. The girl had a lot to answer for, but she deserved to do so as herself. Mary certainly wasn't about to cut her down while she wasn't in control of her actions, but if she couldn't knock out Reiner without hurting Rel, she didn't know what she was going to do.

As soon as she'd let her music falter, Reiner's ugly song had flooded right back in, filling the dead like hands in puppets and calling them to the pond, where they immediately started impaling themselves on the giant spikes of lavender crystal that filled the water to make Reiner a safe path to shore. This was better than attacking Josie and the others, but Mary was sure the respite was only temporary, and she didn't know what she was gonna do when it ended. Reiner was the canker at the heart of everything, but she could think of no way to stop that monster without killing Rel too. Reiner knew that, clearly, for Rel's face was smugger than ever as she climbed up onto the bridge the dead soldiers had made for her out of their bodies, looking up at the pillar like she could see Mary floating inside.

"I know you're in there, Half-Breed," Reiner announced in that awful, sneering voice that seemed to be the way they said everything. "Congratulations. You've confirmed my oldest and greatest theory. Too bad you don't know what to do with it."

Mary answered with a low whistle that knocked the dissonance out of the corpses just long enough to drop Reiner back into the water. It made a very satisfying sight, but Reiner definitely did not look cowed when Rel's body climbed back out.

"Uh uh uh," they said, lifting Rel's arm to show Mary the bloody gouge one of the underwater crystals had made in her bicep. "Attacking me only hurts her, and I know you don't want to do that. Just think how your beloved Miss Josephine would react if she saw you maiming her *best friend*."

The monster in Rel's body nodded at the base of the pillar, and Mary looked down to see that, sure enough, Josie was watching. She didn't know when her friend had come back to consciousness, but she was awake and on her knees at the edge of the crystal thicket, clutching her bandaged stomach and staring across the glowing crystal at her possessed friend with more fear in her eyes than when she'd been shot.

If Mary hadn't already decided against killing Rel, that look would have cinched it, but what the devil was she gonna do? Reiner was already sucking the color out of the crystals in the pond, turning the lovely glowing lavender black as rotted meat just by putting Rel's hands on it. The crystals screamed as they died, each vanishing voice leaving a gap in Mary's own body now that she was part of them, but she didn't know how to make it stop without more killing, or before Josie expired. She was already slumping to the ground, clinging to the crystal to keep herself upright as she called to Rel in a voice Mary could no longer hear.

Mary didn't know if that was because she could no longer hear voices without crystal in them or if Josie was too weak to make a sound. Either way, it filled her with terror. She was scrambling for something, *anything*, that might fix this when the music began rattling her bones like it was trying to get her attention.

When Mary turned her attention to see what it wanted, the Song snatched it right back to the crystals Reiner was murdering. "I know," Mary whispered, wincing when the words came out as crystal chiming rather than speech. Apparently she couldn't talk in this form. Not that it mattered, since there seemed to be nothing she could—

The Song blared inside her, filling Mary's head with a pounding echo of her own thoughts from just a few minutes before, when she'd sworn to stop giving up just because she thought she couldn't change things.

"You're right," Mary said, duly chastised. "What are we looking at?"

The music directed her attention once again to the blackening crystals but not because she was trying to make Mary feel bad about it. The sense Mary got was that the Song wanted her to watch. Or more accurately, to *listen*, for the crystal Reiner was touching wasn't just losing its light. It was losing its song. The same Song that filled Mary, because these were *her* crystals grown and filled with *her* music. Reiner wasn't all powerful. The bastard was stealing from the Song, draining the sound she'd built up in these stones over untold time, because crystals didn't make music.

Music made crystal.

Mary went still. Of course. All those crystals—the Mother Lode's glittering cavern, the giant clusters of the Deep Caves, even the little shimmering flecks left over in the walls after the miners moved on—they weren't actually little voices singing their own songs. They were just echoing a greater music, bouncing and amplifying the pillar's Song just like they'd reflected Mary's lantern into a sky full of stars.

That was why the cave music always sounded so random! It was echoes, not singing. Echoes of *her* Song, and now that Mary understood that, the solution she'd been scrambling for popped into her head.

Smiling for the first time since she'd left the pillar, Mary whirled her attention back to Reiner. Specifically, she focused on the still-glowing, still-singing crystals deep in the water below Rel's feet, for the monster had already silenced the shallower stones to heal the damage to Rel's body, which was now climbing back up onto the corpse bridge.

"I take it from your silence you've accepted your impasse," Reiner said, shaking the bloody water out of Rel's short hair. "But there's no reason we have to be enemies. I'm sure you think me a monster, but I've only done what I felt was necessary to ensure my survival, the same as you. If you could put aside your prejudice for a moment, though, I think you'll see we're not so different. We both want to understand the music that made this magnificent place, to master its potential. The fact that you got in there first proves you're a better listener than Reliance ever was, so how about a deal? I'll stop my creations and let you rescue your dear Miss Josephine, and in return, you let me come in there with you. We could learn so much from each other! That's all I've ever wanted, you know. To learn, to understand, to no longer be a helpless victim of the ignorance that keeps humanity trapped in the gutter of mortality. Why should minds like ours be limited to the flesh when we could be eternal? We could find the answers together. My secrets for yours, so what do you say, child? Shall we make a truce?"

Mary's answer to that was a single note, though not at him. She was singing to the stone deep below Reiner's feet, to the huge veins of still unmined crystal that drove the Deep Caves' constant changing. All this time, she'd been thinking of the cavern like a bubble, a place of its own, but crystal was a connection.

The Song that lit up this place was the same music that bounced through everything down here. *Moved* everything, for music was never still. It was always rolling forward, shaping and reshaping the tunnels that channeled it like a stream moving through sand. It was that movement Mary harnessed now, singing her own Song at the stones that made up the bottom of the pond until they shifted, too, opening the tiny crack she *knew* had to be hidden down here into a chasm big enough to drive a wagon through.

After that, things changed very quickly. Starting with the insultingly false smile Reiner had slapped on Rel's face, which slid into a look of surprise then horror as the corpses holding Rel's boots out of the water dropped suddenly into nothingness.

Not too much nothingness. Mary was still determined not to kill anyone, but the ground vanishing out from under you was never a good surprise.

The last Mary saw of Reiner, they were sucking in a final breath as the falling water carried Rel's body and all the dead down into the darkness of the underground river below. The same river she now knew fed eventually back into the black lake at the end of the Midway. It'd still be dangerous, but she felt much better about Rel's chances in a washout than if she'd abandoned Reiner in some unknown hollow of the Deep Caves, and she didn't have time for something more complicated. She might have dallied too long already, for by the time she'd closed up the pond again and whirled to check on the others, Lucas had already worked his way out of the bloody crystal thicket, carrying a very pale, very scary-looking Josie in his arms.

"Marie!" he yelled, looking around at the bright glowing crystal with wild eyes. "You're here, yes? I saw that devil Tyrel trying to bargain with you. I'm glad you sent him to a watery grave, but we need to get Miss Price to town *now*."

"Her heartbeat is getting weaker, and I don't know how to get it back up!" Chaucer cried, stumbling out after his lieutenant. "She needs an actual doctor who knows what they're bloody doing."

"We can still save her life, I am certain!" Lucas said, looking up at the bright shining pillar. "But we won't make it back without you. Please come out!"

Mary wanted nothing more. Her heart was breaking at the sight of her friend looking so much like a corpse already, but Mary'd separated from her body when she'd left the pillar and she didn't know how to go back in or how she was gonna get herself out once she did. Her Song didn't seem to have any answers either. She had plenty of ideas bubbling through Mary's mind, but none of them seemed to understand yet that humans and rocks were different. Mary supposed that made sense for a Song that lived in crystal, but it didn't help right now, so she pushed the music aside and focused her ears on the whisper-soft melody of Josie's own song.

It wasn't easy even for Mary's better-than-ever ears. Her friend's music was no more than a murmur, easily overwhelmed by Lucas and Chaucer's louder, more frantic drumming. But unlike the soldiers' unfamiliar strains, Josie's was a tune Mary knew by heart. It was the very first person-music she'd ever noticed, and even then it had been familiar, like a childhood song. Singing along felt natural as breathing, for though Josie's wasn't Mary's Song, she was starting to understand that all the musics she heard—cave song, people song, even Reiner's awful noises— were just new sorts of the same thing. They were different instruments, but they were all playing the same notes, and those were the ones Mary sang now, using the same music she'd sung to move the caves and light the pillar to lift up her friend's fading melody.

Mary's effort wasn't enough to heal her like Reiner's cursed song seemed able to, but the extra volume brought a bit of color back to Josie's face. Her breaths grew stronger, too, giving rhythm to the music and buying Mary space to switch her attention back to the cave. Her plan this time was a lot bigger than what she'd done with the pond, but even with

Mary singing to her the whole way, Josie was never going to make the long journey back to Medicine Rocks like this. She needed a quicker path than even Mary's ears could find, but if there was one song Mary knew better than any other, it was the music that took her back to town.

Reproducing the cave's random chiming was a lot harder than singing along to a person. But while Mary'd only been listening to Josie for a few days, she'd hung her life on this song for years. It might not be an actual melody like the pillar sang, but even echoes had a pattern if you listened long enough, a way they liked to be.

Mary knew those quirks and turns by heart. She parroted them now, singing the music she'd always listened for hardest until the rock of the Mother Lode's walls shifted, the glowing crystals shuffling aside to form a new tunnel that hadn't been there until just now. One made from the same pale sandstone as the Front Caves.

Lucas must've recognized the color, too, 'cause he ran over to the new cave before the rocks had stopped moving, carrying Josie like a treasure against his chest. It looked like he was gonna run right through, but he paused at the last step, looking back at Mary's pillar even as Chaucer tried to drag him forward. "I'll come back for you!" he promised. "Stay right there!"

It was kind of him to say. But while Mary had changed her opinion of the lieutenant enough to believe he meant what he said, connecting a song that stretched through miles of stone was a lot harder than singing to rocks that were just a few dozen feet below. It also didn't help that there was practically no crystal left in the Front Caves to sing to, leaving Mary struggling with all her might to hold the passage together.

Fortunately, Chaucer had the good sense to recognize a collapse when he saw one. He shoved Lucas through, pushing him into the quiet stone caverns of the actual Front Caves just before she lost it. The impossible tunnel caved in a second later as Mary keeled over, crashing back into the whiteness of the pillar and the body she'd left inside as suddenly as she'd fallen out of it.

The change was a lot less graceful this time. Turned out, bodies didn't like it when you left 'em. Leaving had been easy as walking through fog, but getting back in felt like trying to shove her hand into a jar of frozen honey. Every part of her flesh felt like a foot that'd fallen asleep. Even her lungs were full of pins and needles as Mary sat up with a gasp, shaking her arms and kicking her legs to try to get the numbness out. She was still at it when a black shape came charging out of the brightness, knocking Mary right back over as Bear Woman's furious muzzle filled her vision.

"Where have you been? I told you to wait here!"

"'N I told you I couldn'," Mary said, the words coming out slurred on account of the tingles that were still crawling all over her numb face. "I had to save my friends!"

"Did you have to be so *loud* about it?" the bear growled. "There won't be a power left that doesn't know what you are after that performance."

"Is that bad?"

"It was reckless," Bear Woman huffed, sitting back on her haunches.

The music tittered in Mary's head, and her tingling face split into a grin. "Calamity says you're the soul of recklessness."

"She's one to talk," the bear said with a snort. "And never give away your Song's name, not even to people you trust. Particularly not *that* name."

The music slid through Mary in a motion that felt like a shrug, and Bear Woman sighed.

"As promised, I have brought help. See that you listen and do as she says."

"Okay," Mary said, biting her lip as she looked 'round the white nothing. "Um, is she still coming? 'Cause the only folks I see right now is us."

"You will have to go to her," Bear Woman said, getting back to her feet.

Mary chewed her lip harder. "But I don't know how to—"

"Figure it out," the bear snarled. "You were the one who chose this dangerous path. If you can't at least walk it well, you have no right to be in this place."

That seemed a little harsh, but Bear Woman had never been known for her kindness. She was already gone again anyway, leaving Mary worrying alone inside the whiteness with her Song spinning apologetically inside her.

"It's all right," Mary said, patting her chest. "Ain't your fault she's growly. You've done amazing, letting me make a tunnel all the way back to town. Now I just gotta figure how to make one outta here."

The music puffed up proudly at the praise, but Mary was getting a little worried. Moving the stones outside had been as easy as breathing, but the white crystal didn't budge when she pushed on it, which was gonna be a problem 'cause Mary's stomach was already starting to feel empty. Was it possible to starve in this place? And if she did, would she still keep her Song if she died and became an actual ghost?

Mary wasn't keen to find out. It would've been nice if Bear Woman had actually shown her to the person she'd supposedly brought to help, but the bear was long gone, so Mary undertook the task herself, running her hands along the hard edge of the white nothing that she now realized must be the crystal's outside. She was still searching for a sign or a door or *something* when she heard a noise that sounded a lot like knocking.

For a wild moment, Mary thought Lucas had actually made good on his promise to come back for her. When she ran over to the sound and cupped her hands against the crystal wall to squint through the brightness, though, the shape standing on the other side wasn't the lieutenant's. It was a Lakota woman.

Not an old-fashioned ghostly one like Bear Woman, neither. This was a normal-looking girl about Mary's age perched on top of the pinecone crystal. She was wearing a lovely doe-skin dress with a yoke of glowing crystal beads stitched tight as corn kernels around her neck. Leather thongs strung with even larger chunks of crystal decorated her long black hair, which was braided and bound away from her face with a bright-colored leather strap decorated with yet more crystals carved to resemble bear claws.

All of this made her looked like a terribly important person, but her smile was friendly as she spotted Mary's face pressing against the stone. After waving wildly to make sure Mary was paying attention, the girl then took her hands and placed them both palms down against the pillar's smooth face. Curious, Mary slid her own hands down to match, lining them up with the other woman's finger to finger. When they were mirrored to each other, the girl on the other side opened her mouth and began to sing loud enough to shake the crystal. It was a clear, happy tune that Mary remembered from her brief time with the Lakota: a song of welcome for the ones returning home.

The moment she recognized what it was, the music inside her answered with a joyous leap, and the hard crystal suddenly turned soft as water beneath her palms. Her hands slid through a moment later, crashing into the woman's, who grabbed them tight. It happened so suddenly, Mary didn't have even time to be surprised before the woman yanked her free, popping her body—her real, living, flesh-and-blood body!—out of the crystal pillar and into her arms.

"I found you!" she cried in Lakota, hugging Mary like she'd never been hugged before. "I finally found you, my sister!"

That last word crashed through Mary even harder than the pillar's music, leaving her gape-jawed in the cavern's rainbow light.

Chapter 26

Josie woke up in what appeared to be someone's attic. Someone's very well-lit attic, for in addition to the sunlight—blessed sunlight!—streaming through the skylights, all manner of mirrored sconces were nailed to the walls. The combined brightness was so staggering that, if it weren't for the discomfort of the hard cot under her buttocks and the tingling ache in her midsection, Josie would've worried she'd passed on to glory. She was still trying to figure out where, exactly, she was and what, exactly, could have brought her to such a place when a short woman dressed in severe widow's black entered the room from a door that had been hidden by the glare.

"Oh," she said when she noticed Josie looking at her. "You're awake. Interesting."

Considering the last thing Josie remembered was clinging to a bloody crystal, trying not to die while the evil thing in Reliance's body shouted at Mary about songs from atop a bridge of corpses, "interesting" wasn't the word she would have chosen. "Miraculous" felt like a much better fit. So did "perplexing."

"Where am I?"

"At my surgery," the woman replied, prying Josie's eyelids wider with her cold, papery fingers.

"And who are you?" Josie asked, resisting the urge to jerk her head away.

"A doctor."

She had the strangest way of talking, as if every word had been stamped out in a factory before being released to her mouth. Her intonation was similarly monotonous, making her speech difficult to follow, even though her enunciation was the clearest Josie had heard yet in Medicine Rocks. That could have been because of the wooziness in Josie's own head, though. She'd never been drunk before, but this certainly felt like what she'd imagined.

The doctor must not have seen anything worrying in Josie's eyes, for she let her eyelids go and walked to the cabinet on the wall to Josie's left. She was so short-statured she had to employ a stool to reach the third shelf, rising on her tiptoes to select a small, glittery object from the backmost row.

"Take this," she ordered, shoving the thing into Josie's hands, which she'd just realized were resting on top of her naked chest.

Josie covered her exposed body with a yelp. The reaction was involuntary and, it turned out, unwise. The sudden movement jostled her bandaged stomach, sending up a wave of stabbing, nauseous pain that, while not nearly as bad as the initial wound, was still enough to make her retch.

"You shouldn't move," the doctor advised belatedly, snapping a basin under Josie's mouth just in time. "The bullet punctured several layers of your small intestine. I pinned everything back in place, but you still shouldn't jostle things until the tissue has a chance to heal over."

"Pinned?" Josie repeated shakily, wiping her mouth. "There are *pins* in my intestines?"

"Crystal pins," the doctor said, setting the sick basin aside. "Very effective, *very* expensive."

"Very safe?" Josie prompted nervously.

The doctor shrugged. "There's always a chance of complications. My pins are carefully tuned, but crystal can behave unpredictably when it's left inside a body. I can take them out if that's unacceptable, but removing the pins will almost certainly kill you, so take that into account when making your choice."

"I'll keep them," Josie said quickly, lying back on the hard cot, which she'd just now realized was actually a padded table. "Um, thank you for saving my life."

"I didn't try very hard," the doctor replied flatly. "I've been wanting a female cadaver for some time, and it seemed impossible you would survive given the amount of blood you'd already lost. But despite there being no logical reason for it to do so, your heart kept beating, so here we are."

A frown ghosted over her face as she said this, the first expression Josie had seen her make. It seemed the unlikeliness of Josie's condition bothered her enormously, but Josie just felt blessed. Things had gotten spotty at the end, but she clearly remembered a beautiful music filling her back up with warmth just as she'd slipped into the cold. It had certainly felt miraculous at the time, but then so had the glowing crystal that drove away the dead. It seemed she'd been the recipient of a whole heap of blessings, none of which she was ungrateful enough to question, however much the doctor might frown.

"I'm just happy you were able to bring me back from the brink," Josie told her politely. "Will there be any long-term damage?"

"Not if you follow your regimen," she said, handing Josie the sparkling object she'd grabbed before the retching had interrupted everything. It turned out to be a glass medicine bottle with *Dr. Emma Pendleton, Crystal Physician and Pharmacy* written neatly across the pasted paper label. The bottle had no other information, but Josie had been in Medicine Rocks long enough at this point to recognize the mirror-bright flecks swirling through the thick, reddish-brown liquid inside.

"Is that crystal?"

"Half an ounce ground in solution with laudanum," confirmed Dr. Pendleton. "Take two spoonfuls twice daily before meals. No solid foods for the first week and absolutely no music of any sort, not even humming to yourself. Follow these instructions and get plenty of bed rest, and you should make a full recovery."

That was a relief to hear, but Josie's tallying eye had already noted that taking four spoonfuls a day from a bottle that only looked to contain eight was going to add up quickly. Add in the crystal pins already inside her and the undoubtedly sky-high fees of a doctor who used such advanced tools, and Josie started squirming with a discomfort that had nothing to do with the wound in her stomach.

402

"About payment…"

"What about it?" the doctor said, moving down to examine Josie's bandaged abdomen with her cold, prodding fingers. "There's always the possibility I'll discover something new, but your current treatments have already been paid for in full."

"Really?" Josie said, shocked. "By whom?"

"Your manservant," Dr. Pendleton said. "He gave me a whole chest of silver when you came in."

That was good to hear, but, "Manservant?" Josie frowned. "I don't have a—*oh*, you mean Mihir! Oh no, he's not my servant. He's…"

She trailed off, searching for the right term. "Company manager" was accurate and appropriate, as was "friend." But both of those felt utterly inadequate for someone who'd given all the money he'd had—money that could have been used to pay his own way out of this town that had been so unkind to him—for her sake.

"He's my family," Josie said at last.

"Whoever he is, you're paid up," the doctor said, brushing her gray-streaked black hair away from her ears to insert her stethoscope, which she then used to listen to Josie's stomach. "I don't normally take silver, but he was most insistent, and he had a cavalry officer with him. The military's support is critical to my work, so I decided it was in my best interest to accept your case. Now drink your crystal."

Josie eyed the medicine with trepidation. "Are you certain that's wise? I've heard what drinking crystal does to your insides, and considering I'm here for a gut wound, I—"

"I don't need a lay person telling *me* the complicating factors," Dr. Pendleton snapped, a flicker of crossness disrupting her monotone at last. "Some additional damage is unavoidable, but ingesting supplemental crystal is necessary to ensure the pins I put in you stay in tune. Let the pitch drift and you could well end up with needles through your stomach, which will do you a lot more harm than a bit of crystal scarring."

All of it sounded dreadful to Josie, but paying for an expert was pointless if you weren't going to listen to them, so she dutifully took her two sips, wincing at the horrid taste and even more horrid noise that burst into her skull. It sounded like exploding glass, and she swore she could feel the bits of ground-up crystal slicing all the way down her throat. Good *Lord*, was this what Rel put up with every time?

The thought of her lost friend made Josie feel even sicker than the tincture. How had she forgotten about Rel? Had she survived as well? And Mary? Where was Mary?

Josie was desperate to ask, but she was quickly losing the ability. The wooziness she'd woken up to was suddenly back in force, filling her mind with dense gray fog.

"Go back to sleep, Miss Price," the doctor urged, fastening a miner's lamp onto her head as she started unwrapping the bandage from Josie's middle. "When you wake again, everything should be finished."

Josie didn't want to go back to sleep. She especially didn't want this woman anywhere near her body while she did, for she swore she saw the doctor pulling up a tray containing multiple crystal needles and a spool of glittering thread. Obviously, it made sense for a crystal doctor to use crystal stitching, but Josie didn't think she'd ever be square with the concept after what she'd witnessed with the Whitmans.

It was far too late to complain, though. She was already sliding back into unconsciousness, her mind adrift in a haze as blank and changeless as Dr. Pendleton's voice.

~~~

When Josie woke a second time, she was back in her bedroom at Price Mining. Really, it was Uncle Samuel's bedroom that she'd merely taken over, but after the strangeness she'd been through, any familiarity was enough to make her feel at home. She was even happier to discover she was dressed this time, wrapped from neck to toes in a warm flannel nightgown. The thick fabric made her feel marvelously protected, but the true treat came when the bedroom door opened to reveal Mihir carrying a tray with a kettle on it.

"Miss Josephine!" the dear man cried. "You're awake!"

"Just Josie is fine," she said, sitting up in bed, which she was most relieved to discover caused her no pain. "*Please* tell me that's coffee."

"Just beef tea, I'm afraid," Mihir said, setting the tray on the table beside the bed to pour her a cup of clear brown liquid. "I didn't want to stress your stomach with anything stronger."

She did feel rather delicate, though Josie suspected that was more because of the horrid crystal tincture than her wounds. "How long was I asleep?" she asked, taking a sip of the extremely mild, savory soup.

"Six days," Mihir replied, taking a seat in the worn armchair that was clearly his bedside vigil.

She nearly shot the liquid out her nose. "Six *days?*"

"Not all at once," he assured her. "You've actually woken several times since Dr. Pendleton released you from surgery, though this is the first you've been able to hold a conversation."

"Good Lord," Josie muttered, running a hand through her tangled hair. "How have you managed? I know you spent all the silver on—"

"Don't worry about the money," Mihir said firmly. "It was worth every penny to get you back, and we've still got the crystal from your first trip. That should keep us solvent until you're well enough to go back down."

Josie's hands tightened on her teacup. "Back down?"

"To the Mother Lode," he clarified, his smile slipping. "You *do* still want to mine? I mean, I'd understand if you didn't, but you were so insistent before, I just assumed…"

"I'm not giving up," Josie said quickly. "It's just…" She sighed, struggling for how to put the feelings into words. "I think I finally understand why Uncle fired all his miners."

"You do?" Mihir said, sitting up straighter in his chair. "Can you tell me why? Sam never could explain it."

Josie understood why. How did you explain a life-altering experience to someone who wasn't there? But there was one part Josie knew he'd be familiar with, so that was where she started.

"I heard the music."

"Are you sure?" Mihir asked, shifting uncomfortably. "You have been drinking a lot of crystal."

"This was well before that," she said. "I heard it in the cave. I think it's what saved my life. There's magic down there, Mihir. *Real* magic! Ask the cavalry officers if you don't believe me. We all saw the cavern light up like a Christmas tree! It was..."

She trailed off, unable to find the words to adequately describe how it felt to see the cavern come alive and banish the bloody darkness with its breathing, rainbow light. Or when the song had entered her mind and lifted her out of death. The situation was all too much, too overwhelming, but one truth rang clear in her head.

"There's a difference between crystal in the ground and the crystal we cut," she said, clutching her teacup with both hands. "It's like the difference between a living tree and a pile of lumber. Both have value and purpose, but I see now that mining the Mother Lode to sell the crystal is like cutting down a sacred grove for firewood. I'm starting to wonder if *all* crystal isn't like that. What if we've been woefully shortsighted about this whole business?"

"It is a rush," Mihir said with a shrug. "They're shortsighted by nature."

"That doesn't mean it's right," Josie argued. "Imagine you discovered the lost tomb of King Solomon, but instead of celebrating the art and wonder of the treasures inside, you melted everything down for the gold. Sure, there's profit, but at the cost of something infinitely more valuable. Something irreplaceable. That's how I feel now about mining crystal."

"Do you want to stop, then?" he offered gently. "Because I wouldn't blame you at all if you did. I never wanted to come out here in the first place, and I'm getting very tired of seeing people I care about get eaten by those awful caves."

"They're not awful," Josie said, placing a hand on her injury. "And I'm not ready to give up. I came out here to take over my uncle's crystal business, and by God, that's what I'm going to stick to. But I do think we've been doing things the wrong way. I may not yet understand everything about crystal, but I'm sure now that whacking stones out of the ground is the least efficient use of our claims, and I bet Uncle felt the same. I'm sure the reason he stopped the mining was because he realized just as I have that we might well be destroying our greatest treasure simply by trying to dig it up."

"I do remember him saying something to that effect," Mihir said. "But if we're not going to dig our claims, what *are* we going to do? You say you want to keep the business going, but Price Mining can't operate without mining."

"I know," Josie groaned, burying her face in her hands to keep out the image of Miss Josephine waiting impatiently by the mail slot for word of the fantastic fortune Josie had promised. "I'm not sure what we're going to do, but even if I was still determined to strip the Mother Lode, I can't get there without Mary, and I don't know where she is." Tears began to form behind the wall of her fingers. "I left her behind. Her and Rel."

"You didn't leave anyone behind," Mihir insisted. "You barely made it out yourself."

"But I'm the one who wanted to go back there!" she cried. "I'm the one who was so desperate for profit that I called in the cavalry over Mary and Rel's objections! I bullied them into that death trap, but they're the ones who paid the price. I have to find them, Mihir!"

"You will," he promised, leaning forward to take her hand. "When you are well. You're no good to them until then, Josie. You can't even stand."

He was entirely right, but that didn't make her feel better. Fortunately, what Mihir said next did.

"I don't know what happened to the others, but Lieutenant Lucas has been calling on you every day since you left the doctor's. He's actually downstairs right now. Should I send him up?"

"Oh yes, *please*," Josie begged.

Mihir smiled and rose from his chair. When he returned a few minutes later, Lucas was hot on his heels. The lieutenant was still battered from their ordeal, but the bloody gashes Josie recalled from her chaotic memories had healed to thin red scratches, and his face looked hale, healthy, and very much relieved.

"I can't say how relieved I am to see you awake and aware again, Miss Price," he said with an earnest smile.

"Not half so relieved as I," Josie said, looking at Mihir. "Would you mind giving us a moment?"

He nodded and stepped back into the hallway, closing the door to guard their privacy. When he was gone, Josie pushed up a bit higher on the mattress and fixed the lieutenant with a serious stare. "What happened down there?"

"A lot," he said, taking a seat in the chair Mihir had vacated. "How much do you remember?"

"A good bit more than I should, I think," Josie said. "But I don't recall anything about how we got back to town. How did we make such a long journey fast enough to keep me from dying? And what happened to Mary and Rel?"

The lieutenant's smile vanished when she spoke Rel's name. "Do not concern yourself with Tyrel Reiner. He is a traitor who got what he deserved."

"Rel's not a traitor."

Lucas looked incredulous. "He shot you."

"That wasn't Rel," Josie insisted. "Mary saw the truth first, but I didn't believe her until it was too late. But I've paid for my mistake"—she gestured down at her stomach beneath the blankets—"so please tell me what became of them both."

Lucas heaved a long sigh. "I don't know why you care so much about that murderer, but the last I saw of Reiner, he was falling down a pit that opened beneath the pond at the back of the crystal cave. Where he fell to, I don't know, but I don't believe it was anywhere deadly. I heard... I heard him speaking to Miss Good Crow, and the ringing of the caves in reply. I know it sounds like madness, but I swear she was in the stones, speaking back. It was she who lit up the crystal and opened the path that brought us back to safety. I know it."

"I believe you," Josie said. "Because I heard her too. It was her singing that kept me from death, I'd bet money on it."

"Then I am certain Reiner lives," Lucas said, smiling. "Marie is not a killer, but I'm afraid I don't know her fate. I had to leave her behind to get you to town, for you were fading fast."

Josie frowned. "How *did* you get back so quickly?"

"It was a miracle, Miss," he said, his eyes growing bright. "In the normal run, you never would have made it, but there must have been an angel watching over all of us, for the caves opened a tunnel leading straight to the very front of the Front Caves. Chaucer and I came out practically on top of the tax table. I told the soldiers there to take you to Dr. Pendleton's while I went back for Miss Good Crow, but when I turned, the tunnel we'd come through had already vanished back into the stone."

"That does sound miraculous," Josie agreed. "But how did you know to take me to Dr. Pendleton?"

"She's the one who saved my leg," Lucas said, patting his knee. "I figured if anyone could pull you back from the brink, it was her. I just hope my decision didn't bankrupt you."

"Money's no use if you're dead," Josie said with a shrug. "I'd gladly pay ten times that much if it means I can go back for Mary. Do you think she's still in there?"

Lucas's hands tightened to fists. "I don't know, but if she is, I'm going with you, orders be damned. It's the least I can do to pay back the life she's saved twice over."

"I know exactly how you feel," Josie assured him. "And I'd be glad of your assistance. I can't rest my conscience until I bring them back home, both of them. Mary and Rel are my partners and friends. I will not abandon them to the ground."

"Then I pray for your speedy recovery," the lieutenant said. "If it's anything like mine, you'll be up again before you know it."

"I hope so," Josie said. "Though I'm afraid you'll have to tell General Cook our deal is off. I know I promised to solve your crystal shortage, but I can't possibly mine that cave after what happened."

"I understand utterly," Lucas assured her. "And I don't think you'll hear any quarrel from General Cook. Losing seventy men over two missions has soured his taste for the caves."

Josie could definitely see that, but, "Does that put you in a terrible position? I know the only reason the general agreed to my plan in the first place was because the Sioux had left him no choice. Now that we've failed, is Medicine Rocks doomed?"

"Actually," Lucas said, perking up, "that's the one part of this that *is* going well, at least for our end. We've received several new reports that make us believe the Sioux will not be attacking Medicine Rocks after all, at least not in the immediate future."

That sounded like terrific news, but something about the way Lucas said it gave Josie pause. "Why is that only good from our end?"

The lieutenant's face grew grim again. "Because they attacked the Black Hills instead. Deadwood, the Whitewood Creeks, the gold mine at Homestake, even Fort Abraham Lincoln. The entire American presence in that part of Dakota has fallen to the Sioux, and I don't think we'll be getting it back."

"My God," Josie breathed. "How many warriors did they have?"

"That's the strangest part," he said. "All the accounts we've gotten claim there were no warriors. It was a mist that did it."

"A mist?" Josie frowned. "You mean like fog?"

"That's how it was described," Lucas said, though from the look on his face, he didn't believe the story either. "The reports I've read all say the same thing: a heavy bank of cloud rolled over the mountains against the wind and fell upon our settlements. They knew it was the Sioux's doing because they could hear the drums, but no warriors came out of the fog to cut them down. Instead, everyone who breathed in the vapor was overtaken by a sudden and undeniable urge to go back to the place of their birth. Within five minutes of the cloud's landing, everyone inside it—miners, soldiers, shopkeepers, everyone—had stopped whatever they were doing before and walked away."

"You mean just off into the woods?" Josie asked, incredulous. "With no provisions?"

"Nothing," Lucas said. "That's how we know so much about what happened, because they're still walking. You can ride right up and talk to them about it, for they're perfectly sensible until you try to get them to stop. Some of them weren't even wearing shoes when the mist came down, but they refuse to pause their journey long enough to put any on. They just walk and walk until they fall over from exhaustion, then they get up and resume their journey the moment they are able. The only ones we've found who seem unaffected are children who were born in the area and thus at the place of their birth already. Everyone else seems cursed to keep going until they get back to wherever it is they came from."

"What about those born overseas?" Josie asked. "Will they walk into the ocean?"

The lieutenant shrugged. "We'll find out when they get there. For now, we've got soldiers from the eastern forts riding escort to make sure the walkers don't starve to death, but this whole thing's a debacle. I hate to say it, but miners guarding their claims played a huge part in our control over the Black Hills. Even if we retook the abandoned forts, we couldn't do

411

more than cower inside them, and our scouts say the mist is still roving over the hills. We don't know how the Sioux made it or how long they can keep it up, but so long as the cloud is there, the Black Hills are lost, which I'm afraid leaves us alone."

"Surely not alone," Josie said. "There's still plenty of forts in Wyoming, aren't there?"

"There are, but between the Whitmans, the Sioux, and the total loss of our eastern front, I'm afraid Medicine Rocks finds itself surrounded." He gave her a pointed look. "I know you're determined to find the others, but if you had any considerations about leaving Medicine Rocks, now would be the time."

"I'm not considering anything of the sort," Josie assured him. "My life is here now. I'm not sure what I'm going to do with it after I bring Mary and Rel home safe, but so long as my name is Josephine Price, this is where I belong."

"Then I wish you bonne chance," he said, donning his cap again as he rose from the chair. "I must return to my duties. Recover well, and when you're ready to begin your search for Miss Good Crow, you know where to find me."

"I'll do that," she promised. "Thank you, lieutenant."

Lucas tipped his hat to her and took his leave, opening the door for Mihir, who was still waiting in the hall.

"Nice to see we still have a few good officers left," he said, returning to his chair after the lieutenant had gone. "I take it we're staying for certain, then?"

"I am," Josie said, refilling her cup of beef tea from the kettle he'd so thoughtfully placed in her reach. "But just because I've taken leave of my senses doesn't mean you have to follow suit. You've already gone above and beyond any duty you owed my uncle. If you want to leave Medicine Rocks before this Sioux situation falls apart, I'll help in any way I can."

"I am *very* tired of this backwards place," Mihir admitted. "But I promised your uncle on his deathbed that I would see you safely set up here. I can't say I've done that yet, so I will remain here until I can."

Josie's hand froze on her cup. She hadn't realized how terrified she'd been that Mihir would leave until he'd said he wouldn't. Now that she knew his answer, the relief was almost more than her poor body could take.

"Thank you," she whispered, struggling not to bawl. "I didn't want to ask, but…"

"I would never leave you to face this alone," Mihir promised, reaching out to squeeze her hand. "As I said before, you're like a daughter to me. I'll stay here as long as you need. But just in case you *were* feeling guilty, know that my first thought was that I couldn't possibly move my books without a wagon, and since the Whitmans have been attacking every wagon that leaves town, I was going to be stuck in town no matter what."

It was sweet of him to try to cheer her up, but knowing they were both trapped didn't make Josie feel any better. That said, there was a silver lining even in this, because so long as the Whitmans were attacking every wagon that tried to leave town, she had all the excuse she needed for why she wasn't shipping crystal back to the real Miss Josephine. That wouldn't stop her mistress from expecting it, of course, but it bought Josie time to figure out what the devil she was going to do for money now that mining crystal was no longer an acceptable option.

Mihir had clearly been thinking along the same lines, because his face grew grim again. "If you're serious about staying and not mining, then we've got some figuring to do," he said, scooting his chair closer. "Normally I'd wait until you were more recovered to have this discussion, but—"

"But these things are best handled as expediently as possible," Josie agreed, setting her cup aside. "Especially now that all our reserve silver's gone into me."

"I can think of no better investment," Mihir assured her. "And silver wasn't much use in Medicine Rocks anyway. The crystal you brought back from your first trip will be far more useful in starting a new, mining-independent business."

"It would generate a lot of capital," Josie agreed, biting her lip. "But I can't help thinking that selling it off for cash is the worst use. I've living proof of the miracles even cut crystal can work. Those can't be the exclusive domain of bandits and odd doctors."

"Refined goods do always sell for more than raw ones," Mihir agreed nervously. "But working with crystal is notoriously dangerous."

"All the better to increase its value," Josie said, her mind spinning. "I was in too great a hurry before. I was so focused on mining crystal for sale I never stopped to consider its larger potential. If we could just learn how it does what it does and make something out of that, something useful, then that single bag of crystal might be all we need."

Mihir looked unconvinced, but he hadn't seen what Josie had. She felt as if everything she needed was in her mind already. She just needed time to put the pieces together, and since she was stuck on her back until she recovered anyway, she might as well put the idleness to good use.

"Did my notebook make it back, by any chance?"

Mihir shook his head. "I'm afraid it was left behind, along with the rest of your pack."

Josie groaned in dismay. That book contained everything she'd compiled from years of Uncle's adventures in the caves. She still had all his letters in her trunks, so she supposed she could just remake it, but the first version had taken weeks to put together. Her writing hand was already throbbing at the thought of so much copying when she realized Mihir was still speaking.

"I'm so sorry, what did you say?"

"I said the notebook is gone, but I still have all of Samuel's own notes he wrote during his excursions to the caves, if you'd like to see those."

414

"He wrote *more?*" Josie cried. "Why didn't you tell me sooner?"

"Because I didn't think the information would be useful until we got to the sorting and pricing stage," Mihir said defensively. "They're very technical."

"Technical is precisely what I'm after," Josie said, reaching with eager fingers. "Bring them to me, please! And the pack of crystal, too, if you don't mind."

Mihir nodded and hauled himself back up to do as she had asked, leaving Josie alone in the sunny bedroom to finish plotting her next, better-be-brilliant plan.

Thank you for reading!

Thank you for going with me on this new adventure! If you enjoyed *The Last Stand of Mary Good Crow*, I hope you'll consider leaving a review. Reviews, good or bad, are vital to every author's career, and I would be very grateful if you'd consider writing one for me.

If you want to be the first to know when the next book comes out, sign up for my New Release Mailing List! List members are always the first to know whenever I put out something new, and it's free! I promise never to spam you or share your information, so I hope you'll join us. Or, if social media is more your thing, you can follow me on Twitter @Rachel_Aaron for writing updates, interviews, and general good times.

Need something new to read *right now?* You can see all my books, including my **5** completed series, at www.rachelaaron.net.

Again, thank you so *so* much for coming with me on this journey into a new frontier. Thank you for reading from the bottom of my heart, and I hope you'll stay with me for many more books!

Yours always and sincerely,
Rachel Aaron

Enjoyed the story?
Need a new book *right now*?!

Try one of Rachel's other completed series!
www.rachelaaron.net

The Heartstrikers Series

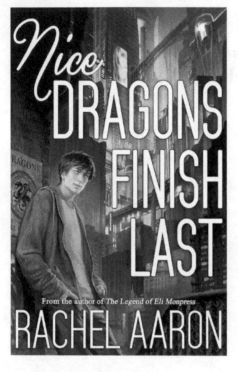

As the smallest dragon in the Heartstriker clan, Julius survives by a simple code: stay quiet, don't cause trouble, and keep out of the way of bigger dragons. But this meek behavior doesn't cut it in a family of ambitious predators, and his mother, Bethesda the Heartstriker, has finally reached the end of her patience.

Now, sealed in human form and banished to the DFZ--a vertical metropolis built on the ruins of Old Detroit--Julius has one month to prove to his mother that he can be a ruthless dragon or lose his true shape forever. But in a city of modern mages and vengeful spirits where dragons are seen as monsters to be exterminated, he's going to need some serious help to survive this test.

He just hopes humans are more trustworthy than dragons.

"Super fun, fast paced, urban fantasy full of heart, and plenty of magic, charm and humor to spare, this self published gem was one of my favorite discoveries this year!" - **The Midnight Garden**

"A deliriously smart and funny beginning to a new urban fantasy series about dragons in the ruins of Detroit...inventive, uproariously clever, and completely un-put-down-able!" - **SF Signal**

Forever Fantasy Online

In the real world, twenty-one-year-old library sciences student Tina Anderson is invisible and under-appreciated, but in the VR-game Forever Fantasy Online she's Roxxy--the respected leader and main tank of a top-tier raiding guild. In the real world, her brother James Anderson is a college drop-out struggling under debt, but in FFO he's famous--an explorer who's gotten every achievement, done every quest, and collected all the rarest items.

Both Tina and James need the game more than they'd like to admit, but their favorite escape turns into a trap when FFO becomes a living world. Wounds are no longer virtual, stupid monsters become cunning, NPCs start acting like actual people, and death might be forever.

In the real world, everyone said being good at video games was a waste of time. Now, stranded and separated across thousands of miles of new, deadly terrain, Tina and James's skill at FFO is the only thing keeping them alive. It's going to take every bit of their expertise--and hoarded loot--to find each other and get back home, but as the stakes get higher and the damage adds up, being the best in the game may no longer be enough.

"Rachel Aaron and Travis Bach have written an amazing story and a realistic LitRPG." - **The Fantasy Inn**

"Excellent characters, an engaging story, and geek humor. What more can one ask for?" - **TS Chan**

The Legend of Eli Monpress

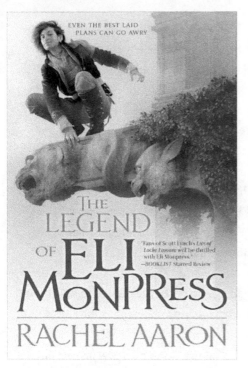

Eli Monpress is talented. He's charming. And he's the greatest thief in the world.

He's also a wizard, and with the help of his partners in crime—a swordsman with the world's most powerful magic sword (but no magical ability of his own) and a demonseed who can step through shadows and punch through walls—he's getting ready to pull off the heist of his career. To start, though, he'll just steal something small. Something no one will miss. Something like... a king.

"*I cannot be less than 110% in love with this book. I loved it. I love it still. Already I sort of want to read it again. Considering my fairly epic Godzilla-sized To Read list, that's just about the highest compliment I can give a book*" - **CSI: Librarian**

"*Fast and fun,* The Spirit Thief *introduces a fascinating new world and a complex magical system based on cooperation with the spirits who reside in all living objects. Aaron's characters are fully fleshed and possess complex personalities, motivations, and backstories that are only gradually revealed. Fans of Scott Lynch's* Lies of Locke Lamora *(2006) will be thrilled with Eli Monpress. Highly recommended for all fantasy readers.*" - **Booklist**, **Starred Review**

The Paradox Trilogy
(written as Rachel Bach)

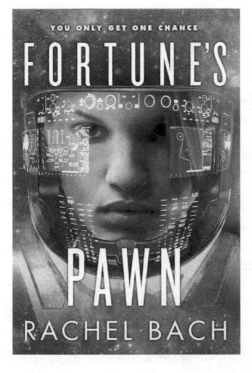

Devi Morris isn't your average mercenary. She has plans. Big ones. And a ton of ambition. It's a combination that's going to get her killed one day - but not just yet.

That is, until she just gets a job on a tiny trade ship with a nasty reputation for surprises. The Glorious Fool isn't misnamed: it likes to get into trouble, so much so that one year of security work under its captain is equal to five years everywhere else. With odds like that, Devi knows she's found the perfect way to get the jump on the next part of her Plan. But the Fool doesn't give up its secrets without a fight, and one year on this ship might be more than even Devi can handle.

"Firefly-*esque in its concept of a rogue-ish spaceship family... The narrative never quite goes where you expect it to, in a good way... Devi is a badass with a heart.*" - **Locus Magazine**

"*If you liked* Star Wars, *if you like our books, and if you are waiting for* Guardians of the Galaxy *to hit the theaters, this is your book.*" - **Ilona Andrews**

"*I JUST LOVED IT! Perfect light sci-fi. If you like space stuff that isn't that complicated but highly entertaining, I give two thumbs up!*" - **Felicia Day**

2,000 to 10,000: Writing Better, Writing Faster, and Writing More of What You Love
(nonfiction)

"Have you ever wanted to double your daily word counts? Do you sometimes feel like you're crawling through your story? Do you want to write more every day without increasing the time you spend writing or sacrificing quality? It's not impossible; it's not even that hard. This is the book explaining how, with a few simple changes, I boosted my daily writing from 2000 words to over 10k a day, and how you can too."

Expanding on Rachel's viral blog post about how she doubled her daily word counts, this book offers practical writing advice for anyone who's ever longed to increase their daily writing output. In addition to updated information for the popular 2k to 10k writing efficiency process, 5 step plotting method, and easy editing tips, the book includes all new chapters on creating characters who write their own stories, plot structure, and learning to love your daily writing. Full of easy to follow, practical advice from a professional author who doesn't eat if she doesn't produce good books on a regular basis, 2k to 10k focuses not just on writing faster, but writing better, and having more fun while you do it!

"I loved this book! So helpful!" - **Courtney Milan, NYT Bestselling Author**

"This. Is. Amazing. You are telling my story RIGHT NOW. Book is due in 2 weeks, and I'm behind--woefully, painfully behind--because I've been stuck...writing in circles and unenthused. Yet here--here is a FANTASTIC solution. I am printing this post out, and I'm setting out to make my triangle. Thank you, thank you, THANK YOU!" - **Bestselling YA Author Susan Dennard**

About the Author

Rachel Aaron is the author of twenty-plus novels and the bestselling nonfiction writing book, *2k to 10k: Writing Faster, Writing Better, and Writing More of What You Love,* which has helped thousands of authors double their daily word counts. When she's not holed up in her writing tower, Rachel lives a nerdy, bookish life in Denver, CO, with her perpetual-motion son, long-suffering husband, and far too many plants. To learn more about Rachel, read samples of all her books, or to find a complete list of her interviews and podcasts, please visit rachelaaron.net!

Cover Illustration by Luisa J. Preißler, Cover Design by Rachel Aaron, Editing provided by Red Adept Editing.

As always, this book would not have been nearly as good without my amazing beta readers. Thank you so, so much to Judith Smith, Christina Vlinder, Eva Bunge, Lindsay Simms, Linda Hall, Sarah Braun, and the ever-amazing Laligin. Y'all are the BEST!

CPSIA information can be obtained
at www.ICGtesting.com
Printed in the USA
LVHW040513050623
748861LV00002B/109

9 781952 367052